What Many Men

Desire

a novel by

Robert L. Grant

What Many Men Desire. Copyright © 2011, by
Robert L. Grant

ISBN: 978-0692256848

Published by the CreateSpace Independent Publishing
Platform

Cover design by Sergio Saucedo –
www.sergiosaucedo.com

Printed in the United States of America

www.whatmanymendesire.com

Let's see once more this saying graved in gold.
'Who chooseth me shall gain what many men desire.'
Why, that's the lady; all the world desires her.
From the four corners of the earth they come,
To kiss this shrine, this mortal-breathing saint.

The Moroccan Prince, in *The Merchant of Venice*

What

Many Men

Desire

I

EVEN AS HE TUGGED AT THE LID, Charles Pierce expected this box to be another disappointment. It was the dowdy librarian's latest—and most likely last—offering and its lid seemed almost willfully to resist him. He'd developed a strong dislike for the woman, a plain, schoolmarm-ish creature, now hovering at his shoulder. She wore her hair pulled back into a bun, without earrings or makeup, convinced, apparently, that feminine adornments were frivolous, or sinful—or both. She had placed Charles at a small desk, squeezed into a corner of the library's main reading room, as if he were an unruly child who needed to be hidden from public view, and she seemed determined to show him just how strict and unyielding a custodian of New York's cultural heritage could be.

The main source of his irritation was that she had wasted, by now, over an hour of his time. He'd made it quite clear that he wanted pictures taken in the early, discovery stages of mining—images of prospecting. Instead, she produced one example after another of well-established mines, bristling with elevators, tramcars, ventilation sheds.

Charles had dressed for effect—dark woolen suit and a conservative tie, highly polished shoes. His thick hair, trimmed, jet-black except for a fringe of gray at the temples, was combed straight back. His intense black eyes and straight nose, the neatly trimmed mustache and unsmiling mouth, completed the no-nonsense air he sought to project. But his efforts were lost on this insensitive pencil pusher.

He'd put his homburg and black kid gloves on the desk, atop the afternoon edition of the New York Times, its headlines trumpeting the Nazi's latest thumbing-of-the-nose at the Versailles Treaty; as he smoothed his hair down, she set the container before him on the desk. It was shoebox shaped, though half again as large. Box and lid were made of pressed paper and veneered in a mottled, black-and-white pattern meant to suggest marble, but falling far short. Charles had worked his index finger under one corner of the lid—at last, with a soft pop, it relinquished its grip and levered up into his hand.

Stale air from the box billowed into his nose, carrying with it the faint, intermingled scents of desiccated paper, old casein glue, and a solvent of some kind. Somewhat stronger was a note of photographic fixer, just acrid enough to make his breath catch. He jerked his head back, his nose wrinkled, a frown stitching his dark eyebrows.

Peering in, he saw the edges of thin, transparent photographic sleeves, closely packed, perhaps two hundred or more. They were 4 X 5s and 5 X 7s and they filled the box from front to back. Some held only a negative but in most, he could make out the thin white edge of a proof print. He glanced up at the stern-faced librarian—she nodded her permission for him to look through them. He withdrew the first sleeve, removed the print and held it up to the light. After a moment, the faintest of smiles bent the corners of his mouth. "Finally," he said, under his breath.

Methodically now, Charles picked through the photos. They were all black-and-white, and showed groups of men and their animals, at work in various landscapes: miners, with pickaxes and shovels, digging into parched and craggy hillsides; oilmen on rigs in flat, barren plains; railroad gangs laying track in steep, mountainous terrain blanketed with snow. They wore an assortment of rough work clothes: overalls, denim jeans and thick cotton shirts, rolled up shirtsleeves revealing the cuffs of BVDs. In the backgrounds, burros and horses lumbered under the weight of tools and bulging sacks, or strained at the traces of heavy wagons.

Charles's focus was on the miners. Some worked underground, attacking rock and earth by hand, with the tools of hard-scrabble mining: picks and shovels, mauls and pikes, and heavy, hand-turned augers. They wore tin helmets with candle lamps perched on top; the photographer had gone to some trouble to get his bulky equipment into these cramped spaces.

But most of the pictures were of campsites or mineshaft openings, which varied from well-framed and marked access ways, to holes that looked like nothing more than the natural entrances to caves. A quick sampling suggested that the box contained photos from perhaps a dozen different claims. The only obvious connection between them was that they all showed men, living and working in the harsh outdoors, scratching for gold or silver or copper or coal, whatever they could force out of the ground.

Bored, the librarian moved to a seat opposite Charles and began examining penciled notes on her stenographer's pad. Moments before, exasperated over Charles's repeated rejections, she'd been about to protest that she had nothing to offer him, even in the vast collections of the New York City Library, when she recalled a stack of cartons that had come in about a month before. An eccentric old man had left his collection to the library—it had been sitting unattended in a corner since its arrival, waiting to be catalogued, and it included newspaper clippings, diaries, and hundreds of photographs.

Ordinarily, she told Charles, she couldn't offer these items to patrons until they were catalogued—however, under the smoldering pressure of his irritation, she offered to make an exception. But it meant she would have to sit with Charles as he went through them, to make certain none went missing.

As Charles picked through the pictures, a group of four-by-fives caused him to slow. They featured three men working a small claim, rough looking men in a barren, sun-bleached landscape, who'd stopped to pose for a picture. They were looking into the lens, unsmiling, as though posed in the photographer's studio, instead of the forbidding landscape around them. Behind them, an irregular entryway was cut into the hillside and framed by three rough timbers. On the lintel, "Paiute" was scrawled, in block letters any grade-schooler could have bettered.

One man leaned on the handle of a shovel; another, with a pickaxe on his shoulder, stood with one foot up on the handle of a wheelbarrow, which brimmed with rocky earth. The third man's brawny arms were folded across the bib of his dirt-encrusted, tattered overalls. The picture was framed off-center, leaving a blank area to one side. Charles pushed the photo back into its sleeve and looked up at the librarian, still engrossed in her notes.

"How long will it take..."

"Shhhh," she said, quickly bringing a finger up to her lips and showing Charles her professional scowl. He affected an embarrassed smile.

"How long," he whispered, "to get a copy?"

"Well, I'm not certain we can do anything before they're catalogued," she admonished. "I'll have to ask my supervisor." As she stood, she kept the angle of her chin high, which left her looking down her nose at Charles. "Let me check the schedule."

She moved to the end of a nearby shelving unit to examine a list, pinned to a corkboard. Peering closely, through wire-rimmed glasses, she ran her finger down one column, mumbling to herself. Charles glanced around to make certain no one was looking. Then, almost in a single motion, he slipped the envelope into the folds of his newspaper and pulled another from the box, laying it where the first one had been.

Returning, the woman bent near. "If Miss Farleigh OKs it," she whispered, producing a thin smile intended to elicit Charles's approval, "…we should have copies for you in about a week. Is this the one?" she asked, pointing to the envelope on the desk.

With a hint of a smile, Charles slid the picture forward.

II

"BE QUICK NOW, AUDREY, it's Mrs Applegate." As Audrey hurried past, ducking through into the shop's back room, Mme Moreau flicked her silver lorgnette in her direction. Juliette Moreau was a woman of some bearing and Audrey found her a little intimidating, even after all these months.

"Hurry, girls. She'll be here any minute now. We do not keep our customers waiting." This declaration was her mantra, repeated several times each day as though it were a celestial command. Audrey couldn't bring herself to care. The phrase had become a joke among "the girls"; they gave themselves the giggles, trying to see who could do the best imitation.

Audrey had never been so fatigued. Typically, she was tireless—the others marveled at so much stamina in her small frame and joked that she must be using something illicit. She prided herself on her ability to handle all the physical demands of her job, whether sorting and stacking bolts of fabric on the shelves, redressing the display windows, or racing "Upstairs" to the sewing room and back, carrying armfuls of frocks. But today, she'd had to skip breakfast and the exertions of the morning had simply exhausted her.

Audrey often mused over the differences between areas of the shop. "Out Front", where she and her co-workers served the Applegates and Astors, the walls, cabinets and display tables were clad and topped in veined travertine. The floors were a checkerboard of that same pink marble, offset by light gray squares of granite. The space was open and welcoming, inviting and comfortable. Fluted limestone columns framed the doors; the windows and the many long mirrors were draped in brocades worthy of any European palace. Lights hidden in soffits in the ceiling spread a warm glow throughout the space, which was subtly divided so that two customers, relaxing on the plush divans, could view their choices without interfering with one another, and could discuss, in discreet tones, the qualities of the garments demonstrated by the parading models.

Through the curtain, in "The Back", opulence was superfluous. Downstairs, the floors were a thick wooden planking, darkened with age, and scarred and splintered from years of hard use and neglect. It was cramped, the floor space crowded by work tables cluttered with half-finished garments and racks hung with dresses, capes, stoles, and suits, separated by aisles too narrow for two to pass side by side. Harsh, un-shaded overhead lamps cast shadows at strange angles; their light failed to reach the farthest corners.

Passing one of the mirrors spotted around the back room, Audrey stopped and combed her fingers through her thick auburn curls with both hands, drawing the hair back from her face. She regarded that pale face, with its intense green eyes gazing back from the glass, and frowned. The circles under her eyes were darker than usual against her freckled skin. A fine film of sweat glazed the sides of her nose; she dabbed it away with the handkerchief she kept tucked in her sleeve. She thought she looked awful.

"'Can't get enough of that pretty mug?" Sally, her comrade-in-arms in the ongoing guerilla war within Chez Moreau, had come up behind and jabbed her softly in the ribs. Smiling, Sally parked her chin on Audrey's shoulder so the two heads, one red haired, one blond, sat side by side in the mirror. "You're pretty enough–don't worry about it."

"I look like something the cat dragged in," she answered, with a sigh. "That's what I feel like, anyway."

Audrey sniffed at the imperfections of her image. She could never see herself and not wonder at the mixture of genes that had produced what she saw in the mirror. She was pretty, she knew that, but in a quirky, curious way that drew a lot of attention. The freckles and the red in her hair, plus the full shape of her mouth, were her Grandpa Wilson's input into her alchemy. The surprising green of her eyes was a family mystery but their almond shape and sharp brows, and the fine line and slight flare of her nose, came straight from West Africa through her father. The slightly too prominent cheekbones were from the Cherokee, through her grandmother; sometimes she thought her most appropriate look would include a beaded headband and an eagle feather.

She looked over at Sally's reflection. "Why do we put up with this, Sally? Slavery's outlawed, last I heard."

"That's just for some, Honey. The blacks are free but Park Avenue shop girls are a dime a dozen–a baker's dozen." The women rolled their eyes and laughed.

Audrey was fond of Sally. She came from somewhere down near Texas and lent the shop an air of brashness, a welcome counter to the pretensions of its owners. But as much as she liked her, Audrey wondered what their relationship would be if Sally knew the details of her heritage.

The women scurried back to their jobs while Mme Moreau amplified the din with her urgent pleas for more speed. Juliette Moreau was an imposing presence, with her mane of graying hair piled above a high forehead, a straight nose and strong chin, always held up at an unnatural angle. Plus the ever-present lorgnette, useful for close inspection of stitches and fabric, and for looking down on her staff. Her husband's death had produced a small inheritance, which she'd used to buy a minority stake in this Park Avenue shop that catered to New York's wealthy. It allowed her to pretend to be one of them.

Audrey ducked into the makeshift changing room. Thea, Moreau's head seamstress, was there, making fine stitches in the three dresses hanging from the overhead rack. This space, not much bigger than a good-sized closet, was formed by drapery clipped to a railing and suspended from the ceiling in an already cluttered corner.

Audrey began stripping out of the high-neck, pleated-front blouse and black, ankle-length skirt that comprised her shop uniform. The lack of privacy in this space was a problem for her when she began the job. While changing, she was often all but naked and, since they were usually racing the clock, it was that much harder for her to do anything toward preserving her modesty. Her many appeals to make it safe from leering eyes were heard—and ignored. It wasn't until Sally clued her in to the fact that Mr Clayton, co-owner and the only male she might encounter in The Back, was not aroused by the bodies of women, that she stopped worrying about it.

Mme Moreau continued her carping. The fuss had started when an urgent call came in: Mrs Applegate was being chauffeured downtown at that very moment to look at frocks for a garden party gala—she had intended to skip it but changed her mind at the last minute. She simply must have a new dress and Mme Moreau had picked out three for her inspection. And as usual, Mrs Applegate had insisted that Audrey should model them. Fiona Applegate was one of the shop's most regular and free-spending customers so it was important, especially in these difficult times, not to disappoint her.

With help from Sally and Thea, Audrey struggled into the first gown, a belted green taffeta calf-length with a gathered belt. Thea and Sally set to work strategically placing a handful of pins for the showing, shaping it to Audrey's slim body. It looked great on her; it would not sit nearly so well on Fiona Applegate's bulbous figure.

Modeling was an occasional extra—and unpaid— task for Audrey; assisting Thea was her main job. Thea was a Portuguese immigrant, middle-aged, short and solid, with mahogany-tinted skin and a strong, etched face framed in thick black hair, streaked now with threads of gray. She wore it in two pigtails, plaited with colorful ribbons and wrapped in a bundle atop her head. To Audrey, she looked like a cross between her Grandma Sarah and the man on the Indian-head nickel.

But Thea could work magic with a sewing machine. During much of the day, Audrey lugged bolts of cloth back and forth from the storeroom and fetched all the other things needed so Thea could remain at her Stitchmaster, turning sketches into richly detailed garments, or churning out alterations. "Sewing" was up a steep flight of stairs and only the large dumb waiter that connected the two levels saved Audrey from having to climb them carrying Thea's supplies. Even so, she climbed them dozens of times each workday—lately, with an increasing sense of frustration.

III

CHARLES SAT ON A STOOL near the end of the photography shop's counter, stiff in his smartly tailored, dark gray suit. His homburg and black leather gloves were on the counter and his Burberry overcoat, with beaver fur lapels the color of deeply polished walnut, was draped across his narrow shoulders. Determined to make the smallest possible impression, he was screening himself behind the late edition of The Times.

He turned the pages as quietly as possible while the shopkeeper served the only other customer, a frail, elderly man. He knew the man would have only a vague impression of him; if enough time elapsed, he might have no memory at all of Charles's presence in the shop. But, as he turned a page, the brittle rustle of the newspaper stirred the large, marmalade cat lounging in the window, next to a display of boxy Kodak cameras, and soaking up the meager heat of a lowering Manhattan sun. His eyes barely open, the cat yawned, stretching one mottled foreleg to its full length and briefly arcing the points of four sharp claws into view. Then, as Charles took in the details of the Depression's latest turn, the cat slumped and relaxed again into sleep.

The jangle of bells over the door announced the other customer's departure and the shopkeeper turned his attention to Charles. "Now, Mister, uhh... Mister Blake, yes?" A thin smile curled the line of Charles's mouth and he nodded as he folded the newspaper. The man went to a long rack of small, oak drawers behind him, each bearing an alphabetic label. He slid open the "B" drawer. Charles stepped to the counter.

"Yes, here they are, Mr Blake." The man was proud both of the efficiency of his filing system, and of his ability to remember his customers' names. Because of such people, Charles often used an alias, even in simple transactions—Blake was one of his standbys.

The black silk back of the shopkeeper's vest shimmered in the afternoon light as he turned from his file drawers and came to the counter opposite Charles. He laid a medium-size manila envelope face down on the glass and, with thin, deft fingers, unwound the string from beneath its cardboard button. Opening the flap, he withdrew three smaller glassine envelopes and three sepia-toned prints, and placed the prints next to one another on the countertop.

Noticing that Charles was encumbered by his homburg, the shopkeeper nodded toward a bentwood hat rack near the door. Charles shrugged off his overcoat and hooked it on the rack, along with the hat. Then he stepped back to the counter and bent to examine the prints.

The shopkeeper leaned back against his stack of filing drawers and watched, pale blue eyes wary behind gold-rimmed pince-nez that clung to the end of a slender nose. He was a small man, perhaps a full head shorter than Charles. He passed a hand through thinning gray hair, waiting to hear whether his work had passed muster.

Charles studied the photographs carefully, taking his time. A smile tugged at the corners of his mouth but he quickly suppressed it, his face again becoming a flat, unreadable mask.

"Of course, a glass provides the acid test..." said the shopkeeper. He reached near the register and picked up a 3-inch magnifier, clasped in a silvery metal circle with a black wooden handle. He offered the handle to Charles, "...although this is the sort of thing I presume you want to be accepted at face value."

"Hmmmm," mumbled Charles, glancing up at the man as he took the glass, not pleased to hear him openly making assumptions about his motives.

Returning his attention to the prints, Charles took in every detail, switching between the magnifier and his naked eye—the steady rhythm of the large Regulator clock, on the wall above the door, was the only sound in the room.

The images were three versions of the photo he had pilfered from the library: three workmen, proudly posed in front of a mine called "Paiute." But now there was a fourth man, Charles, standing an arm's length off to the side. He was dressed in something suggestive of an engineer's or a surveyor's kit: jodhpurs and dusty riding boots; a campaign hat, its broad brim casting a sharp shadow across his face. The dust mottled shirt, probably tan and of a coarse material, with epaulets, showed stains of sweat at the armpits. He held a clipboard and was smiling broadly at the camera, while gesturing with his free hand toward the other three, as though to fête them.

Charles examined his own image in the pictures and compared it with the others, concentrating, taking great care, oblivious to distractions. The clock ticked on. Finally, he looked up from the pictures and stood to his full height. He was tall, and knew how to use his height to intimidate.

As he handed back the glass, his expression revealed nothing of his feelings. He separated one of the prints from the other two and looked down at the shopkeeper. His sharp, black eyes met the man's squarely. With a nod, he allowed a smile to appear on his lips as he handed him the picture.

"You've done a fine job—first-rate." His crisp English accent carried a trace of East London, alloyed with Oxford or Cambridge. "I believe you've made three copies from each of these negatives?"

The man nodded. Charles handed him the print he had culled.

"This is the best—very good, indeed. Destroy the others, negatives *and* prints."

The shop owner hadn't realized that he'd been holding his breath. He allowed the air to escape and smiled faintly, a gift of self-approval. Then he found the negative matching Charles's choice and returned it to the manila envelope. "Will three copies be enough? I can easily produce a few extra."

"No. No, I'm sure these will do. What do I owe you?"

The man secured the envelope with its cord before moving to a note pad next to the big cash register. He took a pencil from his vest pocket and began jotting down figures.

"The prints are not very expensive," he said. "Fifteen cents each. Of course, the main work was in melding the images. That, I'm afraid, took rather a lot of time to do convincingly—the better part of a day. It's very much a trial and error process and, uh..." His voice trailed off as he concentrated on the tally, tapping the pencil's eraser lightly against the side of his nose.

"Let's see. The photograph itself, intermediate negatives, et cetera..." He scratched out the numbers. "Total of seventeen dollars and fifty cents."

Charles hesitated for an instant while he ran a quick comparison in his head between what he'd expected to pay and what the man was asking. "Well, given the result, I'm not offended by the price." He dug into his breast pocket and extracted his billfold, found two ten-dollar notes and laid them on the counter.

The register was clad in ornately tooled brass, kept polished to a mirror finish. The shop owner pressed a few keys on the big machine and the cash drawer shot out, accompanied by a loud chinging of bells. He delivered the change into Charles's manicured hand.

"There you are, Mr Blake." Pushing the envelope and the prints across the counter, he nodded, with an engaging smile, toward a display of photographs. "As you can see, we're regarded very highly in Manhattan for our portraiture, but we do everything in the photographic line. If there's any other need you may have, I trust you'll let us know."

Charles began working himself back into his overcoat. Although his natural caution would prevent his ever returning to this shop, he took a moment to look critically at the line of poses. It was a gallery of New York's upper crust, with all their self-importance on display, their wealth implied in their dress, their feathers and jewelry, and the opulent rooms in which they were posed. Duly impressed, he turned back to the man with an appreciative smile.

"You may be assured of it." Charles picked up the packet of photographs. He pointed to the rejects. "I want these destroyed. Right away."

"Of course, sir." The man hurried to gather up the rejected prints and negatives. He took a pair of large scissors from a drawer and began cutting them into small pieces, taking care to stand so Charles could clearly see the cuttings, as they spilled into a waste bin at his feet.

Smiling, Charles took his hat from the stand. "Good day sir, and thank you." The man nodded as Charles turned to leave.

The door produced another clanging of bells as Charles stepped out to the sidewalk. He tucked the envelope of photos into the breast pocket of his suit. Then he set the homburg on his head, taking care not to muss his hair. Slipping his hands into the comforting leather of his gloves, he glanced back through the shop window, where the marmalade cat still lay. It didn't stir but Charles saw its lidded eyes shift slightly, and knew the cat was fully aware of his presence. With a grin of admiration at the animal's ability to be at rest and alert all at once, Charles turned and set off down the narrow street, toward Seventh Avenue.

His light step signaled his satisfaction at the results of his business in the shop. Watching him now, so elegantly dressed, so purposeful and forward in his gait as he emerged onto the noisy thoroughfare, crowded mostly with men surging along in pursuit of their commerce and bundled up against the chill of a late Spring afternoon, it was hard to imagine this worldly gentleman making common purpose with the three, unkempt men in the photos, which now sheltered in his breast pocket. The three were nothing less than ragged, at home in torn, dirty denim as they posed before the hand-cut entrance to a mineshaft.

The pictures did show him there—the fourth man—but in truth, he had never been there, wherever it was. He thought "there" might be somewhere in Colorado. He wasn't sure, but Colorado is where he intended to say they had been, the four of them together—near Leadville—he couldn't resist the association with one of Colorado's most storied strikes. And he had no idea who those three men were, nor did he care. But their photograph served his purposes perfectly. *His* image, in an outfit cobbled together in a theatrical costume shop, had been spattered here and there with dust and fake sweat, carefully posed and lit, and then seamlessly inserted in the tableau by the meticulous little man whose shop he had just left.

IV

THE FITTINGS OVER, and Fiona Applegate charmed and satisfied, eleven o'clock struck and Audrey, now back in uniform, fled through the back door at the first sound of the hour, ringing from the ornate clock that stood, tall and solemn, just inside Chez Moreau's front entrance.

"Don't be late back, Audrey," Mr Clayton called as the door into the alley closed behind her. She pretended she hadn't heard.

As she bolted from the shop and down the cobbled alley, the weak sunlight, on this hazy spring day, provided little warmth. She tugged the shop's functional black jacket over her lace-trimmed blouse as she hurried away—she'd left behind the straw boater that completed the outfit. At the end of the alley, she turned eastward along 32nd Street.

She had found the plainness of the uniform's jacket unbearable and, without asking permission, had thinly piped its lapels and sleeves with a silk ribbon of dark magenta, turning it into a garment with some claim to elegance. She was proud of it and liked the way it made her feel—special, unique, above the common run of shop girls that heavily populated this part of Manhattan. Clayton hadn't noticed the improvement, while Mme Moreau liked the look but didn't want to encourage individuality in "the help," and so said nothing. Later she would have all the jackets enhanced in the same way without ever mentioning that it was Audrey's innovation, though all the girls knew it.

When she began the job at Chez Moreau, her future seemed bright, her prospects open-ended. Now, three years on, she saw her dreams fading. Much of her work was drudgery. And although she handled and cared for fine clothes every day, neither Clayton nor his partner, the widow Juliette Moreau (for whom, and purely for its Parisian cachet, he had named the shop), gave her much opportunity either to show her creative talents, or to study design or the techniques of manufacture—although she picked Thea's brain at every opportunity. The only time they involved her directly with the shop's business was when they used her— exploited her—to model dresses for their wealthy customers.

Besides her unique attractiveness, Audrey had personality; people were drawn to her. And her small, trim figure and striking looks—those short, thick reddish curls framing a pale, slightly boyish face—often provided the best setting for the gowns. Yet she had never felt that her job was secure, or inclining toward anything that she could call a career.

At a brisk pace, Audrey made straight for Barney's Midtown Diner, where she knew, at this early hour, she could beat the luncheon crowd and find a table. Going to Barney's carried a certain risk but it had by far the best food of any place she could both afford, and reach on foot, in her short lunch period. Barney Regan, its big, red-faced Irish landlord, would see to it that any men who took lingering notice of a young woman sitting alone in what was essentially a bar, would not interfere with her.

She reached the diner and pushed through the oak paneled doors into its dim interior. A handful of men stood drinking at the bar; others sat in small groups at tables sprinkled around the room. The only other women there, a trio of twenty-year-olds wearing identical costumes, were absorbed in conversation at a table in a far corner; Audrey recognized them as elevator operators in one of the nearby skyscrapers, which were popping up like mushrooms these days in Manhattan.

A pall of cigar smoke had already begun to form against the ceiling and was slowly engulfing the heads of the standing men. But the smoke couldn't ruin the scent of lamb on the skillet, roasting potatoes, and fresh-baked bread drifting in from the kitchen; the earthy aroma made Audrey realize how very hungry she was.

She felt the gaze of men following her, assessing her, daring her to look up, as she maneuvered toward her favorite table. She carefully kept her eyes down, avoiding their stares, threading a direct line down the row of small tables along the wall, leading in from the door. A long padded bench, with a matching backrest attached to the wall, provided one of the seats for each table, with simple bentwood chairs opposite. Audrey slipped in behind the last table and took a deep breath.

She settled back. Success. She had broken free from the stifling atmosphere of Moreau's and now could spend a little time savoring life. With luck, LaVerne would show up and they would have a pleasant half hour or so chatting and giggling about men and clothes, and recovering from the stresses of the morning.

LaVerne hadn't been very reliable of late. She was in love, or thought she was, and spent a lot of time with her Timmy. Her mother disliked Timmy so their meetings were mostly restricted to lunch hours. LaVerne's father distrusted Timmy, believing that he wanted one thing from LaVerne, which had nothing to do with marriage. But LaVerne's eyes were shrouded by her infatuation and Audrey had given up trying to sweep that shroud aside.

"Hello, Audrey my darlin'. It's a delight to see you." Barney stood across the table from her, grinning. His cheery, booming brogue was a welcome sound—he made her feel cocooned and protected.

"Barney. My hero." She rose and threw her arms around his thick trunk and squeezed him happily. He was a big man, and solid. His arm, draped over her in a shy, momentary return of affection, felt like a stout oak branch across her shoulders. Legend had it that Barney never needed a bouncer—when The Man himself was on the premises, it was unwise to start trouble. The last man who did, a brawny ironworker who earned extra money boxing in Saturday night barroom match-ups, had over-estimated his own prowess and was still in the hospital.

"Ah, hero indeed." He waved a dismissive hand. "If only it were so, my dear. I keep telling my Molly, 'If I were ten years younger, you and me might've got hitched and...'"

"Well!" She looked up into his craggy face, parking her fists on her hips in mock rebuke, all part of the game they liked to play to express their mutual affection. "I can't think your wife's too happy to hear you saying things like that, you big lug."

He scratched his head. "You don't imagine that's the reason she keeps slingin' plates at me, do you?"

They laughed together and she felt happy, part of the real world.

As Audrey settled back into her seat and leaned against the backrest, Barney bent down as if to share a deep secret. "The lamb chops are particularly fine today, Audrey. Will you be givin' them a try?"

"Yes, I thought I sniffed them when I came in. I can't resist."

"And a glass of my finest?"

"I'm going to risk it."

A grin transformed Barney's rugged face, as though her acceptance of his lamb chops were a blessing from the queen. "Coming right up." He turned toward the kitchen and strode purposefully away.

She smiled at his broad back, feeling a bond with him that contrasted sharply with most of her other interactions in Manhattan. Then, remembering where she was, she composed her face in a neutral expression and brought her gaze to her hands, clasped on the tabletop. Careful not to look up in the direction of the bar, which stood opposite her and stretched across the length of the room, she picked up the pair of faceted glass salt and pepper shakers. Focusing intently on making them toe an imaginary line on the table, she let her mind drift back to her situation at the shop.

At the beginning, she dove into her job with energy and purpose. She had a flair for clothes and an eye for design, and for the way colors blended. Her girlfriends back home had depended upon her to tweak and adjust the details of their outfits when any important occasion—a dance or a party involving a new beau—called for extreme measures.

But she knew that her own parochial experience and raw talent could take her only so far. What she knew about clothes she'd pretty much taught herself and it wasn't enough; she was constrained by the insularity of her Baltimore suburb, which seemed cut off from the mainstream of American culture. She wanted to learn everything about clothes—designing, manufacturing, marketing. That meant New York, and after that, her long-term goal of London or Paris—preferably both. The job in the tony Park Avenue shop was only a start.

But New York, like the rest of the world, lay in the grip of an economic freeze. People were homeless, living off handouts, or jobs that paid next to nothing—

sometimes only a bartered meal or a pair of worn and patched dungarees.

The Depression had not spared Park Avenue. Sure, the regulars still came. They shopped as though they had few concerns about money, as though the Depression were someone else's little problem. But for most, the true story lay in their shopping behavior, in the difference between what they spent hours looking at, evaluating, trying on, clucking over, and what they actually bought.

A movement in the periphery of her vision brought Audrey's attention sharply back to the diner. It hadn't been that long ago that no young woman could sit unaccompanied in a place like this, without it being automatically assumed by the passing men that she was available for their gratification at a price.

Audrey had often been confronted, and on a couple of terrifying occasions, groped by a boorish lout, usually well into his cups, and had to bring her sharp wit and tongue to bear in her defense. Once, she had added the sharp toe of her shoe to her response, applied with force on the shin of a particularly insensitive Lothario. And another time, Barney had to intervene with his massive presence—augmented by the cricket bat he kept behind the counter.

So she never completely dropped her guard here and it wasn't by chance that she now sensed the gaze of a tall, well-dressed man in a dark suit standing at the front end of the bar. He must have been there when she came in but she hadn't noticed him; perhaps now, some gesture of his had caught her eye.

Being alone and idle at the table was the worst situation to be in—she wished she'd remembered to bring a book or magazine to read. And where was LaVerne?! Her anxiety flashed to irritation when she remembered why LaVerne was missing.

The man made no move toward her but as she caught his reflection in the mirror behind the bar, she could see that he was looking in her direction. She resented not being able to relax and look forward to her meal and the foaming glass of beer, whose earthy flavor she had just learned to appreciate, and to lose herself in thought, instead of having to fend off yet another leering idiot.

Usually she let a man stare—they often gave up if they couldn't catch her eye. Something about this one was different. Even in the brief glimpse she caught in the mirror, she saw that his clothes were too fine for this laborer's bar. Then too, he wasn't boisterous or unsteady from drink and he wasn't wagering shots over whether he could successfully approach her. Why, she thought, were men so arrogant?

She decided to stare him down. She set her face in a stern, confrontational expression and brought her eyes up to meet his—and regretted it immediately. When she locked eyes with him, he didn't look away, nor did he put on that, "Yes, I'm just the man you've been looking for" face that so infuriated her. Instead, he looked at her steadily, an amused smile on his lips. He nodded and held her gaze, a few beats too long for her comfort; she found a sudden interest in the fine print on the beer poster on the wall, off to her side.

Maureen, Barney's niece and chief waitress, scurried up, balancing a tray crowded with tumblers of whiskey and pint glasses of foaming, amber-colored beer. She greeted Audrey cheerily and plunked a brimming glass down in front of her; a tongue of white foam licked down its side and soaked into the square paper coaster. Maybe with Maureen there, the man would keep his distance.

"Audrey. Great to see you. You OK? You look worried."

"Hi, Maureen." She tried to indicate her tormentor with a subtle nod. "Yeah, it's that guy at end of the bar. He's been staring at me. Do you know him?"

Maureen lowered her voice. "We've been wondering about him—too well dressed. None of us have ever seen him before." She brightened and winked at Audrey. "You know what to do if he gets pushy."

"Sure." She needed to change the subject. "You've had your hair cut. Looks great." Maureen ran her fingers through her straight dark hair and shook her head.

"Just a trim, really. Summer's here. I hate all that hair on my neck in the hot days."

"Yes, I..."

"I have to run, Audrey. That silly Margaret's late again and I'm all alone. Let's talk later." She spun and hurried off.

Audrey looked down at the glass on the table. Frost had formed on its sides, turning its honey color into a softer hue. She brought it to her lips, careful to keep her gaze from straying toward the bar. But as she took a sip and sensed the brew's yeasty, grainy brightness on her tongue, she noticed out of the corner of her eye that the man had put a coin down on the bar and picked up his glass, along with his hat and gloves. He was now moving in her direction, weaving between the tables. She steeled herself.

"I hope you will forgive me for staring but I have to confess, I am mesmerized by you." She listened to the voice without turning, trusting that the obvious snub would make him go away. But he pressed on. "Will you allow me to sit with you a moment? I assure you, I'm no masher."

She looked up, challenging, hoping her coldest stare might do the trick. But he stood his ground and he was smiling—not leering—at her. Determined not to respond, she turned again to the poster and sipped at the beer, but her ability to appreciate its flavor and foamy feel in her mouth were blocked, her attention pirated by this intruder.

"You know, in such a large city," she heard him say, as if chatting with a friend, "we have only one chance to meet; our paths—yours and mine—are unlikely to cross ever again." This excursion into philosophy took her aback, and intrigued her in spite of herself. Again she looked at him, wondering where he would take it. To her disquiet, she found his smile warm and engaging and she had trouble maintaining her challenging attitude.

The man used her silence as permission to join her, dropping into the chair opposite her! This was new and alarming. Typically, by this time, the offender would have made a clumsy or indecent proposition, perhaps even offering her money, or have crowded drunkenly into the seat at her side. This one was the first to make a polite request to join her, even though he hadn't waited for her consent.

He was different, too, his accent—not New England, but English, she thought. And his appearance—he seemed to be a man of means. She knew something about men's clothes and his were top-drawer, impeccable and expensive; starched white collar, the thin silk tie, not black but a deep blue and lightly flecked with a nacre-colored thread, a dark blue-gray wool serge suit with subtle pin stripes, and tailor-made. His dark hair and mustache were neatly cut and trimmed and he was perfectly manicured, his nails clean, filed and, she noted with interest, buffed. If appearances meant anything, he was a gentleman by the definition of the day. And yet, here he sat, apparently attempting the ungentlemanly act of taking advantage of a lone woman in a café bar.

No sooner had the man arranged himself in the chair than a presence materialized at his elbow. Barney. He placed the plate containing Audrey's lunch in front of her, then turned to face the man, whose eyes were fixed on her. She noticed the cricket bat, hanging loosely at Barney's side in his massive, gnarled hand and she couldn't suppress a slight smile at his timely intervention. But as she picked up fork and knife and prepared to cut into her lamb chop, she also found that she was curious about this man, and hoped Barney might be able to scare him, without scaring him away.

Just as the man tilted his head back to scan the looming form above him, Barney bent forward—their faces were separated by inches. Barney rapped the end of the bat sharply on the floor; the man blinked hard, his eyes wide, and Audrey thought she heard him gasp.

"Pardon me, your Lordship," Barney's brogue sharpened in moments like this, "but my daughter does not want to be disturbed. I'll be askin' you to move along."

Wide-eyed, the man glanced at the bat and began a stuttered appeal. "I... I... I merely..."

Audrey surprised herself by stepping in on his behalf. "It's all right, Barney." She smiled affectionately at her protector and laid a soft hand on his forearm. "Thank you. We're just chatting. He appears to be harmless—not like the typical riff-raff you let in here." She enjoyed teasing him about his clientele and he allowed himself to be teased by her.

Barney looked at her closely, to make certain her assurances were genuine. Satisfied, he looked sternly back at the man, then bent toward him again and spoke softly, but still with a note of menace. "So long as the young lady vouches for you..." He straightened and flicked the bat against his leg with a soft but definite strike. "Mind your manners." With a meaningful glare at the man, and without looking again at Audrey, he headed back to the kitchen.

"He's not really my father," she confessed with a faint smile. "He owns this place and he thinks of himself as my protector. Actually, I've needed him on a few occasions."

"I'm pleased you have him," he said, with an air of perfect sincerity.

What was it about him and the way he spoke that made her lower her defenses? There was no emotional pang; she was in no way smitten. But something about him appealed to her, as though they might be old friends or distant relations.

"My name is Charles," he offered his hand. She hesitated for an instant, then offered hers. It surprised her that his was so near her own in size, thin for a man's hand, much softer than that of any working man.

"Audrey," she offered, flatly.

He smiled. "A beautiful name."

Audrey smiled back shyly. She'd no idea what to say to her visitor so she returned to her meal, assuming he would state his purpose.

But he didn't speak. He sat and watched her, smiling, for several long minutes as she ate. His scrutiny only irritated her—mildly at first, but it turned to aggravation as it continued. She couldn't concentrate on the taste of the perfectly cooked meat and Barney's famous mashed potatoes. Finally, she sat back and glared at him.

"Was there something you wanted to say? I don't understand why you've come—certainly not to watch me eat my lunch."

"Actually, in a way, that is exactly why I've come."

"Now look..."

"Let me explain," he held up a hand to stay her, then motioned for her to continue eating. She thought briefly about calling out to Barney but checked the impulse. She held his gaze for a long moment, irritation flaring in her eyes, then trained her attention again on her meal, determined to enjoy it in spite of him. Charles readjusted his position in the chair and leaned forward.

"I'm in search," he began, "of... an assistant. Not just anyone—a young woman, with a touch of... refinement, and more than a touch of beauty and charm. I'm wondering, Audrey, whether you might be she."

She didn't register the compliment. "An assistant?! For what?" Something about the way he couched this notion irritated her further. "What on Earth are you talking about?!"

She looked toward the kitchen. Barney was inspecting them, squinting from behind the counter near the kitchen door, and she saw him reach for his bat. She waved an OK sign at him, then returned her gaze to Charles. Now, just above a whisper, she said, "You're saying you want me to be your assistant?! You want to hire me?!"

"You *have* a job, I'm sure." He said this with an assured air, as though he knew all the details of her life. She cocked her head to the side—God, he was getting under her skin! "Yes, I do," she said firmly. "A very good job."

"Do you like it?"

Unexpected. She hated being thrown off balance—she needed to be in control in situations like this.

"It's fine. It's... it's none of *your* business, is it?"

"Not really," he said, still smiling.

She plunked down her knife and fork—they clattered loudly on Barney's chinaware plate. "Oooh," she said in frustration. "What in heaven's name...? What *are* you getting at?!"

Charles laughed softly at her outburst. "I told you. I need an assistant. Do you want to hear about it? I think it will... it may... interest you."

While he waited for her answer, he reached inside his coat and withdrew the manila envelope. He unwrapped the tie and tipped the envelope down; a photograph slid into his hand. Looking at her intently now, his smile fading, Charles turned the photo toward Audrey and handed it to her.

She took it tentatively and brought it nearer, turning it to catch the light filtering in through the windows. The picture showed three ragged and sweaty workmen posed before a mine entrance, plus a fourth man, in boots and jodhpurs, standing nearby and gesturing toward the others. She wasn't sure but she thought the fourth one might be the man sitting opposite her.

She leaned against the backrest and regarded him. Something about this situation felt wrong, edging on improper, but having prevented Barney from showing this odd stranger the door, she couldn't come up with an excuse now for refusing to hear what he had to say. With a curt gesture, she invited him to continue.

V

WILLIAM CLARINGTON PRUITT III was having trouble extricating himself from Sadie Collins's shabby little room. Having pulled his clothes into reasonable order, he was itching to leave but every time he made a move that edged him closer to the door, Sadie dissolved into yet another flood of tears and wails. Worse yet, she refused to do it quietly and, despite his appeals, she seemed bent on making as much noise as possible.

William—Billy—feared he'd be recognized as he left the creaky tenement and would find his name in the gossip columns again. His father would not appreciate that and Billy would be forced to do penance for several lean weeks—his allowance cut nearly to zero. He desperately wanted Sadie to understand his distress and keep her anguish contained within the squalid room that served as their amorous retreat.

She sat on the narrow, rumpled bed in her bra and slip, trying to find a place on the tattered top of her stocking still sufficiently intact to accept the button of her garter. Billy watched. Though Sadie's face was twisted in anger and he could not look at her without discomfort and guilt, her body remained the magnificent conjunction of curves and lines and clefts that he was so in thrall to.

"It's not fair," she whined as she worked to secure the stocking. "What've I done but give you everything a woman can give a man? What?!" she demanded. "Tell me?!" She began winding up again, louder and more shrill all at once, like the end of a Rossini overture badly out of tune. Billy hated it.

"Sadie, it's not the end of the world. Can't you just... Look, I'll be back before you know it—two months, at most." He stepped toward her, intent on comforting her with a stroke of his gloved hand, but something prevented him from closing the gap completely. It felt too much like knowingly walking within striking range of a coiled snake.

She looked up at him. "But why do you have to go at all? Why you? Your stinking father's got loads of people he can send over there. It doesn't have to be you. Shit!"

He was too much of a prude to be comfortable hearing such words coming from a woman, even a woman who made her meager living by giving men everything a woman has to give them. He rolled his eyes and stepped back. He wanted very much to be out of that room, out of that building and into the open air, where he could draw a full, clean breath.

It took everything he had to stand and explain himself to this gutter-mouthed, classless girl, this prostitute. Moments before, she was a willing, pliable, sweet-smelling voluptuary who felt delectable beneath him, her thighs clamping him and meeting his steady thrusts with thrusts of her own, emitting gasps of the deepest pleasure. It was then that he thought he could love no one as much as he loved her. But now, those sweet sensations were a fast-fading memory, replaced by her tear stained, sour, indignant face. The mouth that had been so inviting to kiss, and which had so lovingly and hungrily engulfed his erection and brought him to his climax, was now a grotesque hole from which belched a stream of censure. It sounded all too much like a version of his mother's disapproving tirades, shriller and cruder to be sure, and more of an offense on his ears and to his psyche—the relentless rasp of fingernails across a blackboard.

This was the trouble with sex, he'd found. You couldn't just do it and enjoy it and leave. There was always some major emotional flare-up surrounding it that drew all the pleasure out, leaving a bad aftertaste. It didn't seem right or fair. All the men he'd known who talked openly about it, like Mario, his father's mechanic, and George, the gardener's helper, could discuss their sexual adventures at such length and with such detail that Billy often mused that his father had hired them only for that—they appeared to do little else. These men never seemed to have this same kind of trouble with their women. Their stories detailed the exquisite pleasure of using women for their own needs, and how the women were dedicated to making them feel good. Mario even claimed that his favorite prostitute often refused to take any money from him—she just gave him her body because she liked him so much.

Billy was one of the wealthiest men in New York—well, his father was. Shouldn't he, of all men, be able to have exactly what he wanted from a woman, from a whore, just like Mario? Shouldn't those twenty-dollar bills, held down by a jar of skin cream on Sadie's dresser, purchase his freedom from any responsibility for her vulgar emotions?

"Look, it's... it's like... sorta like training. I'm going to... probably... going to be taking over the business one of these days and Pop wants me to know all about it."

Her laugh was derisive, serrated. "You? Take over his business? In a pig's eye." If she had to suffer, she would take him along for the gritty ride.

"Now, don't be like that," he pleaded.

"You don't even realize what's going on, do you, Billy?" She'd tugged on her blouse and was pulling on her plain black skirt, the one with a gap in the seam where the thread had broken. He'd been wanting to point it out to her but didn't know how to say it without it sounding like an accusation. Her blouse remained unbuttoned and her breasts, those perfect breasts, lay, cupped in the thin bra, just under the silk, the nipples poking at the fabric in a way that mesmerized him.

"Your father's getting you out of town, you sap. Getting you away from the heat—away from me."

"I... I don't think..."

"No, you don't!" She was buttoning the blouse now and the tears started again. She stood and the black fabric of the skirt swirled seductively around her knees and clung to her thighs as she stepped to the nightstand to get her handkerchief. Those thighs, that ass—they formed a supple sculpture of curves and dips and ridges of flesh brought into relief by the sheen of the skirt. They defied description and they boiled his blood. If he could just shut her up and press her back onto the bed, and take her once again before he left. No love talk—he simply wanted to take her. He was rigid again, his erection straining against his trousers, but her anger kept him at bay.

She stepped into her slippers and moved to the dresser. She was piqued when she saw her disheveled hair in the bureau mirror. She stabbed at it with a long, tortoise shell comb.

"You just day dream and go around making defenseless girls pregnant," she said, addressing his reflection. "You don't care what happens to me."

He took a hesitant step toward her. Maybe there was a chance he could play out his renewed urge if he could embrace her and run his hand inside her blouse and touch that fascinating breast, that taut, pink nipple.

"But I do, Sadie. When I get back, we'll..."

Her contemptuous glance stopped his advance. She really kind of liked him, but she couldn't stand that he was such a baby—so stinking rich and so stupidly naïve.

Sometimes she allowed herself to fantasize about becoming his wife. A big wedding. 'Mr and Mrs William J. Pruitt II request the pleasure of your company at the wedding of their son, William, to Miss Sadie Bradford Collins of Pittsburgh, Pennsylvania...' All she had ever known was work and privation and humiliation and hunger, and men who felt she should be grateful because they could pay to use her body. She let them use her because she believed she had no real choice. And here stood yet another one, a pale and pudgy and useless baby who, if he had the courage, could change her life, could bestow on her the dignity that had always remained beyond her grasp. Fat chance.

No, it wasn't fair. She did like Billy. She liked the way he felt, lying between her open thighs. They fit each other well and she could sense his urgent, child-like need. She found herself wanting to respond to him, to mother him, even as she worked hard to be his whore.

But her resentment had grown too strong. Before long, her belly would swell with the results of their carnality and her life would move in a different direction, one, she was sure, that would make it another notch worse.

In the mirror, she saw the mixture of discomfiture and anxiety in his face and her tears flooded back. She covered her face with her hands. "I'm the sap here," she spluttered.

Billy strained forward to hear. "What?"

"Just get out of here. Go on!"

He almost tripped as he turned and moved toward the door.

"Look at you. You can't wait to leave. Can't wait to turn your back on your child and its mother."

He turned back toward her, determined to challenge her. "Well, look, now. How do we... I, even know...? I mean you could be... How do you know it's...?"

The first thing that fell under her hand was the small, dense, dark blue jar of skin cream, the one weighing down the money he had placed there so ostentatiously. She hurled it at him with all the force her rage could put into it. Billy ducked and threw his arm up in front of his face; the jar missed him by inches and smashed against the door jam, exploding into shards of sharp blue glass coated with the sticky white cream.

"Get out! Get the hell out—what are you waiting for?! Go get on your boat and make your escape. I can't stand you!" A new torrent of tears washed across her face. She turned back to the mirror and resumed the attack on her wild curls with the comb, all the while snuffling and bawling so that her words sputtered out like a misfiring engine.

He turned and opened the door. Sadie tried to stifle her crying; she had lost control of herself and of the situation, and disliked herself because of it. She couldn't resist a last jab at him as she resumed the attack on her hair.

"Tell that bastard father of yours that this is going to cost him. He can send his little boy to Europe if he wants—I can't stop him. I just get to live with the results. But he'd better be ready to pay to keep his useless, spoiled little brat's name out of the society section. It's going to cost plenty!" She snapped her head around and shouted at him.

"I told you to get out!"

Billy lurched into the hall and drew the door closed against any new missiles. He fled down the three flights, twice nearly tripping on the tattered carpet covering the wooden stairs. Several doors cracked open as he lunged down the stairwell; he prayed no one he knew lurked behind any of them, especially not a reporter who would recognize him, with his Graphlex at the ready.

Safely on the street and apparently still anonymous to those in Sadie's grim apartments, William Pruitt III adjusted his coat, pulled on his gloves and tried to relax, savoring his release from Sadie's fury. He parked his hat on his head and took a moment to think what the best route to his bank might be. He would embark for England in the morning on the Queen Mary and needed a substantial amount of cash to insure the maintenance, aboard ship, of his terrestrial life style. He understood from more traveled friends that first class on the Queen Mary would be sumptuous and hedonistic, and he was determined to take full advantage of its delights. Smiling in anticipation, he ambled off in the direction of Wall Street.

VI

TWO IN THE MORNING. Except for the clerk, the Western Union office on Houston St was deserted, just as Charles had expected—and hoped. He wanted his message to be at Western Union in Lambeth, just south of the Thames, when Alvin got there, but didn't want it sitting around any longer than necessary. The late hour also helped him send the message under the least scrutiny.

The clerk sat at his desk behind a counter, which stretched from wall to wall of the small space and was topped by a thick plate glass barrier. Charles took his scratch sheet to the window and tapped to get the man's attention. He was middle-aged, white haired, with a green eyeshade pulled down over his eyes. His white shirtsleeves were tied with bands, the cuffs hidden under protectors.

When the clerk stepped to the window, Charles pushed his scratch sheet through the slot at the bottom of the glass. The man picked it up and examined it through his narrow reading glasses.

"Uhmmm, let me see... Addressee: Mister Alvin Grayson," he quoted. "We'll need an address, sir."

"I'm sorry, my good fellow, I haven't one. Mr Grayson is expecting this message. I'm sure he'll come for it."

"Oh, I'm sure you're right, sir, but..." He shrugged, looking up at Charles. "Policy. You know how it is. I need something—a, uhh... telephone number?"

The man appealed to him from beneath his eyeshade, trying his best to be helpful but needing to make sure his job was done as commanded—all the necessary spaces filled in.

Charles wanted him to stop being a bureaucratic slave and do what he was asked. But to make any sort of scene would ensure that this functionary would remember him, a result he definitely did not want.

As he mulled this over, his hand fell on a matchbook in his coat pocket and he remembered that he had got it in a favorite London restaurant. The phone number would do as well as any to fill the space on Western Union's form.

"Ah, yes, I think I do have his number on a note here." He pulled the matchbook from his pocket but held it below the level of the counter, out of the clerk's view, and rattled off the exchange and the digits.

The clerk brightened as he jotted down the numbers. "Good. No use stirring up the powers-that-be, you know what I mean?" He winked at Charles. "Let sleeping dogs lie, is what I always say."

Charles nodded with an appropriately conspiratorial smile and thought what a pathetic creature this poor fellow was. He noted the man's shirt, so heavily starched it seemed to be constructed of stiff panels. Charles guessed that it had to last him through the week; he'd probably alternate it with an identical one, paying a washerwoman to wash, starch, and iron it over the weekend. It was possible his wife did this for him but he wore no wedding band. He might have a third shirt for special occasions but Charles thought this man's small life contained few such occasions.

The clerk mumbled through the message, which told of a happy reunion with a Mary Weldon, who sends her love. It was signed, Martin Chase. Charles confirmed that the man had it correct.

The surface content meant nothing, of course. The coding signaled his associate, using the name Alvin Grayson, that he would be on the Queen Mary when it sailed the next day and would put their scheme into motion.

Charles paid the clerk, thanked him, and left.

VII

WHITE GULLS, SOARING on long, bright wings, found a quickening thermal and wheeled high above the Hudson in the morning sunlight, squawking and yammering. With the sun still low in the East, the city's tall buildings cast long, dark shadows over most of the broad pier, but one bright ray slipped through a concrete-and-steel-lined canyon and splashed over scurrying trucks and freight carts, and the gathering crowd of people waiting to board the new ocean liner, the Queen Mary.

The pier's thick planking shuddered and groaned when the biggest of the vans rolled across it, with last-minute deliveries of goods to pallets lined up next to the Queen's hulking, black-painted side. Burly longshoremen loaded the pallets with food and soap, wax and paint, milk and wine, towels and newsprint and ink, and all the other things needed to keep 2,000 people content for five or six days on the Atlantic. When they had the pallets stuffed and netted and tied, the men clipped them to drooping hooks, waved an arcane signal, and the cranes drew them aloft and swung them into the ship's vast hold.

Fresh breezes snapped the colorful pennants, attached to lines radiating from the Queen's imposing bridge. Watching them, David Bowen thought that, one of these days, he would ask Benny to explain what the various shapes and colors and insignia meant. For now, fluttering in the wind, they looked like party streamers celebrating the ship's departure for Europe and he didn't need them to hold more meaning than that. David's mood was light—he felt happy and optimistic, a rare indulgence for him these days.

He was at the rail, one deck above the gangway where the first-class passengers come aboard. He began every voyage here, looking down on the toffs as they ambled on, the women and girls in mink or in fine wool coats enhanced with fox stoles, the men and boys in heavy overcoats with fur-lined lapels, some of them affecting spats over patent leather shoes. As they paraded by, followed by porters and chauffeurs carrying their heavy cases, David took his inventory. Wearing denim trousers and a pea coat, he did his best to look like a sailor on watch. A well-worn, black Greek fisherman's cap covered his short, curly blond hair. He *was* on a watch of a kind—pale blue eyes, behind tinted glasses, searching for the monied men he hoped to see boarding the ship, men who liked to play poker.

He expected this voyage of the Queen to be special. The ship had gone into service only a month earlier and was the pride of the Cunard and White Star fleet, so a good number of well-heeled passengers with a special destination, the upcoming Olympic Games in Berlin, were sure to be sailing. These were some of Europe's and America's fattest cats and, before they got a chance to cheer on their favorites in Berlin, David intended to trim several of them in a succession of high-stakes poker games.

A handful of America's Olympic athletes were sailing, as well. White Star and Cunard had hastened to imply the prospect of rubbing elbows with them in their ads, to lure in even more high-paying customers. Not only did America have high hopes for its athletic heroes, this Olympics would offer a chance for men of business to get a closer look at the new and troublesome regime in

Germany. Many of them had extensive interests in Europe and were anxious about National Socialism and its fiery, belligerent standard bearer.

David's guess about the concentration of wealth on the voyage was proving correct. He recognized many of the passengers from articles in the business and society pages of the New York and London papers, all of which he scoured routinely to keep track of their rise and fall, their comings and goings, their successes and disappointments, their shifting fortunes in tough economic times.

He'd already spotted Samuel Riverson, recent heir to the Salient Oil fortune; Felix Hansen, whose company built many of Manhattan's growing population of high-rise buildings; Nelson Chandler, who, following Kellogg's example with corn, had promoted wheat as a breakfast cereal with astonishing success; and Milton Brownlow, head of Lake Eastern Bank.

Brownlow, in particular, was known to be an avid card player. People wondered, half joking, if he ever tapped into his depositors' accounts, so much had he lost—and so often—without apparent concern. The plain truth was that he had vast personal resources and losses that would devastate other men were of little consequence to him.

David wondered what went through the minds of men like Brownlow when they rubbed up against people still caught in the grip of the Depression. Bread lines and soup kitchens remained a fact of life in New York, though by now the worst had passed. Brownlow's chauffeured trip down to the docks from his Park Avenue apartment would have taken him past numbers of homeless families, desperate men looking for hand-outs, people fighting over some two-bit job. To see them, he only had to lift his eyes from the Business Section of the Times, as his limousine carried him south.

Like Brownlow, the wealthiest arrived in their own limos, the shiny broughams and phaetons and Silver Ghosts and other chrome- and brass-accented, over-sized machines now lined up, nose to tail, along the wharf below, each attended by a uniformed driver. Other passengers slated for first class arrived by taxi, about a dozen of which formed a second line of cars next to the limousines. This line, noisy with bleating horns and barking cabbies, was in constant flux, the drivers scuffling to avoid being trapped there for long when they could be trolling for new fares uptown.

Even at this distance from the dock, some five stories overhead, a young man, hatless, vigorously shaking the hand of the chauffeur at the wheel of a large, shiny black Rolls Royce, grabbed David's attention. He stood out not only because of his expensive clothes, but also because of his obvious youth—twenty, perhaps twenty-one. Young people of wealth usually didn't travel alone. Typically, a family sent a companion along to keep the youth out of trouble.

Then an older, somewhat portly man, in a homburg and a fur-collared overcoat, approached the boy and he turned. He took the youth by his shoulders and they stood there for a moment in conversation, the older man doing the talking. David couldn't hear their dialogue, of course. Nor could he see much of the man's face beneath the brim of his hat, but their interaction had the earmarks of a serious father-son talk. From the slump of his shoulders, the cant of his head, David thought the son didn't much like what he was hearing.

Then the father thrust out his right hand and the young man clasped it in a handshake that had a look of desperation about it. Abruptly, with a nod, the man disengaged, slid into the limo's back seat, and closed the door. The car jerked away, and David sensed that, as the youth watched it go, he had to stop himself from running after it. When the limo swung around a corner and disappeared, the youth turned slowly and sidled through the crowd to the gangway.

Downcast, the lad made his way up the ramp, and David scoured his memory for a match to this face. It was a blank at first but, as he came closer, it clicked. Yes, that expression, often glassy-eyed, had shown up many times in the newspapers, usually in connection with some run-in with the authorities—a party gone out of control, an engagement called off, a questionable business venture—and best of all for David, blows exchanged over gambling debts. It was William Pruitt III.

A notoriously bad poker player, the gossip had it that Pruitt had left thousands of dollars on card tables across Manhattan without regard for where those dollars had come from—the clamoring cash registers of Pruitt Mercantile, his father's nationwide chain of cheap-line department stores. On one much talked-about occasion, Pruitt had trouble making a fellow player understand that he'd have to wait a day or two before Pruitt's debt could be settled—that is, before he could talk his father out of the money. He was fortunate that he wasn't playing in the Bowery or Hell's Kitchen at the time. This game had taken place at an uptown party thrown by one of his college chums and his naiveté only cost him a split lip. David smiled to himself. If only half of what he'd read about this feckless young man were true, the down payment on David's farm might be assured.

Next up the ramp strode a handful of richly dressed women who boarded without escorts, chattering excitedly with each other. They waved to David with knowing smiles as they reached the top of the gangway— he waved back.

Then came an intriguing couple, along with a porter trundling their cases on a handcart. The couple was unknown to David. The man was tall, dark haired.

As they, too, reached the deck, David saw that he was expensively but not ostentatiously dressed. David could easily imagine him as the successful owner of a growing industrial enterprise, destined for the top tier of the newly wealthy, though perhaps not there quite yet.

But it was the woman on his arm, a fresh young beauty, who caught and held his attention. Clearly, she was new to this experience. She was almost giddy, as she looked excitedly from one new feature of the ship to the next, the man patiently explaining each one. Her short, curly hair was an earnest reddish-brown and her skin was cream-like, set off by a full and sensual mouth. Her eyes were gray, or maybe green, at this distance he wasn't sure but they held a current of mirth and of passion that shone as if from beacons. She wore a conservative day dress that revealed a trim, almost athletic figure, with a narrow waist accenting modest breasts, carried high on her frame. He had never seen a woman so arresting.

David looked at the man again. Though far from old, he seemed too old to be her husband but this could be misleading. Many a new millionaire's first attempt to display his money's buying power came by marrying the town's most desirable young woman. This sometimes led to a match that became the topic of derisive chatter behind raised handkerchiefs, or in smoky rooms to which the man still found himself barred.

But if this couple was New York's newest pairing in the world of the *nouveau riche*, why, David wondered, hadn't he run across a picture of them in the papers? In tough competition with each other, especially in the society pages, the city papers never missed (and many were not above manufacturing) an opportunity to post a picture of a woman as attractive as this one. So why was she totally unfamiliar to him?

David pegged the man as not among the truly wealthy, yet he had an almost regal air about him, and his clothes were too well arranged, like a mannequin in the window of a Park Avenue haberdasher. Something about the way the two interacted negated any notion of husband and wife; they lacked the air of easy intimacy that married couples present. They seemed happy—untroubled—yet not involved with one another. Or was this wishful thinking?

David doubted that they were father and daughter; they didn't appear to be that far apart in age. He was confused, not sure what their relationship might be and hoping that it wasn't romantic.

At the top of the gangway, the woman turned the wrong way when something toward the bow caught her attention. The man called to her: "Audrey!" She stopped and spun around, confused. "This way." With a giggle, she danced back and grasped his offered arm, and they sauntered off to find their berths, with their porter in pursuit.

David was done in. Audrey. His mother's name. A beautiful name for a beautiful woman. His inventory of the toffs suddenly took a back seat—he'd catch up on it later. His objective now was to find out all he could about Audrey.

He scrambled down the stairs and fell in a few yards behind them as they entered the superstructure and, along with the other passengers, plus porters, chauffeurs and other helpers, made their way down to the berth decks to search for their cabin. Walking behind, David focused on Audrey's figure and, despite the stole draped across her back and hips, which veiled her shape, he was mesmerized by her form and by her movements as she walked. When she turned her head to throw a comment to her escort, the arc of her long neck and her profile seemed almost too perfect to be real. She astonished him—he discovered that his throat had gone dry.

But there was something out of kilter—she appeared too fresh and exuberant to be society. Society women behaved with reserve, determined never to become the subject of "talk." This young woman didn't care about that. This was all new to her and she was enjoying its newness thoroughly—"talk" be damned.

Her escort? ...beau? ...father? He was another matter. He had an air of certitude and command about him that struck David as somehow wrong, in relation to the woman on his arm. He looked every bit the man about town, a person of breeding, a master of men. There was nothing about him—not his manicured nails, his neatly trimmed hair, his polished shoes without a hint of wear at the heels, his impeccable creases, the kid gloves, the Saville Row suit—nothing that spoke of anything but solid, mercantile success. But David didn't buy it; he found, with no clear idea why, that he did not like the man. Something he could not put his finger on told him there was something important to be known about this "guy," blank pages that needed to be filled in.

Checking the signs and arrows on the walls, the pair made their way to the middle cabins on the A Deck, joking with each other, Audrey never losing her light grip on her escort's arm. David hung back, dodging other searching passengers, and luggage temporarily stacked in the narrow passageway, and pretended also to be looking for a cabin. The couple seemed to behave more and more like lovers as they continued—laughing, on a mutual lark. David sank into despair as they continued. But just as quickly, his spirits were lifted—when they found their berths, they entered adjacent but separate rooms.

David was astonished at how relieved he was. He leaned against a bulkhead and let the coolness of the ship's metal structure, hidden beneath the paneling, seep into his back. His heart was beating fast and although the morning was cool, a rivulet of sweat slid down between his shoulder blades. He took a deep breath and turned away, trying to get a grip on his emotions. He'd never reacted like this before to a woman. It bothered him—he liked to be in better control of his emotions.

He made his way out of the first-class cabins to the stern and down two decks to his own, Tourist-class berth. He never tried to appear as a bona fide member of his traveling companions' set by booking first-class accommodations. All he needed for his role was the right costume: A tuxedo, of which he had three; a cigarette case—Alkin was *haut couture* this season; and the manners and speech that allowed him to pass as one of the privileged. Despite the disadvantages of his upbringing, David had acquired enough social polish at college to move comfortably in this milieu.

He was making this particular voyage for one reason—to win as much as he could off the poker players in first class. That was always his mission, of course, but there was special intensity in it this time. He'd grown tired of his gambler's life, with its endless round of trips across the featureless, sometimes treacherous Atlantic. He'd been at it for almost ten years, so much of that at sea that his mother and two sisters had nearly become strangers to him. But he'd done well financially, his poker skills providing him a comfortable nest egg, now stashed away in a bank in Cornwall. He wanted to top it off with a big deposit so he could finally pull the plug, and this trip might do it for him.

When he was last in England, he went down to Truro, where his family had its roots, and learned that his grandfather's old farm was up for sale. He took it as a favorable sign that he should do as he so often threatened: retire. A small corner had been chipped off the farm for an expansion of the new A39/390 roadway toward London but the rest was intact, including the original wattle-and-daub farmhouse, built around 1750. David put down a deposit and the estate agent, a family friend, agreed to hold it off market as long as he could while David pulled the remainder of his down payment together. He planned to live on it, grow beans and millet and raise sheep or cows, and forget he ever knew anything about poker.

When he first crystallized that daydream and began slipping into it in relaxed moments, just before falling asleep or in the morning as he shaved, there was no one else attached to it—he was there alone, except perhaps for a pair of adoring border collies. But now, without willing it, his imagination made space in the dream for another person, a laughing, sparkling young woman with curly auburn hair.

VIII

LEONARD BATES HAD NO SUNGLASSES and no one there on the docks needed them more. The familiar pain was building at his temples. If he kept his head down and stayed in the shadow of the man behind him in the line, he found he could keep the bright sunlight from burning holes in his skull.

The sun had just pushed through a thin haze and now bathed the flanks of the massive ship, the docks, and the throng of people saying their goodbyes in its reassuring warmth, a warmth that Leonard's alcohol ravaged brain made it impossible for him to feel.

He'd never been so unsure of himself. Standing in the line of loud and scruffy people, shuffling toward the gangway for the third-class passengers, he hardly had any idea what he was doing. The ship would soon cast off and carry them all down the Hudson, point its prow toward the morning sun, and set course for England. In less than a week he would step off the gangway at Southampton. Beyond that, he had only a vague notion of what his next move would be.

Why in hell was he going? He'd spent a big chunk of his limited money to buy passage and its chief result would be to separate him from what little he still had in the way of roots, of connections with other people.

On the surface, it seemed senseless but in fact, it was the one thing that did make sense in his life right now. Leonard's connections with family and friends were in tatters. He had no idea where his wife was—his ex-wife.

She divorced him while he was still behind bars and he couldn't blame her. And to the extent he was anything at all to his son, Teddy, he was an embarrassment.

He'd had only slight contact with his sister when he went inside, then she moved without sending him her new address. She wasn't there waiting when they conducted him out through the prison gates this time. A profound feeling of hurt and shame swept over him and he understood that he had exhausted all his familial capital with her and was utterly, irredeemably alone.

He figured his best course was to leave and start again, somewhere on the other side of the pond. After the Great War ended, Leonard had knocked around awhile overseas. He spent time in England and Ireland, trying to get something started. Now he thought he might be able to work himself into some sort of game there, most likely in London. He'd heard there were always schemes that needed a rich American businessman to lend a note of expertise, combined with the exotic, and that was a role he knew how to play. If he could make a decent score, a few thousand, he could come back to New York and perhaps re-enter his son's life as a prosperous man, no longer needing to sponge off him. The last he heard, Teddy was married and about to become a father. Leonard wanted to see his grandchild. Maybe, eventually, he might even be a part of the kid's life.

But now there was little to keep him in New York. He didn't think he could make an honest living here, or anywhere in the US. "Honest" was an important criterion; he was under pressure to avoid anything that would get him arrested again. The rules of his parole made it too easy for the bulls to rush him back behind bars. He was in jeopardy if they caught him with another felon, even if all they were up to was helping a blind man cross the street.

Leonard and good fortune had been strangers for much of his life but a bizarre bit of luck had come his way a couple of months back. Although it was well into spring, a freak cold snap had blown in and settled over the Northeast. It was late on a Sunday—twilight—and it was snowing. Leonard had only a sport coat and a cap. Hurrying toward his shabby apartment down in SoHo to escape the cold, he stumbled upon a guy lying in the alley behind a vacant furniture store, frozen stiff.

The alley and street were deserted and Leonard was alone with the corpse, which lay just far enough from the street to escape the attention of most passersby. The poor sap had apparently drunk himself into a stupor. His clothing was even thinner than Leonard's and he'd hunched into the corner of a low porch at the back of the store, apparently trying, without success, to fend off the wind, and equally unsuccessfully, trying to warm himself with a quart of rot-gut whiskey. When the liquor closed its grip around his brain, he slumped onto the icy pavement, where the rains soaked him through before turning to sleet, and then to snow. When Leonard came upon him, curled up under a thick, snowy blanket, he looked more like a child's toy igloo than a human being. Icicles hung from his nose and from his ice blue fingers, which still clutched the empty whiskey bottle.

Cars rattled by but no one in them allowed his attention to linger long enough to register the minor tragedy playing out in that darkening alley. Leonard approached the white heap and knelt, one knee dropping into the cold powder. He brushed away some of the snow, down to a pair of threadbare trousers, and turned the guy's pockets out. All he found were a few coins.

He tried to avoid looking directly at the guy—he felt you shouldn't look at a mark when you're picking his pocket, no matter that he was dead. But curiosity overtook him. He brushed away the snow from the man's head and the sight of the pale face brought him up short. Peering closely, he had the sensation of looking into a ghastly mirror—similar jawline and prominent cheekbones; same dark brown hair, cut short; a dark mustache speckled with gray. His eye color, as near as he could tell, was close to Leonard's brown—close enough. He couldn't be sure but it seemed there wasn't more than an inch or two difference in their heights. In all, the resemblance was enough to fool anyone taking a casual look.

Leonard searched the clothes more carefully, looking for a wallet, but found none. He scanned the ground, now covered in several inches of new snow. A white lump in the corner, where the stoop joined the building's brick wall, looked like it might be the missing billfold, tossed there by whomever had beaten Leonard to it. He stepped over the body, at the same time reaching for the switchblade knife in his hip pocket. He flicked the knife open, whisked the covering of snow away, slid the long blade into the fold of the wallet, and lifted it out of the snow. Given where it lay, he expected it to reek of piss but, sniffing it cautiously, he caught only the scent of damp leather.

Leonard rifled through it. No cash, of course, but the driving license was there. He pocketed the wallet and walked further into the alley; he wanted to get some distance from the body while he took stock. As he sheltered in an overhung doorway, the dull pain at his temples, which had been crouching just outside his senses, now throbbed its way to the front of his brain. His right eye felt as though someone was stabbing it with an icepick. He yanked a flat pint bottle of whiskey from his coat pocket and guzzled a large mouthful. He scrinched his eyes shut as the booze burned its way down his gullet. After an excruciating minute, the alcohol surge in his blood succeeded in beating back the pain in his head. His hands shaking, he lit a cigarette and took a long, deep drag.

Calmer now, he dug into the wallet. Frederick Michael Steffens. An address in Queens. Born in 1896—Leonard was a year older. He noted that the few elements of physical description on the driving license agreed more or less with his own.

It didn't take him long to make up his mind. He hurriedly transferred most of the notes and cards from his own wallet into Steffens's. He left behind his Department of Corrections registration card and his driving license, plus a few useless odds and ends. And for a little dramatic effect, he also left a couple of wrinkled dollar bills.

Checking again to make sure he was alone, he returned to the frozen body, his footsteps crunching in the snow. The light was fading from the skies, turning grey clouds toward a menacing black; Leonard could feel the air begin to bite.

He pushed the turned-out pockets back in and returned the coins he had found. He took off his glasses and arranged them plausibly in front of Frederick Steffens's lifeless eyes. After another look around, he shoved his wallet into Steffens's back pocket.

It was almost dark now and the snow was falling heavily in large, wet flakes. He turned his face up into it and closed his eyes. Snow fell onto his cheeks and eyelids and into his open mouth; their prickly cold refreshed him. He realized, with a smile, that the snow was his ally; it would help mask his crude rearrangement of the macabre scene. The cops could be counted on to trample the remaining clues. He rose and walked away from the still, cold form of the late Frederick Steffens.

As he crossed over the street that the alley gave onto, he dodged an old Tin Lizzie, rattling uncertainly down the slushy pavement. Sheltered in the entrance of a shuttered storefront, he could see both the body, which was once again becoming a shapeless, snowy mound, yellow tinted in the dim reach of a streetlamp, plus the view right and left along the street. He needed to keep watch, to make certain some other guy looking for a little luck didn't happen along and spoil his tableau before the cops found it.

The cold stung and Leonard wasn't dressed for it. His feet grew numb; he stamped them continuously, turning in small circles. A tune forced its way into his head to match the beat of his feet and he started singing to himself, just above a whisper. "Camptown ladies sing this song, Doo-dah, Doo-dah. Camptown Racetrack five miles long, Oh, de doo-dah day..." He swayed from side to side to the rhythm as he circled.

He wasn't certain he could stick it out. He had to fight off the growing pain at his temples, urging him to take refuge in the bottle of comfort nestling in his pocket; he knew it would be a mistake to cloud his judgment with more booze.

A torturous half hour passed and a blustery wind got up, whipping snow around Leonard's head. Even with his coat collar turned up, his ears ached from the cold. It didn't help that, having left his glasses on the corpse, he couldn't see very well. Still, he thought he'd be able to make out the distinctive long-coat and cap of a New York cop, if only one would show up.

He was on the point of giving it up and leaving the rest to chance when the beat cop turned the corner at the end of the block and headed in his direction. "About damned time," he growled under his breath. He pulled his coat collar closer around his face, clamped down his cap and walked briskly toward the cop, trying to look like he might be late for something important. As he neared the policeman, who eyed him warily and held his billy club in front, ready to use it, Leonard pointed behind him and called out, "'Looks like you've got a stiff in the alley down there, copper." He hurried on.

It had gone as well as he could have hoped. He knew his parole officer, the only person left on Earth who would give a damn, would eventually get the news of Leonard Bates's unfortunate but predictable death.

Still, it didn't solve all his problems and it created new ones. He now felt exposed, here in the city. Any slight mis-step or a chance encounter with someone from the parole office, even a secretary, could blow the ruse apart. Having been stripped of his license to practice law, he would have to make his living as a laborer if he stayed in New York and now, in the teeth of the Depression, there was no shortage of men willing to swing a pick or carry a hod. Besides his strong distaste for actual physical labor, Leonard was far from being skilled in any of the trades. Better to leave, at least for a year or two.

So now, two months later and resolved to his self-imposed exile in the person of Frederick Steffens, a stranger he was still learning to become, he shuffled forward among the scraggle of people waiting to board the Queen Mary; men, women, chattering children, each clutching a piece of paper that promised a berth aboard the huge, floating steel edifice.

The sun was fully up now, above the tall buildings, flooding the pier and its mass of people in dazzling light. Leonard tugged his cap down further. The sun blazed like a torch he couldn't escape and it was burning out his eyeballs. That familiar, persistent pain stabbed at his temples again and his throat was dry and itchy. He'd already emptied his last pint and couldn't buy another one this early. He ached for a slug and didn't care what kind.

The docks teemed with people, some grim faced, some smiling in anticipation. They poured out of the subway and the streetcars, through the turnstiles and onto the docks. Most were men, but women too, and families with young kids in their mothers' arms, the little ones whining from anxiety, while the older ones raced around the pier at break-neck speed, squealing in anticipation of the coming adventure. It was a rich stew of humanity; young, old, well-dressed, shabby, and carrying all manner of luggage, from fine leather grips to brand new cases in faux leather, and many threadbare carpet bags. Leonard's own grip was a nondescript suit valise with a busted handle he'd picked up cheap at a pawnshop. A machine screw and some washers had made it serviceable.

Young men heading for England and beyond to go to college hugged their parents and tried to look brave. Occasional pairs and trios of soldiers and sailors from various nations walked past, embarkation orders clutched in their fists.

A small group of giddy young women and their chaperons scurried around trying to figure out, despite the huge lettering high on its flanks, whether the big black hulk in front of them was, in fact, the Queen Mary. When they finally convinced themselves that is was, they set to fussing about whether they should use this gangway toward the stern or the one at the bow, or was that reserved for the cabin class passengers?

Leonard noticed that, up toward the bow, three to four hundred feet away, the toffs had their own version of this chaos. Taxis were doing their best to get rid of their fares and get back onto the street. They were frustrated by the big showy cars of the wealthy, whose chauffeurs were in no hurry to get out of anybody's way and whose main goal was to avoid scratching or denting the Bentleys and Rolls and Duesenbergs they were in charge of. Even at this distance, the din of car horns was relentless and irritating.

As Leonard neared the base of the gangway, the line was disordered and confused. Ahead of him, men shouted and shook their fists. His irritation grew when he saw the cause of the hold-up—only one man was there to handle the crush. "How hard could it be?" he muttered to himself. They knew how many people to expect and when they would be coming. A simple calculation would show how many agents were needed to forestall this chaotic jam and all these pissed-off passengers.

The anonymity of the crowd created this insensitivity to people's needs, one of the many curses of being poor. Leonard's whole life was about his need to avoid being one of the faceless dupes and he was painfully aware that that was exactly his current condition.

His need for a drink now slewed toward desperation; the first thing he would do after getting aboard was to make a beeline for a bar. He struggled to keep himself under control. The ache behind his right eye felt like a stiletto; he thought he might crumble at any time. The next guy to bump him, the next over-active kid who ran up and shouted something stupid at the top of his lungs was in danger of feeling Leonard's switchblade in his ribs. Aware he was edging toward losing control, he relaxed his grip on the knife, which was in his hip pocket. He withdrew his hand and dug into his coat for his cigarettes.

He lit up, sucking the smoke deep into his lungs; for a while, at least, it would help him get a grip on his nerves. With an effort, he tried to divert his attention from the pain by looking for faces among the crowd at the forward entrance. There was sure to be a handful who had turned up in the society pages at one time or another; many of those in first class would be sailing now to get to Berlin in time for the Olympic Games. But with the forward gangway at such a distance, he wasn't sure he'd be able to recognize anyone.

Then a figure caught his eye, a man whom, if it was in fact him, Leonard had a personal interest in. He couldn't be sure at this distance; his eyesight had gotten worse in the pen and, even with his new glasses, his world was often blurred. Nonetheless, something about this tall man, with a red-haired woman at his side, just going up the gangway, was intriguingly familiar. The way he moved his body and carried his shoulders, somewhat stiff and challenging, reminded him sharply of Charles Pierce. He shaded his eyes and squinted, trying hard to bring the man into focus. Frustrated, he had to give it up; his eyes weren't up to it.

It was so unlikely to be Pierce that he decided not to spend any more energy trying to verify it now. He had little else to do over the next few days than to look around the ship for his former partner. That would be complicated by the fact that the operators did their best to keep their high rollers separate and safe from the riffraff below decks, but Leonard knew how to get around such obstacles.

"Ticket! Come on, Mack, you're holding up the line."

Leonard turned sharply and found the agent's hand reaching in his direction, his fingers skiffling in a gesture of impatience. Leonard recoiled–his hand went to his knife... then he caught himself. Embarrassed, he recovered and fumbled in his coat pocket for his ticket and handed it to the man, who had fixed him with a look of curiosity. After examining the billet, the agent tore off the stub he needed and, still regarding Leonard strangely, motioned for him to mount the gangway.

As he climbed the steep stairs, Leonard craned again toward the Cabin Class entry but the man he had seen had now disappeared into the ship. What were the chances? In his penurious condition, if it was Pierce, it would be a great stroke of luck. Charles Pierce owed him a large sum of money, and money was the least of it. And boarding with the toffs, it probably meant he had a substantial amount of money in his possession.

Leonard reached the top of the gangway and studied the signs, which pointed to various places in the ship's interior, searching for one that promised a quick path to Jack Daniels.

IX

A RAUCOUS CHORUS of call and response between deep-throated steam whistles, louder than Audrey ever imagined possible, burst from the tugboats as they eased the Queen Mary away from the docks and got her pointed down river. An airborne choir of equally raucous gulls, though not nearly so loud, hung languidly on invisible currents and let the world of the river know that they, too, were to be noticed. Now, as the ship steamed through the mouth of the New Harbor and past the Statue of Liberty, holding her torch high against the morning sun, Audrey leaned against the rail and did something she seldom did. She questioned her own judgment.

When she began at Chez Moreau, she had felt optimistic and successful, embarked upon a career whose pinnacle could be as high and heady as she could imagine. All her mother's predictions of defeat had proven wrong. She *could* survive here, she *could* thrive. Now she was leaving it all behind; Chez Moreau, New York, America.

Audrey had bunked with her Aunt Jessie's family when she first arrived from Baltimore. But Jessie and Daniel had three adolescent boys and not much space; they couldn't accommodate her permanently in their home. Jessie helped Audrey find a room in a boarding house nearby.

Her mother would have burst into tears had she seen its crumbling Victorian facade and its seedy surroundings but it concealed a set of small comfortable rooms on two upper floors, with bathrooms at the ends of carpeted halls. On the ground floor, the large parlor—full of overstuffed couches and chairs—and the ample kitchen, accommodated a dozen or so unattached women who worked in the burgeoning city as waitresses, telephone switchboard operators, hotel maids, and school teachers.

The landlady, Mrs Elmira Walker, was a widow whose husband had been deacon of the Upper Manhattan Christian Congregation. She was a fitting tribute to his evangelical legacy; straight-backed, her hands and face the only part of her mahogany-toned skin ever visible. She kept her frizzy grey hair in a tight bun, pinned, incongruously, with a pair of lacquered, decorative chopsticks–always the same ones.

Few of her tenants had ever seen Mrs Walker smile. She rented only to young Negro women and made it her mission—with strict rules on comings and goings and limits on how far males were allowed into the building's interior—to safeguard both their persons and their reputations.

When Jessie brought Audrey to the boarding house, Mrs Walker couldn't hide her surprise and discomfort. Frowning, her eyes narrowed, she bore into Audrey, looking for signs of black heritage. But after Jessie introduced her as her niece and Audrey greeted her with her natural charm, Mrs Walker accepted her warmly and she went out of her way to help Audrey settle in and get to know the other boarders. Audrey felt secure there; it was a good base from which to face the hazards of the city.

She made friends quickly among her housemates and they, in turn, quickly involved her in their lives. Soon, her weekend nights were filled with visits to Harlem's fabled nightclubs, where they saw exotic, sultry stage shows and heard vibrant jazz rhythms from Duke Ellington, Ella Fitzgerald, Louis Armstrong and the like. The Depression had claimed a lot of Harlem's historic clubs but some survived; the Hot Spot, Connie's Inn, the Apollo Theater, the Cotton Club. It was Shilly and Mae, her two closest friends from Mrs Walker's, who told her that, although the performers at the Cotton Club were all Negroes, until Ellington complained, Negroes couldn't enter as patrons. Audrey was amazed.

One Saturday night, the three of them huddled at the High Spot, sipping exotic cocktails and watching an energetic group of dancers on the stage. They were giggling, behind their hands, at how the girls managed to remain legally covered while wearing almost nothing, when a commotion erupted at the entrance and two couples swept in, dressed in formal evening clothes. One man was a familiar figure, tall and imposing, with dark skin and a broad grin, and accompanied by a light-skinned woman. Shilly screeched, "Oh, it's him! Paul Robeson!"

The club's owner, normally the very essence of cool, tripped over himself showing the revered actor, singer, and activist to a table near the stage. Audrey and her friends, along with the entire room full of patrons, forgot about the show and basked in the reflected glory of their black hero. The emcee stopped the orchestra and gave their visitor an extravagant welcome—everyone, patrons and performers alike, stood and applauded. Waving affably to each corner of the room, Robeson accepted their accolades with all the grace he could muster under such awkward circumstances.

"Well, I don't know about you," Audrey declared, springing up, but I'm going to get his autograph."

"Girl, you can't just walk up to him like that," said Shilly. "What will he think? I couldn't be so forward."

"Let's all go," Mae gushed.

"Yes, come on. We'll all go," insisted Audrey, bubbling with excitement. "Come on Shilly, don't be such a ninny."

The club's printed showcards, detailing the evening's entertainers, were spread around the tables. Audrey picked up three and grabbed Shilly's hand, dragged her out of her chair, and led a parade over to Robeson's table. She introduced herself and the others and implored him to autograph their cards. Robeson was charmed and happily scrawled something on two of them. He took Audrey's last and lingered over it, holding her there while he stole looks at her. The presence of his wife at his elbow prevented him from making more of the encounter. Smiling seductively, he handed the showcard back to her. The three young women rushed back to their table, chattering happily.

Unescorted women were under constant pressure from men in the clubs, looking for a night's wooing and more, and Audrey was a special target. She was always quickly noticed and the patrons sometimes reacted resentfully to her presence, to the sudden appearance of a white woman in their midst. But as they took in her easy interactions with dark-skinned friends, saw how tight she was with them and that she spoke their same patois, and showed no signs of being sadiddy, they relaxed and accepted her.

Then the young men zeroed in, like bees to nectar—handsome and confident young men, with skin tones that varied from creamy whites, nearly as light as hers, to rich mahogany and all shades in between. Dressed in flashy and expensive clothes, they had the gift of gab. She accepted some of their offers of champagne and cocktails and moonlight rides but she was determined not to become involved—certainly not intimate—with any of them. Marriage would be the end of her hopes for a career in the fashion world, something she would not put at risk. She walked, and talked, and danced with a few, found a handful interesting, and kissed one or two, but she and Shilly and Mae always got back to the boarding house safely within Mrs Walker's curfew.

Her experience of always being taken at first for white at the clubs repeatedly made her face this uncomfortable fact about herself. In her determination to see if the New York fashion world had a place in it for Audrey Simmons, there was one thing she hadn't fully thought out. She would not only have to leave Upton, a relatively protected suburb of Baltimore, and face the uncertainties of New York City, she'd be forced to do something she abhorred—she would have to "pass."

She knew others who had done it and she knew it could be fraught with pain, anxiety, and humiliation. Those who embraced it completely had left the family and friends who protected and shaped them, and set up an alternate life, a life without a true past, a life with a hollow litany of false background details. They were constantly on their guard against revealing things that didn't fit with their assumed identities. The worst was the need to be ready to turn their backs on friends or family, as though they meant nothing to them at all—less than nothing—should their paths happen to cross in public.

Audrey hated the idea, but if she wanted to reach her goal, she had to apprentice in tony shops and ateliers, places where blacks were tolerated only as menials—if at all. She decided she had no real choice—she would take advantage of her appearance for the sake of her ambitions. On it's face, there was nothing untoward about this. It's what many people did; actors, performers, politicians, anyone who had to establish a public persona. People changed their names or fudged their date of birth. But, of course, here, in America, it was different where race was the issue; the lines were not to be blurred with impunity.

She determined to engage in this charade only at her workplace. She would let her employers and co-workers make their assumptions about her; she focused on getting down to work and demonstrating her talents, and letting them speak for her. Whatever else happened lay in God's hands. If someone challenged her about her race, she could always cite her Cherokee heritage; for some reason, having Indian blood in your veins didn't carry the onus of African ancestry. But if she were to encounter a relative or friend in a situation that might expose her secret, so be it. Despite her appearance, she was a Negro, and so were her people. Jessie's and Daniel's roots were plainly African—she couldn't imagine running into them on the street and turning her back. Her father, whom she had loved deeply, was a beautiful, proud, brown-skinned man. She could never have denied her connection to him.

But she never felt totally at ease. When she took the subway out of Harlem each work day, she also took a cultural sidestep. She joined the crush of blacks descending into the station as a light-skinned Negro woman, laughing and chatting with her friends from the boarding house, whose skin tones were an earthy variety of copper and ebony and bronze. Minutes later, she surfaced alone in midtown among throngs of whites and they took her to be one of them.

Typically, no one asked her about her race and she never felt a need to raise the subject herself. But every so often, the reality of her situation burst in upon her, like a tree suddenly blown down across her path. She'd find herself closed in a room or packed in a subway car next to an aggressive racist, who saw it as his or her mission to entertain those within earshot with jab after jab at some hapless minority.

These people were seldom selective when they got started and they always had plenty of poison to sling—at Negroes, Jews, Italians, Irish—whoever was unlike them enough to be "other," to be powerless. Audrey hated her impotence in these situations. She felt unable to oppose these racists, fearing it would put her own situation in the spotlight.

She was doing what she had to do to reach her goal but she could never escape the fact that this aspect of her life was a lie. People said that in England and Europe, she could relax about her race; it wasn't the issue it was in the U.S. Still, as she stood at the rail of the Queen Mary and watched Lady Liberty slip by, then turned her gaze forward as the ship aimed its prow into the broad expanse of the Atlantic, other questions weighed on her mind and forced her to wonder whether she was making a mistake.

Charles had given her little time to prepare—he said he had to sail within a week. With all the shopping and fittings and other arrangements, she'd had time only this morning to send a quick telegram to her mother, telling her of her journey.

Although she'd never felt fully appreciated there, she did have a job in a fashionable dress shop on Park Avenue. And although she was concerned about the arc of her ambitions and how much she had fallen short of achieving them, she was more or less content with her situation. No one had the perfect job, especially now—that didn't exist, except in the storybook world of ladies magazines.

Then, over the last handful of days, her life had changed in a way that happens *only in* storybooks. A handsome, forceful, purposeful Englishman had stepped into her life and offered her a job—a "position"—as his assistant. She thought it was a hoax at first, an imaginative ruse for meeting women, but he worked hard to convince her. She allowed him to take her to some of the best dress shops in Manhattan (steering him away from Mme Moreau's) where, to her surprise and delight, he bought her a half dozen outfits, all of the highest quality and fashion. Jewelry too, mostly costume, to be sure, but of good quality. He had, as he liked to say, "decked her out," and she had the unusual experience of seeing herself lifted, dress by dress and shoe by elegant shoe, to a high social station. The shop assistants treated her with deference and brought out the latest fashions by name designers for her to try on, all under Charles's watchful and appreciative gaze

She went along with it, wondering when the game would end, when her horses would turn into mice, her coach into a pumpkin. But as her wardrobe expanded, as one seamstress after another set to work molding fine silks and chiffons to her measurements, she started to believe in the fantasy. And she took the first tentative step of her own toward making it real: she withdrew most of the money from her savings account and stashed it in an envelope, ready to go into her valise if the day came that she actually started packing.

And best of all, it was in preparation for a trip to Europe! At first she didn't believe Charles's offer of a voyage to England on the Queen Mary, in first class, no less. He responded by taking her to the Cunard-White Star office, where he purchased two tickets, for separate first-class cabins, and solemnly presented one to her. She was speechless.

England! London, and then possibly, Paris, where she could seek an apprenticeship in the very hub of the fashion world. She could hone her skills there and maybe, one day, be a recognized designer. When she came back, if she ever did come back, she just knew it would be as a star of women's *haute couture*.

She conjured up that day, imagining herself interviewed by the fashion reporters of the New York press while Mme Moreau and Mr Clayton sat at the back of the room, wishing they could take credit for her success. But they would not dare to speak, for fear of being treated with the same indifference they had shown her.

Was all that merely a tantalizing fantasy? What had she done—what had she dared? She'd had to prepare to sail in less than a week. She raided her meager savings to buy a moderately priced set of matching luggage. And she assembled a collection of drawings she had worked up of her dress designs, and splurged on a black leather portfolio case for them. Then she steeled herself for an intense heart-to-heart with Aunt Jessie and Uncle Daniel that would confront her with how her decision looked through other eyes.

Audrey's mother, Lerita, and Jessie were sisters and when they finally agreed that Audrey could come to New York to pursue a career, Lerita extorted from Jessie a promise to watch over Audrey. There was no question about what this meant. Lerita imagined New York to be a cauldron of sin and Jessie's solemn obligation, in Lerita's mind, was to protect Audrey from it at all costs.

Audrey spent weekdays at the boarding house but Sundays, she went to be with Jessie and her family. On this recent Sunday, she met them at church, the New Amsterdam AME, and spent a cathartic hour praising God with exuberant singing and clapping, just as she had done back home. Afterward, they all went back to Daniel and Jessie's clapboard cottage on Convent Ave and she and Jessie set to work preparing dinner. As she strung beans and shucked corn, carefully picking out the fine threads of silk that clung to the plump yellow kernels, she was apprehensive and a little sad; she probably would not see Jessie and her family again for a long time.

Jessie served up one of her classic feasts—fried chicken, the green beans cooked with lemon slices, corn-on-the-cob, mashed potatoes and gravy. Its rich aroma infused every corner of the modest home. From all her bustle in recent days, Audrey was ravenous and ate two large helpings.

Later, while Daniel and his boys listened to a Yankees game on the large console radio in the living room, she and Jessie did the dishes, chatting and catching up on each other's lives. As they worked side by side at the sink, their familial connection was unmistakable; despite the difference in their skin tones, it would be easy to take them for sisters. They shared the same red in their hair, with Jessie's a little darker and more tightly curled. Audrey's eyes were a dazzling green; Jessie's were hazel, a look that lent a sense of intensity to her expression. Where Audrey's skin was a creamy white dotted with freckles that she hid beneath powder, in Jessie's, those freckles had merged into a patina the color of burnished copper.

As always, Jessie talked mostly about her three boys, 15-year old Jeffrey, Delano, 12, and Michael, 10. She worried about how they were doing in school and whether their schools, almost completely segregated, were the best ones for them. Daniel had hung on to his job with the transit authority doing track maintenance but he didn't make near enough to send the boys to private school. They had tossed around the notion of putting them in Catholic school, which had a good reputation, but they didn't want their kids indoctrinated in that ritual.

As they restored the kitchen to order, Audrey listened and clucked with Jessie about the boys' future but her own problem distracted her—Jessie didn't have her full attention. Finally, as she made a stack of the well worn, sturdy white china dishes before lifting them into the glass-front cabinets over the counter, she broke in. "I need to talk to you about something, Aunt Jessie."

Jessie looked up from the pan she was scrubbing and found a troubled look on Audrey's face. "What's the matter, Sweetheart? You sound serious."

"Yes, Auntie, this *is*." Audrey turned to make certain she caught every nuance of her Aunt's reaction. She took a deep breath. "I... I'm going to Europe."

Jessie stiffened—her brow knitted in a frown. "You're what?! Going to Europe?! What do you mean, child?"

"Well, a man has asked me to work for him, to be his assistant. He's in mining, and he's going to England in connection with a new strike, and... well, he wants me to go with him."

Jessie dropped the pan into the soapy water and gripped the edge of the sink, leaning her weight on her hands. She couldn't have been more astonished if Skittles, their cat, had jumped up on the counter and begun reciting Genesis. She gazed at Audrey, trying to read her expression, looking for a hint of the joke she had missed.

Audrey turned her gaze onto the plates in front of her, hoping Jessie would respond. Finally, the weight of the silence became too heavy and she tried to fill it. "I met him at that café where I have lunch. He told me about the job and he wants me to..."

"Wait, wait," Jessie broke in. "You *have* a job, Audrey, in the business you wanted to be in—high fashion, hoity-toity clothes. It's why you came to New York. How is it you suddenly want to give all that up and be somebody's "assistant?" Assisting him with what, exactly?"

Audrey knew this wasn't going to go down well; her face reddened with embarrassment. "Well, that's it. I *do* want to be in the fashion world and my job at

Moreau's isn't getting me there. I've been there three years and I've gone as far as I can go—as far as they're going to let me. Going to England, I can look for work there, or better yet, I can get to Paris—that's the center of things."

"So, you're hooking up with "a man"—a perfect stranger—just to get to Paris? Have you lost your ever-lovin' mind?!"

"Auntie, please, don't be too quick to judge him. He's a good man. He treats me good, he's a gentleman and... well, I trust him."

Jessie scrubbed her hands dry on her apron and crossed to the kitchen door. The sounds of the ballgame filtered through as she opened it and called into the living room. "Daniel. Come here, please." She waited only a few seconds, then added, sharply, "Daniel!"

This brought Daniel to his feet. When he came into the kitchen, looking puzzled, Jessie closed the door. He was an imposing man, tall and muscular in slacks and a white undershirt. Broad at the shoulders, his body tapered to a narrow waist and, though well into his forties, his work in the subway kept the fat off.

"What's up?" Daniel's sharp, black eyes looked out from a handsome, chocolate brown face. His nose was broad and flattened above full lips, which usually curled into a warm, boyish smile, but now were set in a flat line, anticipating bad news.

"Your niece has gone crazy, that's what's up!" Jessie leveled a disdainful look at Audrey and perched one fist on her hip. "Tell him," she demanded.

Audrey gave them the best account she could of her encounter with Charles Pierce and of her intention of taking up his offer. She left out a lot of the details about the new frocks and jewels, pretty certain they would not work in her favor. When she finished, a heavy silence hung over the small room, broken only by the rhythmic sound of water dripping from the faucet.

Daniel was now expected to say something. But he had no idea what to say that would make an ironclad argument against Audrey's crazy notion. He didn't understand why anyone wanted to go to Europe. Deep in thought, he stared down at the scratched and chipped linoleum, and stroked his lower lip with his thumb. Finally, he focused on the one thing that felt most out of kilter. He folded his arms across his chest and leaned against the doorjamb. "What do you know about this Pierce guy, Audrey?"

She lowered her eyes and thought for a moment. This was the weak link—she knew virtually nothing about Charles, beyond what he had told her. How do you find out about another person, a stranger, who isn't known by anyone you know? There's no gossip, no lore to ferret out. On the strength of his apparent sincerity, the stories he told about prospecting, the clothes he had bought for her, the ticket for a first-class berth on an ocean liner, which lay beneath her undergarments in her bureau drawer—given all these, she had decided to trust him. "I... I don't know much about him. He tells me he's in mining, and he showed me pictures of him at a mine. I don't know... I wish I had a way to find out more, but I don't." She looked up and held Daniel's gaze as steadily as she could. "I believe him."

Daniel pushed away from the door and stepped to the table. Calmly, he turned one of the walnut stained bentwood chairs and straddled it, draping his muscular forearms over its back. Audrey remained propped against the drain board. Daniel cocked his head to one side as he examined her face. "This job—as his assistant—what's that mean? What exactly will your duties be?" His dark pupils, surrounded by whites so bright they were almost blinding, bored holes into her.

"Well, it's... he needs someone to take notes and things. He..."

"Are you a stenographer, Audrey? Shorthand?" His gaze was unflinching.

"No, I..."

"Do you type?"

"No, no..."

He continued drilling into her with questioning eyes, challenging her wordlessly. It felt as though he never blinked.

"Well... well, he's going to teach me everything I need to know. First, he needs a woman, he said, someone uhhh... pretty, he says... to help break the ice with the wealthy men he meets... investors."

"I'll bet!" Jessie's sarcasm could etch steel. Noisily, she resumed scouring the enamel off the saucepan in the sink. Daniel looked at Audrey carefully, as though trying to understand exactly which piece of her had broken.

"Tell me, girl, does this guy, Pierce... does he know you ain't white?"

Audrey colored and looked away; she shook her head. Jessie glared at her from the sink. "I knew it! I've always said that skin of yours would get you in a whole lot of trouble one of these days. What you gonna do when he finds out?"

"I'm not in any trouble, Aunt Jessie," Audrey protested, her embarrassment starting to slip into anger. "And why should he find out? There's nobody to tell him." It had become an argument—just what she had hoped to avoid. She was desperate to make them understand, to get their blessing, but she knew what a stretch it was for them—and would be for anyone. "He's been completely forthcoming. The secretary things are secondary, he *told* me that."

It was Audrey who had not been completely open. So far, she had ducked the question of whether to tell Charles about her origins. It was easy for her to let things continue this way—the way it went in most of her interactions outside of friends and family. Like everyone else, Charles had assumed she was white. He didn't ask her—no one ever did. Just leave well-enough alone.

But this was different. It wasn't just about whether to associate with her or hire her. Charles had *invested* in her, rather heavily. Didn't he deserve to know what that investment got him—all the salient facts? Still, she hadn't asked for any of this—it was all his initiative. No. She hated the lie she was telling Charles by her silence but she'd didn't want to risk scuttling this chance. It was all about appearances, anyway—it was possible Charles wouldn't even care about her race. But she'd decided not to test that notion.

Daniel's voice broke into her thoughts. "I don't think you can do this, girl," he said. Audrey wished he didn't sound so much like a judge passing sentence. "It don't seem legit. This guy could have any kind of scheme up his sleeve."

Jessie broke in. "I can't believe you'd be so naïve, Audrey." She turned from the sink, waving a soapy hand, her anger a product of her concern for Audrey and her solemn promise to her sister, Audrey's mother. She fought back tears. "This is New York, girl... and desperate times. People do desperate things."

"Aunt Jessie, please. I know you're worried about me..." Audrey went to her with extended arms. Jessie tensed at first, then let Audrey embrace her, hugging her in return. Audrey spoke softly, her mouth at Jessie's ear. "I believe in this man, Auntie, in what he told me, and I need to grab this chance—it's too good an opportunity." She stepped back, holding Jessie at arms length. "If I don't go with him, how am I ever going to get to

Europe? To Paris? It certainly won't be on the wages I earn from that tightwad Clayton at Moreau's."

"Maybe we can find out something about this Pierce," said Daniel, tentatively. "I know a guy over at the po-lice, might get us some information on him. When you planning on going?" Daniel was a peacemaker by nature—and he was missing the ball game.

"Uhh, the ship sails in about three weeks." This was the only lie she told them. In girding herself for this talk, Audrey didn't know how stiff their resistance would be, or how long Aunt Jessie would wait before picking up the phone to call Baltimore. She wasn't going to take the chance that her mother would turn up to stop her. Although the Queen Mary would sail for England again in three weeks, it was an earlier departure, two days away, that Audrey was ticketed for.

And so, two days after her earnest talk with Jessie and Daniel, a talk that had failed to get her the blessing she had hoped for and which left her feeling guilty for deceiving them, Audrey boarded the Queen Mary. That morning, she composed a telegram to her mother; sending it was the most difficult thing she had ever done. You couldn't say much in a telegram; the whole notion was to trim the message of any nuance. But it was just those nuances that she would need to explain what she was doing and why, and that she would be all right and wouldn't bring shame on the family. She felt miserable, a disobedient child running away from a safe and caring home. She ached to tell her mother face to face what a rare opportunity had suddenly been placed before her.

Lerita would have forbidden the trip, of course; that was a given. At 24, Audrey could go despite her mother's objections but she had not yet reached the point of open defiance. If Audrey had faced her mother and she had said no, Audrey would not have gone. So the timing allowed her to claim that she'd had no choice—

Charles had to go, she would say, with or without her. She would explain it all in the letters she promised to write, that she most certainly would write, once she found her feet in England.

She imagined her mother opening the telegram, itself such a novelty that she would be astonished—and frightened—to hear that it was for her, and would insist that it was a mistake. Finally accepting it, she would take the message to the window of their tiny living room in Upton and, standing next to the lace curtain, anxious, she would tear it open. As she read, her hand would rush to cover her mouth and she would sob. A long wail of pain would escape her, a sound she would not even know she had made. She would read and re-read, trying to make sense of a message saying that her Audrey was about to step onto a ship and sail away. She was going to cross an ocean as big as the universe, leaving her home, her roots, and her, the mother who loved her, and to whom she meant everything. Everything.

Audrey cringed as she ran those painful images through her mind. She had left out any mention of Charles; that would have to wait for the letter. In a letter, she would have ample space for elaboration and reassurance. Now, as she stood at the rail of the Queen Mary, a fresh breeze tugging at her clothes, Audrey snugged her coat around her and tried to find a place for her conscience to rest.

Her mother could not want her to miss this chance, would not want to restrict her beloved daughter's dreams. Lerita Simmons knew how talented her daughter was—that she had a gift and, despite her reluctance to let her go to New York on her own, she knew how desperately important it was to Audrey that she pursue her goals. That the dream included going to Europe to live for… what? A year? Two? More, perhaps? That distant, unimaginable notion wasn't raised when she agreed to let Audrey go to the city. New York was already much farther away than she was comfortable with but, she rationalized, Jessie was there to supply some level of protection, stability, and a sense of familial connection.

Of course, Lerita knew how Audrey's beauty attracted men, men ready to spoil her purity, to shame her, and the fact that she looked white just made things worse. She had long ago decided that beauty, which all the young women sought, was a curse, and the cause of so much Godless behavior. Audrey had been cursed with exceptional beauty. Cherokee, African, and Scotch-Irish blood flowed through her and the combination had produced a woman whose singular, off-beat appearance turned the head of every man she came near, young or old, white or black, the way a lodestone commands the attention of a compass needle. Lerita had seen it when she and Audrey shopped together on Howard Street, and even on Sundays, at church—men could not keep their eyes off her.

If Lerita was certain of one thing, it was that God would not forgive her, and she would never forgive herself if, by giving in to Audrey's ceaseless pleas to go to New York, she had sent her into a hell of dissipation and carnality. Please God, not that.

All this, Audrey knew, would race through her mother's mind as she read the telegram. She would do everything she could to ease her mother's anxiety, to reassure her and make her proud. That meant writing as often as possible, at least every week. She wished she could do more but she would certainly do that.

X

AFTER A BUSY MORNING rubbing shoulders with the first class passengers and whetting the appetites of possible opponents, David was again dressed in his denims, with his pea coat buttoned against the chill of a damp ocean breeze. He checked to see that no one was watching before he popped through a door marked Crew Only.

David's act at the poker tables depended on the perception, however vague, that he was upper class and he had to be careful not to be seen mingling with the ship's staff—members of the upper class did not mingle with common seamen unless forced to. To allow his relationships below decks to become known above would blur the lines.

On his way to the crew mess, he made a detour down to the very bottom of the hull and entered one of the vast boiler rooms. Every once in a while, he felt the need to see and touch the workings of the ships he sailed in and this one, the spanking new Queen Mary, was particularly impressive. It was a floating behemoth, so massive that it seemed to be sitting firmly on land, instead of out on the Atlantic and smaller than a cork in a bathtub. The world of the ship's innards—of boilers and tubing and wires and steam—fascinated him; they were the obverse of all the fragile pretense up in the salons.

There were 24 boilers, each the size and approximate shape of a small house, distributed among five large rooms at the bottom of the ship. At any given time, half were alight, heating the water for the steam turbines. Their interiors glowed red and orange, and they created a din that made normal conversation impossible. They fed steam to four turbines, each one fifty feet long and over two stories high. These massive machines supplied the energy that knifed the ship's bow forward into the Atlantic's cold green water. Seeing them, and feeling their heat and sound and vibration, gave David a sense of a connection to Man's greatest accomplishments, the wonders of the modern world. Men just like him had designed and built this juggernaut. They fashioned these boilers and turbines and stupendous brass propellers, they set the ship in the water, and challenged the miles of heartless ocean that stood in their way. The joke among the crew was that, milling about on the ship's various decks were some 2,000 people oblivious to the juxtaposition of wrought iron, milled steel and cast bronze, drawn copper and processed oil, all at work so they could imagine they were safe on land.

He left the boiler rooms and made his way forward to the mess. As he went, he mulled over his experience of the morning. He felt he'd done well, identifying the men he wanted to lure to the poker table later on. He needed a break now, to get his mind off business, and shooting the breeze with the crew was his favorite way to do that. He was much more at home among the men who made the ship run. They looked at the world with a fresh perspective, open-eyed, and they lacked the fat, debilitating layer of insulation from real life that money provided the rich.

He poked his head through the doorway to the crew mess; "Right, mates, Ps and Qs—your favorite card sharp has arrived!"

A chorus of exaggerated groans and mock epithets erupted from the five men eating there—David had to dodge a couple of well-aimed bread rolls.

"Hey! That's Her Majesty's property," he protested.

"So's my arse," replied Jamie. "You see where she's stashed that, God bless her."

As their laughter subsided, Carl, the ship's engineer, piped in. "What's it like up there, Davie? The toffs all safe and secure, are they?"

"Bugs in a rug," replied David as he pulled out a chair and sat, pushing aside plates and cups from the remains of the men's lunch to make some elbow room. "This is quite a group. The Olympic Games cleared out all the stalls."

Carl was a compact man of 50, older than the average seaman on the ship. He gestured toward the galley, "Grab a plate, mate. The roast beef is worth a go."

"No thanks, Carl. I need to take lunch with the high rollers up in first class—part of my research, don't you know. But I'll join you in a cup of tea if I may." He plucked a cup and saucer off the china shelf; Carl slid the big teapot across the table.

"So what's of interest?" asked Benny, the second mate.

"Well, for me, there's the usual contingent of men with a lot of money and little talent, although none of them seems all that interested in poker so far. And as I say, there are more of them than usual on this voyage. Nelson Chandler is one of them–Chandler's Mills? All that cereal you blokes wolf down every day? He makes a good amount of it."

"Well I'll be blowed," bellowed Jamie. "Chandler. I've a mind to rush up and pin 'is ears back. Piece of rock the other day almost took a tooth out."

"But listen, lads." David's cabalistic tone got their attention. "I have to tell you, there's a redheaded girl in first class who's so... so incredibly gorgeous, I thought I was going to have a heart attack."

"Oh, come on, Davie. We've heard this blarney before"

"No, really. You have to see her. 'Name's Audrey."

"Uh oh. D'you hear that?" Jamie, chief steward for tourist class, smiled knowingly at the others. "He knows her name already and we're not even a day out of port. This is serious."

"So what's she like?" asked Benny. "You've talked to her?"

"Well, not exactly talked. We exchanged pleasantries—'Beautiful day...' 'Smooth going, so far...' you know the script. As for what she's like, well..." He gazed at the ceiling, recalling his impressions of Audrey. "She's small and, what's the word, lithe, like a cat. And a smile that... Oh, I don't know how to express it. I've never seen anyone like her. Best of all, she doesn't seem to have any idea how beautiful she is. Wherever she goes, men of means—the toffs—pile up around her like a rugby scrum. I don't know anything about her, except that I want her to be the mother of my children."

They broke into hoots of laughter and derision. David laughed with them, but part of him was serious in a way he'd never been before.

"Where's she from?" asked Carl.

"I don't know. New York, I suppose."

"Well, there's an end to that, then," Jamie piped in. "No chance you're gonna get hooked up with a Yank."

"Why ever not?"

"David. Son. I mean let's not take leave of our bloomin' senses. You know I've made it my personal goal to get you married off, but it's got to be to a fine daughter of the Empire. An American just won't do. Look, I know you're almost a Yank yourself but I'm doing my best to ignore that. What would the Queen say?"

"Well I am a Yank, and bugger the Queen if she can't appreciate this peach of a girl." The room erupted in a howl of mock outrage and indignation.

Still laughing, David pulled out a deck of cards and shuffled them with a flourish. "All right, me hearties, shiver me timbers. Who's up for a game?"

Jamie shook one of his massive fists in David's direction, "I'll shiver your bloody timbers, mate. I wouldn't play cards with you if my life depended on it."

"You can pretty much bet that it would, you old coot." Grinning, Jamie waved him off.

"Who's in?" asked David. "Penny stakes."

Mack, one of the cooks, was always up for anything that would keep him out of the heat of the galley for a few extra minutes. Benny was trying to learn to play poker at David's level, to impress his girl.

"Deal me in," Benny said. "Come on, lads, show a bit of backbone."

Carl eyed him, "Let me tell you, laddie, there's a time for backbone and there's a time to show your backside—on your way out the door. Gambling with him," he declared, nodding toward David, "is the latter."

"It's just pennies, you goofs." David and Benny were moving dishware aside to clear a space on the table.

Jamie rose. "You'll have to excuse me but her Royal Buggery does not pay me to sit here jawing with the likes of you lot. I actually have a job to do."

"Me too, lads," said Carl. "Now don't stay here too long," he warned, wagging a finger at Benny and Mack. "You'll find you'll be missing your trousers when you stand up."

David picked up a half eaten bread roll and winged it at him. "Go on, you old spoiler. How can I trim these guy's sails if you're going to warn them off?" He began dealing out the cards.

XI

DAVID'S WORK RESUMED at the first meal, lunch, as the tips of the tallest buildings on the New York skyline, far astern now, were blurring into a low-hanging streak of clouds. He scanned the male passengers gathering in the first class dining room, deciding which of them he should sit near, trying to guess who might be open to the temptation of a poker game later that evening.

This could be tricky, particularly if he had played with them on earlier voyages. That burn-out quotient was another factor in David's decision to quit the gambling life. A limited number of the *nouveau riche* traveled the Atlantic at any one time. Games with modest stakes were no problem—he could easily scare up one of those. But he never tried to run the hustle, pretending to be just a casual card player, and once it got around the ship that he was a pro, he had a harder time setting up high stakes games.

So far, from the looks of this bunch, he was in pretty good luck. One or two of his former marks greeted him with wary smiles as they shook hands. They were quick to let him know, with embarrassed looks and self-conscious laughter, that they wouldn't be sitting down to cards with him if there were any significant money on the table. None of them bore him any malice; they'd known what they were getting into. By and large, they had lost with grace and no small amount of respect. So although David had walked away from the table with a lot of their cash, they hadn't felt cheated and didn't consider it their duty to warn off other players. They were more inclined to remain mute in order to watch him play, perhaps to learn something, maybe so they could say they were there if anyone actually got the better of him.

David had an ironclad rule: Never cheat at cards. It was so easy for disappointed losers to throw that charge at him—he had to be especially careful. His mentor, Milo Clark, had tripped over that stump. Milo had been at the top of his game and ruled the poker tables on the Atlantic when David was starting out. But he made the mistake of beating a spoiled English twit too soundly and, in an unguarded moment, joking about the man's amateurish play.

The fellow's ego was too fragile. To get even, he put it about, with no evidence at all, that Milo had marked the cards. He waved an ace around at the crowd of men that had responded to his raised voice, displaying a card with a knick in one edge that neither Milo—nor anyone else there—was sure he saw. Milo tried to fight the charge, treating it with derision, but it was no contest. Milo was a card sharp, the twit a titled English gentleman—poor as a church mouse but still a peer of the realm.

Word spread fast and Milo soon found he couldn't find anything beyond penny-ante aboard any Cunard or White Star ship after that. If he managed to convince his fellow players to raise the stakes and get a real game going, he soon found himself staring into the frowning face of the captain or first officer. It took him a while to realize that every time he came aboard, crewmembers, detailed to keep an eye out for him, quickly reported whenever any real money appeared on the tables.

So as David came into the restaurant and began chatting up new prospects, he also sized them up, getting them to reveal who they were and, subtly, for those he wasn't familiar with, the source of their money. He was culling them, switching tables if necessary—usually on the pretext of having spotted an old friend—to meet and vet as many of them as he could as early as possible. He had five days and nights to make it all happen. His program had a natural arc and timing was critical.

But he had to be patient. After hinting at his interest in poker, he tried to wait for the marks to suggest "a friendly game," as they so often put it. He played it a little reticent at first, not wanting to find himself sitting down with second- and third-tier people, whose resources would be quickly exhausted. A number of the first-class passengers were pretenders at some level, traveling first cabin for the purpose of looking rich and hoping the pose itself would lead eventually to hard cash.

Only a few were truly wealthy. They were known to their peers by sight, through long association in the social circles that money automatically made them eligible for—if their complexions were white and they prayed to the right god. David hoped to net these men, along with any others who, though wealthy, had kept themselves off the society pages, and so were not well known.

He wanted the biggest fish, of course, those who didn't care how much they lost because they had so very much. These tended to have another useful trait; if they played at all, their commitment to the game was strong. And although they didn't care about money, face was another matter. These men were used to winning, whether at poker or anything else, and they always imagined themselves to be the best at whatever they put their minds to. They seldom understood the extent to which others—not only those in their employ but also the less wealthy people in their circle—pandered to their expectation of coming out on top. So they often got breaks that better players would never see, simply because no one wanted to be downstream of the consequence that ensued if they failed.

Then there was the machismo that goes along with poker. Many men who play it seriously feel they should be good at it—that it somehow demonstrates their virility. This has no logical basis, of course; you wouldn't get far trying to make the argument for this idea.

But the primal urges always nudge rationality off the stage, particularly the ones involving sex. If you win the stakes, you leave the table with a triumphant smile and a potent swagger, while those you've vanquished are left dejected and flaccid. And you leave with a fattened bankroll, the sign to the women posed around the perimeter, women who like to be kept in expensive frocks and jewels, that you are indeed the guy with the biggest balls.

In the minds of most men, this had no down side. Whether philandering in his wife's absence or sowing wild oats, his sex appeal spiked when he left a high stakes table with all the money. During the crossings on these luxury liners, these men were very well laid.

XII

BILLY PRUITT WAS ENJOYING a new sense of freedom. He was elbow to elbow with the most admired members of American society, all headed to England, the hallowed seat of Western culture, and he was one of the gang, one of "the boys." Problem was, he didn't *feel* included. Instead, he had the uneasy sense that the other first-class passengers took little notice of him and, when they did, it was with an undercurrent of disdain.

He decided to forget what these people thought of him. Who were they, after all, to look down their noses at him—who were they to judge him? He could buy and sell most of them twice over—well, his father could. And didn't his father send him on this voyage so that he could learn the business? Certainly his father didn't intend him to be a monk while he was learning the ropes in the various company offices.

Sadie had insisted that his father really wanted him out of the way while the mess with her pregnancy played itself out. Billy refused to believe that. He believed what his father said—that it was time for him to begin the process of becoming the next head of Pruitt Mercantile. He didn't see why he had to go abroad—there were half a dozen Pruitt stores within an easy drive of their headquarters in Bridgeport. But his father insisted that he start in England, where the company had recently opened two stores, its first ever outside the US.

"Dowling's the ticket for you, Billy." He and his father were standing near the bottom of the Queen Mary's gangway, next to the Rolls. They had just returned from locating Billy's cabin in the ship, and watching as the porter and their chauffeur brought in his luggage and stacked it in a corner of the small space. Back down on the dock, William Pruitt II grasped his troublesome boy by the shoulders and held him at arms length. "I know you don't understand why I insist on this, but you will. Malcolm's a savvy customer and he'll straighten you out about retail. You and he get along OK; he has more patience with you than I have. Pay attention to him; he knows how to sell." His father grasped his hand and squeezed it, hard enough so it hurt. Then he turned and slid into the back seat of the big car and closed the door. He glanced quickly at his son as the car jolted away—Billy wasn't sure if he had smiled.

So it was off to be Malcolm Dowling's protégé. So be it—he would make the most of it, and he certainly didn't mind a respite from Sadie's anger, nor the chance to replace her with someone more agreeable. He didn't care what it cost. He would begin by taking full advantage of the pleasures at hand on this magnificent ship, and one of these was a very attractive, auburn-haired girl who seemed to be with, but not intimately attached to, a tall Englishman who had something to do with mining. He'd never seen anyone like this girl. Contained within her small frame was a bewitching conjunction of curves, of arcs of flesh at her hips and breasts and along her lithe form, all of which moved under her clothes in subtle undulations that took his breath away.

He was seated in the lounge; she stood near the bar at a distance of some 30 feet, her back toward him, talking with Dolly Chandler, the cereal king's wife. She was dressed in tan slacks and a silk blouse that shone in the reflected sunlight, washing in through the windows. In his imagination, Billy peeled away her clothing, working to define her naked shape. Her slacks fit snuggly and revealed every sensual line of her buttocks, her hips, and the tops of her thighs. He didn't know a woman could stir his blood so; not even Sadie had this effect on him.

As he examined her, Mrs Chandler walked off. Audrey stepped over to a large lounge chair next to her escort and slid into it, pulling her feet up underneath her.

Billy stood, smoothed the wrinkles in his shirt, and closed the distance between himself and the luminous object of his lust. Her escort was chatting with Cedric Worthington. He caught Billy's approach out of the corner of his eye and turned to him.

"Good afternoon." Billy blurted. "I... I've been wanting to... well, may I join you? My name is Billy. Billy Pruitt." The thrust of his hand toward Audrey was so abrupt that she almost recoiled, but then she took it and shook hands, smiling tentatively.

"Hello. I'm Audrey. This is Charles."

The two men shook hands; Charles eyed Billy the way a hawk eyes a vole.

"Uhh... Pruitt. Pruitt. Ahh! Pruitt Mercantile, right?

Billy cleared his throat and began to demur.

"Ahh. Well, I'm impressed," said Charles. Sensing that Billy was susceptible to flattery, he turned to Audrey. "Audrey, Mr Pruitt is the head of one of America's most successful enterprises."

"No, no. You mustn't... I mean, it's not me. It's my father. He's the head of the company. I'm just... well, I'm learning the business."

"Well, I have to say I did wonder that you were so young. That explains it, of course. Have a seat, Master

Pruitt." Charles waved him toward the chair on the other side of Audrey.

Billy sat, obediently, and stared at Audrey, his mouth hanging open. A long moment passed and Audrey became aware of Billy's gaze. She hoped he would get hold of himself and start a conversation. Finally, she turned to him and raised her eyebrows.

Billy started: "Oh, I'm sorry. I didn't mean... uhhh... to stare. It's just that... you're so... uhh..."

Audrey broke in to save him. "What have you learned so far, Mr Pruitt?" She smiled, hoping it would put him at ease.

"Well, you see, I... I've only just started my practical education. It's a big company, lots of branches and... hundreds of products. There's a lot to learn.

"I'm sure that's so." She hoped he would pick things up from there, but he remained tongue-tied.

Billy could not find things he thought worthy to say to Audrey–everything that coursed through his head sounded like drivel. He never really talked with Sadie; they just had as much sex as Billy could handle. He wanted to tell Audrey how beautiful she was and how smitten he was with her but he knew well enough that it would ruin his chances. Charles rescued him.

"So, Master Pruitt. How long will you be on your education tour?"

"Uhh, well, could be as long as a year–that's what my father says."

"You don't sound happy about it."

"To be frank, I don't think it's all that necessary but my father is quite opinionated."

"Yes, I believe I've heard that about him."

The silence returned. Finally, Billy couldn't take it. He wanted only to talk with Audrey and he couldn't think of a single appropriate thing to say to her. He jerked to his feet.

"Excuse me. There's a friend—I have to talk with him." He stuck out his hand and hastily shook both of theirs. "Pleasure meeting you... both."

Audrey and Charles smiled as he wheeled and bolted away.

"Sweet boy," said Audrey.

"Rich boy," said Charles.

XIII

PLACEMENT AT TABLE in the first-class dining salon was never pre-arranged. No ship's functionary would dare try deciding who sat next to whom amongst these well-heeled, pampered, influential people. Except for invitation to the Captain's table for dinner, White Star judged it best to leave it to the passengers themselves to work out their pecking order. Charles's early goal was to enter the dining room as these decisions were being made because they were always accompanied by introductions.

It was luncheon, their first meal at sea. As Charles and Audrey walked in, three other parties milled around a table near the door and Charles wondered whether he'd struck the richest vein in history.

He recognized Nelson Chandler first, founder of the wildly successful breakfast cereal juggernaut, Chandler's Mills. Nelson Chandler had been a modestly successful neighborhood pharmacist in a suburb of Albany, New York. One day, his wife, Dolly, an avid baker, turned out some softened and rolled kernels of wheat she thought might liven up an old bread recipe. The experiment went awry but, by chance, Edward, their hyper-active 10-year-old, whom everyone called Sonny, grabbed a handful off the baking sheet as he ran through the kitchen, and wolfed them down. Later, he begged his mother for more. Pleased there was anything resembling wholesome food that he would actually ask for, she made up batches for him to have at breakfast.

Sonny's delight in the toasted wheat never flagged and Nelson took notice, thinking he might be on to a new health food. He asked Dolly to make extra, which he bagged up and sold at the pharmacy. His customers would come in for their medicines and ask if he had more of those funny little flakes. They didn't know what to call them—needing a name, Nelson dubbed them "Sonny's".

It wasn't long before Dolly was overwhelmed trying to keep up with requests for Sonny's and they realized they had a commercial tiger by the tail. Before long, every day across America, in cities, on farms, in grimy tenement kitchens, in middle class homes, in the dining rooms of sprawling mansions and in their servants' quarters, children who craved an alternative to the corn cereals produced by William Kellogg, sat down to a breakfast of Sonny's Wheat Flakes or Chandler's Wheaty Bites. And each little bun of processed and baked wheat or flattened and toasted wheat kernel—millions upon millions of them every day—put another mil or two in Nelson Chandler's accounts. And oh, how those mils added up.

Charles strode directly up to Chandler and his dowdy wife, with Audrey on his arm. "A very good afternoon. May I introduce myself—I'm Charles Pierce, and this is my niece, Audrey Simmons."

"A pleasure, Pierce. Miss Simmons. I'm Nelson Chandler. This is my wife, Dolly."

Hands were shaken all round. Charles took note of Chandler's reaction to Audrey—his eyes were glued to her. Dolly frowned.

"Uh, Nelson Chandler, you say. Not Chandler's Mills?" Charles was a natural actor–his tone of uncertainty mixed with curiosity was as good as anything Barrymore could have done.

"Uh, yes. Guilty as charged."

"Well, sir, it's indeed a pleasure," said Charles cheerily. "Not only has your fame spread across the ocean, so have your products. I enjoy them often myself." It was true enough; they were difficult to avoid. He would soon find that they were on offer on the Queen's breakfast menu, along with other traditional fare. "I must say, you're really giving old Kellogg a run for his money," added Charles, in an attempt to display a knowledge of business.

"That's good of you to say."

"Not at all," he said, tamping out his cigar in a nearby ashtray. "It looks like we're in for fair weather and smooth sailing," said Charles. He was always ready with small talk, determined to make certain there were no awkward silences.

"Yes, I think we'll be OK," replied Chandler, trying hard not to stare at Audrey. "Are you going over for the Olympics?"

"Oh, no, I'm afraid not, although I hate to miss it. No, pressing business matters bring us on board."

"May I inquire as to the, uhh...?"

"Oh, it's a matter of capital. I'm in mining, you see, and I've made a rather good strike, silver—at least, I believe I have—and I'm at pains to get back to London to brief my partners and secure additional funds to develop the mine. There's a great deal to do before we can get at the ore."

Smiling, he fell silent and let the image of an active silver mine settle in for a moment. "But, please, I beg you, let's not allow business to usurp our conversation. We should talk of loftier things, don't you think, as we enjoy the modern miracle of this splendid ship?"

"Quite so, Pierce. Well said. Business should occupy the place of business, and none other. That's what I always say, don't I, Dolly?"

She gave her husband a questioning look. "He does say that–and sometimes he means it."

Charles laughed appreciatively and Chandler helped.

"We were about to take this table for lunch," said Chandler. "Will you join us? Our son's wandering around here somewhere. Where is Sonny, Dolly?"

"Oh, you know how he is. I expect he'll be delivered to us from the bowels of the engine room any minute now, most likely covered in oil from head to foot."

"Yes, he does get into things," mused Chandler. "Fortunately, while we're on the ship, we know there are limits to how far he can wander. Please join us." He gestured to suggest they all sit.

"With pleasure," said Charles. He motioned Audrey toward a chair, noting that Dolly was not entirely pleased to be graced with their—or more precisely, with Audrey's—attractive company.

Before long, the railroad tycoon, Thomas Anders, and Felix Hansen, skyscraper financier, joined them. If it all went this well, Charles thought, as he spread his napkin on his lap, he was on track for a substantial pay-off.

XIV

DAVID HAD BEGUN TO WORRY that no one was interested in poker. When he finally got a game started, shortly after the midday meal, the stakes were the smallest he'd ever seen aboard the liners; one- and five-dollar limits, action no serious player would be interested in. Real poker requires a sense of danger—the twinge of fear evoked by the possibility of significant loss. David had put the word out earlier and had indications of interest from several of the ship's high rollers but, as yet, none had shown up. Instead, these guys had kept the betting low and were shooting the breeze. Frustrated, he voiced a lame excuse and stole away.

Now, just after dinner, he sat at a table in the starboard gallery, a long room adjacent to the main ballroom, and resorted to a stunt he disliked, showing off his technique for shuffling a deck of cards. He favored this modest room for its intimate feel and muted sound, the result of a splendid, russet-toned, deep-pile carpet. Three sets of double doors pierced the long inner wall leading to the ballroom, each framed by handsome, tropical themed, low-relief carvings in Honduras mahogany. Floor-to-ceiling curtain hangings covered most of the opposite wall, further damping the orchestra's energetic tunes as they filtered in from the ballroom.

The gallery was furnished with square tables and matching upholstered arm chairs, both finished in combinations of ash burl, pear, and other light, fine grained woods. The tables were a little small but otherwise perfect for cards.

Small groups in formal dress, couples and trios, dotted the room, smoking and sipping cocktails, creating a low hum of chatter and clinking glass. A man in a white dinner jacket was at the piano, playing a reasonable rendition of a rag. Waiters scurried back and forth between the tables and the bar, which was in the salon on the opposite side of the ship.

David chose his table with purpose. It was close to a framed placard on the wall that read: "Passengers Are Advised To Use Caution In The Choice Of Partners In Card Games And Other Games Of Chance." He sat with his back against the wall, the sign almost directly above his head.

He handled the cards so adroitly, it looked like sleight of hand—they were a blur as they riffled from his arched hands and cascaded into place. He performed many, flamboyant variations, then he put the deck on the table and fanned it into a broad arc with a single sweep of his hand. If you hadn't watched him do it, you'd swear he'd spent the previous hour meticulously placing the cards, making certain that the portion of each one showing, and the angle it formed to its neighbor, was identical from end to end.

He knew this open challenge would catch a few flies and let him get a substantial game started; he hoped they would be serious gamblers. Continuing, he became absorbed in the manipulation of the cards and the voice caught him slightly off guard.

"How about a game?" Milton Brownlow and Nelson Chandler had sauntered up to the table and were admiring David's show.

"Uhhh, sure. Swell, have a seat." With a welcoming smile, he indicated the empty chairs to his right and left. He swept the cards into a tight stack and pushed them into their pasteboard box. A waiter hurried past, bustling toward the bar—David caught his eye. The waiter came and took orders for drinks and, as he was turning to leave, David checked him, holding up the pack of cards. "Two fresh decks, please." The waiter nodded and hurried off.

"That's OK," Brownlow protested as he slid into his seat, "we can play with these."

David looked him over with a mixture of amusement and concern; was there a hustle hidden behind this offer? He extended his hand.

"I'm David Bowen."

"Milton Brownlow. And this is my friend, Nelson Chandler."

Brownlow's grip was a little tentative. He was a smallish man, with graying dark hair that was thinning at the top. When he was settled, he pulled a pair of gold-rimmed reading glasses from his breast pocket and perched them on his long nose, carefully tucking the wired, recurved temples over his ears. Chandler had a real grip, the kind of firm strength that generates confidence. He was square-jawed, large-framed, but now going a little paunchy. His greying blond hair was combed straight back. He also wore glasses, bifocals. Like David, both men wore the white dinner jacket and bow tie that was the virtual uniform in first class after sunset.

David turned back to Brownlow. "I appreciate your gesture of trust, Mr Brownlow," he said, with a hint of a smile, "but if you'll allow me to offer you advice, since I'm one of its targets..." he pointed to the cautionary placard, "you'd be wise to take these signs to heart." He watched Brownlow closely as his gaze flicked up to the sign and took it in—his look of surprise seemed genuine. "Even in a place like this," David went on, "first class on a White Star liner—you can't trust everyone. Because of that sign, and the events that put it there, I insist on starting with a fresh deck."

Brownlow regarded David with a look of mild shock; Chandler was similarly bemused. Brownlow sputtered. "This does you credit, Mr Bowen. I..."

"David. Call me David, please, I insist."

"David, then. Please call me Milton." He grabbed David's hand again and shook it vigorously, but without any increased strength. "I'm honored."

Chandler nodded at David and smiled admiringly. Brownlow was visibly embarrassed but went on, trying to cover his discomfort. "Is this really your... your work, David? Playing cards on ocean liners?"

Some found it beyond belief that anyone could have such an occupation—it was like claiming to be an underwater house painter. David had been obliged to answer this question so many times, it no longer rankled.

"Yes, this is what I do. And you?" He knew who Brownlow was, of course, and was merely making small talk. He threw the question at both men but Brownlow responded.

"Not much, really. I'm in banking."

Chandler chuckled and piped in, "Uhh, Milton is being coy, David. He's actually the chief financial officer of one of our largest commercial banks, Lake Eastern."

Brownlow shot a transient look of irritation in Chandler's direction, then looked down at the carpet.

"A pleasure, sir," said David. He was glad to have Brownlow at his table, since he was known to enjoy playing poker and to not be very good at it. David didn't take seriously the gossip that his losses were covered from bank funds but he did hope that he had with him a chunk of cash that David could make a significant dent in. He turned his attention to the other man.

"What about you, Mr Chandler? Chandler's Mills, isn't it? Cereal?"

"Tons of it, I'm afraid," said Chandler, with a smile.

"Do you also find it hard to imagine a man making his living playing cards on the high seas?"

"Not at all. What better place? Call me Nelson, will you?"

"Of course."

The waiter returned with the fresh decks and the drinks. Now David wanted to get down to business. One of the most important things Milo had taught him was to develop a precise plan to insure that he came out the winner and leave as little as possible to chance. He took it seriously, starting with what he drank during play. He always ordered rum and Coke but, if he was in a game, all the waiters knew to hold the rum. Later, they would pocket a ten spot for remembering.

When the game was underway, his first tactic was to try controlling the pace of play. He wanted things to start slowly and for the intensity to mount during the trip, peaking on the last night. He had to adjust this program for each ship, depending on how long it took in the crossing. Each new ship was faster than its predecessor; for the Queen Mary, it was down to just over five days and this was a critical moment in it. His first job was to pick out from among the ship's wealthiest men those interested in making high-stakes poker their onboard pastime. He needed to define this group quickly, cultivate them, and plant the notion that if they were interested in some good poker action, his table was the place to get it.

David felt that these men were about as promising a core group as any he had seen; others would no doubt meander in and out during the voyage. As the men were settling themselves around the table, Michael Gallagher, one of America's leading industrialists, walked across at the far end of the gallery, headed for the ballroom. Something drew his attention to the group—he changed course and made a beeline for the table. "Good evening, fellas. Am I mistaken or is there a poker game brewing?"

"No, you're quite right," said Brownlow, cheerily. "Pull up a chair."

Gallagher was a short, balding man, but broad and muscular. There was something aggressive and challenging about the way he carried himself—David was prepared not to like him. In the Manhattan social set, Gallagher was regarded as arrogant and coarse. But there was no doubt that he was financially sound; he was the outright owner of Bessemer Allegheny, second only to US Steel.

An unsavory reputation followed him. Stories circulated about his aggressive rise to power in the steel business and they included a persistent, though unsubstantiated rumor. Before the fledgling company got its fancy name and was on the cusp of breaking into the lists against Big Steel, Gallagher's partner, with whom he was known to be somewhat at odds, died in circumstances that were a little suspicious. But no charges were ever filed.

Despite his earlier fears, David had now met his initial goal—a group of high rollers in a warm-up game on the first night out. Now he angled to create a relaxed atmosphere that would put the men off their guard at the outset. He wanted to keep the stakes at a moderate level for these first games. At the same time, he assessed his pigeons, looking for their tells.

On day one, David always left the table a loser. It was folly to scare off fat pigeons when the pots were still low. Instead, he'd cede to the more self-confident, arrogant players—at least one of those always turned up—and fold some hands that showed promise. Then, in the following days, he would ratchet up the betting—and the accompanying anxiety. Only on the final night of the voyage would he push the stakes to levels that drew in crowds, hanging breathless on the turn of every card. Then, of course, he wanted the pigeons' nerves to be as taut as violin strings.

So an early question always was: How high could he start the betting without making the other players jittery? Besides starting at the right level, it had to be the right game with the right players—men with lots of money to throw around and who enjoyed putting that money at risk.

Sam Riverson and William Pruitt emerged from the ballroom and, like Gallagher, sniffed out the game. "Room for one more?" asked Riverson, cheerfully. Everyone quickly agreed. This time, they pulled over another table to make space and Nelson Chandler tipped a waiter to bring one of the ship's big banquet table covers.

David wondered why Riverson only asked about including one more. It became clear when, after timidly greeting the players, Billy stood outside the circle and folded his arms across his chest. He offered that he felt out of his depth, saying he'd only played in dorm-room games and wanted to watch for a while. He would join later, once he felt more sure of himself.

David wondered why Pruitt felt it necessary to tell this lie; did he believe it would somehow gain him an advantage once he decided to risk sitting in? Knowing the depth of the Pruitt resources, he hoped Billy wouldn't remain shy for long.

He was pleased to see Riverson, knowing how much he could add to the pot. He hoped Riverson's youth equated to inexperience. Also, he brought the group to five, a good number for poker, although a sixth man, with the right level of capital, would be even better.

As he cracked open the fresh cards, David, angling now for a substantial start, made an important strategic overture to the group. "Seven-card stud?" It was a statement disguised as a question; he tried to make it sound as though no alternative was worth the bother.

As David hoped, none of the men had any particular stake in the version of poker they played. Seven-card stud was easily the most popular form of the game and his opponents acquiesced with nods and grunts. But David was not indifferent. This was his working game—it produced the largest pots and more than any other, it gave a skillful player the winning edge.

He fanned the cards across the table for a quick look to make sure the new deck was complete. Now, shuffling the cards to work the stiffness out, he moved methodically. He took his time, waiting, certain that another call would come, one that had become inescapable recently.

"How about jokers wild?" There it was—with Brownlow the culprit. For amateurs, it seemed a tantalizing sense of danger existed in the risk of significant money in a game where cards were "wild"—as though it helped the player feel *he* was maybe a little wild, too.

No one else was interested in this option; several grunted objections. Wild cards were an irritation; they added to the influence of chance on the outcomes. This countered David's edge and he was glad he didn't have to be the one to object.

The group appointed Brownlow banker for the session. Because of his profession, this happened almost anytime he sat in on a private game; he had long since stopped grousing about it. David pushed a set of poker chips in front of Brownlow, which he'd secured from the salon—despite their cautions, the shipping lines provided their passengers with gambling paraphernalia.

The men quickly set their ground rules, part of the ritual of poker at the start of play. £20 to ante, same as the minimum bet. The maximum bet—£200, with a limit of three raises per round. They pegged white chips at £10, red at £20, blue at £50.

David would have preferred an unlimited game but for him to suggest it at this point would make him seem too aggressive. But players often abandoned the limits as a session heated up toward the end of a long night, and they became desperate to recoup their losses before the session ended.

They chose Sam Riverson to start the dealing. Sam was a tall, lean young man with light brown hair, trimmed short. His eyes were pale blue and he would have been film star handsome, were it not for an unflattering hook to his nose.

"Ante up," he announced. The players each tossed in a white chip and the first game of the cruise was underway. Riverson began the deal; two "hole" cards, face down, plus a third, face up. Even before he got all the cards out, Brownlow began to chatter.

"Did you all catch the headlines today?" Condensed versions of the major papers reached the ship by radiotelephone. "I'm worried about this guy, Hitler." He directed his comment mostly at his friend, Nelson Chandler. "He's put his soldiers back into the Rheinland—plus, this thing he's got against Jews is a bad business."

David glanced at Brownlow with annoyance. Amateurs often talked too much during a game and it looked like Brownlow might be the chatterbox this time. Bravado and friendly jibes were the norm when a group of men got together but David's experience was that the crucible of the poker table brought out something else— the more insecure you were about your skills, the more you nattered on. He'd seen players gab so much that they lost track of play, with real money sitting on the table, and suffer the embarrassment of having to ask where the betting stood.

He'd learned long ago how to join in this patter without losing his concentration but the talkers always rankled him. His work was beginning and he needed to concentrate.

The players checked their down cards and did their best not to let their faces give anything away. Michael Gallagher, on David's left, had the highest card showing, the jack of diamonds. This gave him the lead bet; he checked his hole cards a second time and bet low, £20, testing the waters. This surprised David, who had him figured for the aggressive type. But it was early days, yet.

Brownlow, Chandler, and Riverson called, bringing the bet to David. While he contemplated whether to raise, Chandler picked up the conversation. "I agree with you, Milton," he said. "'You think we're going to have to step in and slap him down?"

"Oh no, my friend. We're staying out of this one. Far as I'm concerned, those Europe guys can fight each other all they want. We don't have to get in it."

David's bet—his initial salvo in the five-day skirmish. Since his object in these early games was to lose enough to appear harmless, he had to make a careful choice. His cards weren't especially strong. His up-card was a six of spades and it was paired with another six in the hole—hardly the most challenging hand at the table.

The simplest way to avoid winning was to avoid playing, by folding early, but a sound strategy required more finesse. He was in the spotlight. As the acknowledged professional, he was automatically intimidating and his every act and word were under scrutiny. At the same time, he was the special prize— each of his opponents would love to boast that he knocked off the pro on the Queen Mary. He decided the right start for this crowd was a modest raise. "I'm in for an extra twenty," he said, sliding two white chips into the center.

David's question was how far into each of these early hands he should play before ducking out. He could simply stay in as late as possible each time but the later he stayed, the more money he had in the pot, all of it sacrificed on the fold. He also felt forced to stay pretty far into two or three hands at least, to maintain a sense of full participation; a player's not truly in the game unless he plays—he has to risk something. So by the end of the second day, David always had a substantial cash investment in his strategy.

He got a ten of hearts in the next round, which gave him an opportunity to look a little aggressive at low cost. Sam Riverson had led with a £20 bet, which the others called. David tossed two red chips into the center. "There's the 20, and 20 to raise." The others matched him but no one went higher.

Meanwhile, Nelson Chandler continued to worry about Nazi Germany. "Yeah, this Hitler's a new kind of threat," he said. "He's not only talking expansion—grabbing land and such, like they always do. No, he's got this Aryan thing, whoever in hell they are, and if you aren't one of them, you may as well pack up."

"OK," Riverson called, trying to keep the game moving. "Going to Fifth Street." He dealt out the fifth cards, again face up.

Gallagher's hand was starting to look strong; he'd paired up with a jack of hearts. It didn't give him a lot of courage—he only bet £30; again, Brownlow, Chandler and Riverson matched him. David also called but, when his turn came to match another £30 raise from Gallagher, he paused for a dramatic moment, then folded, tossing his cards into the dead pile.

Gallagher cast a glance at him from under thick eyebrows. "So, Mr. Bowen. Not so tough as advertised, I see." He was smirking.

David puzzled over the cause of his hostility but he wanted only to deflect it. "Advertised?!" he said, with a mischievous smile. "Is my face on a billboard around here someplace?" He turned to Gallagher. "Oh, I know! It's that "Wanted" poster. Darn," he said, in mock self censure, "I thought I got them all."

Everyone except Gallagher chuckled at the joke; he remained on the attack. "Well, your reputation seems to be all smoke," he said, with unmistakable contempt. He turned his attention to Brownlow. "I second you on staying out of it, Milton," he declared. "We don't want a war. It would be a disaster for business."

The sudden change of topic defused the tension but David was left wondering why Gallagher was picking a fight with him.

"Well, I don't know about that," said Chandler. "As it happens, war's usually pretty good for business. But that's beside the point."

Now on the sidelines, David surveyed the table as Riverson continued running the game. Chandler had a king and a pair of nines showing but, with his two jacks, Gallagher's hand looked the strongest and he clearly felt in control. He and Chandler kept the betting going, raising each other in £30 increments, with Brownlow and Riverson along for the ride. Starting the final betting rounds, Gallagher went for the maximum, tossing in two blue chips. Then he repeated a gesture David thought strange—he pushed his glasses up the bridge of his nose using his thumb, as if he were about to poke his own eye.

David studied him. His demeanor at the poker table was all bully and bluster, hardly the thing for a consistent winner. But more troublesome was the too-obvious enmity from a man he had no quarrel with, and who could buy and sell him many times over. He wondered how he should handle it.

Brownlow called Gallagher's bet but didn't raise. Chandler cleared his throat and fidgeted in his chair as he rearranged his cards. Then he also called, and added a blue chip, a £50 raise. David wondered if Chandler was always this transparent when he held a good hand.

Brownlow couldn't get Hitler out of his mind. "Y'know, he's banned all non-Aryans from the German team. Apparently he wants the Olympics to show off the new *Deutschland*—expects to win it all."

Riverson's play now. He took another look at his cards, sighed, and threw them into the dead pile, alongside David's.

Gallagher said, "Well, I think we'll make a pretty good showing at these games. Did you know some of *our* boys are on the ship?"

"Really? The team's sailing with us?" Brownlow was excited.

"I don't think it's the whole team," said Chandler. "Just a few who're going across a little early."

At the turn, Chandler had a nine-high straight that no one had seen coming. It took the pot and he began gathering in the chips. David thought Gallagher was a little too unfazed, since he had clearly expected to win the hand. He was going to be tough to figure.

Gallagher took advantage of the break in play to light one of the huge cigars he affected. Once he got it going, he leaned back in his chair. "Adolph Kiefer, the swimmer, is one of them." he announced. "I understand he intends to work-out everyday in the pool."

"Plus there's most of the guys on the basketball team," Chandler added.

"Adolph Kiefer? Sounds German," said Brownlow.

"He was born in Chicago," said Riverson. Except for his calls as dealer, Sam Riverson hadn't said a word 'til now and all eyes shifted to him. "Wouldn't that be a joke for *Herr Hitler*, if a German from Chicago whipped the pants off his champion?"

David was puzzled by Riverson, a bright young man whose demeanor was too reserved for a lad in his twenties. He, too, was difficult to read and David wondered if he might be his toughest opponent in the end.

Chandler found it hard to joke about the German Chancellor. "I wish that was all it would take to keep Hitler from starting another war. Like Milton says, his troops are back at the French border now, just like before."

"But he's all tied up by the Versailles treaty, isn't he…?" asked Brownlow, hoping it was true. "You know, from the end of the war in '19?" He tipped his chair onto its back legs and lit a cigar. "You can't fight a war with just rifles, these days."

Billy Pruitt decided he wanted to test his luck and asked to sit in. The men were a little surprised—Billy just seemed too young for serious poker—but they made room for him. David smiled at this new opportunity.

Gallagher now had the deal and was feeding out the cards. An unbroken rope of blue smoke rose from the pipe he held between his teeth, making it difficult to understand him. "No, he's ignored all that. He's putting together a first-rate fighting machine; planes, modern tanks, subs, the works. It's all supposed to be hush-hush but you can't hide that kind of industrial activity. Now's the time to check him but... well, so far, nobody's stepped up."

"Still, I can't see why any American boys should have to die to stop him," Brownlow insisted. "What do you think, Gallagher. How's it look from where you stand? You have a lot of government business."

"Well, I can't say I'm too worried." He was chuffed to be asked for his opinion. "Not that I'm any sort of expert, you understand." The opening bets were down and Gallagher again had the highest cards showing. He tossed four blue chips into the pot, the maximum bet, and glanced around the table as though he'd just laid a big, gilded egg. He puffed on his cigar and squinted through the resulting pall of smoke. "I don't think I'm going to lose much sleep over a few Hebes getting hassled but I do think that, once we get together and let this Hitler know we won't stand for any Kraut nonsense, he'll tow the line." Gallagher didn't notice Brownlow's reaction to his anti-Semitic reference.

David didn't keep up on politics much but, from what he had read and heard, Gallagher was being amazingly naïve. He turned to Chandler. "I think you're right, Nelson. I fear it's only a matter of time before we're up to our tits again in another European mess."

He didn't venture more; he wanted to stick to business—what the hell could he do about Adolph Hitler, anyway? He turned his attention back to the poker table. It looked as though the pots were going to build to a useful size. He wasn't going to fight for this one but he knew that a substantial pot on the table this early in the voyage meant a truly big one later, when it really counted.

Sam Riverson had high cards now and he came on strong, betting the maximum and then raising aggressively by the time the fifth card was out. He smiled as he raised again, and glanced around at the other players. David regarded him quizzically; he'd analyzed the cards in this round six ways from Sunday and couldn't find any reason to believe Sam knew something he didn't. If Sam thought this was effective bluffing, he was in for a big disappointment.

David rather liked Sam Riverson. He was a decent sort, young and inexperienced but earnest—a work in progress. David had followed his story in the papers, which couldn't resist the youth-inherits-huge-fortune angle.

Sam's father had gone out wildcatting in eastern Texas and Oklahoma. He got a reputation for knowing where to drill and his company, Salient Oil, had the lowest percentage of dry holes of any in the territory. He needed that innate sense because the land he was punching holes in, near Kilgore, never was the quivering bubble of crude, waiting to be pricked, that the early prospectors found in places like Beaumont. There, folks liked to joke that you had to be careful knocking in a fence post for fear of hitting a gusher. Around Kilgore, a fence post churned up nothing more than a cloud of dust—to get oil, you had to be a good deal more aggressive.

The oilrigs had a particular meanness to them. Rag-tag groups of thin, hungry-eyed men moved from one to another, hanging around, hoping for jobs. They sat in small groups, smoking and playing cards or dominoes. They never said it out loud but they were all waiting for some poor bastard to let his attention wander for a second or two and get himself smacked by a swinging drill line, or his leg caught in an arresting chain, and be carried away on a stretcher. They'd quickly crowd around the platform boss, offering to fill the gap. A lot of guys worked with cracked ribs and crushed fingers because that was the only way they could keep their jobs. There was no job security, no union contract. If you were injured, someone took your place and that was it—he was in, you were out.

Beyond all this, Riverson Sr had to deal with scavengers, hucksters selling drilling rights to land they didn't own, scammers faking strikes in dry holes, and no small number of women ready to use liquor and sex to get hold of his purse. He'd survived all that and made a pile of money, and brought in a bunch of steadily producing wells, only to die when one blew out and a section of drill pipe, driven by 6,000 pounds of Paleolithic pressure, pinged off the rig and bashed him against the wellhead like Babe Ruth connecting with a fast ball. He was dead before his body slumped to the oil soaked deck.

His wife, Marie, sold the business on very favorable terms, including an irreducible percentage, in perpetuity, of the output of every well, present and future, developed on Salient holdings. The ink had barely dried on the documents when the 1928 flu epidemic, a relatively tame one, swept through and caught her in its path. All that money devolved upon young Sam, a teenager at the time.

Now in his mid-twenties, it had all come into his hands. He'd hardly had to think about money before and now, he had to figure out what to do with a mountain of it. The fortune was growing larger every minute, as dozens of Salient pump-jacks bobbed against the Texas sky. It would essentially never stop growing.

With his parents now interred in the hillside overlooking their Virginia homestead, Sam, fresh out of Geology at Yale, decided to book on the Queen Mary and head for Europe. He'd take in the Olympics, do the Grand Tour, and see if he could clear his head enough to think it all through. A friend had urged him to get into the flickers—maybe buy a controlling interest in one of the small studios that were popping up all over the place, now that the movies had sound. Sam was considering it.

He'd played a lot of poker at college but, despite studying the game with a lot more enthusiasm than he applied to Geology, he was always the butt of jokes over a nearly unbroken record of losses. The money, of course, was never an issue but he yearned to develop the knack. His friend, Kelly, was good at the game and Sam wanted a winning percentage that at least approached his.

Kelly came from a working-class Irish family and he'd virtually battered his way into Yale with his intellect; he and Sam hit if off from day one. Sam got serious about poker then and, with Kelly's tutoring, he began to improve. Before long, Yale's well-heeled scholars were losing their ample allowances to him at a heady rate.

But despite all the money behind him, Sam had grown up working-class and it showed in his manners and speech. Some of the rich Yalies found it easy to call him a cheater, typically behind his back. One spoiled, soft-skinned son of a grocery chain owner lost his whole month's allowance to Sam one night and accused him openly.

Sam was on the verge of attacking the kid but Kelly pulled him aside. He convinced Sam that, instead of punching him, he'd score a lot of social points with a classier response—he should challenge the kid to a duel. Sam liked the idea—he literally threw a glove at the lad's feet and issued a challenge. The boy, who was a minor star on the wrestling squad, compounded his error by accepting: Fisticuffs, bare knuckles, the Quad, high noon. Sam and Kelly made certain word got around and they put down some good-size bets; by noon on the day, the bulk of the undergraduate class crowded the Quad.

Nobody recognized Sam at first. He arrived in style, in an open carriage, with a liveried coachman driving a matched pair of cockaded white horses. He was decked out in formal dress, complete with a top hat—Kelly and another friend as seconds; the crowd of eager college boys broke into cheers when they realized who it was. With great drama, he descended from the carriage, stripped to the waist, shook hands with his accuser, then humbled him in the first round—the boy didn't land a single solid punch. Sam and Kelly became roommates and, from that point on, whatever their academic interests, they minored in poker.

Tonight, Sam felt pretty good. As the clock ticked on toward midnight, over £1,000 sat in the pot and Sam was pretty certain he was going to walk away with it. Although Billy Pruitt felt he had gained a sense of the table, it was soon clear he was in over his head. He was playing too conservatively, scared, folding hands any seasoned player would have coveted.

Only David, Gallagher, Sam, and Billy were still in the current hand. It was David's play and he appeared to be struggling with his decision, a fact that Sam tried to mask his pleasure over.

"I'll stay," said David, weakly. Every game was a performance for David and he had fine-tuned the level of energy and enthusiasm of his calls at the table. Tonight he wanted to sound a little stressed and unsure of himself.

David didn't expect to draw the third jack that probably would have won this pot and that was exactly the way he wanted it. Even if the jack did come up, he'd simply not show it and fold the hand—he wanted Gallagher or Sam to take the game. He would let the money he had on the table go. Tomorrow, he'd try to break about even.

The time to start winning was on day three. By then, with David's subtle assistance, he expected his happy tablemates to develop a sense of invincibility, along with the conviction that they didn't have to take David seriously as an opponent. Then they would abandon caution—that was the time to bear down.

The following night, his injured opponents would be champing at the bit for a shot at getting even, certain that David's success had been a fluke. But they would lose again, and more heavily. The night after that, their last night at sea, with David in possession of just about every loose pound, franc, or dollar among them, the more desperate ones would be virtually gasping to get some of their money back, some to save face, others because they'd over-extended themselves and risked being in Dutch with a business partner or, possibly worse, a disapproving wife. David, of course, would be perfectly amiable and sympathetic, he'd wonder at his own good luck, marveling at a run that he would suggest had never happened to him before. And he would be ruthless. He thought his winnings for the week might top £15,000.

The seventh card slid to a stop in front of him face down—Gallagher was dealing and he looked up at David, squinting through the smoke swirling out of his cigar. The cigar was such an obvious affectation that David had to squelch an urge to reach over and smack it away. He saw so much pretense in the people he played cards with that he had little tolerance for it anymore; often his response was to trounce the offender even more soundly.

Gallagher was too obviously gloating over his hand and David's concerns about his skills were dissolving. Michael Gallagher, the head of Bessemer Allegheny, US Steel's only significant rival in the States, was looking more and more like a petulant, spoiled child. He had grown up on the streets and wrestled and schemed his way into the business world, sharply aware of every advantage and always quick to grab it. He'd grown up in the rough and tumble neighborhoods of Boston's Southie, where he'd had to fight for whatever he wanted.

David didn't know much more about him; Boston society didn't get much exposure in the New York press. What he saw of him, and was coming to know of him across the card table, he didn't much like.

Though Gallagher tried to affect an air of polish and breeding, he had the underlying character of a bully.

David had seen this before. Some men, after scratching their way to the top, were at ease with their new wealth and had a certain level of humility, aware that their new position owed at least as much to the help of others, and to luck, as to their own wits and skill. But others, perhaps most of them, David thought, looked with disdain on those less successful, those still struggling, those they had "beaten." They behaved as if they had merely fulfilled the destiny that fate—or God—had marked out for them. Other people were to be used, directed, suppressed, and never allowed to forget their place.

It seemed to David that Gallagher was intent on disparaging him in particular, apparently believing David had no place in a poker game with men who ran huge enterprises and made large sums of money. The notion that David, despite his lack of status in business, was regarded as the "pro" and might be the best player at the table, irritated Gallagher. David resolved to be careful in his interactions with him, even as he contrived to lighten his wallet.

David picked up the new card and allowed a look of disappointment to flit across his eyes. He looked at Gallagher. "What do you have?"

Gallagher smiled, too pleased with himself, and laid down a high straight. David turned over his cards—two pair, a loser against Gallagher's cards. He pretended to be miffed. "Well, Mr. Gallagher," he said, doing his best to be chummy. "I don't know if you've been gulling us but you're plenty hot tonight."

"Somebody said it, my expert friend," Gallagher replied dismissively. "You can't win them all." As he scraped the pile of chips toward him, he glanced briefly at Pruitt, who looked as though his pet dog had just died.

Gallagher didn't bother to commiserate; he felt Pruitt had no business to be playing with grown-ups.

As Gallagher methodically sorted his chips into their denominations, David smiled wanly and stood, announcing himself tapped out for the night. As he took his leave, he had only one real concern—was he the only gambler aboard ship? He could never guarantee it, but there weren't that many poker professionals on the liners these days.

Most didn't like being so footloose and preferred to play at the various clubs, legal and not, that drew the high stakes players in the larger cities of Europe and America. A few who would have been happy to be on the Queen had been banished by White Star and Cunard–the only lines that counted–for straight-out cheating. That left just a handful, including David; so far on this trip, he'd seen nothing of the others.

But he'd become aware that the man whom Audrey was attached to had some sort of game going, though it didn't involve cards. He worried that his own background had brought out his cynical side but he had that strong feeling that Audrey was the bait in some kind of scam. And she was succeeding. Wherever she and her escort turned up, crowds of hormone driven young men formed, buzzing around her like hornets. Earlier that evening, with the social heat turned up to maximum, a knot of tuxedoed hopefuls had swarmed around her, all but drooling. Though dismayed at the attention focused on her, Audrey handled it well, never allowing any of her admirers to think he was her favorite.

Each time he saw her, David's interest deepened and he wondered whether *he* stood any chance of becoming her favorite.

XV

CAREFULLY ADJUSTING HIS BOWTIE, Charles looked in the mirror of his small bureau and ran through his mind the men he'd encountered that afternoon. He'd been at this long enough to know that several of them, perhaps more than he could comfortably accommodate, would allow themselves to be lured into his net. But he'd always found it difficult to predict which ones it would be. Too often, for his comfort, the one he guessed would take the bait was the one who showed the most reticence, either out of fear, or natural skepticism. Often the inhibiting effect of a watchful wife made the difference, which was why he now had Nelson Chandler in the questionable column.

Billy Pruitt, of course, was high on his list. Charles prayed he was as well buffered with cash as he was naive. Felix Hansen looked like a real possibility. He was on board alone, his wife having decided at the last minute to accept an invitation in the Hamptons instead of sailing with him. The rumor mill had it that it was an excuse to spend two unfettered weeks with her lover, and that Hansen had caught wind of the affair. Many times, Charles benefitted when a husband reacted to his wife's infidelity by becoming reckless with money. He hoped this was another such instance.

Then there was Sam Riverson. He was in oil, which lately was making new millionaires at a prodigious rate, although it was his father who had actually made the fortune. Charles didn't know whether Riverson Jr. was ever involved in the business. Still, he thought the natural association between oil and mining might make Sam enthusiastic about the prospect of a vicarious win.

Satisfied with his tie, Charles slipped into his dinner jacket and checked himself again in the mirror. Shoulders back, a direct gaze, that knowing smile beneath a stylishly trimmed mustache—the packaging was complete. He stepped to the door to the adjoining suite and tapped. "Are you ready?" After a moment, the door cracked open.

Audrey stood there in a shimmering green silk gown that perfectly complemented her auburn curls and caressed her curves. A matching band of silk stretched across her forehead and held the radiant center of a peacock's feather. On one wrist, diamonds from a thin bracelet caught the light. An emerald pendant dangled from a silver chain around her neck and rested between her small breasts, which swelled discreetly at the gown's scooped neck. She was dazzling.

Charles grinned broadly. She shone and sparkled, exactly as he had planned. She smiled at him and struck a pose, one slender hand on her hip, the other holding a cigarette she pretended to smoke. "What do you think?" She knew what his answer must be.

"You are ravishing. You will draw them in like bears to honey."

It took a beat for her to realize that, despite her lack of romantic interest in him, she was miffed that Charles wasn't captivated by her. She wanted to see a spark of sexual interest in his eye, to justify all her careful preparation. All she got, after his initial smile, was business-like approval.

And though she hid it, she was stung by his "bears to honey" remark. She hadn't fully understood that her role was that of a lure; maybe she didn't want to understand that. Faced with it now, she didn't like the idea.

She turned abruptly and marched into her room. "Charles, I don't understand what I'm supposed to be doing. Is this really what you hired me for, to wear pretty clothes and jewelry? You said you wanted an assistant—what am I actually doing here?"

"It couldn't be simpler, my dear." He clasped his hands behind his back and showed her an avuncular smile. "I do need you to tell the white lie that you're my niece; that's just to keep tongues from wagging. And, because of your ample secretarial skills, you are my assistant, as well. Thus, though we travel together as family, you work for me and draw a salary. The arrangement is mutually beneficial."

"But what am I assisting you with?"

"As I told you, I have been prospecting in Colorado and I'm pursuing those mining interests. You will handle correspondence and my dealings with assay offices—you know what assay is." It was more a statement than a question.

"Well, sure, where they tell you about your mining, uhh... stuff. The ore. How good it is."

"Just so. The results come back as a ratio of the amount of plain earth to the gold or silver or tin—silver, in our case. It's never more than a few ounces in a ton of the assayed material."

"I can't help feeling there's something fishy about this—I have no experience in mining matters."

Still smiling, he grasped her shoulders and held her at arms length. "But you will, my dear. No one starts out knowing what his job is all about; it takes time to learn the ropes. I'll see to your training as we proceed. In the meantime, I need you to exude class and beauty—something you have no trouble doing—along with a small measure of acumen. Do that and the men I'm interested in talking to will flock to us.

"But suppose one of them asks me for details—like who your associates are. I'm going to look like a dolt."

"Don't worry, you'll absorb it. Meanwhile, simply explain, should anyone bother to ask, that you've only just started. Now that's true, isn't it?"

She nodded, not entirely satisfied.

"Now then. Are you ready to go to dinner?"

She shrugged.

"I'll meet you in the passageway."

Pouting, she backed into her room and closed the door.

Charles paused a moment, wondering whether he was tutoring Audrey correctly. He didn't want her to know the whole picture too soon. Things would build as the voyage continued and he felt it best if she didn't twig to the realities of her situation just yet. He had to be careful—a wrong word from her could blow things apart.

He decided to let the matter rest for the moment. Things were going well for this stage of the journey; the next few days would demand all his skill. He stepped to the cabin door and went out.

XVI

AUDREY WAS BORED. It was after dinner and she and Charles had spent more than an hour in the dining room making small talk, while Charles smoked his cigars and talked business. Several youngish men drifted by to get a closer look at Audrey but Charles's presence scared them off. They usually left for the salon. Although the band played well enough, Audrey had grown weary of their collection of colorless dance music, which constantly filtered in from the ballroom. She found herself longing for the lively jazz riffs at the clubs back in Harlem.

"I'm going to the powder room, Charles."

He smiled at her. "Hurry back."

The opulence of the women's lounge was another in a string of surprises in the grand ship's repertoire. The anteroom was sprawling and pink, done up in the latest art deco fashion. The walls featured an exquisitely painted skyline scene that stretched around the room; Audrey wasn't sure if it represented a real city or an imagined one.

"Beautiful, isn't it?" The sultry, British-accented voice came from a woman who had entered after Audrey and now leaned against the wall behind her, puffing on a cigarette set in a black lacquered holder. She took a long, thoughtful drag as she examined the panorama. "Don't know how you get the talent to create something like that, eh?" The woman pushed away from the wall and sidled up to Audrey. She had a luscious figure enclosed in a revealing, backless, pearlescent chiffon that draped to the floor. She was one of two or three women who inhabited the first class lounges and bars but who, Audrey had noticed, appeared to be without escorts.

"Yes," said Audrey. "It's amazing. Is that England?"

"Sure, luv. It's London, isn't it. See that," she pointed with the cigarette holder, "that's Big Ben next to the Parliament building. Over there is St. Paul's."

"I'm not that familiar with foreign geography."

"Foreign?"

Audrey caught the tone. "I'm sorry. I'm afraid I'm a little green. I've never been out of the States before and I..."

"Well, don't worry about it, luv. It's natural. My name's Christine—call me Chris." She offered a cigarette; Audrey declined with a shake of her head.

"I'm Audrey."

Chris tugged the cigarette stub from the holder and took a long time grinding it out in a nearby ashtray stand, while eyeing Audrey closely. "I've noticed that man you're with. Splendid-looking bloke. Are you two married?"

The notion that she and Charles might be married took her by surprise and she giggled. "Oh, uhh... No, no, he's my uncle, sort of." A twinge of fear gripped Audrey's stomach. Without realizing it, she had dreaded this moment. She had to start speaking "the story" now and she wasn't sure she was up to it.

Chris's eyes narrowed. "What do you mean, 'sort of'? Is he?"

"Well, he is, but so far removed, I'm not sure it means anything." She had to take a deep breath.

Chris nodded her understanding. "I'm having trouble making up my mind about him. Is he well provided for?"

Audrey bristled at her frankness. "Aren't you direct?"

Chris wasn't in the least deterred. "We don't have a lot of time, luv. This trip only lasts five days. I'm trying to determine if I should give him a tumble."

"Give him a tumble?"

"A girl's got to earn her crust, doesn't she?" She busied herself fitting another gold-tipped cigarette into the holder. "So is he rich, or is he just putting on a good act?"

Unable to sidestep Chris's prying, she affected an air of coldness. "Well, I'm not sure I know, for certain. If I had to guess, I'd say it's somewhere in between."

"Hmmm, too bad," said Chris. "It's better when they're good looking *and* rich." She took a match from the small holder, set into the rim of the ashtray, and lit the fresh cigarette. "I appreciate your candor, luv. We girls have to stick together, don't we?"

"Uhh, yeah..." Audrey thought she heard a serious note beneath this remark but she couldn't be sure. She wanted to ask exactly what she meant but Chris had already turned and was headed toward the door.

"See you later," Chris said with a smile, and glided back into the salon.

XVII

CHARLES STOOD IN THE DOORWAY connecting the two rooms, buttoning his cuff links, as they prepared for a late-night return to the salons. Audrey was arranging a tortoise shell comb in her hair and following his movements in the dressing table mirror. "She said 'we girls have to stick together.' Stick together over what?"

Charles folded his arms across his chest and regarded her as she worked with the comb. "Well, I think this is probably going to upset you, sweetheart." Audrey stopped fussing with the comb and fixed her gaze on his reflection. "Christine was talking about herself and her friends, and their business here on board. They're prostitutes."

Audrey swung around. "You can't be serious! You've seen her—she's beautiful! Elegant!"

He smiled at her fierce innocence. "Yes, elegance and beauty are what the men we're traveling with require in the women they bed." He shrugged. "They can afford it."

She stared down at the combs and brushes on the dresser, not seeing them; she felt her life had suddenly veered off course. She looked up at him again, in the mirror. She was coming slowly to realize that Charles regarded everyone with the minimum of sentimentality and she was trying to see him in that same way. "Is that what life is for you, Charles? Just money? Just business? Just what can be 'afforded'?"

He took a step into the room and looked at her reflection, his smile fading. He thrust his hands into his pockets. "In a way, yes, Audrey, I'd have to say that it is, by and large. I'm only trying to educate you about some of its realities."

"It feels more like you're dragging me through the gutter. What is it exactly I'm supposed to learn? To be... tolerant?... of prostitution!?... If that's really what she's doing." Audrey could hear her certitude about Chris's innocence dissolving.

"Hmm, seems this has caught you off guard. Let me suggest that, for now, you step back from making moral judgments about it. Try looking at it in commercial terms."

"*Commercial* terms?!"

One of Charles's cufflinks refused to snap into place. He extracted it and worked the mechanism.

"Look. Take Felix Hansen." Charles walked up behind her. He laid a hand gently on her shoulder as he spoke to her reflection. "He's married, but his wife isn't sailing with him."

Audrey braced herself for some unwelcome revelation about the Hansens. Charles went on.

"Why? We don't know. Maybe her mother's ill. Or maybe they can't stand each other."

Audrey scowled up at his image in the mirror.

"So Felix Hansen, a wealthy commercial real estate developer, is sailing alone. My dear, that's a market, by any definition."

"A market?!"

"Of course. Markets are a result of needs or wants. This ship, for instance. Hansen, Chandler, Brownlow, and the rest—you and me, for that matter—plus many nameless others enclosed within this vessel, we all want access to England and Europe—transport across the Atlantic. And we want it enough to be willing to pay for it. All its opulence aside, this ship is an ocean-going bus—the marketplace's answer to that need."

"But love isn't... transport... or beer or butter."

"Love?" He chuckled softly and paced along the three open sides of the bed, refocusing on the balky cufflink. "I've said nothing about love. Who's to say what love is? You? How many people have you known—couples—who were genuinely in love?

She'd asked herself this many times before and she knew the number was small. Jessie and Daniel surely loved each other. She wanted to say that when her father was still alive, her parents had been in love, but she wasn't certain. They respected one another, of course, but she wasn't sure about love.

"I've known one or two my whole life," Charles offered. "None at present. I've nothing against it but love is not what I'm referring to." Finally, the cufflink clicked into place. He secured his collar button and took up the challenge of his bow tie. "The commodity I'm talking about is sex. Chris and her friends are trading in sexual gratification—in all its forms."

Behind her again, he put both hands gently on her bare shoulders but she shook them off. He shrugged at her reflection. "I'm just trying to explain it."

"None of that makes Chris a prostitute."

"Let me finish," he said, softly.

The tie had come out uneven and, as his pacing resumed, he tugged it open to begin again. "As I said, Hansen's needs—taking him as an arch example; there are many others onboard—his needs or desires comprise a market and as usually happens, someone—Chris and the others—has popped up to fill those needs, to take advantage of their existence."

Watching in the mirror and listening grudgingly, Audrey followed Charles's progress around the bed.

"People like Hansen buy at the top of the market. You saw him. Remember? He arrived at the dock in a big Rolls Royce, a dark blue phaeton with brass accents—and a uniformed chauffeur."

"Why are you talking about cars...?"

He held up his hand. "Just listen. That car has six seats and four forward gears. The engine has eight cylinders if memory serves.

"I don't care about...!"

"The point is simply this, Audrey. I can think of plenty of cars that have all those things and cost perhaps a tenth of what that Rolls set Hansen back. Now if there's one thing I know for certain about Felix Hansen, he's no fool; he has a sharp eye for the value of things. So why did he buy the Rolls?" He paused for her answer but she didn't respond. "Because the Rolls, unlike any other car, loudly announces: 'I can afford the best.' And of course, by implication, it says, 'You cannot' to everyone else."

He had stopped behind her now, bending to examine his tie-tying progress in her mirror. He checked to gauge her reaction—she was pouting.

"Don't you see? The same goes for his choice of companion. The women who've come on board to address Hansen's needs when he goes shopping for sex understand that he's not interested in Chevrolets—rolled down stockings, garish make-up, loud and vulgar talk. He's a Rolls Royce man. That means elegant gowns, cigarette holders, pearls and emeralds, Chanel, and all the sophisticated manners that go with them. Chris and her friends do their best to supply that. I don't know if you agree but I'd say they're possibly the most elegant women on the ship."

She did agree. The one whom Chris seemed closest to, with short, dark, hair, had a special flare for clothes. But Audrey didn't want to give him the satisfaction of hearing her admit it. "That doesn't make prostitution acceptable, right in our faces."

He got the tie right at last and with a shrug, he turned to go back to his room. "Have it your way. You said you wanted to know what was going on."

"But this is the Queen Mary! How could they be doing that right out in the open? They wouldn't allow a..."

"Oh dear, Audrey," he chuckled. "Allow? The ship's owners encourage it."

"*What?!*"

"Now I grant you," he said, gesturing broadly as he ambled back into the room, "they don't run ads for sexual services. But they do nothing to curtail it. They do keep an eye on it, informally, but only to make certain there aren't too many such women onboard at one time, and that they're up to Cunard and White Star standards of dress and decorum. It's all part of their program to ensure that their highest paying customers have the best possible experience at sea." Charles looked down at her; she seemed defeated.

"I'm sorry to burst your bubble," he said, with real feeling.

"What on Earth have I gotten myself into?" she said, mostly to herself.

"I don't know that you've got yourself into anything. No one's suggesting that you should engage in any such business, although I dare say there are a dozen or so men on board who wish that you would." She snapped her head around and gave him a look she meant to be withering, but he ignored it. "Anyway, that's what Chris meant."

Audrey needed to move. She rose and stalked to the armoire at the end of the cabin, and paced. Embarrassed that she had been so naïve, she still couldn't understand Charles's cavalier attitude. "Charles, it's not right. Don't you care about it at all?"

"There you go again with your judgments." He softened his tone, trying to console her. "So far as I can determine, I'm not injured by it. Are you? Think, now. How are you affected if, say, Christine shows Felix Hansen a good time?"

Audrey knew there was ready answer for that but, when she opened her mouth, no words came. She *felt* injured. The fact that she was no longer in the safe embrace of her God-fearing mother, and the upright parishioners of the Bethel AME back home, washed in on her like a storm surge. *They* would have known how to answer him.

She slumped back onto the stool. She wouldn't make eye contact with him so he turned away and spoke into the room. "Look, Audrey. There's a lot of money on this boat; greenbacks, five- and ten- and twenty-pound notes—so much I'm surprised the thing doesn't sink with the weight of it all. It would be astonishing if there were no one onboard who wanted to lay hands on some of it. As I said, that's what White Star and Cunard are doing. They provided this boat and its appointments and amenities, in exchange for a good helping of that cash. That's what Chris is doing too, and rather well I understand. And in no small way, it's what you and I are up to, so don't disparage."

Her eyes stretched wide in surprise. "What do you mean?!"

"Only that I'm also interested in that pool of wealth. I need investors to help me make this mining venture work—there are several men sailing with us, any one of whom could easily give it the start it needs, all on his own. So I, too—with your help—am eager to exploit this market."

"Well, looks like I'm just an ignorant hick. You'd better explain again exactly what you mean because I have no intention of stealing anybody's money."

Charles reacted to the word but recovered, forcing a light laugh. "Stealing? Who said anything about stealing? Is that what you think? When Chris takes money for her sexual favors, she's stealing?"

"It... I don't know—it seems so. Yes... in a way..."

"Well, I can't say that I understand that logic, but all I want is for some of these men to invest in my mine."

She felt tied in knots. "Certainly you could complain to the Captain!"

He threw up his hands. "What on earth would I say? 'Captain, raise the alarm. There are people having sex on this ship! You must stop it at once!'" He couldn't squelch a laugh, though he knew it would upset her more. He sat next to her and spoke in his most calming voice.

"I'm afraid you haven't understood, Audrey. The Captain works for the owners of this ship. Their interests lie in maintaining the custom of Felix Hansen and those like him—all those moneyed aristocrats. They pay the bills; they keep the ship afloat. For example, you've noticed the signs in the salons warning against gamblers?"

"Yes, I saw those."

"Have you seen any warning about prostitutes?"

The implication hit her squarely and she fidgeted as Charles went on.

"The owners aren't interested in complaints of the kind you suggest. They would very much prefer that such complaints were not brought."

She was subdued and confused. She thought she knew about prostitutes. The ones her mother had pointed out to her back in Baltimore, and those she had seen in Manhattan, were unkempt derelicts, women who had lost all sense of dignity and pride. To her, prostitution was a desperate act of survival that took place in slums, in back alleys and flop houses, not among prominent society people. Could it really be that White Star condoned, even welcomed, prostitution on the Queen Mary, the pride of the British passenger fleet, symbol of Britain's status in the world? It just didn't seem possible.

XVIII

THE ACCOMMODATIONS in the Queen Mary's first-class areas were a rich and exquisite Art Deco landscape. Whether in the main salons, lounges, bars and restaurants, private dining rooms, panel after panel of exotic and expensive woods—maple, ash, pear, mahogany—covered the walls and ceilings and wrapped around the pillars. Several lounges sported practical fireplaces, kept stoked and tended by the staff in the evenings. Etched and frosted glass panels lit by lamps hidden in their bases or sides contained *bas-relief* scenes of lush landscapes, flocks of geese on the wing, beautiful young women at the bath. Cast bronze doors featured finely wrought scenes of mermaids and gods and other mythical creatures. And everywhere, plush chairs and settees upholstered in thick fabrics welcomed the backsides of wealthy travelers.

Moving through the ship on the Promenade Deck, Audrey mused that she had never seen a place as plush as this on land—not even the toniest of the salons in Manhattan. Only now did she have the sense of the Queen as a floating hotel. She'd seen something of the opulence in a few of New York's best hotels, all the crystal and paintings and marble, but none of them overshadowed her current surroundings.

Charles had picked out a corner set off from the main salon area by a low wall and settled into the largest armchair, positioned so he could watch the parade of people as they strolled past or found seats nearby.

Audrey folded her small frame into a cushioned chair near him. The waiter brought her a sweet sherry, along with Charles's scotch.

Even as she listened to Charles's banter with the people near them, she felt the pressure of the gaze of many men. They sat or stood in small groups around the salon, nursing their bourbons and scotches and making small talk, trading bits of personal information, "breaking the ice," but several of them found it hard to keep their eyes from straying to her. She picked up a magazine and fixed her attention on it.

One man broke away from a knot of mostly older men at the bar and walked casually in their direction. He was younger than the rest and wore a white dinner jacket in the new, thin-lapelled style. He smiled faintly at Audrey as he approached, but walked up to Charles and stuck out his hand.

"Martin Bascomb," he said, without preamble.

"Charles Pierce." Charles smiled and grasped the hand. He started to rise but Bascomb stopped him with a gesture.

"No, things are formal enough around here, don't you agree?"

He had an easy manner, a reserved self-confidence, and Audrey thought he was not bad to look at. There was a sense of playfulness in his black eyes. His hair was dark and had a slight curl to it. His mustache dipped slightly at the corners of his mouth. Audrey liked his mouth. His lips were full and red, and fixed in a slight smile, as though he knew a secret that would amuse her. She thought it might be fun to get him to tell it to her. Charles settled back into his chair and drew on his cigar.

"I couldn't agree with you more, Mister Bascomb. Quite formal enough," he said, smiling broadly.

"Please. It's Martin," he admonished, with a cartoonish wag of his finger. Then he turned and smiled warmly at Audrey, and stepped to her, extending his hand. Charles offered the introduction.

"This is Audrey, my niece."

The man took her hand and bowed subtly, while looking intently into her eyes.

"A distinct pleasure, Audrey. And a relief." His eyes twinkled.

"A relief? Now what am I to make of that?"

"Well, I was afraid that Mr Pierce was going to tell me that you were his wife. Had he done so, I was prepared to run straight through that door," he bucked his head toward the double doors behind him, "out across the deck and hurl myself into the sea. So naturally, I'm relieved." He continued his grip on her hand and showed her a smile that she could not help returning.

"Well, in that case, I have to say that I too am relieved. That would be an awful consequence."

"Unspeakable." His smile deepened.

"I agree," said Charles. "Take a seat, Martin. Here. Have a cigar and tell us about yourself."

Bascomb pulled up a stuffed chair and sat, and leaned over to help Charles get the cigar lit. He had a physical grace that attracted Audrey. She wondered whether he might be a dancer, then decided he was... too masculine. In New York, she knew several male dancers who were the partners of ballerinas in the dance companies. They were all graceful but, typically, in something of a feminine way that robbed them of their appeal. Martin Bascomb, she thought, had the grace of an athlete.

"I hate talking about myself," he protested, as he arranged himself in the chair. "I'm boring."

"Oh, I somehow doubt *that*," Audrey interjected.

"No, it's true. I'm disgustingly ordinary," said Bascomb, smiling mischievously.

Audrey found Bascomb's playfulness refreshing in the Queen Mary's stuffy environment and she hoped she would get to know him better.

Charles eyed Bascomb carefully, a look of amusement on his face. He was certain that, whatever Martin Bascomb might be, it was not ordinary. What was he concealing? Was it a secret, or was this a ploy to start a conversation that would reveal how other than ordinary he was, to the delight of his listeners, in general, and of Audrey in particular?

"You'll have to come clean, Bascomb. What is it that you do?" Charles smiled, sure that Bascomb was stretching it out for effect.

"Well, not much—as little as I can get by with. Interesting that you mentioned coming clean—nominally, I'm in soap."

Audrey couldn't help giggling and Bascomb turned his warm smile on her.

"I'm afraid it's true, Audrey. It does sound silly, doesn't it? I told you I was ordinary."

Charles was intrigued. "What do you mean by 'nominally'?"

"Well, my family's in soap. Lots of it. Mounds of it. It's fair to say we are up to our eyeballs in soap, and even that's an understatement. I have nightmares about sinking into a huge vat of the stuff, Calla Lily, bubbling and churning away. Then I'm sucked into the pipes that feed it to the molds and the wrapping machines and the casing machines and the... oh, it's too much." He brought the back of one hand to his forehead, as if he were on stage.

"Aha! Calla Lily," said Charles. "There's the clue—everybody knows your brand. Samples & Son."

"Oh, I use Summer Scent all the time," Audrey squealed. "It's heaven." She couldn't have been more excited if Bascomb had turned out to be a movie star.

"I'm afraid that is my game," said Bascomb, in mock humility.

"But the name?" Charles challenged. "Bascomb?"

"Phinnaes Samples sold out to my father about 15 years ago. There used to be some Samples around the plant—a cousin, I believe, and a grandnephew. But the cousin wasn't really interested in the business, or any business for that matter. He went on safari in Africa, determined to shoot a passel of lions and such. We heard that instead, he fell under the spell of a tribal princess—beautiful, and black as a lump of coal."

Audrey had been staring at the carpet but this brought her gaze up sharply. She focused on Bascomb, fearing she would see an indication that he knew her secret, but there was no hint.

"Apparently he chucked his khakis and campaign hat in exchange for lion skins, and settled in. I imagine that by now, they've produced a cluster of rather attractive mulatto children."

Bascomb told the story in such a way that it was impossible to accept it at face value; something about the cant of his head warned, "Don't believe a word I'm saying." But he was amusing and charming enough in the telling that they listened raptly anyway, laughed heartily, and found they weren't too concerned about its truth.

"You mentioned a nephew," said Charles, hungry for details.

"Yes, the grandnephew, actually. He, I'm afraid, experienced my nightmare for real, poor man."

There was a peculiar note in this lament that made Audrey's breath catch. "What do you mean?" she asked.

Bascomb grew serious now, apparently trying to be solicitous of her feelings. "Well, I'm afraid it's not a pretty story." He hesitated, as if asking for permission to continue.

"Go on. We're un-shockable." Charles rolled his cigar between fingers and thumb.

Bascomb settled back in the chair. "Well, Bardwell Samples—they all had weird first names—Bardwell was known to wander the plant at odd hours; we're in Canton, you may know. He was a chemist and was always experimenting with new formulations and processes. Some of the things he came up with were, well... the craziest things: Soap that didn't foam; sticky soap you could smack against the tub and it would stay put; odd stuff like that.

"Anyway, he was working on something special. He told me he'd come upon a new formula and it was sure to revolutionize the business. 'People will never wash themselves the same way again,' was his boast. This was at the start of a weekend. He told his wife—yes, despite his oddities, he actually was married—he told her not to expect him home, he'd probably spend the entire weekend in the lab."

Audrey was convinced this tale, too, was mostly artifice but she liked Bascomb's mischievous way with words.

"Well, no one really knows what happened. He was all alone over the weekend—no evidence that anyone else had been there. But the early shift on Monday found him face down in a vat of Spring Rose. Somehow the heat had been turned off under the vat and the soap had set up. They had to chip him out."

"Oh, how ghastly," cried Audrey.

"Not so awful, actually. Compared to your typical cadaver, he smelled exceptionally good." Bascomb broke into a vigorous laugh and Audrey joined in. Charles laughed too, but he kept a corner of his mind at the pragmatic level.

"But your family kept the original name?"

"Consistency, Pierce. If Calla Lily by Samples suddenly became Calla Lily by Bascomb, customers would have wandered away, convinced they were getting an inferior product—we did a test that established that beyond doubt. Brand loyalty is very important in the soap business."

Charles was curious. "What sort of test would that be?"

Bascomb leaned in to Charles, as if he were about to share a vital secret. "It really was interesting—ingenious, I thought. What we did—we chose one of our ordinary soap brands—Spring Bouquet, one of our middle-of-the-road sellers. We picked a new name for it—Summer Breeze, if I remember correctly. We also came up with a new wrapper for it, a simple design, not our typical florid, baroque look, you know. The soap looked like nothing Samples had ever sold—that was the idea. Then we made up two batches, each of 100,000 units. Now the wrappers were identical in every way except one." He leaned toward Audrey. "Can you guess the difference?"

After a moment of surprise at being asked for her thoughts, she collected herself and pondered, but came up with nothing. She shook her head.

"It's a matter of brand, remember," said Martin. "One batch read Samples's Summer Breeze, the other said Carter's Summer Breeze. Same typeface and all. Same soap. That one name change was the only thing different about them."

"Aha," said Charles. "Yes, I see." He stroked his chin. "But how then, to present them so that shoppers would encounter them on equal terms?"

"The very nub of the matter, Charles, and a challenging problem." Dragging the mystery out, he took a long drag on the cigar and blew a perfect smoke ring. Then he continued. "We arranged with our largest retailers that they would make room on their displays, in eight different cities, for the period of a month, putting the Carter's at one end of the shelves and Samples at the other. Moreover, half the stores started with Carter's at the left, the other half started on the left with Samples. They swapped places mid-month."

The curious experiment had drawn Charles in. "And the retailers. They didn't object?"

"Oh, some did, rather loudly. We had to buy their cooperation—cost a pretty penny." He took another toke on the cigar. "You'll never guess what happened."

"Well, I think I can guess," Audrey ventured, "based on what you said before."

Martin had addressed his comments mostly to Charles and was surprised when Audrey spoke up. "Take the plunge," he said, smiling. "If you turn out to be both beautiful *and* intelligent, I shall have to seriously rethink my pledge of bachelorhood."

Audrey blushed, then recovered her poise and addressed herself to the challenge. "Well, I'd guess that you found there was very little interest in Carter's. It's not surprising that people, especially women, the main shoppers, are loyal to brands. It's a simple matter of economy, or perhaps I should say, efficiency. There's nothing more infuriating than spending time comparing and testing, worrying over a new product that promises to solve all your domestic problems. Then you get it home and discover it's a fraud. My bet is that the Carter's sales were sluggish, at best."

"Brav-O," exclaimed Martin, clapping his hands. He turned to Charles. "By George, isn't she a peach!"

Audrey cast a rueful glance at Martin, then feigned an examination of her nails. She disliked being referred to the way he'd just done, and as if she weren't there. Martin caught the disapproval in her look and when he spoke again, a softness had crept into his voice—he was apologizing without saying so.

"You're right, Audrey. The Carter's soaps were a flop. By far the majority of them were dumped back in the vat." He leaned toward her in the same manner of confidentiality as he had with Charles earlier. "One interesting detail. Although it hardly sold well at all, Carter's did better when placed at the left. Oh, and it beat Samples handily in one town—Fairfield, Connecticut. We have no idea why."

Charles allowed himself a long and hearty laugh over this, a laugh that spoke of his general contempt for people.

"I suspect that if you could discover why," Audrey said softly, her eyes still on her nails "you'd know something useful." At that, she looked directly at Bascomb, with a hint of disdain in her expression.

XIX

AUDREY SNUGGED INTO HER COAT against the stiff, salt-tinged breeze spilling across the deck. Mid-morning sunlight bathed the ship and spread light and warmth into the shadows as she made her way forward on the starboard sun deck. She stopped at the rail, beneath a lifeboat suspended from a davit arm that arched overhead, and took in the vast expanse of the sea. Leaning against the stout teak railing, she watched the bow shove aside a churn of green water and white foam as the ship wedged its huge bulk forward.

Looking into the distance, she marveled at the immensity of the ocean. Except for the faint profile of another ship on the horizon, steaming across their path, all she could see was water, in any direction. And she knew that if she were where that ship was now, a featureless expanse of water would still be all there was to see, no matter where she turned. Despite its imposing mass, she realized what a small thing the Queen Mary was, afloat like a fallen leaf on all this water.

She resumed her course forward and found an opening in the superstructure that led to the wide entry vestibule connecting the port and starboard decks. Opening off its aft wall was a broad, double-flight staircase. Opposite the stairs and framed by ornate, sculpted brass doorjambs, were four elevators, two on the starboard side, two to port.

She could easily have taken the stairs down but she wanted to know how it felt to ride an elevator on an ocean liner. One of them had just discharged its passengers and its open door invited Audrey in. She stepped into the waiting car and pressed the button for A Deck. The doors closed on a small but elegant area, carpeted, with wood paneling and brass accents in the ship's Art Deco theme. Warm, soft light from the coffered ceiling bathed the small space.

Three levels down, she stepped out into a cozy foyer leading to the staterooms. Here, the two passageways running fore and aft were both long and unexpectedly narrow. They were darkly paneled and dimly lit, and they stretched away into the distance, not straight, curiously, but curving upward as they went so that at the greatest extreme, the floor merged into the ceiling. Audrey had the sensation of walking into a shrinking rectangular tube that she might have to back out of. Even narrower branching halls led to the stateroom doors.

After some searching, Audrey found Chris's door. She hesitated. Leaning against the wall, she folded her arms across her bosom and rubbed the knuckle of one finger lightly against the underside of her nose, as she tried to imagine what she might face when the door opened.

She wasn't sure why Chris was so eager to have her come round this morning. For coffee, Chris had insisted, politely and even with a certain charm, but insisted nonetheless, there was no other way to put it. Audrey wondered whether she shouldn't just turn and go. She was a little fearful of this meeting and didn't fully understand why. She was jealous of her independence and didn't want anyone to think they could command her presence. Since throwing her fate in with Charles, she had become uncertain that she could maintain that independence—it might already be a thing of the past.

But she was intensely curious about Chris and the others like her in first class—a handful of young women, beautiful, elegantly and expensively dressed, and sailing alone. She wasn't sure, even yet, that she believed what Charles had told her—she didn't want to believe him. She didn't like thinking that she might be a prude but the idea that someone as beautiful and sophisticated as Chris could actually be selling her body, her sexual intimacy..?! Audrey couldn't accept it.

She formed a picture in her mind of what it would be like to do that, to go into a room with a strange man, boozy, probably stinking of cigars, whose sole attraction was the size of his bank account, and pretend to like him, to kiss him, and let him put his demanding hands on the private places of her body, and then... The thought made her gorge rise. She willed the image away.

But she had to know the truth. She took a deep breath and rapped on the door. She turned and stepped away, back to where she could look right and left along the main passageway. Had she come too early? Was Chris even awake yet? She imagined that women in her trade slept late. Then she heard a noise and spun around to face Chris, who leaned out of the cabin doorway, wrapped in a shapeless dressing gown, her hair disheveled, shading her eyes against the glare of a hall light that seemed dim to Audrey.

Chris's vision came into focus and recognition flashed on her face. "Oh, Ducky, it's you. Come on in." She stepped back and pulled the narrow door open. Audrey felt a need to show she wasn't a pushover and she strode in with as much swagger as she could manage. But when she stepped across the threshold, she was enveloped in a thick pall of smoke; she tried to inhale but her diaphragm balked and suddenly she was coughing uncontrollably. Chris quickly saw the problem.

"Sorry, ducks. We smoke a lot, here. I'll put it out." She crushed out her cigarette in an overflowing ashtray on the nearby bureau and propped the door to help clear the smoke.

"Thanks," said Audrey, her throat still in rebellion against the smoke. She looked around the tiny room and spotted the dressing table stool, and headed for it, still trying to get her breath under control.

Chris glanced at her watch. "Right on time. I'm impressed. Hungry? I was about to call down for something."

Audrey didn't want to commit herself to staying long but she was hungry.

"Coffee and toast?" She slipped off her coat.

"Hmm," Chris smiled knowingly. "I see how you keep that figure."

Chris sauntered over to the phone and dialed. Audrey thought she heard her order for three. She found out why when Chris went to the connecting door and knocked; a voice came back and she cracked the door open.

"The kid's here."

"There in a jiff." Audrey didn't recognize the voice.

"That's Molly, my partner in crime," said Chris. "You've probably seen us together once or twice, up in the salons?" Audrey had noticed that Chris and another of her unescorted friends, a dark-haired woman with an understated figure, often huddled in the corners of the ship's lounges.

"I didn't realize you roomed next to each other."

"We always try to, anyway. Helps us look after each other, doesn't it. Comes in handy, sometimes." Chris sat down on the edge of the bed and crossed her long legs. "Sometimes the guys get a little... stroppy. It helps to have someone nearby who knows the score."

She winked at Audrey in a conspiratorial way but Audrey didn't know how to respond, and looked away.

Seeing Chris like this, dressed down, no make up, her hair in disarray, Audrey appreciated her physical gifts and understood why men were drawn to her. She had the classic hourglass shape and her skin was slightly tinted, as though she were always tanned. Her breasts were full and, even without the help of supporting underclothes, they filled her dressing gown and pressed her nipples against the thin fabric. She needed very little help to be irresistible in her underwear.

The connecting door opened and Molly walked in. Audrey had only ever seen her in evening gowns; she wasn't prepared for this Molly, in dark gray gabardine slacks and a pale yellow silk blouse—simple but stylish. Her skin was like nacre, slightly glossy and underlain by a warm hue not quite the strength of primrose, and set off by close-cropped, jet black hair. Her full lips, even without lipstick, drew the eye. She was stunning—not as full figured as Audrey imagined men preferred, and perhaps a bit short in the leg—but stunning nonetheless. Now, dressed in trousers, her look was feminine, but with an edge.

"Hello. I'm Molly." She extended her hand.

"Yes, I've seen you upstairs. I'm Audrey."

"I know." She settled into the only chair in the room, against the wall near the foot of the rumpled bed. She pulled a slim pack of cigarettes from a pocket and started to light up.

"She don't smoke," said Chris. Molly stopped short and looked quizzically at Chris, and then at Audrey. She tapped the cigarette back into the pack. With one foot, she pushed against the bed and levered the chair against the wall, balancing it on its back legs, and leveled her gaze at Audrey.

"Well, lassie, I see no reason to beat around the bush. What's your game?"

The question came sharply, without a hint of friendliness and it made no sense to Audrey. "What do you mean? What 'game'? I don't have a game."

Molly threw a faint smile in Chris's direction. The smile was gone when her eyes settled again on Audrey.

"Look, lassie. I don't..."

"I'd appreciate it if you'd stop calling me that!" Audrey sat up straighter and lifted her eyes to engage Molly directly. "I'm not a child. As I said, my name is Audrey."

Chris hastened to reassure her. "Don't get testy, luv. She don't mean nothin' by it." Her British accent had shed a degree or two of refinement.

"What's this about? I didn't know I was coming here to be cross-examined."

Molly showed little concern for Audrey's feelings. "We're curious about you, las... sorry, Audrey. Frankly, I see you as a threat and I'm trying to decide what we should do about it."

"A threat? What are you talking about?"

"I'm talking about your game. I'd like to know exactly why you're on this ship."

Audrey got to her feet, grabbed her coat and started for the door. "I don't believe I'm required to justify myself in order to travel on this boat—certainly not to you."

She had to get past Molly to reach the door. Molly let her chair drop onto four legs and in the same motion, she was up and squarely in Audrey's path, her jaw set, unsmiling. Chris came to her feet behind Molly. They were both staring her down.

Audrey stopped short. Molly stepped closer— Audrey uttered a faint gasp. "I have some questions to ask you, luv. I don't think you'll find them especially difficult but you're not leaving here until I get answers."

Her expression was flinty. Audrey doubted that she could fight her way out of the room if it came to that and she didn't really want to try.

"What do you want to know?" She wanted to make it a challenge but it was subverted by an involuntary catch in her diaphragm. She'd lost control of her voice and though it lasted only an instant, it was enough to demolish the notion that she had any power in the situation.

"I told you, deary," said Molly. "I want to know your game." She gestured toward the stool. "Why don't you sit back down."

Audrey held her ground and met Molly's gaze. Molly took another step closer and poked her finger high in Audrey's chest.

"You and your 'uncle' aren't here on any fucking pleasure trip, deary. You're working, but I haven't figured out what you're up to yet. Oh, I've watched you; it's clear you're job is to draw the flies for your old man's scam. What I'm not sure is whether you're taking them back for a quick knock."

Audrey stammered. "I don't..."

"Frankly, I have to say you're well suited to the job–none of these punters can resist you."

Molly closed in—her eyes cold and threatening. Audrey drew back. "Thing is, luv, this is our boat—Chris and me. We claim dibs on the toffs in first class." She poked Audrey again. "Sit down," she ordered.

Audrey stumbled backward onto the stool—her face was on fire and a knot of fear gripped her stomach.

"You're clearly new to the trade. Well, deary, here's something else you have to learn." Molly leaned in close.

"There's territory in this business—your pimp should know that. Like I said, *this* territory belongs to Chris and me, plus our friend Sarah. We don't like competition—and we don't put up with it." She took a small step back. "You're welcome to second class if you think you can make anything of it. You'd be a hit there, that's for sure, but the money's scarce." She backed up a step but remained on her feet.

Audrey could hardly believe what she was hearing. "You think...?" She leaned back; her hand went to her mouth. "My God." She looked at the two women, who now seemed far off, foreign, and no longer threatening. She wanted to both laugh and to cry.

Molly and Chris traded looks. Then Molly parked her fists on her hips. "So, are you saying you're not in the game? You're not here turning tricks?"

Audrey looked up, her eyes wide. "Certainly not! No, I'm not... I can't believe you thought..." Suddenly she was crying; she dug into her bag for a handkerchief.

Molly and Chris glanced at each other, then they sat and waited, watching while Audrey's tears abated. Molly reached for her cigarettes again but remembered and stuffed them back in their pocket. She leaned back in the chair and folded her arms. Chris finally spoke.

"So just tell us. What the hell are you and Pierce up to?"

"He's, uhh... I don't really know," she blurted. "It certainly isn't prostitution."

"OK, let me get this straight," demanded Molly, "so there's no misunderstanding." She leaned toward Audrey. "You and... what's-his-name, Pierce... you aren't here peddling that pretty ass of yours?"

Even though she no longer kidded herself about this new reality, Audrey was still shocked that anyone could think of her in such a way.

"Most certainly not!" The tears threatened to flood back. She sprang to her feet but the two women still blocked her way to the door. The bathroom door was at her elbow and she rushed through it. At the sink, she opened the cold tap and splashed water on her face. Its coolness braced her and she was able to calm herself a little.

She examined the reflection of her wet face in the mirror; the woman she saw there was unfamiliar. She was older, her brow creased, her mouth taut. It was an Audrey whose sense of the world, of the way it was ordered, had been marred by realities she was not prepared for.

Her mother had instilled in her a horror of prostitution. All her warnings about men, all her whispered comments about loose women who dressed and behaved provocatively, and all her anxieties over Audrey's move to New York had this one concern at their core. She loved her mother but she was never able to be at ease with her until, as she was preparing to leave for New York, her mother said something that let her know she no longer feared that Audrey was corruptible, despite what else might befall her there.

Now, having taken an audacious step to advance her career, a step so brash that she'd denied her mother any chance to quash it, she discovered that the situation she was in was not so genteel as it was painted, that the high society set she was traveling with included elegant and beautiful women who were unabashed prostitutes— the idea astounded her. And then, to add to the injury, these women had mistaken her for one of them!

She daubed at her face with a towel, drawing comfort from the soft terrycloth against her skin. Then Chris opened the door and Audrey faced her reflection in the mirror.

"Sorry, luv. We were sure you were here setting up shop against us. We couldn't just let it go, could we? I hope you understand."

Audrey nodded.

"The room service is here. Come and have your coffee."

The steward, a tall, towheaded boy of about 17, was laying the silver service on the small table opposite the door. With two of its sides pushed into the corner, there was room for only two at the table.

The steward moved slowly, trying to stretch the task so he could stay in the room as long possible. Chris had tied her dressing gown loosely and her breasts tested its restraint, threatening to tumble out. When she bent over the bed to smooth the coverlet—without apparent need—the boy was treated to a long view of her cleavage.

Chris looked up into the young man's eyes, catching him, as she knew she would, gawking at her. He looked quickly away and busied himself shuffling cups and silverware. When he looked back, he found her smiling at him suggestively and lighting a cigarette in a provocative way.

She took a pound note from the pocket of her wrap. "Here you are, Ian." She walked up to him and pulled her shoulders back, making the dressing gown gap even wider, and slipped the bill into his pocket. Then she placed a finger under his chin and lifted his head, forcing him to transfer his gaze from the landscape between her breasts to her eyes.

"You're a handsome lad, Ian. Do you suppose we could have a stroll together one of these evenings, after you get off work?" Ian didn't realize he was licking his lips.

"I... I..."

"Knock me up when you have some time." She guided him to the door; his eyes remained fixed at the level of her breasts until the closing door cut off his view.

Still smiling, Chris turned into the room and leaned against the door. "Cute lad. I'm going to enjoy screwing him." She took a drag on the cigarette, then remembered Audrey and stubbed it out. "Do you think he's a virgin?" she asked Molly.

Molly thought about it for a moment. "Mmm, don't think so. But I'd bet he's never been with a real woman."

Chris nodded. "It's my duty to correct that, isn't it?" She and Molly laughed and Audrey couldn't suppress a smile of her own.

Chris turned her attention back to Audrey and sat at the foot of the bed. Leaning over onto one hand, she said, "Well, luv, I must say you surprised us, didn't you." She threw a knowing look at Molly. "So. You're not in the business..." Audrey shook her head.

"That certainly works in our favor," offered Molly. "Bit of a waste, isn't it; you certainly have the stuff for it." Audrey felt chuffed, then caught herself, thinking she probably should resent this compliment.

Molly filled three cups from the silver coffee pot and handed one to Audrey, whose curiosity about these two "working girls" still lingered. She wished she could stop herself from going red at every sexual reference but she wanted to ask them about sexual things—she wanted to know what it meant to do what they did.

"So... you really are... uhh, prostitutes?"

Chris chimed in, cheerfully. "Prostitutes. Hookers. Ladies of the night..." She cackled. "'Show girls.' One of my punters introduced me like that to his mum—as a show girl." She and Molly shared a long laugh. "Yes, that's us, take it or leave it." She lay back on the bed and stretched out like a cat. "We're in it for the money."

"Not whores, though—at least, not me," Molly added, with a grin. "Now Chris is a bit of a whore, isn't she." Audrey glanced at Chris, expecting her to take offense. Instead she was smiling. She had found a brush and was sitting up, working at her hair.

"Is there a difference?" Audrey asked.

"Oh, there's a big difference," said Molly. "A whore enjoys it, doesn't she. Nothing wrong with that, I suppose, but you end up giving a lot of it away. Bad for business."

"Molly's all business," Chris retorted. "Me? I admit it—I've got to get some enjoyment out of it, at least sometimes. So, every once in a while," Chris went on as she worked at her hair, "some lucky bloke gets a bit of Oedipus Rex without having to pay for it, and I get to feel... like a normal woman."

Audrey was completely confused. "Oedipus Rex?!"

"Cockney slang, luvvy," said Molly. "Never heard of it?"

Audrey shook her head.

"Don't know how it got started, but Cockneys do it all the time. Got a rhyme for most everyday words. A tit-for-tat is a hat, a drink's a tiddly wink or kitchen sink—like that. Oedipus Rex? Sex."

Audrey got the gist.

"So is that so bad, giving a little bit away?" asked Chris. "I'm pretty sure Ian's my next charity case."

"I don't see how you can do it at all," Audrey said, softly, hoping she didn't sound too much like a puritan. Chris stopped teasing her hair and looked over at Audrey.

"Ah, luv, your problem is you take it too seriously. It's the most natural thing in the world, isn't it, and a lot of fun with the right bloke, don't you think?"

Audrey was silent. She studied the nap of the carpet, her cheeks reddening.

The weight of her silence made Chris glance up and she immediately understood. "Oh, I'm sorry, luv. You've never... uhh, never had a man, have you?"

Audrey tried to make it a statement of honor. "No. No, I've never had... uh, been with a man... that way." Before now, in any circumstance she could have imagined, she would have made the same statement with a quiet pride. Now, it embarrassed her.

She had to get away. She rose and stepped to the door. "I have to go. Thank you for the coffee. I'll see you later." She didn't wait for their reply. She was through the door and into the passageway almost before she realized it.

As quickly as she could, she made her way back up to the Promenade. She hurried to the rail and leaned against it, taking in gulps of fresh sea air. After her nerves settled, she ambled aft toward her cabin, her mind still back in the smoky room, dealing with all the things she had just heard.

She thought of her mother, who taught her that women who sold their bodies were wretched, tortured souls, unable to hold their heads up in the presence of God. The Reverend Thomas had painted them as the worst creatures imaginable—handmaidens to the Devil. When she was 12 and 13, Audrey and her girlfriends would whisper together about fancy-dressed young women they saw on the streets in their neighborhood, and made a game of guessing which ones were hiding tails beneath their skirts.

Now, at 24, she was no longer that protected child from Upton's evangelizing pews. She'd been exposed to life and experienced some of its realities; she no longer saw the world in storybook ways. Yet in all her daydreams about mixing with the smart set aboard a grand liner, she never imagined it could turn out to be a floating brothel. Moreover, she couldn't understand why she remained so uncomfortable with the idea while no one else seemed to care.

She looked down into the roil of water streaming from the bow. A white seabird, a gannet or an albatross, bobbed on the surface and allowed the rills to bump and knock it about as they clashed, creating a chaos of mounds and troughs in the foamy sea. Audrey fixed her gaze on the bird, fascinated that it was so unfazed while the towering ship surged past and it was swept away aft.

The two bow waves, joined by the backwash from four massive propellers, combined at the stern to create a broad, turbid wake. The bird floated there, bobbing, stoically it seemed, in the choppy water amid scoops of foam, its head pivoting from point to point, its black eyes on constant alert. Something edible floated nearby and the bird lunged for it, just as two others appeared from overhead and dived toward it too. Whatever it was, it seemed to appear out of nowhere, then Audrey realized that someone in another section of the ship must have tossed it in.

The floating bird won the prize and remained in the wake, picking at its bounty while its two adversaries circled above and squawked their complaints. The bird was shrinking in her sight and before long, she couldn't distinguish it in the churn.

Then without willing it, Audrey's imagination placed herself there in the water, where the bird floated. What a small object she would be on this sweep of ocean, she thought, and how hard for anyone on the ship to see her. She tried to imagine what her head and waving arms might look like in the wake, if she were struggling to get the attention of someone on board.

She only knew the bird's position now because of the two others circling above it and it was clear that unless someone knew exactly where to look, they would not see her. She would struggle there, in the ship's wake, watching her only reach of safety steam away, leaving her to drown, or become the prey of whatever creature might be lurking beneath her flailing feet. The stark truth of it made her shiver; she stepped back from the rail and pulled her coat more tightly around her, then turned and ducked through a doorway into the warmth of the ship's interior.

XX

WHEN DAVID WRAPPED UP his stint at the poker table, he ambled into an adjacent salon, ordered a full-strength rum and Coke, and ran through the details of the night's games. Brownlow and a few others wandered in and scattered themselves among the tables.

It was after midnight. The energy in the room was low and those less serious about partying, or who had already found their night's companions, had left. The hardcore night owls remained and that included a group huddled around Charles Pierce, with Audrey sitting nearby.

Looking into the mirror behind the bar, David witnessed an amusing scene when Audrey announced that she was tired and wanted to return to her cabin. A brief skirmish broke out among the young men there for the right to escort her. One muscled the others aside; Billy Pruitt would have crashed to the floor if he hadn't fetched up against a post. The aggressor escorted her away; the down-in-the-mouth losers turned their attentions back to Pierce.

David wondered if Pierce had given Audrey a signal to leave. He certainly wasted no time capitalizing on her allure to engage the men around him.

"She's really something, isn't she?" he said, smiling as though he were showing off a spiffy new car.

"Quite," enthused Cedric Worthington, head of Britain's largest coal mining company. His grandfather was the man who first brought England's coal to the surface, after William Smith invented geology and showed everyone how to find it. "Your niece, you say?"

"Yes, many times removed, as the phrase goes. Daughter of a distant American cousin." Charles took a last draw on his cigar and stubbed it out. "I was interviewing for a secretary when I met her, rather by accident, in Manhattan. I immediately offered her the job. You should have seen the cow I nearly hired." The men shared a laugh at the expense of the imaginary contender.

"Gosh, what a find. A jewel," said Pruitt, his hormones visibly astir, memories of Sadie's body swirling in his brain.

Charles was always prepared to exploit such an opening. "Yes, I dare say, a diamond more beautiful than any I ever stumbled upon out in Colorado."

Felix Hansen, builder of sky-scraping office towers, took the bait. "Colorado? What in God's name took you out there? Pretty desolate, isn't it?"

"True enough, but that's where the rich ore is. Actually, diamonds aren't common there at all. You find a sprinkling of them now and then, and other gemstones, seldom of any quality. You'd lose your stake betting on diamonds or other gems in that God-forsaken place. But metals? Ah, now that's a different story." Smiling amiably, he crossed one leg over the other and tugged his trouser cuff down—no matter what he did, Charles managed to look ready to have his portrait painted.

"That's the stuff to prospect for in Colorado. In fact, I've hit some veins of silver that look very promising." He smiled broadly, settled back into his armchair, and lit another cigar—time to be quiet now, and draw the pigeons in.

There were seven men ranged around Charles and at the mention of silver, David could almost hear the sound of their ears snapping to attention, their heads turning sharply on thin necks. A marked silence followed. Charles released a thick pall of cigar smoke into the room and relaxed further into the chair. It would have been easy to believe he had nothing more to say about silver and would have been happy if someone changed the subject.

"Silver, you say?" Milton Brownlow leaned forward eagerly. His bank had been behind a number of rich mining ventures, including some of Hearst's. It was regarded as the only game in town when it came to backing mines.

Sensing that this would be a rare moment, David left his perch at the bar and moved closer to the group. He settled into a chair, lit a cigarette and while pretending to read The Saturday Evening Post, he eavesdropped as Charles expanded on the subject of his silver strike in Colorado.

Their own tests, he claimed, proved its value to the satisfaction of himself and his fellow prospectors, so he'd left immediately to return to England. His agreement with his investors, he said, required him to appear in person if he found anything worth developing. And, he added, they also gave him a time limit on prospecting with their money; the deadline was only weeks away.

As he laid out his tale, Charles reached into the hip pocket of his jacket and pulled out a brown envelope, closed with a flap tied by a waxed string wound around a paper button. He pulled out a handful of photographs and passed them to Billy Pruitt, sitting next to him.

Resuming his story, Charles explained that he'd left half the ore samples with a partner, to get an official assay. He'd brought the other half with him for an independent evaluation in England, again as per his agreement.

As Pruitt passed the photographs on, Charles drew an elongated leather pouch from his jacket. From it, he took a sachet of dark red suede, folded and secured with a leather thong. A lamp on the table at his side cast a warm circle of light and Charles placed the bundle there. He untied the thong and slowly, for maximum effect, unfolded the bundle. In it were three long glass vials with cork stoppers, tucked into pockets sewn into the sachet's inner face. Inside each vial was a small rectangle of paper bearing an inscription, carefully handwritten in black ink. Charles slid out one vial and held it up to the light. It contained something earthen; Charles's audience of seven leaned in for a better look.

Brownlow reached forward slowly, silently requesting permission to take the vial. Charles placed it in his hand. The banker brought the vial close to the lamp and examined it with a small silver magnifier he carried, attached to his watch chain. He took his time, nodding silently, clearly impressed.

"I'm expecting a telegram with the official assay results," said Charles, smiling amiably. "Probably in a day or two."

Brownlow looked up expectantly. "What's the assay on... What's this say?" He squinted at the writing on the vial's slip. "Kiowa?"

Charles shrugged. "Yes, we had to call the veins something. We named them after Indian tribes." He puffed on his cigar again and knitted his brow ever so slightly. "The assay remains the big question. We're confident of their quality, from our own tests. But they're unofficial; it wouldn't be proper to bandy those numbers around. You understand."

David thought Charles could charm a baby out of its mother's arms. A show of ethical reserve—waiting for the official assay—the perfect touch. The man was either on the up-and-up or a first-rate con man. David favored the latter label.

"As I headed for New York to catch the Queen," Charles continued, "my partner—he's the one who took the pictures—he was to set out for the official state mining office in Boulder, the state capital, for the assay—also to make certain our claim is airtight. I headed east to a nearby railway head but he faced a difficult trek, westward over harsh terrain."

"Did he make it?" asked Worthington.

"Well, that's the trick. I don't know yet whether he got there safely or not. He probably did—the dangers of the American West tend be exaggerated. If he didn't, these samples are all I have." Charles's manner was diffident, confident, with no hint of ballyhoo.

"It took us 10 days to get to the mine site from Denver, so it must have taken him at least that long to get back. I had the advantage of a straight if rather steep trail to negotiate on my own—me and my horse. He had to get the other men, along with the animals and all our kit, back down the mountain."

Charles's audience hung on every word. David watched, fascinated. Here were seven smart, experienced businessmen, between them representing a significant chunk of America's new wealth, and for all he could tell, to a man they were totally enthralled with this fellow's unlikely tale. Hadn't any of them ever been gamed?

Gallagher, he knew, certainly had not been coddled. He was wily. He'd fought his way up in the streets of Boston, leveraging minimal funds until he had enough to buy a decrepit mill that had slipped into bankruptcy. You don't build that sort of start into a multi-million dollar, international empire without gaining some smarts along the way. Yet there he sat, spellbound.

The Gold Mine was a well-worn scam. Pierce's ingenious touch, David thought, was to make the strike silver. Apparently changing the color of the swag was all it took to disguise such a simple-minded dodge; David was 95 percent sure Pierce's cuff links contained more silver than any mine he might have title to.

David rose and left the salon, shaking his head in wonder at Man's infinite capacity for gullibility. Of course, his own success depended on similar weakness but his playing field was level; his fortunes rose or fell on his talents.

He strolled out to the deck and leaned against the ship's rail, pulling on a cigarette and watching the moon's reflection dance across a calm black sea. Maybe it was the context, he mused. Here, in the first-class section of this grand ship, these men were unable to entertain the notion that a fellow passenger who, outwardly at least, was of their station—and with a British accent for good measure—might be a flim-flam artist. From the look of it, they had completely dropped their guard. Hansen, Gallagher, and several of the others had been of "their station" for only a short time, maybe a decade or so. They'd rushed to suppress the memories of the dodgy aspects of their own pasts. That willful turn away from their working class origins now worked against them.

David had no intention of blowing the whistle on Pierce; more power to him if he could gull this impressive club. To be sure, he couldn't be absolutely certain that the man wasn't on the level. There *was* silver in Colorado; perhaps he'd really stumbled onto some that the mining companies already there had somehow missed. David's concern was that to the extent these men paid attention to silver ore, they were not playing poker. There was little he could do about it and it intensified his dislike for Pierce. He wouldn't go out of his way to expose him but if an opportunity came along, he'd be ready to send the right signal.

Pierce's presence did have one positive aspect—Audrey was attached to him. David resolved to learn more about her.

XXI

IT WAS APPROACHING MIDNIGHT. The activity in the salons had hit a natural low that occurred every night at about this time. With energies at their ebb, people went away to freshen up or reconnect with traveling companions. Some retired, of course, but the true night owls would soon reconvene, order new bottles of expensive liquor, and revive the atmosphere of non-stop, playful abandon they were so determined to maintain.

Feeling pleased with himself, Charles, having seen Audrey back to her cabin, paced the Promenade deck near the stern, in waning moonlight, pulling thoughtfully on his cigarette.

Things were going well. Worthington was more than a little interested in silver and doing a poor job of hiding it—Charles was certain he would ask to buy in. He wasn't sure about Hansen, who had displayed some skepticism, though he was not overtly antagonistic.

Edison Cheadle, the other banker on board, was eager to make a killing. Charles guessed that the money Cheadle would use actually belonged to his bank, and that he saw the anticipated profits from Charles's mine as a way to get his books in order, before a surprise audit tripped him up. That meant he'd face ruin when the truth came out. Charles lamented this facet of his business but he couldn't concern himself with the fate of his marks. Cheadle would have to face his own music when the time came.

Young Pruitt was the perfect dupe. Famously profligate, he was now out to impress his father, who correctly judged his son as hopelessly bad at worldly affairs, and especially so at business. His image was bound to suffer further in his father's eyes after this.

Charles's ambling brought him around to the port side, where he leaned against the rail and looked out. On this eastward journey, the moon did its magic on the water mainly to starboard. Off the port rail, which faced more or less North, it was typically darker, with the sea often shaded by the superstructure through much of the night. Now, except for an occasional flash of weak moonlight reflecting off distant waves, Charles had the sense that, just beyond the reach of his arms, the world ended.

He peered into the darkness, trying to make out details of what he knew must be there in the distance, but the view remained black and formless. Then he sensed someone else at the rail nearby, a few feet off to his left. Tensing, he felt for the snub-nosed revolver he carried in his jacket pocket. He turned slowly. The outlined figure of a man, an inch or so shorter, dressed in dark clothing and wearing a fedora, congealed out of the black night. The man spoke.

"You're doing well, Charles."

Charles recognized the voice immediately. "Bates?! My God, man, what a surprise!"

Yes, surprised, and not a little chagrined. Nothing could have darkened his mood so quickly as the unexpected appearance of this particular man. "I have to say, I never expected... Last I knew..." He stopped to look across the deck into the shaded corners, where people often sat alone at night. The darkness made it impossible to see anyone but he didn't want to assume they were alone, so he dropped his voice to a whisper. "Last I knew, you were headed to a term in Patterson."

Bates matched his low tone. "I got myself paroled. A good lawyer is worth his weight in gold."

Leonard Bates and he had been partners in a charity scheme that went bad when a bank clerk, by sheer dumb luck, happened upon a suspiciously large funds transfer. The news accounts mentioned Charles's name but the cops only arrested Bates. He took the brunt of the legal action while Charles made himself scarce, along with what funds they had managed to get away with— not an inconsequential sum.

Bates was himself a lawyer, although he'd been disbarred in several states. It didn't surprise Charles that he'd found a loophole that shortened his term.

Bates took a step closer and Charles stiffened. He pulled back as Bates's outline loomed larger, a black silhouette against an inky sky. He tightened his grip on the gun and pointed it, through the fabric of the jacket, at Bates's belly. He could now see the man's eyes dimly, though not well enough to read his expression, but the coldness in Bates's voice told him all he needed to know. "I don't have any illusions, Charles, about our relationship. I'm sure I'm the last person you wanted to see. It's completely accidental but, as you've said so often, facts are facts. We have to settle up."

Charles didn't know which part of this intrusion he resented most, its possible damage to his scam or its effect on his mental state. He needed to devote his whole attention to the flock of cosseted sheep he was about to shear. Although he'd be a corrosive influence, it was clear now that Bates didn't intend to attack him. Charles loosened his grip on the pistol.

"Well of course we must," he whispered, "but I'm very... uhh... entrenched in my current venture. And I certainly don't have any extra cash."

"You can't imagine how sorry I feel for you, Charles..." Bates's flat inflection weakened his sarcasm but Charles understood the message. Bates went on. "But having stumbled upon you here, I'm not about to let you go without getting square. You would do the same."

Bates inched closer and Charles smelled the familiar stench of cheap whiskey on his breath. His mind churned. He wanted nothing more than to be rid of Bates—wishful thinking now. Bates was right, of course. If the tables were turned, he certainly wouldn't let Bates out of his grasp. He needed a diversion. Something took shape in his mind and he turned to Bates with some excitement.

"You know, I think I may have the perfect solution to this little problem." He looked about nervously, conscious that the flare of a cigarette lighter spilling into the darkness might reveal several people within earshot, though most would be focused on the difficulties of mating without undressing. Charles lowered his voice further. "This could work but we can't talk about it here."

Bates tried to read his ex-partner's features in the darkness. "Look, Charles, don't try to hustle *me*—I know them all, remember?"

Charles slid in closer. "No, listen. I don't know how much you've observed but my scheme is going perfectly—smooth as silk. And with a shill, the score could be even bigger. You'd be perfect."

"Shill, eh? Isn't that what that pretty piece of ass you're working with is supposed to do? What's the game?"

Charles grabbed Bates's arm and squeezed. He spoke now in a harsh whisper. "No. We can't talk here. If any of my marks see us together, it's all up in smoke." He released his grip and turned back to the dark ocean. He drummed his fingers on the rail. "Are you in first class?"

Bates laughed. "Afraid not, Bucko. Can't afford it, thanks to our last adventure."

"How'd you get up on this deck?"

Bates chuckled. "Oh, you know. For the right... what's the word... emolument?, you can always get somebody to turn his back at the right moment."

He pulled a pack of cigarettes from a coat pocket and offered one to Charles, who refused. He lit one and sucked in a lungful of smoke. In the match's yellow light, Charles got his first real look at his former partner—he was stunned at the deep lines a few years in prison had etched into Bates's face.

Bates flicked the match into the sea, plunging them again into blackness. "You know, I thought I saw you when we boarded in New York," he said. "I wasn't sure and I was nosing around last night when I saw you, lathering up your..."

"For God's sake, man!" Charles hissed. "Keep your voice down. Look, it'd be best if we could talk it over in your berth. You're alone?"

"Well, not really. I'm berthed with a stinking Dago, but he's in love and spends all his time rutting with his girl." He waved his hand toward the shadows. "Probably out here, somewhere."

"It'll have to do. Look, I've got to get back inside and wiggle the bait. Can I meet you in your berth in about an hour? What's the number? I'll lay it all out for you."

"D243." He took a long drag on the cigarette, trying to read Charles's face in the orange glow. "An hour, you say?"

"Give or take a few minutes."

Bates had been leaning on the rail but now stood to full height. His liquor-laden breath, even as he whispered, assaulted Charles anew. He closed one hand around Charles's arm and squeezed, as he glared into his eyes. "I don't have to play the heavy with you, Charles. You know the score, and you know me. I took that rap in

Chicago and kept your name out of it. I know you sent a few bucks to my wife. I'd put that down to an attempt to salve your conscience, except I'm fairly certain you don't have such a thing." He flicked his cigarette away. "I expect to be compensated and I won't be trifled with. I hardly need add that, given our present circumstance, there's no possibility of your slipping away. Make sure you show up tonight. If you don't, I'll take it as a sign of insincerity."

Charles knew many men who maintained a level of bluster to keep physical intimidation at bay. He didn't take many of them seriously but Leonard Bates was an exception. He didn't need Bates's grip on his arm to know that he was in a real bind. "Don't worry, Leonard..."

Bates broke in, whispering. "I'm Steffens now. Frederick Steffens. I'll tell you all about it later."

"Uhh... Frederick Steffens. OK, Frederick... Fred. As I was saying, the more I think of it, the more I think this'll work very well. There's a lot of cash on this boat, my friend." He edged away toward the salon. "Get going, before somebody sees us. D243. See you in an hour."

Charles's mood was black as he made his way back to the salons. He stopped and punched the wall of the passage in frustration. "Bugger me blind!" he hissed. "Why in blazes..." His scam was going well and he had no interest in sharing it, certainly not with his contemptible former partner. Back in Chicago, when Bates was preparing for his court appearance, Charles thought he was rid of Bates in about the best way imaginable. He made small overtures to him, through Lena, his common-law wife, about giving him some sort of payment when he finally got out. He'd left Lena a commiserating note containing some cash and assurances that promised more than he ever intended to deliver. Then he stopped paying attention and lost track of the proceedings. Now, suddenly and uncomfortably, Bates turns up, in the flesh and in the way, and with his hand out.

The shill idea actually had promise, although he wasn't confident that it would produce enough extra to make it worthwhile. For now, while he tried to think it through, it should give Bates something to do and Charles time to come up with something better. Ideally, it would be something that would remove Bates from the picture altogether. He wondered whether Bates's proclivity for drink might prove useful.

XXII

DAVID STRETCHED AND STOOD UP, throwing his cards into the dead pile at the center of the table. "That's all for me, gentlemen—it's past my bedtime." He stepped back and pushed his chair to the table's edge, as though saving the place for his return. "I hope I'll see you tomorrow," he said, with a broad smile. "Maybe I can win back some of the money I've spread around this table tonight."

His four tablemates chuckled. "Don't take it too hard, old sod," Gallagher smiled with smug satisfaction. "Think of it as instruction."

David smiled back as he took a cigarette from his case and lit up. "Oh, I do, Mr Gallagher, indeed I do. Good night, all." He strolled away in the direction of the starboard deck. Leaning against the rail, he took a long pull on his cigarette. The moon was nearly full and its fractured reflection sparkled in the black sea.

David smiled, remembering Gallagher's parting words. Instruction, indeed. He was right on plan. This evening, he played slackly at first and went into the hole by about a hundred pounds. He worked his way back to just short of even, although to his fellow players, he complained that he'd lost rather a lot. Now he was ready to make his move. Gallagher was going to take some painful instruction of his own over the next three nights.

David watched a roil of foam as it cascaded off the ship's flanks and swept aft. As he followed it, his gaze fell on a figure, a woman standing alone at the rail, seventy or eighty feet away. Had it not been for the bright moonlight reflecting off the silvery satin of her gown, he would not have seen her. It was Audrey.

He had spoken to her once before—a quick greeting in passing and a brief exchange of chatter. Now was his chance to get to know her. He straightened his tie and smoothed his shirt, and set off in her direction.

He tried to think of something clever to say when he reached her, but nothing came. He hated his faltering tongue, which always acted up at times like these. In his whole life, he'd never been able to find the right words with a woman he wanted to impress; he'd managed to sound foolish more times than he could bear to recall. Now Audrey was just a few steps away and he desperately needed the right words—and he knew that desperation was his enemy.

Audrey heard his footsteps and turned toward him. A smile brightened her face.

"Audrey. Hello again. I thought it was you." He extended his hand. "We spoke briefly before. I'm David."

Her smile broadened. "Yes, of course. Hello." She offered her hand.

Her smile reached in and touched his heart. Something about her, something he had no words for, was so perfectly right and fine—and utterly desirable. He had often seen women at a distance and thought them at first to be wonderfully attractive, only to be disappointed when he drew close. Eyes too severe, mouth too thin, worse yet, a personality that belied their good looks.

But not Audrey. It wasn't only her looks, though he thought her amazingly lovely. No, it was her entire aspect; the way she moved, the cant of her head as she stood in conversation, her choice of hairstyle, the sparse, careful selection of jewelry, the elegant cut of her gown and the indescribable way her body moved in it. And now, her voice, low-pitched but bright, articulated, musical, and a ready openness, an absence of formality, a desire to connect with others. She seemed flawless.

"Yes. Audrey. I think I knew that—I heard someone call out to you. I've always thought it was a beautiful name—it's my mother's."

"Oh, that's very nice," she said. "The most profound compliment. Thank you."

It was in that instant that he began to love her. He couldn't speak for a moment. She turned and looked out again at the sea, a faint smile on her lips. He stole a look at her profile, outlined in the moonlight's reflection off the water, and thought he had never seen anyone so exquisite. He ached to embrace her—he gripped the rail instead. He wanted to say something now, the perfectly right thing for this precious moment but as usual, words escaped him. He was tongue tied—his mind a useless whirl. Audrey broke the silence.

"You never see the moon like this on land. You don't realize that it lights up everything—just like the sun, only not as bright. Isn't it gorgeous?"

David dragged his gaze from her and looked out at the sea; the moon's light revealed the facets of the waves and its elongated reflection stretched out into the darkness. He found his voice. "Yes. It is gorgeous—one of those things you never get tired of looking at."

"You don't belong here, do you?" She had turned and was looking directly at him.

"Uhh... I don't... What do you mean?"

"You're not like these men, are you? Rich, I mean, a society boy, rolling in money."

He laughed. "No. If that's what you mean, you're right, I *don't* belong here. I'm embarrassed to know it shows so much."

"So what are you doing here?" He didn't know how to answer her. He needed a way to tell her he was a professional gambler.

"Is that too personal a question?" she asked. "Forgive me," she pleaded, turning back to look at the sea. "I'm being boorish."

"No, I... I don't mind. With you... I don't mind." She glanced at him and smiled faintly, then looked away again. "It... Well, I guess the question is so infrequent, I have to think about it—what in blazes *am* I doing here?" He took a deep breath. "What I'm doing is making a living."

"You, too."

"What's that mean?"

Her mouth tightened. "I just found out there're some women on this ship who aren't exactly what they seem. They're, uh... 'making a living', as you say."

"Oh, you mean Sarah—and Chris and the others."

"So you know them. You make them sound like a troupe of... Girl Scouts. How many are there?" A troubled look clouded her expression.

"What's wrong?" he asked.

"Oh, it's just that I'm such a chump. I thought I knew about people—something about them, anyway. I thought I could spot the good ones and the bad ones. It's a shock to find that the world is so full of pretense and... well, bumpkin that I am, I'd no idea a woman could look as elegant and refined as any on Park Avenue—better, even—and actually be selling her body to the highest bidder."

She was quiet for a moment. "So tell me, how many are there?"

He heard a new note of cynicism in her voice. He wanted to console her but felt he shouldn't sugarcoat it—she was after the truth. He chose his words carefully.

"Well, I'd say three serious ones, Chris, Sarah, and Molly. I think there are a couple of dabblers, sort of trying it on for size, you know. I don't know their names."

"Dabblers! How does a person dabble in... in prostitution?"

"Well, as I say, I... I guess they're trying it on, trying to decide if they want to make a life of it."

She frowned at him, then heaved a heavy sigh and looked down at her hands. He felt a surge of guilt.

"Look, can I buy you a drink? I don't know about you but something cold and fizzy would go very well right now."

They moved across the deck and into the salon, which had a fully staffed bar even at this hour. They sank into a pair of soft chairs. David lit a cigarette and ordered a rum and Coke. Audrey sipped a tall ginger ale.

David felt he'd skimped on his explanation. "Look, I know it sounds... well, life is... sometimes... not what it seems. I think it can be a mistake to judge others by your own circumstances."

She reacted to the implied accusation and he rushed to explain. "Sarah's a perfect example. We've talked about this—I know something about her history. She grew up near Bristol and had a perfectly normal upbringing until her parents were killed in an auto accident. Suddenly, she was an orphan—all alone at sixteen.

"What about her family—uncles, aunts?"

"She had one uncle; he and his wife took her in. The next thing she knew, one day when the wife was out shopping, she found herself fighting him off with a kitchen knife." The look of scorn on Audrey's face began to soften. "She was interested in acting so she ran away to London to see if she could make her way there—it didn't go so well. She struggled, sponging off friends, sleeping in attics and closets, sometimes in alleys."

"You'd think someone would help her."

"Ummm. I don't know. Some people are harder to help than others—obstinacy, distrust, pride. It's hard, sometimes." He drained his glass, and beckoned to a passing waiter to bring another round.

"She met some wealthy guy at an audition. He offered to take her on a trip to America—bought her clothes, jewelry." David saw something tweak her brow but he continued. "She had enough talent as an actress to be convincing as a society girl. Since she had no other prospects, she sailed with him. Of course, the deal was that she was... available to him, more or less on demand. She saw no real alternative and she liked the man well enough—at least, he didn't disgust her. So she took the deal.

"Aboard ship she met Chris—she was already in the game. Chris told her that as long as she was trading in sex, she should do it for her own advantage—she was missing out on a lot of scratch... uhh, money. It made sense to her so when she got to New York, she dumped the guy. Now this is her job. She's saving up—has her eye on a bed-and-breakfast back in Bristol."

Audrey was silent. She stared blankly into the distance, biting her lip.

"Do you think she's an evil person?" he asked.

"I don't know. No, I suppose not. It's a shame."

"It's odd, I think. Some people just seem to fall through society's cracks."

"What about you, David, what do you do?"

"Me. I'm a prostitute of another kind."

"Don't joke that way, please." Her tone was serious.

"Sorry."

"Where I grew up, women like that were the worst creatures imaginable, the devil in the flesh. People didn't speak to them. Of course, they didn't look glamorous or anything like that—just the opposite."

The waiter appeared and swapped their empty glasses for fresh drinks. Audrey sipped at hers as she examined the corners of her life. "I've never thought about how a girl comes to do that. I guess, if I had, I would have said it was something... you know, a perversion, something they liked doing."

David studied the bubbles in the caramel liquid in his glass. "Well, I've known a few, all of them like the ones here—classy women. I've never talked to any who actually liked doing what they do. But they like the results. They like the clothes, the jewelry, the champagne, the attention, the parties with sophisticated people. More than anything, I think, they like their independence. I don't think there's one who'd trade in her freedom for a pinafore and apron."

He took a last drag on his cigarette and stubbed it out. "I think they have to play a mental trick on themselves." She looked at him. "Seems to me they close off a section of their minds, and don't think too much about what they have to do to get all the things they like about it."

Audrey scanned the room, now nearly empty. David waited, sipping at his drink and stealing looks at her when he could. A long moment passed before she spoke. "I still don't know about you."

"Well, in a way, Chris and Molly, the others, and I—we're all doing the same thing—that's kind of what I meant before. What we're doing is trying to separate the first-class passengers from some of their money. The gals have their looks, their luster, their sexiness; I happen to be good at poker."

She stiffened and sat up. David felt that a curtain had dropped between them.

"What? What's wrong?"

Audrey rose and walked away briskly, heading back toward the Promenade Deck. David scrambled after her. He found her at the rail, gazing out at the sea, a look of concern on her face. He settled an arm's length away. He lit another cigarette and studied the moon-dappled surface of the Atlantic. After a long silence, he looked at her again, taking in the details of her profile, but he continued to wait her out. Finally, she spoke.

"So you're the guy those signs are talking about. You cheat at cards."

"Don't take liberties!" he snapped. "I didn't say anything about cheating!" He was surprised that he'd lashed out at her so sharply. But the accusation, and the look of disapproval that she turned on him, brought back the unpleasant parts of his relationship with his mother, times when she had made him feel guilty and unwanted.

"I'm... I'm sorry," she said, startled and embarrassed.

Again silence. She was confused. Tentatively, she asked, "You make your living playing cards but you don't cheat?"

He took time with the answer. The question alone was enough to stir him up but the tone of accusation was gone from her voice.

"Do you know anything about poker?" he asked.

"I'm finding that I don't know much about anything."

He smiled, and then continued. "When poker's played right—played well—it involves skill. It's a game of bluff—each player tries to make the others think the hand he's holding is unbeatable, regardless of how weak it might be. So you need a little psychology, a sense of what makes people tick, knowing... *sensing*... when they'll chase after a bad hand, or stretch a bet beyond a reasonable limit. And it *is* a sense. I don't know exactly how I know some of these things but I pick up clues. It's funny really. You play a few rounds with a guy and after a while, you realize he's telling you whether his hand is any good or not, just by the way he looks around, or the way he fidgets with his tie.

"Plus, you have to pay attention to the way he bets—that can tell you a lot about what he's holding. If you're good at it, you can win a good proportion of your hands; cheating isn't necessary. It happens that I'm pretty good at it."

Audrey looked up, surprised to hear someone brag about something she'd been taught was wicked.

"More to the point," he lowered his voice, "and this is my secret—you have to promise not to tell..." With an amused smile, she raised her hand in the scout's honor salute. "Well, very few of the people I play against on the ships—virtually none, in fact—have any real expertise at the game. They're dilettantes.

"They like playing poker. What they like is the camaraderie, the give and take, the manly bravado—cigars, whiskey, all of that. They've played a lot—like at college and in their clubs—and had some great times doing it, so they think they know the game. What seldom dawns on them is that all their experience is against people as mediocre as they are. And, lucky for me, a lot of the ones traveling in first class on these boats have plenty of money to put behind those pretensions."

"You're so smug."

He looked at her, fearing he would find censure in her eyes. Instead, she was smiling, and he realized that her tone held a note of appreciation.

He turned and looked back to the sea, smiling, feeling he might be getting to know this fascinating woman in just the right way now. They were silent for a while, then David spoke.

"I've noticed you're with that tall fellow. What's his name? You work for him?"

"His name's Charles. Yes, I do—in a way."

"Uh, oh. That sounds odd."

She laid her hand on his arm. "I'm going to bed, David. It's very late."

"But won't you tell me what you mean by that, by 'In a way'?"

"No. Not now, please, I'm asleep on my feet. Another time."

"Can I walk you to your room?"

"No. I need to get to bed. I don't want to be tempted to do anything else." She smiled shyly at him. "Goodnight. I'll see you tomorrow." She turned and walked past him, heading toward her berth.

His growing confidence abruptly turned to disappointment—maybe it wasn't going as well as he'd thought. He called to her as she strode away. "Good night, Audrey." He wanted to add, 'I love you,' but caught himself. "Sleep well."

She looked back and smiled. Then with a small wave, she turned and walked into the darkness.

XXIII

CHARLES WALKED DOWN the narrow companionway on D Deck, picking his way toward Bates's cabin. He paid attention to the turns and connecting passages, mapping them in his mind to make certain he could retrace his route.

Things were a lot more pedestrian here in third class. Instead of exotic woods, the walls were of metal coated in a glossy beige paint. The thick carpet in the first class stateroom hallways was replaced here with a grit-encrusted gray membrane, whose chief appeal was that it was nearly impossible to slip on. Charles felt the narrow passage walls pressing in on him.

He was dressed in the dungarees he had packed—this was no place for a tuxedo. And in case something went wrong, he'd brought along his pistol.

His guess was that he wouldn't encounter anyone at this hour and so far he was right. One concern was that an officer might challenge him, believing, dressed as he was, that he was a seaman. But the big worry was Bates's roommate. Charles hoped he was still out enjoying the intimate gifts of his girlfriend.

He found room 243 and put his ear to the door but heard nothing. He knocked. After a beat, the door jerked open and Bates stood there, looking a little surprised. Charles stepped inside quickly. In this small space, it only took a second to see that Bates was alone.

"I'm glad to see you," said Bates.

"I told you not to worry, old man."

"Oh, I still worry. Nonetheless, I'm glad to see you. Drink?"

"What have you got?"

"A very common grade of whiskey." He walked, a little unsteadily, Charles thought, to a table next to a set of bunk beds and picked up a bottle. He held it up for inspection.

Charles hated drinking cheap liquor but this was no time to hold out for high standards. His job here was to get Bates's confidence—to re-acquire it—since his actions in the Chicago case had revealed just how callous Charles could be. "Good. Yes, I'll join you."

Charles watched as Bates stumbled to the sink to retrieve a glass. He took a quick look around. The room was tiny; he'd have gone mad if he had to spend five days in it with a stranger. Like the passageway, there was no carpet here. Instead, linoleum in a *moderne* pattern covered the floor. A steel conduit ran across to the center of the ceiling and into an electrical box, holding a utilitarian light fixture. A bulb with a small, clip-on shade was screwed into it.

There was little furniture in the room, only a small, plain bureau against the wall at one end of the bunk bed, near the door, and at the other end, a matching chair for the table. Bates was washing a glass in the small basin, which hung on one wall, beneath a mirror, opposite the bed. There was no separate bathroom; the toilet and shower were down the hall. Charles found it grim.

With a slight stagger, Bates returned from the sink carrying two small glasses. He poured a couple of fingers of whiskey in each and they drank to their anticipated score. Then they sat down to business. Charles took the chair while Bates sank onto the lower bunk. Bates emptied the glass into his mouth and poured a refill. Charles eyed him closely.

When Bates approached him on deck, Charles had been aware of the whiskey on his breath. Now, watching him toss down another shot—and who knew how many he'd had before Charles arrived—his old impression of Bates was confirmed. He'd always believed Bates's weakness for liquor played a part in their Chicago fiasco, which had helped Charles decide to abandon him those years ago. Charles now determined to use it against him.

"Look, old man," Charles leaned the chair back against wall, affecting an air of comfort and confidence. "There's a great opportunity here." He pulled the wrapped vials from the pocket of his denim jacket and dropped them on the bed next to Bates. Bates stared at the bundle for a long moment before picking it up.

"I shan't make you guess. Those are ore samples, silver. They'll assay as high as 16 ounces to the ton.

"Whose samples are they?" he asked, as he untied the leather knot.

"I had them, uhh... constructed. I'm running a mining scam on these blokes and, I have to tell you, they're going for it in a big way."

Bates wondered whether Charles was up to running such a scheme successfully. He decided that he was. He opened one vial and tipped a small amount of its sandy contents into his palm. "Silver, you say?"

"The real thing. I thought I'd better have something that would pass scrutiny in case I ran into someone who really knew what he was looking at. Lucky thing, too. One of the dupes is rather knowledgeable in this area. His approval, in fact, has helped bring the pigeons flooding in."

"Why didn't you do gold?"

"No, no, no, my good friend. Too obvious." He waved a dismissive hand. "Subtlety is what's called for here. Gold sets off alarms in even the most naïve. But silver—who's ever heard of a phony *silver* strike? See what I mean, old man?"

"Of course," replied Bates, dully. The whiskey was well at work.

"I was going to make it copper but the market's glutted now." Bates gulped down more whiskey; Charles wondered whether Bates had worsened since their last business, and whether perhaps he was now too much in the grip of booze to be reliable.

Bates stared at the ore samples with half-glazed eyes, then with a look of irritation, he laid them back on the bed. "You've got them where you want them. I don't see how I can help."

"Oh yes, you can, my good man. I've been thinking about this since I saw you earlier, Leonard, and..."

Bates raised his hand and Charles stopped. "It's Fred. Frederick Steffens."

"Ah, yes, Steffens. Well, let me tell you, Mr Steffens—Fred—that this is a great bit of luck, our turning up together on this voyage. I expect I can settle my debt with you and then some—many times over, in fact. Now listen." He leaned in closer. "You, as you Yanks like to say, are going to be the icing on this cake."

XXIV

AUDREY SAT ALONE in one of the private dining alcoves spaced around the perimeter of the first class restaurant. The brightly lit room was nearly empty. A handful of uniformed waiters were re-setting the tables in preparation for the lunch service. The chink and clatter of plates and flatware scraping together mixed with the low hum of the waiters' voices.

Audrey was dressed for comfort—tan slacks and a simple cotton blouse. After she and Charles finished their breakfast, he had left to track down a possible investor, while she lingered over a cup of the fragrant, full-bodied coffee the Queen Mary's galley seemed able to produce at any hour.

Molly entered through the main door, at the far end of the room, apparently in search of someone. When she saw Audrey, she came over, her heels tapping on the polished parqueted floor. "Hi," she said, breezily.

"Hello," said Audrey, a little surprised. She glanced around, expecting to see Chris.

"Looking for Chris? She's not here, but I expect her. May I...?" She indicated the chair that Charles had recently vacated.

"Sure. Sit down. Just finishing." She pulled her cup and saucer closer to make space.

Molly wore a simple day dress in light brown, topped by a midnight blue blazer. She had a flair for making simple look sexy—Audrey thought her outfit perfect for the "down-time" in her profession.

Molly arranged herself in the seat and leaned forward, smiling. "Chris and I... well, we wanted to apologize for the other day. We were too hard on you."

Audrey demurred. "No, no. You don't owe me any apology. Heck, I'm the naïve one—I probably should be apologizing to you."

Molly waved away Audrey's protest. She produced a pack of cigarettes from her black leather clutch and held it up. "'Mind?"

Audrey didn't feel she could protest, here in the dining room. "Go ahead, please."

When she had the cigarette going, Molly leaned back in the chair and regarded Audrey with a quizzical smile. Like many smokers, she held the cigarette between long fingers, just off to the side of her head, as though it were important that it never get too far from her mouth.

"I'm sure you still think my friends and I are the most evil things you've ever seen."

"Wait, I never said that..."

"No, you never said—you didn't have to." She shifted her position. Leaning closer, still smiling, she lowered her voice to an intimate level. "Look, I know it's a surprise to find women like us, Chris and me, so matter-of-fact about it, as if we were a pair of librarians or something. I just... well, I..."

Audrey sensed her discomfort. "What is it, Molly?"

"Well, we were tough on you. I guess..."

The alcove was set off from the main salon by a low wall with an opening at its center. A waiter appeared in the opening and addressed himself to Molly. "May I bring you something, ma'am? Coffee?"

"Please, luv. A cup of coffee would be smashing."

"Certainly, ma'am. Here's today's breakfast menu." He opened the menu and placed it on the table, then left.

Molly brought her attention back to Audrey. "I guess I want you to understand how it is, about being a..." She looked around to make sure no one could overhear. "About being a hooker. You do understand, don't you?"

The question surprised Audrey. "Understand?" she said. "No, I can't say that I understand." She looked away, trying to sort through her thoughts. "I've thought about it a lot. I... May I ask you something?"

"Sure."

She wondered whether Molly's story was similar to what David had told her about Sarah. "How, uhh... how'd you get started, doing... that?"

Molly hesitated a moment, then rose and walked to the low wall and looked out into the dining room, which was empty except for a family in a far corner, loitering over a late breakfast. Her back to Audrey, she sucked on her cigarette, shifting her weight from side to side. Audrey examined her back—she felt something unpleasant was coming.

Molly turned and looked at her with a serious expression. "Well, I don't know that it's a very interesting story," she said, sauntering back toward the table, "but, you're welcome to hear it."

Chris appeared, looking even more casual than Molly, in slacks and a peach-colored silk blouse that enhanced the erotic effect of her full breasts. Whether she was working or not, Chris made certain, with varying degrees of subtlety and the aid of a variety of thin silk blouses, to keep those breasts on display.

"What's up, luvvie?" she said, cheerily, to Molly.

"I'm giving Audrey my life story. Shouldn't take more than a minute." Smiling at her joke, she turned to Audrey.

"I suppose you believe there are no circumstances that would make you open those thighs for money." She pointed a long finger in the direction of Audrey's crotch.

Audrey had been perfectly certain of that a few days ago. Now, in the company of two women who, from appearances, were no more morally deficient than any of her old friends and acquaintances, her certitude had taken a pounding. Still, she clung to an idea of proper conduct for a woman, which went by the name of chastity. "I... no, I don't think I could. I'm sorry," she added quickly, trying hard not offend. "I don't mean to..."

Ignoring her apology, Molly moved in and sat across from Audrey, on the edge of the chair, leaning forward on her elbows.

"I was married, once. Yep," she said, seeing Audrey's surprise. "I was pretty young. We were only married for a few months—looking forward to starting a family. He had a decent job—a quarryman; earned a pretty good packet. Best of all, we were happy. He was an average sort of bloke but a good man, and handsome," she winked at Audrey, smiling. "Yeah, a real hunky guy—all my friends were jealous. Best was, I never doubted that he loved me." Remembering, she took another drag.

"Then he left for work one morning on his bicycle, like he did every day, carrying his lunch pail with the sandwiches I'd made him. But he never came back. Some kind of accident on the road—a passing truck? A blind corner? No one knew exactly what happened."

Audrey looked up. "Oh, Molly. I'm so sorry."

"Yeah, poor bloke," Molly sighed. "Probably never knew what hit him." She pulled on her cigarette again and blew a long stream of smoke into the air. Even in this open space, Audrey was starting to feel the effects of the smoke.

Molly eased back into the chair. "I had no other family—Mum and Dad long since passed on. My brother disappeared into the muck of some trench in the Alsace during the Great War. I was alone. Luckily, we didn't have any kids yet but I had no skills to speak of. Jobs were short and the one job I did find didn't pay near enough. But I noticed that one thing kept being offered because I was a widow now–in other words, young and unattached—and no longer a virgin." She rose again and resumed pacing, patrolling the line separating the alcove from the main salon.

"Just about anytime I met a man of any substance—married or not, it seldom seemed to matter—he, uhh... suggested, hinted, intimated, that he was willing to pay—and rather well, I was surprised to learn—for an hour or so of my very private, very personal time."

She continued pacing, puffing on the cigarette. "I resisted, of course. I had my pride, didn't I, and my morals. I even slapped a face or two. But the bills mounted up. The one or two jobs I did know how to do—sewing, secretarial work, laundering—when I did find one of those jobs, there were dozens just like me, fighting for them, so they didn't pay enough to keep the constables away.

"Then, once again, a man—a 'gentleman'—appeared. He was reasonably appealing, not at all hard to look at. And, without being too boorish, he makes that offer again, an attractive sum in exchange for..." Molly cocked her head and arched an eyebrow; Audrey felt the gestures were more lascivious than if she had spoken the words.

"And this time," Molly went on, "I didn't slap and I didn't scowl. No, I smiled. Inside, of course, I was crying. Probably if you were standing on the Tower Bridge at the time, you'd simply climb over the rail and leap off. But I wasn't standing on the bridge, and anyway, I'm too much of a coward.

"So there you are. You're still woman enough to know how to be coquettish, and you find that talent and bring it forward and put it to use, because it gets you some level of... comfort, and of control over your life. You're out of the rain, off the streets, and you have enough for a little coal for the fire and a scrap of food, if you mind your pennies, for another couple of weeks."

Still pacing, she puffed on the cigarette; Chris was smoking too. The alcove's ceiling hung lower than the main room, trapping an expanding pall of smoke. It was beginning to make Audrey nauseous but she didn't want to complain.

The waiter returned and set Molly's coffee on the table. "May I get you something to eat, ma'am?"

"No thank you," she replied, smiling warmly at the man. Audrey sensed that simply out of long habit, every interaction Molly had with a male involved an attempt at seduction.

"And you, ma'am?" He had turned to Chris but she shook her head. He dallied, wiping down the table and straightening chairs, while stealing glances at Chris. She gazed straight at him suggestively the entire time, daring him to return her look. Finally, aware it was a contest he couldn't win, he fled.

The room was quiet now; the family had gone and the waiters had finished their set-up and left for other duties. Audrey, Molly, and Chris were the only ones left. Molly picked up the narrative. "And something else, luv, something unexpected: I learned after a few experiences that these... these couplings... don't stay with you. You don't *like* them, not one bit, but incredibly, you find they're bearable, and easy enough to put out of your mind. They don't seem to turn you into something... untouchable."

Again, Audrey tried to imagine herself in Molly's situation—a strange room, some man she hardly knew stroking her, kissing her, trying to push himself into her. She shivered.

"Don't get me wrong," Molly broke in again. "I did a lot of crying, especially at first. I don't know exactly what I expected but, to my surprise, as time went on, in the mirror I never saw a hideous wretch looking back at me. And you know," she added with a smile, "I discovered the redeeming value of a long, hot bath. Most important: I discovered that I'd become independent—a businesswoman of sorts—in control of my life for the very first time."

Audrey smiled thinly at Molly before looking away, mulling over what she'd heard. She connected strongly with Molly's desire for independence and found herself nodding with her.

"So that's me, deary. Older and wiser today, to be sure. Chris, too, more or less."

Audrey examined these two bright and elegant—and likeable—women, straightforwardly engaged in prostitution in this luxurious setting, and began to grasp how divorced from reality her own view of the world was. "And you're going to go on... doing this...?"

Molly sniggered. "Still having trouble with the notion, eh? Well, yes Missy, I'm going to continue doing it. I take no great pride in saying so but I do take pride in the fact that no one owns me, and I'm not begging for handouts in the East End. I'm well aware..." she turned and nodded toward Chris, "*we* are well aware... that our attractiveness is on the wane. New blood, fresh and delicate young creatures—creatures like you—will soon walk in and spoil our party. They'll sweep us aside without the slightest conscience, not even realizing that they've cut us out and left us with the poor mugs in second class." She ambled over next to Chris and put a hand on her shoulder.

"So we're saving up, preparing for that day."

Chris chimed in. "That's why we're so protective of this territory."

"Yes, I see," said Audrey, with a nod. "It's certainly more lucrative here."

"That's not the half of it," said Chris. She was working on her nails with an emery board. "These men are the real thing—truly loaded. Even with all the extra expenses, gowns and shoes and sparklies, we couldn't do nearly as well anywhere else."

"Diseases too, luv," Molly added. "They're less of a problem here, though not as little as you'd think. Turns out some of these fancy men have stuck their tools in some pretty grimy holes."

Chris scowled. "Ain't it the God's truth."

Audrey couldn't stay any longer; the smoke was making her ill. She stood and pulled on her jacket. "I have to go." Picking up her bag, she smiled at the two. "I'm sorry if I..."

Chris broke in. "No, honey, don't give it a thought. If you're not used to the idea, it can come as a shock."

"No, no," Audrey quickly insisted. Even now she wasn't really sure being in their company didn't compromise her. She needed to get away from the smoke, and the weight of this new world they'd laid out for her. "Thanks for putting up with my questions."

Chris answered with a dismissive wave.

"Forget it, luv," said Molly.

"I'll see you later?" Audrey offered. "Tonight?"

The women nodded. Audrey smiled weakly and hurried away. She crossed the restaurant, threading her way through empty tables *en route* to the foyer. She pressed the button for the elevator but she was too agitated to wait for it and took to the stairs, almost running up the three flights to the Promenade. As she walked out onto the deck, which was shaded by the Sun Deck overhead, the briny scent of the morning air revived her. She looked out to sea, bright in the morning sun, rushing astern. It didn't frighten her as it had before.

She wondered what she would have done if she'd been in Molly's shoes. Suppose she found herself alone in the world—her mother, Jessie and Daniel, her other relatives, all gone. No skills to speak of. And men offering to rescue her, if only she would grant them certain privileges. What would she do?

Tears welled in her eyes. She pulled a handkerchief from a pocket and dabbed at her face. The tears were for her innocence. She wasn't prepared for these realities; she'd refused to accept them when Charles pressed them on her. Now, hearing them from women who were actually dealing with them, she had to face facts.

But facing them did not make her comfortable with them. She had always looked down on women like Chris and Molly, women who apparently ignored all moral strictures and offered their bodies up for cash. She now had to accept that it wasn't nearly so simple and she chided herself for passing judgment so carelessly.

The whole picture was so much more complicated and laced with ambiguity. Clearly the men who solicited these women had much to answer for but it wasn't them alone. The men who owned and ran the ship, and the system of commerce in which it functioned, shared complicity in the lives Chris and Molly led.

And was blame even the right notion? Was prostitution really the evil she had been taught it was? Or was it the obvious response to a need, to strong human desires which, as so often occurred, was then corrupted into a mere matter of commerce, as Charles proclaimed with his unsettling coldness? Where was solid ground? Was there anything she could count on? Or was the entire world of morals and decency built on sand that shifted with every change in the wind?

She re-entered the ship and found her way to the small library and writing room, near the stern on the Main Deck. A woman was scribbling out a letter at one of the four writing tables; they nodded at each other as Audrey entered. The wood paneled, softly lit room was lined with leather- and cloth-bound books. A plush green carpet covered the floor.

A writing table occupied each corner; Audrey sat at the nearest one and flicked on the shaded desk lamp. A wooden fixture beneath the lamp held a sheaf of writing papers, a dozen or so envelopes, and a bottle of dark blue ink, fitted into a shallow depression. A round container held pencils and serviceable nibbed pens, their black wooden shafts inscribed with the ship's name in gold-leaf.

Audrey smoothed a sheet of paper on the desktop. A drawing of the Queen Mary, with a trace of smoke winding from its stacks, steamed along its bottom edge. She un-stoppered the ink bottle and dipped in the pen. "Dear Momma," she began. "So much has happened in my life in the last few weeks, I hardly know where to begin..."

XXV

BENNY GLANCED AT HIS WATCH and moved toward a nearby door. "I've got to get back," his voice rose above the engine room's hum. "Use this door when you're ready to go. And don't touch anything." At the door, Benny glanced at Audrey, who had turned to look more closely at a gauge, and winked at David with a nod of approval.

"Thanks, Benny," David responded with a wink of his own. "See you upstairs." Benny turned and disappeared through the doorway.

They stood on a catwalk in the forward engine room, where two of the ship's four steam turbines produced the power pushing the Queen through the water. Two men in white overalls worked at the other end of the catwalk, tending gauges, valves, and graphing machines. Bright bulbs cast pools of light into this dim, steel-walled space; no sunlight penetrated this deep into the ship.

This was the last stop on a tour of the Queen's innards David had cajoled out of Benny as a way to get to know Audrey, without having to compete for her attention with all the heavyweights up in first class.

"This is one of the prop shafts." David pointed down through the grate at a long, horizontal, polished steel shaft, twice as thick as a man's thigh. It ran, spinning, from the back of the turbine through a large, bright steel ring bolted to the aft wall, just beneath their feet. David worked to get his voice above the turbines' thrum. "One of four. It's hollow."

"Hollow?" Audrey asked. "Why on Earth?"

"Less likely to snap, they tell me." Audrey strained to hear him. "Helps handle the changes in resistance the props encounter in the water."

They moved toward the center of the catwalk, away from the turbine's noise. Immersed in the insistent hum and the warm, moist air, they perched against the railing. David was fascinated by the power of this machine. It was huge—as big as a house. Even in their position up on the catwalk, it towered over them, hot, dense, solid. The turbine, plus its condenser, which looped from its top like the craning neck of an ungainly swan, seemed to bulge as it reached to fill its half of the vast room. It looked like something out of a Jules Verne fantasy, dull, black, misshapen, inspiring awe and fear. Each turbine drove one of the four propellers and, despite the Atlantic's tireless resistance, they would soon bring England into view on the horizon.

But Audrey's interest was in David. She wanted to get to know him and was glad that Benny had to leave. Standing next to David at the guardrail, she watched his expression as he scanned the engine room.

"Who *are* you, David?" she asked, simply.

The question startled him. No one had ever asked him that before—and he'd never asked himself. He looked at her quizzically. "What do you mean?"

"I don't know anything about you—are you from Mars or something? I didn't know you existed three days ago."

He didn't want her to see his unease. He thought for a moment, not knowing exactly how to answer. Finally, "Well, fair's fair. If I tell you who I am, you have to tell me all about *you*." He hoped this would give her pause, and let him off the hook. Instead, she thrust out her right hand, a challenging smile in her eyes.

"That's a deal."

David was unsettled. He didn't like talking about himself—he felt he had no story to tell. But he extended his hand to meet hers and they clasped—he was committed.

The feel of her hand was a gift. Despite her small size she had a firm, assertive grip. He looked down at the hand—she made no attempt to withdraw it. Even in the dim light, he could see its perfect form; long, lithe, the fine long bones making discreet ridges beneath her tinted, lightly freckled skin. Her fingers tapered toward delicate pads. Her nails were perfectly shaped arches, coated with a clear, matte polish.

He noticed a thin scar behind the knuckle of her middle finger where something sharp had nicked her. It was almost an inch long and parallel to the bone. He was curious about it but felt he didn't know her well enough to ask her about it yet. He hoped that would soon change.

He released her hand reluctantly and focused on her challenge. He would tell her about his father, about how Raymond Bowen had moved the family from a tiny English village to New York just before David was born.

"There was this guy, Merchasin, that my dad worked for—owned a drayage company. Hauled all kinds of stuff: furniture, sacks of flour, gallon cans of olive oil he picked up at the dockside and took into town. Ice, beer..."

"Beer?" She'd never given any thought to the precise way beer found its way into her glass at Barney's, beyond the tap whose long, polished wooden handle she'd seen Barney pull a thousand times. "You mean... bottles of beer?"

"No, I'm talking about *beer!*" He made the shape and size of a barrel in the air with his arms, with a grimace to show that his air barrel weighed half a ton. "Fifty-gallon barrels! He loaded 'em up at the breweries, rolled them onto the wagon, and delivered them to the bars and pubs. These big, beautiful draught horses drew the wagons," he stretched his arms, palms spread, to suggest the horses' size. "My dad drove them and took care of them."

"Did you get to ride with him ever?"

"Lots. Summers, Saturdays. It was the best fun. If I got lucky, and hadn't misbehaved lately, he'd let me handle the reins."

He slipped into a reverie and was lost to her for a minute. Audrey felt a surge of admiration for him.

"You like horses."

The simple statement broke his spell. He looked down at her and smiled, and he found that his reticence had dissolved; he actually liked telling her about himself. He turned his gaze back to the turbine, remembering.

"Yeah. Something about their size—and their strength."

"So how did you misbehave?" She poked his arm playfully.

"Oh, you know, throwing rocks, skipping school. Boy stuff."

He met her eyes again. She fascinated him; each time he looked at her, her offbeat beauty took him by surprise. A convergence of lines in her brow, her cheek bones, her full mouth with its playful little smile, combined in ways he could never express but which sent a surge of emotion through him each time.

He forced his mind back to the subject. "I do like them—horses. If you treat them well, they're your best friend."

She chuckled softly and decided he needed more teasing. "So, you grew up tending horses and delivering 'beer'"—with her thin arms in a circle and a comic set to her jaw, she parodied his beer barrel mimicry. "Then you decided it wasn't for you—too tame, I suppose," she said, with a mischievous look. "So of course, the next step was gambling on the high seas."

"No-o-o. First I did a stint as a lion tamer for Ringling Brothers," he gave her a sidelong look she hadn't seen before. "But the cats and I never got along." David had worked his coat sleeve to make it flop over, as though it contained a stump, and he turned and thrust it at Audrey. She jumped back, startled, then they shared a long laugh.

Turning serious, he said, "What happened was, my dad got blindsided by the horseless carriage."

"What? Oh, David, I'm so..."

He held up his hand. "No, no, I don't mean literally. No, poor guy—although when he did die, it was in a particularly bizarre way. No, it was more tragic than that. What I mean is, he became New York's best farrier just when motor cars were pushing horses aside."

"Oh, my. Yes, I see," she sighed, as though, somehow, her own life had been affected.

With those few words, spoken in that quiet, sympathetic way, David knew that he was falling in love with her and he had no idea what to do about it. He didn't know what to say—he could almost feel his tongue tying itself in knots.

She laid her hand on his arm with a barely perceptible pressure; a new flood of warmth swept through him and stole his breath. He hoped she would assume he was just gathering his thoughts; he also hoped she would never want to take her hand away.

When he was able, he went on to flesh out the brief, grim history of Raymond Bowen's fortunes in the

New World. How, after the family arrived in New York, Raymond got lucky when he looked in at the door of Merchasin's Drayage in the Bowery. One of his men had tied one on the previous night and failed to show up for work. Merchasin was rehearsing a litany of earthy, vivid, and original curses for him when he turned and saw Raymond standing there, tools in hand, looking capable.

David smiled at the memory. "According to Dad, neither of them could make much of what the other one said. Merchasin talked in thick, Yiddish-accented English; Pop spoke his West Country dialect from Cornwall. But Merchasin did get across that he needed his two Fresians shoed and in the traces on the company's big beer wagon, ASAP. Of course, this was right down Dad's street. These are big animals, 17-, 18 hands—dangerous if they get spooked. But they took his lead as though they'd known him their whole lives. He did the job fast and he was hired.

"We were OK for a while but it didn't last. More and more loud, clanging, gear-grinding machines on rubber wheels careered around the streets of Manhattan, belching smoke, backfiring."

"It's strange," Audrey broke in. "It seems to me there have always been cars and trucks."

"Yeah, you grew up with them. Me too, mostly. Not my dad. He grew up with draught animals, leather harnesses, horseshoes, and hay. Not long before he died, he told me that, before he picked us all up and came to New York, he'd seen *pictures* of motorcars but he'd never actually laid eyes on one.

"Golly."

"Well, one Monday morning, when the men showed up for work, there was a truck in the yard, brand new. Dad said Merchasin was kinda skulking in his office—couldn't come out and face the men. The atmosphere was gloomy that day, and many more days after."

"David." He had drifted off again and her voice brought him back to the humming, warm interior of the Queen's engine rooms.

"Sorry. What?"

"You said earlier that he died in a strange way—your father. What happened?"

"Yes. Ironic," he drew a deep breath. "He was kicked by a horse."

She gasped. For an instant, she thought he was playing a crude joke but the look on his face told her he was in earnest. "Oh, David! No!"

"I know. Weird, isn't it?" he sighed. "Let's get out of here."

They made their way up into the bright daylight on the sun deck and went to the rail. Audrey pulled the cool sea air into her lungs, flushing out the heat and damp from below. David lit a cigarette. They looked out at the rolling Atlantic, reflecting the azure sky of a perfect summer day. Then, no longer needing to raise his voice above the turbines, he continued his story.

"I was about 13 when it happened. Mom was a wreck. Money was already tight and she didn't know what to do. There were my two sisters to take care of..." A strained look clouded his expression and he shifted his gaze from Audrey to the horizon.

"We had a few rough years there. I wanted to quit school and help but Mom wouldn't let me; all she could do was take in washing and sewing. She worked herself to exhaustion. Saturdays, I peddled newspapers; later I pumped gas. Funny. I felt strange doing that, since the cars had ruined my dad's life. The worst part was watching the way it affected my Mom—she couldn't earn much and she sort of blamed herself for our situation."

"I think I understand that," Audrey said, softly. She was looking out to sea but she turned and caught a pained expression on his face. "What is it, David?"

He was torn. He had never talked to anyone like this before, never laid his life out to another person. But doing it for her was different; it felt right, though he couldn't have said why. He wanted her to know everything about him, and he wanted her to want to know. Still, he was aware that parts of his background weren't pretty.

He glanced down at her, then looked out again at the sun-flecked water. He took in a breath.

"Well, one day, I came home late from school and there was a guy there. He'd sort of made himself at home, if you know what I mean?" He glanced at her and she gave a nod.

"Over the next few weeks, he kept showing up at the kitchen table at dinner time and then sticking around. I kinda liked him at first; he was like my dad in a lot of ways. He was a steel worker—on all those tall buildings in the city. He had a ton of great stories about 'high steel,' balancing on I-beams a hundred stories up, and dodging glowing hot rivets tossed from the forges.

"But he was a rough bastard—liked his drink. And he had a temper. He stayed on good behavior at first but then he got comfortable. After he'd knocked back a few bourbons, he got to batting me around— sometimes my sisters too." David took a long drag on his cigarette and bit his lip. "We had a couple of big run-ins, him and me." He looked down and picked distractedly at a fingernail, then he took a deep breath. "My mom saved his life, I guess you could say, though she didn't know she was doing it."

"Saved his life? What do you mean?"

David turned and settled his back against the rail, facing the ship's brilliant white superstructure. Two middle-aged couples strolled by, arm in arm. They nodded greetings that Audrey and David returned.

David watched the couples as they ambled away, unable now to look directly at Audrey. He took a last, deep pull on his cigarette and flicked it into the sea. "I'd had enough. I mean, who the hell was this guy to come into our home—not that it was much of a home, but it was what we had and he'd had his feet under our table lots—who the hell was he to come in and start using me for a punching bag? I got a knife—a long one, and I sharpened it. I was determined to bury it in his heart if he ever touched me or my sisters again."

"Ohh, David...!" She understood suddenly that she wanted to respect David, and to be able to love him. She didn't know where that expectation had come from, she hardly knew him, but there it was, real and urgent, and this new part of his story roiled her picture of him. "I'm so..." She looked away, searching for the right words. "You... you seem so calm about it," she said, so sadly that it was almost a rebuke.

He looked into her eyes, afraid he might have lost her in his clumsy way. Despite his skills at the poker table, he didn't know how to mask his character, to dissemble. And everything—everything between them—had changed since this day began. Lying to her, in any way, was now out of the question. He felt defenseless. All he could do was go on with his story.

"I suppose I *was* calm. That happens when you realize there's something you can't run away from. I had to defend myself, my sisters, my Mom. I was the Man in our family, forchristsake; if he hit me again, I was gonna kill him or die trying."

He tried to read her reaction but she turned away and looked out at the ocean, trying to hide the tears brimming in her eyes.

It was well after noon. The shadows had lengthened and the sea had taken on a golden tint, as if trying to help soften their mood. But David was angry at himself—he couldn't believe he'd pushed her to tears when all he wanted was to regale her, to bring smiles to her radiant face. Silently, he cursed his clumsiness. As softly as he could, he spoke:

"I'm sorry, Audrey. I..."

She shook her head to stop him. Upset with herself, she wanted to back up and start again. Before this, the day had been perfect and her time getting to know David had been delicious. Now, his flat, homicidal declaration had turned her emotions upside down.

She had gone beyond her intent. She accepted his invitation for a tour of the ship because she wanted to get to know David, realizing that she had started to care for him. Now she questioned all her judgments about him. She was confused and needed to get her feelings under control.

Forcing a smile, she looked up. "What happened?"

A feeling of dread tugged at his stomach. He wanted to soften the tale, to pluck her out of her sadness and coax that smile back onto her face. He didn't think this story was the best way but he couldn't find a way to make it pretty. He shifted his weight.

"Well, like I said, my mom saved his life. I didn't know it but she'd had enough, too; turned out he had socked her a couple of times. She didn't say anything to me because she wanted to be loyal to him—you know, that 'man of the house' thing. She needed a man of the house and, before he showed up, even though I was only about 15, I thought it was me. Seems she demanded he stop hitting us and he promised her, but it didn't mean anything 'cause he was a quick temper kind of guy.

"It was at dinner again and he'd been drinking. Something came up and he went for me, caught me on the ear and sent me head-first into the wall. Mom yelled at him. Before I could do anything, she grabbed the meat fork and she held it in that street fighter's position—you know, sort of cocked, close to her side, and threatening to jam it in his face. She was shielding me and screaming at him—words I was surprised she even knew. She was fierce, Audrey, like a tiger. My sisters were shrieking— you should have seen her!

"He was scared; he got his coat and cleared out. Then she grabbed me and hugged me—real tight, crying. She felt the knife and when I showed it to her, she just fell apart, sobbing, more even than at Dad's funeral"

David now looked at her, afraid he'd ruined his chances. Instead, though her cheeks were damp with tears, her eyes held a look of admiration. He let himself breath again.

He turned back to the rail and lit another cigarette. "Not long after that, a kind of miracle happened. My mom discovered a bankbook at the back of a dresser drawer with my name in it. It turned out Dad had salted away some money to send me to college, if I ever turned out to be the college type."

Audrey reached for his arm. He looked down at her and opened a space so she could thread her arm through his.

She smiled back. "Well, did you? Go to college?"

He nodded. "Seton Hall. You know it?" She shook her head. "It's a Catholic college in New Jersey. Dad's money wasn't much but it helped. My high school grades looked pretty good and they offered me a scholarship. We weren't all that pleased with the Catholic thing—we were Church of England if anything—but Seton Hall had a good rep and it was close, across the harbor at South Orange."

David didn't say that it was his only good offer. He had applied to several colleges, including many of the Ivy League schools. He preferred Princeton because it was so close. He would have been a pretty good choice for any of them. But the Ivy Leagues were reluctant to accept someone like him, a farrier's son and a horseman himself, a man who knew about physical labor. There was, after all, a privileged class in America and Princeton, Harvard, and the others were the gateways into it. Those who labored with their hands occupied the lower ranks, where they were expected to remain without complaint.

David pulled on his cigarette and let the smoke spill out slowly through his nose. "Princeton and those others—they're not interested in a bloke like me, guys whose talents don't go much beyond how to shoe a horse or place a bit in its mouth."

A hint of regret had crept into his eyes. Audrey laid her hand softly over his. He hooked her thumb gently with his own.

"It was an easy choice," he said, with a shrug. "I took the offer at Seton Hall. I studied accounting. Graduated with honors, as it happens." He allowed himself a timid smile; Audrey smiled with him.

"My studies didn't take up all my time. Evenings, in dorm rooms and in taverns, I drank a lot of beer and learned how to play poker. I had a real knack for it."

XXVI

DAVID STROLLED THROUGH the retail arcade off the Promenade Deck, marveling at the offerings in the shop windows. Its Corinthian columns flanked broad expanses of plate glass etched in art deco designs, all scaled down in size to meld into the ship. One could easily imagine oneself in an arcade off London's Regent Street.

Most of the shops offered expensive women's attire—dresses from the finest couture houses, millinery, jewels, furs. The single men's haberdasher also carried luggage. Here in the middle of the Atlantic Ocean, hundreds of miles from anywhere, it felt surreal and incongruous.

David glanced in the window of the men's shop as he passed and saw Charles Pierce standing at the counter. He stopped short and took a step back, hiding himself at the window's edge. He wanted to speak to Pierce; this was his chance. He moved across the small atrium and pretended to concentrate on the hats arranged on busts in the milliner's display, using the reflection off the window to track Charles's movements behind him.

He didn't have to wait long. Charles exited the shop carrying a small leather case, like a doctor's satchel. David hurried to catch up with him.

"Excuse me. Mr Pierce." Charles stopped and turned. "A brief word, please."

"Ah. The gambler."

"Yes..." David smiled as he approached, "...the gambler. David Bowen." David offered his hand and they shook.

They walked on together into the passageway leading to the Observation Lounge and Bar. Charles stood two to three inches taller; David tried not to let that bother him.

"What can I do for you, Bowen?"

"Well, I'm not sure. We have a problem, I think. I'm sure it's crossed your mind that we're both fishing in the same small pond."

"Yes, I agree it's a bit awkward but I can't say I have any sort of solution. Have you?"

"My problem is I'm counting on this trip for a large score. I'm getting out of the game. I don't suppose I could get you to, uhh... restrain your ambitions this once?"

Charles chortled in surprise, "My good man, several of these fellows are poised to... to invest a lot of money with me. You can't expect me to damp the fires now."

David pursed his lips. "No. Realistically, I suppose I can't." He was embarrassed—it hit him how desperate and naïve his appeal must have sounded. "I'm sorry. I shouldn't even have broached it."

"No hard feelings, old man." An amused smile fluttered across his mouth. "It's just the way the dice fall. I think we're just going to have to compete with one another. For what it's worth, if you're as good as your reputation, I doubt you'll have trouble reaching your limit. There's a lot of money on this tub." David smiled at the compliment.

"Let me ask one other thing." They stopped and Charles cocked an ear toward David. "Audrey. What are your intentions regarding her?"

Charles was surprised. "Why do you ask?"

"I, uhhh... well, I suppose I have to say I'm very attracted to her."

Charles grinned. "Hmmm. You and a crowd of others. Well, as for 'intentions,' I have none. You clearly know the score—she's the nectar. She draws them in. And I must say, she's perfect for it."

"But you haven't told her the truth about what you're doing." He made sure his tone gave the plain statement the bite of an accusation. "She thinks you're on the up-and-up."

Charles's amused expression faded to a cold stare. "I'm not sure I like your way of speaking, Bowen." His eyes narrowed. "Look, old man. This is none of your business—and I resent your insinuations. Good afternoon." He wheeled and started away, then stopped and turned back.

"Look here, Bowen, stay away from Audrey. I don't want her attitude to shift. Understand?"

"Now it's you who's asking for a lot. I told you I'm interested in Audrey—this is no whim. I have no intention of staying away from her."

Charles walked back toward David, moving in close and glaring down at him. He scanned both ways down the passageway, then locked his eyes on David's.

"Hear me well, Bowen," he growled. "There's a lot at stake here, as you well know. The groundwork is laid and I don't want it disturbed. I need Audrey's full cooperation. If you influence her against me, it will go hard on you. I won't let anything stand in the way of my success here. Not any *thing*... nor any *one*." He held David's eyes for a chilling moment, then turned and walked briskly away, the satchel swinging at the end of his arm.

David bit his lip and slumped away in the opposite direction. He was miffed, feeling he'd handled the situation badly. He hoped he hadn't endangered Audrey.

XXVII

A MILLION PINPOINTS of starlight spattered a black sky. Audrey tightened her thin wrap across her bare shoulders against the cool air sweeping around the ship, as she and Martin Bascomb strolled the Promenade Deck. The waning sliver of a moon, suspended above the Western horizon in a streak of clouds, would soon shake loose and plunge into the dark, calm sea.

"A beautiful night," said Martin.

"Yes, it is. It's gorgeous. All those stars."

He lit a cigarette. "This is your first crossing." It was a flat statement of fact.

"Oh, is it so obvious—my inexperience?" Only part of her was teasing.

"Not an accusation—just an observation. Everyone has to have a first time."

"I suppose you've been across dozens of times, have you? I bet if the Captain died, you could take over for him."

"I'm sorry. Just conversation. Forgive me."

Now she felt bad. "I suppose I really am green. Actually, I envy you your... your worldliness. Men have an advantage." She hoped she hadn't gone too far and queered her hopes of learning more about him. His unlikely tales fascinated her.

They stopped and leaned at the rail, gazing out at the sea. Martin drew on the cigarette. "Yes, I suppose we do, the way society is set up. It angers you?"

She thought for a moment. "When I hear a man taking his situation for granted, like a divine right, and talking as though he owns the world, and women... and me. Yes, that can really get under my skin."

"I surely hope you didn't hear that tone in what I said."

"Yes. A little, I thought."

He didn't want to dig himself into a hole with her; his hopes for the evening required Audrey to be well disposed toward him. He concentrated on the moon's reflection playing on the water. "I must say I was impressed with your understanding of the marketing issues with regard to soaps. Where did you learn it?"

"Before I... uhh... before coming on this trip, I worked in a Park Avenue dress shop. It was important there to have a sense of what makes people—women—decide to buy. I think, despite the difference in price, soap and custom frocks have a lot in common."

"Well then, tell me again—if you don't mind—how you concluded so readily that the new soap would not do well?"

They resumed strolling, passing along the rail. The moon, now free of the clouds, cast weak shadows of the Promenades posts and awning across the deck; the area against the superstructure was deeply shaded. As Audrey started to answer the question, she became aware of a bulk huddled in a dark corner. Normally, it would not have caught her attention but it was moving, bulging out first in one place and then another, like an amoeba. She nudged Martin and pointed at it, questioningly.

Martin concentrated on the shadows for a moment, then he took Audrey's elbow and picked up their walking pace. In a whisper, Audrey protested.

"What are you doing? What's going on?"

Martin put himself between Audrey and the dark lump. He leaned in toward her and spoke softly. "I'm trying to spare us an embarrassment."

This made her more determined to see it but each time she tried to peer around Martin, he moved to block her view.

"What do you think you're doing? I don't need you to 'spare' me anything."

"Perhaps you don't," Martin replied, grimly. "Let me just say that, well, what's going on back there is... an act of love. Do you understand?"

Audrey was shocked. "You mean...? They're...?"

"It's far from uncommon on these cruises. People can't find privacy in the normal way and... well, the deck is dark, and usually not very populated at this hour."

She was intrigued. "I'm not sure I believe you. I have to go and see."

"Audrey! Come now, don't interfere." He put out a hand to stop her.

"I have no intention of interfering. I just want to... to see if you're correct. She sloughed his hand and strode toward the lump, peering into the shadows. She saw that a blanket formed the lump's exterior; she could now hear a woman's guttural moans and a man's occasional grunt coming from beneath it. A deck chair supported this shape but she couldn't make out how the owners of the voices were arranged on it. But there was no question now that Martin was right. She turned and walked quickly back.

Avoiding eye contact with him, she pulled her wrap more securely around her shoulders and resumed the rhythm of their stroll—he fell in step beside her. She tried to sort out how she felt about the goings-on under the blanket and it took a long time before she registered

Bascomb's presence next to her. Aware that they hadn't spoken for a while, she wanted to break the silence.

"Well," she said, carefully avoiding his gaze. "That's a first."

"Shocked?"

"I have to say... yes, I am, a little." She hazarded a glance at him, hoping she wouldn't find him amused by her inexperience. The shadows hid his expression but then, he lit another cigarette and, in the yellow glow from his lighter, there was no hint that he was enjoying her discomfort. "You say this is common?" she asked, her voice low.

He nodded as the darkness enveloped them again and he took a long draw on the cigarette. "There's something about a trip like this, I think, that affects people in a strange way. They fall in love more readily, and I think they'd say, more deeply. Passions run high. Seems these two didn't get the word; it's a lot darker on the other side of the ship."

"But to do... that!... right out here, where anyone can see them..."

"I understand your reaction. I don't know—in the scheme of things, I wonder if it's really important?"

The notion that it might be trivial shocked her even more. "But how can you...?!"

He interrupted. "Think about it this way. Tomorrow, you'll come into the salon for breakfast. You'll sit down and there'll be a man, say, to one side, and a young woman, across the table perhaps, and the three of you will have a pleasant conversation about the trip and their plans and yours and so on." His cigarette, held between two fingers, made a glowing tracery in the air as he gestured to emphasize his points. "And you won't have a negative thought about them because you won't know that they were the couple wrestling under that blanket just now."

They walked in silence for another long moment while Audrey grappled with this idea. Bascomb worried that the attention on the rutting couple was creating the wrong atmosphere for the plans he had envisioned for this stroll.

"Audrey, indulge me, if you will. I want your whole perspective on my company's little marketing experiment. You seem to have your finger right on the pulse of it."

"What can *I* tell you? I'm just a seamstress."

"Please allow me to contradict you—you're very much more than that. There was a sense of authority in what you said that... well, perhaps you don't even realize it. I want to know what made you so confident in your analysis."

She smiled, chuffed at Bascomb's attentions. "I do believe you're trying to flatter me, Martin, but I'll play along." She chortled. "I have to say that, had anyone told me, as I swept out the changing rooms at Madame Moreau's last week, that today I'd be on the Queen Mary, having a conversation about marketing soap, I'd have said they were insane."

"I see your point." They shared a laugh at the incongruity. "I suppose I would feel the same. Still, will you indulge me?"

She thought for a moment, and then began. "It's really simple. A product like a bar of soap is an unknown—a pig in a poke. Except for its scent, you can't sample it. Women face this problem all the time when they shop. They don't want to buy something, then get it home and discover that it's not to their liking—perhaps more important, not to the liking of their husband or someone else in the family. It's not merely an error, it's bigger than that—a betrayal, of sorts. And if you're on a budget, and most women are these days, it's more than just wasteful, it's, well... shameful." She looked up to see if he understood. He nodded.

"So, as for soaps, once you've settled on one that's satisfactory on all counts—smells good, doesn't dissolve into foam the first time it's used, isn't too expensive—what incentive do you have to look under the wrapper of an unknown? If you *do* experiment, it'll be conservatively—in other words, you're not going to look outside a small circle of familiar brand names." She stopped her stroll and leaned on the rail, looking out to sea. Then, glancing at him, she added, "With one exception..." She let the thought trail off.

He waited for her to elaborate but she remained silent, leaning on the rail and gazing at the dark water, the hint of a smile on her lips. After a long silence, he became agitated. "Here now, you're not going to withhold the last crucial detail, are you?" Though he was smiling, he genuinely feared she might leave him in the dark.

"Come on," she teased. "This should be easy for you."

He thought hard but couldn't find the key to the puzzle. "You have me on pins and needles."

She laughed at his impatience. "One exception. If a friend has told you about a wonderful new soap by ABC Company, you'll eventually try it."

He smiled broadly and softly applauded her. "Well, I have to say, Audrey, that may be the most cogent analysis of retail business I've ever heard." The air had chilled more and she drew her wrap more tightly around her. "Here. My cabin's nearby," he said. "We'll get you a sweater."

They were near the entrance vestibule; they took the stairs down to A Deck and along one of the narrow corridors connecting to the staterooms. He opened the door to his room and stood back to let her pass. Audrey hesitated. She rather liked him and wanted to know him better but it was not typical for a woman to go unescorted into a man's room. For an instant, she thought she would ask him to go in and bring out a sweater for her but she felt he might think her priggish. She didn't want to relapse into Lerita Simmons's protected little girl; if she was going to make her place in the world, she couldn't behave as though she were still an innocent. She walked past him and into the room.

Inside, on a small table next to a comfortable upholstered chair, a shaded lamp splashed a yellow circle of light onto the ceiling and another onto the table top, where a cloth-bound book had been left open, face down, to save the reader's place. A bottle of bourbon and a pair of highball glasses stood next to the book. The room looked much like her own but perhaps a bit larger; the ship went in for opulence but, except for the biggest spenders, everyone had much the same opulence.

A bed, its counterpane turned down, stretched along the wall opposite the door. Next to the bed, on the adjoining wall, stood a tall bureau. When Bascomb closed the door, he crossed to the table and picked up the bottle. He filled one of the glasses and offered it to Audrey. "Let's have a drink."

A prickle of concern ran across her shoulders. "No, thank you, Martin. I just need that sweater. Is it nearby?"

He paused and, for an instant, he eyed her, a hint of a smile on his lips. Then he took a swallow from the glass, put it down, and crossed to the bureau. He rummaged in a drawer and came up with a maroon v-neck pullover. "This should do for warmth—we'll have to use our imaginations as far as fit is concerned."

He went to her and held the sweater up against her. She had laid her wrap over a chair.

"The color suits you." His eyes locked on hers and, without warning, he embraced and kissed her. She was not opposed to kissing him, though she did not like being surprised. He worked his mouth against hers. His mustache scratched her nose and she tasted the whiskey on his lips. She brought her arms up, for an instant thinking she might embrace him in return. But then something made her feel that she had better not, that not only was this intimacy occurring just a little to soon, it was being forced on her. If she was going to be intimate with him, she had to reset the balance; it had to be mutual. She placed her palms on his chest and pushed. Reluctantly, he relaxed his grip. He showed her a smile that said he had conquered her, that they would soon be together in his bed. She didn't agree—she took a small step back, and a big breath.

"That was... unexpected."

"Did you like it?" His tone, and the arch of an eyebrow, told her that he expected her to like it a lot. He tugged at the end of his bow tie, undoing the knot.

"Well, yes, in a way. I didn't dislike it. I..." She looked away, searching for the words to damp his expectations without closing off his interest in her. She liked him rather, but she also feared him a little. "Please don't do it again," she said.

He wasn't listening. As she tried to collect herself, she felt his hand encircle her waist, more aggressively now. He pulled her in to him, kissing her roughly. As he sought her mouth, his hand slid to the base of her spine and pushed in, so that she could not miss the bulge of his erection against her belly.

She tried to break away but his grip on her this time was stronger—her efforts had no effect. But then, as she pushed with all her strength, his arm relaxed, allowing her to back away a few inches. But instead of releasing her, the change only provided space for his other hand to move from her arm to clutch her breast. In this instant, she knew that, regardless of her protest, he intended to take what he wanted.

He pinched her nipple—his touch rough and painful. Desperate now, with their mouths still locked together as he tried to force his tongue past her teeth, she drew his upper lip into her mouth. She could feel the hairs of his mustache and the taste of his spittle. She bit down hard.

"Ay-eee!!" He shoved her away. She slammed against the wall and felt a sharp pain in her back—the handle on the closet door. Bascomb lurched back, grabbing at his lip. He came up with blood.

"You bitch!! Look!" He thrust his bloodstained fingers toward her.

"Am I supposed to feel sorry for you?!" she cried. "What do you think you're doing?!" One of the straps on her gown had broken and she clutched it to prevent the bodice from falling open; she still had his sweater in one hand.

Daubing at his mouth with a handkerchief, Bascomb looked intently at her; streaks of blood stained the cloth. But his sly smile returned, along with a look of malice. She no longer cared to know what lay behind that smile.

"So, my lovely little Audrey." His tone mocked her. "You think you have us all fooled, don't you? Little black Audrey—little red-headed nigger!"

She'd been trying to deal with the broken strap and this oath caught her utterly by surprise—he'd given no hint that he had any inkling of her race. She composed a look of bafflement before facing him. "What...? Whatever do you mean?!"

"Oh, that's good," he said, derisively. He walked toward her, one slow, deliberate step at a time. "I almost believe you don't know what I mean. I've seen plenty of nigger gals like you down in New Orleans; most people can't tell them from whites. Is that where you're from, my little white pickaninny?"

Fear clutched at her gut. She struggled for self control, unsure if she would get out of the room alive, or unsullied. She took a step toward the door but he was nearer and easily blocked her.

"Uhn uhh!" he said, wagging his finger and shaking his head in slow denial. "You want to play the tease? The little black tease, passing for white? Out to toy with rich white men? Well, let's play."

"I don't know what you're talking about!" She feigned focusing her attention on the broken strap, to avoid looking into his face. "I want to leave—you're behaving like a lunatic!"

"No, that doesn't work," he threatened. "Not with me." He was eerily calm, his threats coming at her in a low growl. She looked up at him. "You've picked the wrong man, Missy. You're no innocent. Who the hell do you think you are, turning me down?"

The look of scorn on his face twisted his mouth into an ugly breach, tinged red with his blood, oozing from her bite. His eyes had narrowed to dark slits. "Didn't anybody ever tell you you should stay in your place?" he hissed.

He slid out of his dinner jacket and tossed it on the bed, then began removing his cufflinks. "Just 'cause you're pretty and look like a white woman, doesn't make you better than any other nigger bitch." He pointed his wagging finger at her, like a pistol. "Well I've fucked many nigger whores and I'm going to fuck you, just as you deserve."

He hooked his thumbs under his suspenders and pushed them off his shoulders. "I'm sure you think you're the cleverest girl—you really thought you could fool me." He snorted, and continued his slow walk toward her, his right hand now balled into a fist.

As the distance between them closed, her gaze flicked from the fist up into his leering grin—she was terrified. She struggled to regain some sense of control, before this battle of epithets erupted into something far more serious.

"I don't think of you at all!" she challenged, fully aware of how weak this insult was. She had one more chance to reach the door. She drew herself up and looked directly into his eyes. "I don't know what gives you the idea that you can attack me, Mr Bascomb. Is it your money—all that soap—that makes you think you have some special privilege?!" She forced her fear down, and brought the full sense of her self-worth and indignation forward—and she readied her grip on the sweater. "I am none of those... those ugly things you called me." "I am not a whore. There *are* a handful of them on this ship, however, if that's what you want. I believe they're all white!"

She started toward the door. When he reached for her, she threw the sweater in his face and grabbed the half-full glass of whiskey from the table. He was wide-eyed when he jerked the sweater away; she aimed the whiskey there. It only splashed into one of his eyes but that was enough.

"Aaaghhhh!" he screamed. "Bitch!!" He groped his way into the bathroom; Audrey grabbed her wrap and raced into the hall.

She ran up to the open deck and strode briskly toward the bow. As she coursed the ship's length, striding as fast as she could manage and holding the torn ends of her shoulder strap together with one hand, she passed a large shapeless bundle beneath a blanket, perched precariously on a deck chair and pulsating in the shadows.

XXVIII

THE BAR TEEMED with a raucous group of the Queen's first class passengers. With the help of a generous flood of liquor, and a young man who had commandeered the piano and was banging out some hot jazz licks, they were having a great time. Now into the third evening of their ocean voyage, they had found their sea legs and lost their sense of the strangeness of living within the confines of the vessel. Their inner ears had adjusted to the constant but subtle motion, a swaying that, because of the ship's great size, was all but impossible to sense by eye.

Their adaptation liberated them and they crowded the lounges, drinking liberally, chatting with energy, determined to make up for the doldrums of the first two days. The women's dresses were low and revealing, the skin flushed, the lips painted in provocative shades of red. And because they would create unsightly lines in clinging gowns, a considerable number of bras and panties that had seen service the first two nights, had been left behind in the bureau drawers of those women whose bodies didn't require them.

This would be a night of much sexual congress and very few of those in the lounge now would fail to find an intimate encounter. And, whether man or woman, married or single, few of the bodies they found comfort with would be those of their established partners.

When a tuxedoed drunk stumbled against a stool and spilled a drink across the bar, barely missing his sleeve, David searched for a quieter place to do his thinking—his play for the night now over, he had much to think about. Retreating to the lounge, he found a dark corner, far from the sound of the piano. He plunked down in a comfortable armchair and lit a cigarette.

His life had taken an unexpected turn. When he came aboard for this trip, he had a goal–it was all about money. He promised himself that it would be the start of an earnest effort, after years of half-formed notions, at working his way out of a life of gambling on the high seas. He no longer wanted to subsist in the cocoon of the Queen Mary or her sister ships, crossing and re-crossing the cold, seemingly boundless oceans. He wanted to stop. He wanted to settle down, as people liked to say, and experience real life.

Life aboard the Queen Mary was not real. It was an endless party and, like all parties—those worth spending any time at, people turned up in their best clothes, their most precious jewels, and their most quirky behavior. The result was a meaningless series of interactions that would never occur anywhere else, and which the partygoers would either deny, or alter to their advantage in the recounting. Relationships formed aboard ship were artificial. More than once he'd looked up a passenger he felt he'd struck up a friendship with during a voyage, and gotten the cold shoulder. In all his time working the Atlantic, only his friendships with crewmembers seemed to last.

Among the first class passengers, sex propelled much of what occurred between shores and the mores around it somehow weakened within the boundaries of the ship. David couldn't count the times he had witnessed much-admired society women walk off toward the ladies room to "powder my nose," when everyone knew she would go straight past to the room of her paramour, shed her clothes, and settle in to a night of debauchery. Faithless husbands were even more common; he'd even seen them fight over who had first dibs on Chris, or one of her friends. And he'd seen wealthy men cheating shamelessly at cards and dice—he wondered what made them all tick.

The prodigious level of alcohol consumed in the ship's bars and salons intensified this bad behavior. White Star and Cunard encouraged it to keep their well-heeled clients happy, plus they made huge profits from middling champagne and liqueurs sold at premium prices, and premium brands flogged for astronomical sums.

All this might have been unremarkable were it not for the fact that White Star and Cunard, their employees, and the first class passengers themselves acquiesced in it all—the dissipation, the hedonism, the high-stakes gambling—all the while looking down their noses at the people in Tourist and 3rd class, as though *they* were morally deficient. Countless times, David had heard one of these pampered men bad-mouth people he had no real experience of, people he never even caught sight of, though they were traveling together at sea. Then, without the slightest nod to the irony of it, he would excuse himself to go off to play with a prostitute while his wife retired to their stateroom.

Sitting in the half-light of the lounge, David felt a new surge of disgust—he was fed up with all of them and wanted to get as far from them as he could. First, he would exploit the presumptions of those he could lure to his poker table and clean them out of their spending money. He meant to be merciless; with luck, this could be one of his last trips.

In England, he planned to go down to Truro and make a down payment on the farm he had set his sights on, find a nice border collie, and settle in. He knew nothing about farming. But he did know the kind of people he would be among. They were his father's people and he knew they would help him learn the ins and outs of rural life. He wanted to spend his days around horses, with his nostrils full of the smell of manure and hay and leather, the way he did when he was a boy, helping his dad. He wanted to forget the smoke-filled, whiskey stained, sex-charged atmosphere of the ocean liners.

But now Audrey had cropped up and embedded herself in his imaginings about the future. With no effort at all, she had stepped to the front of his queue and she had the power to change everything. A few days before, he didn't know she existed. Now, in his image of his life, Audrey stood at the center. The dream of the farm in Cornwall was sweet and alluring but it would turn sour if she were not there with him.

He knew the chances weren't good that he could win her. He was the poorest man in first class. To be truthful, he wasn't even in first class—he merely mixed with the real ones. He could hold his own in their social chit-chat because he'd learned to speak their language in college and he worked at keeping up on their affairs. But it would have been pretense to imagine he was one of them.

No, Audrey was most likely to be swept up by someone like Gallagher, the steel baron, or Brownlow, the banker with bottomless pockets. Or most likely, Bascomb, a young and handsome bachelor, and rich—all that damned soap! He had seen the interest Bascomb took in her; it was impossible not to notice. Worse yet, he was sure Bascomb wanted Audrey only for his pleasure, to use her, perhaps only for the remainder of the voyage, then discard her. He had a reputation as a womanizer and had left a trail of broken hearts and hymens across five continents. David was distressingly aware that he had little to counter Bascomb's all-too-obvious advantages.

Still, he would try. One thing poker had taught him—it was a mistake to count yourself out too soon—your chances could improve in the blink of an eye. He knew Audrey now, if only a little, and he felt strongly about her—there was a natural fit between them. Perhaps he could reveal himself to her in a way that would let her sense the perfection of that fit. He had to try. If he were both clever and lucky, he just might shoulder Bascomb out of the way.

David had one advantage over Bascomb, and over anyone else trying to win her. He knew she was enmeshed in a situation that was way over her head—that she was in danger, perhaps mortal danger. Knowing this, he was in the best position to help her and, because of this, he was obligated to help her. Even if she were some dowdy old matron, he would have that obligation. But as it happened, she was the most desirable woman he had ever known and reaching out to help her and protect her was the most natural of acts, as easy as drawing breath.

XXIX

"WHAT ARE YOUR PLANS, once you reach England?" David tried hard to seem nonchalant.

"Hmmmm. I don't know. We haven't discussed that at all. I want to look at all the dress shops, of course."

It was nearing 2:00 AM and they had returned to a favorite spot on the starboard rail, looking out at the dark sea. The moon had already dropped below the horizon, leaving the ship alone in an inky blackness.

David worried. He thought it odd that Audrey was vague about her future beyond their arrival in England. "So you've made no plans. I take it Charles hasn't offered to introduce you to the Queen."

"You're mocking me."

"I guess I am, a little."

"Well, please stop it. It doesn't feel very friendly."

David smiled to himself. He admired her most when she was a little piqued. She had grit. Behind that delicate exterior was flint and steel; he was sure she'd be formidable in a tight situation. He liked that toughness, even as he yearned to reach out and hold her, to feel her slight body close against him as he shielded her. But he forced himself to stop this line of thought; instead of creating feelings he could savor, it was a distraction.

He wanted to protect Audrey from a threat she was blind to and he knew he had to be careful—she would not appreciate anything that felt patronizing, or like an attempt at seduction. He thought for a long time about how to phrase his next question.

"What do you do for Pierce? Your job, I mean—do you mind my asking?"

She was silent for a time, gazing out at the dark ocean. She didn't know how to answer. She felt she should be able to say and she was embarrassed that she couldn't, that the job was vague and oddly undefined. She was grateful that it was too dark for him to see her face. "Well, I... I'm his assistant. Sort of." She hadn't meant to say "sort of" but without it, her response was a lie.

"Sort of?"

"Well, I am."

"Have you worked as a secretary before?"

"Look here. What gives you the right to question me?"

David tensed—he had to be careful. "You're right. I've no right at all to grill you. I'm just curious." He shifted, his hands opening as if to catch her anxiety. "I'm curious about you. I want to know everything there is to know about you. Is that so bad?"

She turned back to the sea, a smile on her lips. "No, I... I'm glad that you're interested." She couldn't risk meeting his eyes but she moved closer and put her arm through his. "I hoped you would be."

His heart leapt. He needed to say just the right thing now, the words that would keep this moment alive. But as usual, he had no small talk to offer. All he knew to do was to barge straight ahead. "Please, Audrey, let me ask you about Pierce. It's important. I'm pretty certain it's *very* important."

Annoyed that he returned to this, she withdrew her arm, though she remained in place, their shoulders touching. "Go on," she said.

He'd done it again—ruined a precious moment with his bluntness. He didn't dare protest; he had to keep his focus on her situation with Pierce. With luck, their talk tonight would result in her trusting him—he had to believe in that outcome.

"Do you know why he hired you? Do you have a statement or an agreement about what your job is?"

Her patience thinning, she took her time, to let him know she was not ready to submit to the third degree. "Well, yes. I do. I don't mean on paper or anything like that. I have an agreement; we talked and we agreed, but it is a little strange for a job. I mean, I type and take some dictation, but that's not why he hired me."

"Why, then?"

"Well, it seems to be mostly about looks. He's like everyone else I've met on this ship, trying to whet the appetites of all these wealthy men."

"His mining... venture."

"You know about it?"

"I heard him laying it out to a few of the toffs the other night."

"He usually sends me away when he talks business."

"I'm sure. You'd learn too much about what he's doing and soon figure out it doesn't jibe with what he's told you in private. Plus, you're a distraction. While he's setting them up, he doesn't want his marks thinking about making love to you"

"Setting them up?"

"Just that. So my guess was correct; he hasn't clued you in."

"I don't know what you're talking about. What do I need to be 'clued in' to?"

He faced the sea again, while he thought about how to answer. This was all new to him. He felt responsible for her now. He wanted her to rely on him, even though he'd adopted the mantle of her protector without being asked. When he turned to her, his expression was serious.

"Audrey, I'm pretty certain Charles is running a con. I don't think there is a mine, of any kind. That vial of earth, or whatever it is he shows around, is probably all there is of any silver ore *he* owns."

She frowned. "Is this what happens to men— they assume everyone is a scoundrel?"

"I could be wrong—I admit that. But all in all, this silver mine has the look of a flimflam. And since Charles hasn't brought you into his scheme, I worry for your safety. He's conning you, too."

"What's that mean?"

"I know you have questions about it: the way he hired you, why doesn't he have a real assistant? He chose you for the way you look—that and your pretty manners—not for your office skills. What's that say about how real he is?"

He tried to change to a warmer tone, leaning closer and smiling. "I hope you don't mind my saying that I'm also very impressed with the way you look and I'm not 'hiring an assistant.'"

He looked at her, hoping to see a smile. Instead, he found a tracery of her tears reflecting light from the salon.

"Ohh, I'm so sorry, Audrey. I'm such a... a boor at times. I never know how to put things."

In a quick move, she plucked the handkerchief from his jacket pocket and dabbed at her eyes. He put one hand on her shoulder to comfort her. She shook him off but again, she didn't move away.

"Please, Audrey, forgive me. I... I didn't mean to bore in on you."

"Oh, shut up. It's not you."

Everything this remarkable girl did endeared her to him more. He decided to do as she said. He changed his position at the rail to give her space, lit a cigarette, and stared out to sea, resolved to wait her out. They stayed like that for a long time, he smoking and studying the dark vista, she biting her lip and dabbing at her eyes. Finally, she blew her nose loudly, wadded the kerchief and stuffed it into the hip pocket of his jacket.

"May I tell you something?" he asked.

"What?" she challenged.

"I... I'm..."

"You sound like an imbecile. What is it?"

"I just want you to know that..." He took in a deep breath. "I'm falling in love with you, Audrey. There. It's out."

She turned on him. "You... you midget!" She aimed a kick at his shin that landed squarely.

"Ow! God! That hurt!" Dancing on one leg, he grabbed the rail with one hand and held his bruised shin with the other.

"You can't stand there and show me what an idiot I am and then turn around and tell me you love me! You're a cad, you know that?! C.A.D.! You play with people's feelings!"

His shin stung. He collapsed onto the deck and rolled up his pant leg but couldn't see anything in the dim light.

"I can't feel... Ouch!"

"Oh, David. I'm sorry. I didn't mean to kick you so hard. Let me see. Is it all right?"

"No. Don't. Too dark to see anything, anyway. You have a real kick." He started to reach for his handkerchief to apply to the wound but then remembered how liberally Audrey had blown her nose into it. "Hey, what do you mean, 'midget'?"

"Oh, I don't know. It's the first thing that came into my head. Don't take it seriously." She stroked his cheek and he thrilled to her touch.

"I'm really sorry for kicking you. You didn't deserve that."

Kneeling next to him, her face was only inches from his and he didn't try to resist the urge to kiss her. He leaned toward her and placed his mouth on hers. She flicked her tongue across his lips. A thrill coursed through his chest and shot to his loins. He put his hand behind her neck and drew her to him. She didn't resist. Her mouth was firm and grasping; she held it open and their tongues met. They kissed for a long moment, then he pulled back and gazed into her eyes. Her tears had come again but there was a smile on her face.

"Oh, this is impossible!" she blurted. "I hardly even know you!"

"I'm David."

"Oh, yes. Cynical old David." She crawled into his arms and curled up against him. Her head lay in the crook of his elbow and she looked up at him, trying to make out who this strange, unlikely man was who made her heart race.

He adjusted his embrace to make the fit between them better. She raised her head toward his. This time their mouths locked firmly, tongues searching, each trying to taste the other's essence. Several times, they backed away and searched each other's eyes, then came together again, each mouth reaching for its eager partner. After many long moments, they disengaged.

Audrey closed her eyes and dropped her head on his shoulder. "I don't know what to think."

"So you don't believe me?" he asked.

She opened her eyes and looked into his. "You meant it, didn't you?"

"About loving you? Ohhh-h-h yes! But I mean about Pierce."

"Oh, David." A deep sigh of frustration spilled out. "I know you're sincere. But Charles has been very good to me. I could say he sort of saved me—from drudgery and boredom. It's hard for me to think badly of him. And you said you're guessing. Suppose you're wrong?"

David shrugged. "You're right. I have no direct evidence against him; I'm going on instinct."

"Why would Charles hurt me? I haven't done anything to him"

"You know too much about him."

"I hardly know *anything* about him."

He smiled inwardly, remembering how unaware of the world he once was. "You know more than you realize. Anytime you spend a lot of time with someone, you pick up details about them without even knowing it, just the kind of details the police want to know if he turns out to be a criminal."

"Well, so what if I do?"

"Look. If I'm right, Charles Pierce—if that's his real name—has to get off the ship before we dock in Cherbourg. By then, he expects to have a lot of cash and he won't take the chance that one of his marks will send a wire to his banker or broker, and find out he's being taken for a ride."

"Well, he can't get off the ship, can he now, Mr Holmes?"

"Audrey, please. You need to take this seriously. I'll be happy as a lark if I turn out to be wrong about him, but I don't think that's going to happen." He saw her pout in response to his scolding.

"In fact, he *can* get off the ship. I figure somebody will be waiting for him off the French coast, in a boat, about 24 hours from now—sometime between midnight and dawn tomorrow."

"David, I know you're trying to help me, but you're mad. I mean, listen to you... I can't listen to any more of this. I'm going to bed." She wrestled herself out of his arms and rose to her feet; David remained seated on the deck.

"Audrey. Darling. Please..."

"No, you're confusing me. And you're making me angry and I don't want to be angry with you. Good night." She began to step away but his pained expression stopped her. She stepped close, knelt and kissed him, lingering long enough to make it more than a friendly peck.

"I like kissing you," she murmured. Then she stood and spun on her heel, and hurried off. David watched her pass through patches of light flooding out of the ship's salons, then she was gobbled up in the darkness. Every move, every purposeful step, every subtle sway of her hips sent a thrill through him. That she was genuinely beautiful was beyond doubt—every man on the ship was agog in her presence. What was special about her—what made him so giddy, was that behind her physical beauty he had found both a sweetness and an improbable depth of character, a trueness, that stood outside her physical gifts and made her irresistible.

And to top it off, she loved... at least she liked... him. He could hardly believe it—it overwhelmed him. Still sitting on the deck, slumped against the cables strung between the rail stanchions, he savored this astonishing fact. He leaned his head back, closed his eyes, and recalled their kisses and how willingly and earnestly she had partnered in them. His heart was about to burst.

Grabbing the rail, he pulled himself up. He was stiff with desire for her and glad she wasn't there now to see his too obvious condition. He turned and looked out at the sea, rendered visible now only as fleeting pinpricks of starlight reflected off the shoulders of waves.

His emotions were settling down. He lit a cigarette and took a deep drag, and began to mull over a problem that came, in lock step, with his new relationship with Audrey. Charles Pierce. He was sure Audrey was in danger and that, because of it, he would have a confrontation with Pierce sometime in the next couple of days, a confrontation that would be unpleasant, and possibly a little rough.

He fingered the sore area of his shin. He winced, then the memory of Audrey slipping into the shelter of his arms swept the pain aside. He smiled to himself. Audrey's kick had placed her squarely in his life and they were now intertwined, falling in love, just as he had hoped. Their embrace, there on the deck, the kisses, even her attack on his shin, had been the greatest gift he could have asked for. And at the same moment, they made Charles Pierce his biggest problem.

David tossed the remains of his cigarette into the sea and, limping slightly, walked toward his cramped cabin, intent upon oiling and loading the long-barreled revolver tucked in behind the shirts in his bureau drawer.

XXX

AUDREY'S CONFIDENCE IN HER LOOKS had vanished. The person she now saw reflected coldly in the mirror was someone she hardly recognized. She was an animated rouged doll, red hair fashionably cut, an incongruous tiara setting it off. The image resembled her but she felt no connection with it. She looked in vain for the enthusiastic, bubbly shop assistant she used to know; self-assured, spirited, impertinent. The person who sat opposite her now, encased in shimmering off-white satin, mouth turned down, eyes sunken, was uncertain, defeated, unattractive, a stranger.

Charles tapped on the door and pushed in. "Ready, my sweet. We must be going. This is the big night."

Audrey followed his reflection as he crossed the small cabin and came up behind her. He placed his hands on her shoulders—the smoke from his cigar stung her nose. "You really are ravishing." He continued sweeping his gaze across her image and when he returned to her face, he caught a hint of something tentative. "But something's wrong."

"What exactly are you doing, Charles?" She felt his hands tense.

"What do you mean?"

"Do you really have a silver mine? Any mine at all?"

He took a long pull on his cigar. "Has someone been filling your pretty little head with trash?"

"Don't talk down to me. I asked you if this mine of yours is real. Or are you playing some kind of game with these people?"

Through the mirror, he looked into her burning eyes and saw the determination in them that would make it useless to lie. "No, Audrey. There's no mine. I'm setting up these lofty gentlemen so I..." he made his face into a smile, "...so *we*—can take them to the cleaners."

She regarded his mawkish smile for a long moment, growing more and more angry as he remained there behind her, now fiddling nervously with his bow tie. It was the first time she'd seen him off balance. "There is no 'we', is there, Charles? If I hadn't found you out, you would simply leave me holding the bag."

He stepped back and sat on the bed. She turned to him and he saw the puffiness below her eyes.

"You've been crying. You can't go out there looking like that. We are about to receive some very good news. We have to be especially joyous."

"I'm not sure I want to go out there at all. I have no desire to be part of your racket." She turned back to the mirror and began massaging the skin beneath her eyes.

Charles checked his rising anger. He sat forward and fixed his eyes on hers, through the mirror. "What's your complaint? When I met you, you were a plain little shop girl, working her life away stacking hatboxes and blouses," he flicked the air with his hand dismissively "and changing costumes on mannequins. Your salary barely covered your rent. Look at you now," he gestured to her reflected image. "You're a princess—nothing less." He reached out and pushed his index finger under the strap of her gown, then let it snap back to her bare shoulder.

"You couldn't have dreamed of owning a gown like this two weeks ago. Now it's yours. The jewelry, too.

I know they're not the pick of the lot but they cost a pretty penny, much more than you could have come up with on your own, before we met."

He stood now and stepped close behind her, still holding her eyes in the mirror. "Moreover, you've made friends—if not lovers, yet—among some of the wealthiest men in America." He puffed on his cigar. "If you play your cards right, you'll find yourself married to one of them, or one of their feckless offspring." He exhaled a pall of smoke, which circled around his head. "What have you to complain about? Tell me." He leaned in closer, against her back and, in the mirror, his gaze bore in on her.

"Tell me," he demanded.

Audrey sat up straight and turned to meet his gaze. "Oh, I have plenty. You've dragged me into a dirty scheme. I may have been a plain shop girl, and poor, but I certainly wasn't a criminal. You're planning to run off with those men's money, and when you're gone, the police will be looking at me."

"Oh. So it's not moral outrage I'm hearing. You're complaining about not being in the know. You want a cut, don't you? A piece of the action?"

"You're disgusting." She turned back to the mirror and worked at fixing her make-up.

He pushed against her now, enough to disturb her movements. He glowered at her in the mirror.

"Let me tell you something, my little beauty." As she brushed rouge on her face, he grabbed her hand roughly. She tried to pull away but he held it, fully aware that he was hurting her.

"I do not tolerate treachery. You've forgotten that I have quite a lot of money invested in you. I don't know what you think of me. It doesn't matter to me much anyway. But let me educate you about one thing. More than one person, all of them strong and wily men, have turned on me, gone back on their word to me, crossed me in some material way. Shall I tell you what happened to them?" He let the question hang in the air for a beat. "They're all dead."

In the mirror, he saw a flash of fear move across her eyes. Then he added, in a low hiss, "And they didn't die peacefully, I can assure you."

He released her hand and when she tried to squirm away, he grabbed her shoulders and held her down. His hands gripped her like a vice, his fingers pushing into the bare skin of her shoulders, making her wince.

"You're going to go through with what you've agreed to. You're going to do all the things I've taught you, and you're going to do them smiling, with verve and brio and *bonhomie*. If you behave, we'll talk about an appropriate settlement. If you slacken, if you become sullen, if, in any way, you fail to play your part, you will simply disappear. Vanish. No one will ever hear a thing about you ever again—you will cease to exist. Do you understand?" He gripped her chin and twisted her head around so he could look straight into her eyes. He was strong; she could not break away. His breath, reeking of his cigar, assaulted her. "I asked you if you understand."

She nodded.

He leaned in even closer, his face contorted into a wolfish mask. "Speak! Say the words!"

In the grip of fear, she could not give the words full voice. "I understand," she whispered.

Charles released her and straightened. He glared down at her through the mirror again, a triumphant smile on his mouth. "No doubt that two-bit gambler, David What's-His-Name, has been bending your ear. I'll deal with him presently." He bent down and looked closely at her chin. When he spoke, his voice was soft and there was a queer note of caring in his tone. "You may need an extra daub of powder there; it might come up in a bruise. Finish dressing; we must go." He turned and walked briskly back into his cabin.

"I want my part!" She cast the remark at him through the half-open door. She hardly even knew what she meant by it, except to declare that she would not be his puppet, and that she didn't feel obligated to submit to violence. Suddenly, recklessly, the notion swam into her head that money might restore her sense of righteousness.

"What did you say?" He appeared again at the door. His fists perched challengingly on his hips.

Intimidated, she softened. "I want my part. I'm critical to your success, I'm just realizing. You don't get something for nothing. I expect payment."

A derisive smile flicked across his face. He sauntered back into the room.

"So, your true colors emerge. No more Little Bo Peep, are we?" He stood behind her, smiling at her knowingly as he looked at her in the mirror. She worked to powder the growing purple blotch on her chin.

She was frightened but knew she must hide it. She hated being manhandled; she put her feelings there and found her anger. "You've misled me, Charles, and you certainly have no cause to look down your nose at me. I am not a... a marionette for you to manipulate at will."

She spun around on the stool and glared up at him. "And I'm certainly not someone you can parcel out to you friends for their crude amusements."

She turned back to the mirror and his reflection. "We will have a talk and negotiate what portion of your... your take is due me. Either that, or I will let your victims know what you are doing. I suspect they won't take it lightly."

Charles chuckled to himself. "Very good. Very good, my dear. You should be on the screen."

"Don't mock me, you... lizard."

Charles's brow wrinkled. "What's that you said about being parceled out? What did you mean?"

"Oh, just that your friend, Mr 'Calla Lily,' tried his best to rape me. I don't suppose you care, as long as I'm not outwardly damaged and can still play my role."

"Bascomb!? So..." He turned and paced, deep in thought. After a moment, he returned to his position behind her. "I'm genuinely sorry, Audrey. I hope you don't think I encouraged him." Looking down at her reflection, her anger was palpable but her expression carried no hint of blame. "I shall have a word with Mr Bascomb."

He took his watch from his pocket and clicked open the lid. "Finish dressing; we're late. You do deserve compensation, of course. We can discuss it when we're finished this evening." He went toward the connecting door but stopped before walking through it. "Does that suit you?" His smile was contemptuous.

She cast and angry look at him but didn't answer.

"Leave your ledger here but make sure you can get to it quickly, along with the stock certificates and your largest handbag. We're going to take in a lot of cash tonight." He left her sitting there, stewing.

XXXI

BY DAVID'S RECKONING, Charles Pierce would reel in his pigeons today and he wanted to be on hand to see it. He found an empty table near Charles's normal roost and parked himself there, nursing a soft drink.

Charles had, by this time, made the easy chair in a corner of the main first class lounge his throne. It was held for him through an unspoken consensus; no one else, save the occasional naïve outsider, sat there as the evenings began. Twice, Cedric Worthington, Captain of Industry, Toast of the Town, sitting in an adjacent chair, had all but leapt to his feet when Charles approached, ready, it appeared, to genuflect.

Charles was now installed in the chair, casually as always, one leg crossed over the other, pulling confidently on a cigar and trading conversation with the regulars: Worthington, Anders, Hansen, and the eager youngster, Billy Pruitt. Chandler was there too, along with Brownlow, standing just outside the inner circle. With his bank's history in mining, Brownlow felt he had to be present, after hearing the rumors about Charles's anticipated announcement, though he planned to join the poker game later.

Leonard Bates sat at the bar, a couple dozen feet away, his back to the group. He was dressed in a neatly tailored black suit and vest that Charles had provided the cash for. Charles prescribed the suit, rather than a tuxedo; the role Bates was to play required the appearance of a man who works with his hands. And at Charles's insistence, the drink Bates sipped was pure ginger ale, its lack of any intoxicating effect producing a growing level of agitation in him.

David saw Audrey, dressed in a gown of creamy satin, sitting to one side and slightly behind Pierce, outside the circle of light cast by the art deco lamp at Pierce's elbow. He caught her eye and smiled at her. She smiled back, warmly, but then, Felix Hansen leaned over to whisper something in her ear. It made her laugh and she fell into conversation with him. She didn't look back at David.

The previous night, Charles told his acolytes that he expected a telegram sometime today with the official assay results on his samples. He'd already worked into his chatter exactly how the assay values of ounces per ton translated into the critical numbers he wanted them to remember—dollars and pounds.

Charles pulled his watch from its pocket in his vest. He checked the time and, before replacing it, he wound it deliberately. David sensed something theatrical in this gesture and sure enough, as Charles re-pocketed the watch, Bates set down his glass and, looking very earnest, left the bar and covered the few paces to the edge of the small crowd. Charles was making noises about his anxiety over the anticipated telegram when Bates stepped forward, center stage.

"Begging your pardon, uh... Mr Pierce, is it? Excuse me, gentlemen." He nodded to the assembled men, including them all in his apology. Charles had told him to take as his model a British police detective. Bates had no direct knowledge of such persons—his experience was limited to the American brand—but his rendition was more than adequate.

"No offense, sir. I mean no challenge of any kind but I understand—these things do get about—that you are in possession of some ore samples? Silver?"

Just as Charles had instructed, Bates raised his voice a touch above normal conversation level. The talk around them stopped abruptly and everyone's attention instantly refocused on the two men. In the silence, Bates continued. "If you don't mind, I'd appreciate a look at them. If it's not too much trouble."

In his black suit, in the midst of all those dinner jackets, Bates looked like a lump of coal in a snow bank. The looks directed at him were not at all friendly, layered over as they were with a distinct class prejudice. These mandarins were uncomfortable with what they were hearing; someone not of their station—a working man— was presuming to stand in judgment of them.

Did they have a station to defend? They thought so. That they had succeeded as capitalists proved to their own satisfaction that they were better than other people. People like this man in a plain suit, so obviously in a class several steps beneath them, the sort of person they employed in great numbers but would never chat with or join in a drink. And the American oligarchs were, if anything, more offended than their British counterparts, some of whom had claims, however distant, to actual titles.

Worthington rose half out of his chair, inhaling deeply, about to confront Bates on behalf of his new-found fellow entrepreneur; Charles felt this was the moment to break in.

"Why, yes, of course," replied Charles, breezily, revealing no hint of insult. This stopped Worthington in mid-rise and he settled back into his chair, feeling a little foolish. Charles had pitched himself as an intermediate on the success ladder—not yet an oligarch but a rising entrepreneur. This, he felt, was the kind of train rich men liked to hitch their wagon to, and throw money at.

He dug into his inside pocket and brought out his pouch. Sitting up, he laid it on the table, untied its leather thongs and spread the vials out.

"May I?" Bates asked, leaning down and stretching a hand toward the vials.

"Go right ahead, old man," said Charles.

Bates pulled one vial from the pouch and brought it up to his face, rotating it slowly to make its sandy contents tumble.

Charles watched as Bates, the only person in the group standing, examined the vials, one by one, using a small, brass-barreled loupe he took from his watch pocket—another touch added by Charles. Charles shot a faint, knowing smile at a couple of the men in the circle as they focused on Bates. Then with a subtle air of challenge, Charles settled back into his armchair, re-crossed his legs, and took a long pull on his cigar. "Familiar with mining issues, are you, Mister, uhhh..?"

"Steffens, sir. Frederick Steffens." Bates, turning a vial under the magnifier as he replied, didn't lift his eyes. "Actually yes, I am." A low rumble of surprise ran among the onlookers. "I was the chief hydraulic engineer for Comstock for several years." The group broke into urgent whispers. Bates then looked down and addressed Charles. "I also had the good fortune of spending some fruitful years in Taxco, in Mexico. Have you been there?" At this, he glanced up at Charles, then quickly returned to his examination of the ore.

"I'm afraid I've not had the pleasure."

"A marvel to see, sir. Some of the richest silver veins in the world. You'd be impressed." Charles could hardly contain his pleasure at the perfect tone of Bates's performance; it was as though he was born to it. He congratulated himself for insisting on the ginger ale.

Bates un-stoppered one vial now and poised to pour some of its grey flecked contents into his hand. He raised his eyes to Charles, a subtle request for permission. Charles nodded his consent and Bates tipped out a small amount of the sample. He re-closed the vial and handed it to Charles, almost as though to an assistant—Charles took it with an amused smile. Bates then moved his hand into the light next to Charles's chair and leaned in, squinting at the sample through his loupe, his face hovering close above his palm.

A stillness now settled over this section of the salon; only the clink of glasses and a low buzz of conversation from a distant corner remained audible. Charles had included in his coaching an instruction that Bates should talk as little as possible; he wanted each onlooker to form his own image of Bates as he vetted the sample—the less he said in explanation, the more magical the process would seem.

With studied movements, Bates held the magnifier to his eye and examined the dust. With one finger, he pushed the loose grains around on his palm. Then, appearing to gauge its texture, he pinched some of the ore and, eyes closed, worked it back and forth between his thumb and forefinger. Charles watched, a smile on his face that only he knew contained a strong element of admiration. He rolled his cigar between his lips. The men were riveted; no one stirred. They kept glancing at Charles, waiting for his reaction.

Charles let the tension build. He knew that if the silence dragged on too long, anticipation would be replaced by curiosity, then doubt. He needed one of his pigeons to squawk, or he would have to break in. He thought Hansen might be the one who spoke first but it was Worthington who cracked. "Well damn it, man! What do you think?"

Bates made no response to Worthington's challenge—he kept his focus on the sand, as though he had not heard the outburst. Worthington fuffed, looking around in agitation at the others. After a long moment, Bates held his hand over an ashtray and let the mineral dust fall into it, and scuffed his palms together to clean off the residue. He folded his loupe and returned it to the watch pocket in his vest, then took out a handkerchief and brushed the remaining particles away.

When he looked up, he addressed himself directly to Charles, as though the others weren't there. "Well, sir, it takes a proper assay to tell, as you know. But I can certainly say this looks as rich as any ore I've seen, and that includes Taxco. You should do very well from it. Congratulations." He extended his hand and Charles took it, and allowed his smile to broaden.

A group-sigh poured from the assembled men and they murmured excitedly to each other, like schoolgirls. Several began talking about investing in Charles's mine and most of the talk was not about whether to invest, but how much. With this new element, a good shill, David's appreciation of Charles's skill rose several notches.

When talk of investment was directed at him, Charles waved it off, protesting that nothing was official yet. Hansen persisted and Charles artfully steered the conversation to Worthington and coal mining, with Charles commiserating with him about the undercurrent of labor protest Worthington was currently dealing with.

A steward entered the lounge and began chanting, "Telegram for Mr Pierce." Charles caught the young man's attention with a wave of his hand. The steward hurried over, holding a small yellow envelope at high port.

Charles rose to take the message. After he'd tipped the lad and dismissed him, he held the envelope up, still unopened, and waved it before his eyes. Raising it higher, he took a dramatic deep breath. "Well, gentlemen..." he glanced around at his coterie, smiling like a boy in a candy store, "the moment of truth. I feel I know the news will be good but, I have to confess, my pulse is racing a bit."

It was the pulses of the men around him, of course, that raced. They leaned forward, a few insisting that Charles get on with opening the message, as though it were meant for them. Bates stood to the side, nursing a glass of whiskey now, a thin smile on his face.

Charles played coy for another moment, then looked over at Chandler. "Nelson, you have a pen knife on your cigar cutter, don't you? Let me borrow it." Charles extended his hand for the cutter, controlling an urge to snap his fingers. Chandler, breakfast purveyor to the masses, dug obediently into his pocket for the cutter and placed it in the outstretched hand.

Keeping the envelope high so everyone could see it, Charles slit an edge and took out the pale yellow paper within. It was folded over once; with studied movements, he spread it open and straightened the crease, revealing a half dozen strips of ticker tape glued to the paper. Sipping his whiskey, Bates smiled to himself as he watched Charles on stage. David smiled too, at the performance.

Charles raised the telegram and read: "1620, 6-23-36, DENVER, COLORADO, WU #28. TO CHARLES W. PIERCE, THE QUEEN MARY. ASSAY RESULTS AS FOLLOWS. SAMPLE ONE, KIOWA: 14 PER TON. SAMPLE TWO, PAIUTE: 13 PER TON. SAMPLE THREE, SHOSHONE: 16 PER TON!!" Smiling broadly, he turned the message around and showed it to his audience, pointing. "He added two exclamation points after that one." They laughed and chuckled and slapped their thighs, and Charles returned to the message. "RESULTS CERTIFIED. CONGRATULATIONS! AWAITING INSTRUCTIONS. MARSDEN."

A cheer broke from the crowd and Charles put on his biggest grin. "My God, we've done it! We've done it!!" He grabbed Audrey and hugged her exuberantly.

From his perch, David tried to read her mood. She appeared to share Charles's glee but her smile was labored. She turned away as the men, all laughter and grins, shoved in and vigorously shook Charles's hand. He beckoned to a nearby waiter. "Waiter! Champagne, your best! Three bottles, at least, to slake our terrible thirst!"

The crowd of men slapped Charles on the back and congratulated him; people in other parts of the lounge turned to look, wondering what the fuss was.

"Oh, this is too good," Charles bubbled. "16 to the ton!" Worthington, Brownlow, and Hansen had formed a circle around him. "Can you believe it? That's the richest vein since Comstock!" He had giddy down to an art, David noted.

When things settled down, Charles and Worthington continued talking. Billy Pruitt hovered nearby.

"Well, Pierce, what now? What's your next step?" asked Worthington.

"Oh, I've much to do. When I meet with my partners in London, we must decide what portion of this find we want to put out for public subscription. We need funds to build facilities; the new steam diggers, rails, wagons, drills. Have to build a serviceable road to the mine. It's a dirt track now, hardly more than a footpath, really. But..." he smiled and ceremoniously kissed the telegram before tucking it into his breast pocket. He let his listeners conclude the thought and form their own impressions of how much there would be to divide among investors.

David saw Bates rise and step toward the group of celebrants. He wondered what more he could add to his brilliant turn on stage.

"May I see your telegram, Mr Pierce?" He stood with his arms held behind his back, his manner direct and somber. Charles looked up as if surprised again. The group went silent but made way for Bates, inching back as if it were dangerous to stand too near him. Charles took the telegram from his pocket and, with a slight smile that suggested challenge, handed it to Bates.

Bates took it and read it slowly. He then handed it back and looked at Charles. "Are shares available in this enterprise?"

Charles did an excellent job of appearing shocked. "Why... why yes, of course. As I was telling, uh, Mr Worthington here, we're in need of the funds to exploit this find, so..."

"I'd like to buy in," said Bates. Solemnity was Bates's whole affect so he needed no lessons on how to communicate dead certainty. His audience of high rollers was taken aback by this gambit from a working-class man and Charles knew how to play to their prejudices.

"Uhhh... all right. I hadn't... well, yes, you can make an investment. I have to tell you though, the buy-in price is not small. The partners have set the minimum share price at a hundred pounds—that's about five hundred dollars." Charles stated the figure as a challenge, thrusting his chin toward Bates, his voice raised to make sure all could hear. "On the other hand, when they see this," a subtle wave of the telegram, "it's likely to go much higher."

Judging by the flawless performance, David figured they'd played this and similar games many times before.

"That's why I want to act now," said Bates. He reached into his jacket and brought out his billfold. "I'll take two shares now. Once we're in London, I'll increase that to ten. Do you need a formal pledge?" He extracted a sheaf of hundred-dollar bills from the wallet and held them out to Charles.

Appearing stunned, Charles spluttered. "No, no. No pledge required. Uh..." he turned to Audrey. "Audrey. The stock certificates. You know where they are. Bring me two of them and..."

Billy interrupted. "Hold on! Bring more than that. I want to get in on this too."

Hansen followed on Billy's heels. "Here, here, old man. Please ask Miss Simmons to bring plenty of those certificates."

Charles smiled coyly. "Well, gentlemen. I'm honored but I'm afraid I have only a limited number..." Apparently stunned, he turned to Audrey. "Bring the packet—and your ledger, of course." As Audrey turned and headed toward the cabin, Gallagher asked if Charles would take a check. Charles demurred, making haste to let him know it wasn't personal but that his actions were circumscribed by his partners.

With a broad smile, Charles turned back to the assembled magnates, rubbing his hands together. "Now, where *is* that champagne?"

David rose and left the salon, shaking his head in admiration for Charles—so much enthusiasm over a handful of sand. One of the few lines he remembered from Shakespeare popped into his head: "All that glisters is not gold..." Well, things hadn't changed much. Apparently the sheen of gold and silver could still snag the mugs.

XXXII

EIGHT BELLS WAS STRIKING as David descended the ladder into D Deck. Miles had promised him he would lock the shop door exactly at eight bells and would not be in the passageway after that.

He'd asked Miles to cut the key for him but it was a breach of rules Miles was unprepared to make. This was the Depression; jobs were scarce. If an unauthorized key turned up, its very existence would cost Miles his job, unless he could make a credible claim that someone else made it in his absence. The first class staterooms were loaded with personal treasure: jewels, cash, securities; Miles could be on the hook for anything a passenger claimed was missing. Giving David the means to cut the key himself was as far as he dared go.

David timed his approach to allow Miles about a minute to get clear. Wearing his common seaman's garb, he turned a corner in the passageway and was within a few steps of the shop door when Carl, the ship's engineer, appeared through a hatchway fifty feet away. David's focus on his approach to the shop was so intense that Carl seemed to appear out of nowhere.

"David. What brings you down here at this hour? I always imagine you trussed up in your tuxedo once the sun goes down."

"Carl! I... I needed to clear my mind. This is my big night. I get the jitters. You never know when the cards might turn cold..." He knew that Carl believed in such hokum. "I have to be in top form tonight—there's a lot riding on it. Say, isn't there a head near here?"

"Along there; you passed it." Carl pointed back over David's shoulder.

David turned to retrace his steps. "Thanks. I'm about to burst."

"Good luck tonight, mate."

"Thanks, Carl. 'Appreciate it."

David ducked through the toilet door and listened as Carl's footsteps rang away to silence. For effect, he flushed a urinal, then checked the corridor. It was empty. He looked at his watch—three crucial minutes had just vanished.

David went back to the shop door and slipped inside. In 17 minutes, Miles, perhaps 10 minutes ahead of the watch officer, would come down the passageway and lock this door. David had to be gone by then.

He crossed to an inner door labeled "Lock & Key," went through and closed it. He felt for the light switch in the dark, flicked it on, and faced the workbench. Three large cabinets hung on the wall above the bench. The first one was labeled, "Top – B Deck" and, as Miles had promised, the key was in the lock. On the lathe, the left-side vice held a shiny brass blank—if Miles had been there, David would have kissed him.

David yanked open the cabinet; the master keys were all neatly arranged there in patterns that mimicked the layout of the ship's berths. Moving quickly, he found the master for Pierce's stateroom and secured it in the right-hand vice of the lathe, making sure, as Miles had admonished, to push it snug against the mandrel.

Checking to make certain he'd closed the door, he glanced down and realized that a telling band of light from the gap at the bottom would be impossible to miss in the darkened outer room. He stripped off his coat and spread it across the gap. Then he held his breath and reached for the switch on the lathe. The motor spun up to speed, emitting a whine at a high, nerve-wracking pitch. It wasn't very loud but, in the absence of the normal bustle of activity, the sound stood out like a match struck in a closet—David feared they could hear it throughout the ship.

Mimicking the movements he'd seen Miles perform many times, David grabbed the handle on the vice and inched the blank toward the cutting wheel. When its teeth sank into the brass, they produced a screech so loud it made him jump. He backed the tool off but he knew he had to press on; no noise, no duplicate key. Speed was his only ally. He forced the brass blank against the wheel and pressed it from side to side. Miles had told him to use both hands on the tool to insure a good cut and he followed that advice. The cutter screeched and spit brass chips at his hands and forearms—it seemed to take forever.

When the teeth no longer found fresh metal, David turned off the lathe and looked at his watch. There wasn't time to check the cut; it just had to be right. He returned the master to its hook and locked the cabinet door. As Miles had instructed, he dropped the cabinet key into a small box at the back of the bench.

He took the new key from the lathe, switched the light off and, in the dark, wriggled into his coat. In another minute, he was hurrying down the passageway, his hand clutching the still-warm duplicate in his pocket. Miles would make a small show of the brass cuttings to his mates when he came on duty the next day, cuttings he normally would have swept up before leaving the previous evening. It would be enough to give him cover if this key somehow got discovered before David had the chance to chuck it overboard.

XXXIII

LEONARD BATES, TEETERING on one stockinged foot, was trying to keep his balance on the chair. He managed not to spill the whiskey as he brought the glass to his mouth but, when he tilted his head back to drink, some of it spilled down his chin and dropped onto his shirt and vest. He tried to stand steady, arms and one leg shifting in and out in jerks, to keep his center of gravity in place. Even sober, it would have been difficult on the rolling ship.

"Wait. Wait now, I'm ready. OK." As carefully as he could, he tried to tip the liquor into his mouth without spilling, but the ship's movement defeated him again.

"Foul," cried Charles. "I see whiskey! Wasted! Look! Running down your shirtfront!" He picked up a pencil from the night table and made a check mark in a column of scratches on the pad beneath it. "Points off!" For this second excursion into Bates's territory, Charles had again exchanged his tuxedo for dungarees.

Bates stepped clumsily off the chair and Charles draped an arm around his neck, allowing some of his weight to bear on Bates's shoulders. "Feeding frenzy. Bloody feeding frenzy, that's what it was, old man," Charles said as he took a sip from his glass.

"They were putty in your hands," slushed Bates. He tipped his glass back and drained it. "Twenty tous..." he stopped and concentrated. "Twenty thous-and. Twenty thousand. Pounds. Damned fortune!"

"That's merely the cash, my friend. Another ten in pledges—sadly, we'll never be able to cash in on those. Still..."

"Yes. Still. Twenty thousand," said Bates. "Your turn."

Charles feigned not knowing what he meant. "What. Oh, yes. One minute."

He leaned on Bates heavily as he climbed onto the chair and turned. He held his glass out and Bates filled it.

"There you are. Eyes closed. Drink up!"

Charles put the glass to his lips and whiskey immediately ran down his chin. He coughed and spat liquor across the room.

"No points! Zero," cried Bates with exuberance.

Charles stumbled to the floor, spilling more of the liquor. Spluttering and coughing noisily, he went to the sink, turned on the tap and splashed his face with cold water. He drank deeply from the tap. Slowly drying his face with a towel, he waited, checking in the mirror, until Bates wasn't looking, then he tipped away most of the remaining whiskey. When he turned back, he made certain Bates was watching before tilting his head back and draining the glass of the remainder.

"Listen, I know a batter... uhh, better game," he said. "Give me a rope. You got a rope?"

The fuzziness enveloping Bates's brain made it difficult for him to understand the question. "Rope? What rope? Don't need a rope. You're way behind, my friend. No points at all on that one. Rope won't help you a bit, unless it's to hang yourself."

"Yes. That's it, exactly. Want a rope. Better game. Where's a rope?" Wait, I know. He staggered to the door and yanked it open. "Right. There's one."

Charles pulled a penknife from his pocket and stumbled a few feet down the passageway to the life buoy hanging on the wall. A braided line ran around its circumference. He raised his voice to make sure Bates could hear him as he cut the line off. "This is good. This will do fine."

Bates popped his head through the doorway. "Hey, you're not supposed to do that."

"You worry too much. Need a rope." Charles stumbled back into the room and handed the line to Bates. "Make a noose."

Bates looked at him blankly. "A noose. What's for. Can't. Don't know how. What's it noose?"

"It's for hangman. Good game. Here." He took the rope back from Bates and began to fashion a crude noose. He made sure to make a few mistakes before producing a serviceable one. "There."

"That's not right. Not long enough. Not enough loops." Bates pointed at the half dozen wraps Charles had coiled around the rope.

"I know. Supposed to be thirteen. Rope's too short. This'll do." Charles pulled the chair under the overhead lamp and climbed unsteadily onto it. He pushed the free end of the rope over the steel conduit running across the ceiling, and tied it off. Bates had collapsed clumsily onto the rumpled lower bunk and was looking up at Charles in a fog. With a dramatic flourish, Charles turned and made a show of opening the noose and lowering it over his own head. He snugged the noose around his neck.

"OK. Hand me my glass."

Bates responded mechanically, handing up the empty glass. Charles shook it at Bates and Bates filled it from the bottle.

"Half! Only half. You trying to kill me?"

"Don't know what the hell you mean, my freem... my friend. What game... What kind of game is it...? this...?"

"I'm showing you. Patience. OK. Now I'm going drink this whiskey, see, and then I stand on one leg, eyes closed. Yes, eyes closed... Have to stay on one leg. Thirty seconds. Got it?"

Bates's sloshed brain cranked its way through this information and finally produced a vague understanding. He decided the game was as good as any. "Yeah, got it. Got it. Good. You don't stand a chance, my freem. You forget that I have the reflashes... re-flex-es of a cat."

"Do not count your chickies until all your little eggies have hatched, Mr Bates... ahh, sorry... Mr Steffens, I believe it is. Pleased to meet you, Mr Steffens." Drunkenly, he shook Bates's hand and then gave him an incongruous salute. "Remember, you must keep your balance for a thull firty... a full thirty seconds while fighting off the effects of this fine mash." Charles postured on the chair, lifting first one leg and then the other, like a ballerina. "Are you ready to time me?"

Bates dug his watch out the pocket of his vest. "You may produce... uhhh... you may proceed."

"Get out your knife! Where is your knife. If I fall, you have to be ready to cut the rope." Among the things Charles could count on with Bates was the switchblade he always carried. Charles had slipped a penknife into his own jacket pocket and he needed it to stay there.

"Oh. Yeah. Sure." Bates produced the knife, flicked it open, and held it up high, showing himself ready to come to Charles's aid. "Ready."

"OK. Here goes." Charles threw his head back and downed the whiskey, closed his eyes and leaned over onto one foot. He lurched left and right more than he needed to, making sure his arms flapped extravagantly, and fixed a look of worry on his face.

Now his act became dangerous. He had to make his high-wire dance look convincing but he knew that if he actually did fall, he couldn't depend on Bates to cut him down in time. He'd wanted to fake drinking the whiskey altogether but it wasn't possible; Bates wasn't that far gone.

When Bates wasn't looking, Charles had dropped his pen knife, with blade open, into the left pocket of his coat. Now he slipped his hand in and grabbed the knife. He knew his chances of getting it out and cutting the rope before he strangled weren't all that good but it was better than nothing. Eyes not completely closed, he continued his performance.

"Twenty-five." Bates was counting down the time and it was not passing fast enough for Charles. He was having trouble keeping his balance—the need to keep his left hand in his pocket, instead of out to help stabilize him, added to the difficulty. He had no intention of doing the entire 30 seconds but he needed to push it as far as possible, to give Bates a mark he would surely try to better. He could feel the rope scraping against his neck.

"Fifteen. Ten..."

"Yaghhh!" Charles brought his left foot down on the chair. "Blast! I've gone over a minute many times!" He handed the glass to Bates and reached up to pull the noose open. "Still, I bout... I seriously bout... doubt that you can improve on that."

"You always have... uhhh... rated your shelf... self too high, Mr Pierce. Doing it again..." Charles stepped down and Bates clambered up.

"Nonsense. Your watch... Let me have it." Charles held out his hand. Bates unthreaded the chain from his vest and handed the watch to Charles.

Then Bates pulled the noose around his neck and cinched it down. "...it will prove your undoing."

"Don't be too confident, sir. Here." Charles handed up his whiskey glass and poised the bottle over it. "Ready?"

"Ready, sir."

Taking note of exactly where he touched the bottle, Charles filled the glass to half. "Bottoms up. Eyes closed. Don't cheat."

His eyes already squeezed shut, Bates swallowed the liquor in two gulps and leaned his weight over onto one foot. "Go!"

"Twenty-Five," Charles called. He looked up at Bates, who was already having trouble staying upright. "Twenty." He raised a foot and placed it against the chair back, and pushed.

Charles was surprised at how easily the chair flipped back. Bates dropped heavily and there was a crunch when his neck jerked the line taut. His arms flailed; the whiskey glass crashed to the floor but without breaking. Bates's stockinged feet kicked, uselessly, six inches off the floor. He grabbed at the rope with one hand, his face already twisting into a grotesque, bloating mask, his eyes wide, turning intensely red, looking as though they might pop out. For an instant, his pleading eyes caught Charles's gaze. Charles backed up a step and placed his hands behind his back, and set a mocking smile on his face.

Bates got a tenuous grip on the conduit and Charles thought he might succeed in taking the weight off his neck. He grabbed the other wrist and tugged, pivoting Bates's body around the rope and breaking his grip on the steel tube. He kept his grip on the wrist so Bates couldn't twist around again.

Bates struggled weakly for another moment, then suddenly, he stopped. His free hand dropped to his side; Charles let the other arm go and it, too, dropped, lifeless. The body lapsed into a pendulum swing in answer to the ship's movements.

Charles stepped back and looked up. Without emotion, he pulled a pair of gloves from his coat and drew them on as he regarded the grotesque face of his former partner, the neck pinched tight by the thin rope, the head cramped to one side. Then he turned his attention to the job of erasing all evidence of his presence there.

It was unlikely that the ship's officers had much facility with forensic techniques and he was certain that any investigation into Bates's death would be perfunctory. Nevertheless, there was no point in taking chances. He spent the next moments making the room look as though Bates had been its sole occupant. With his handkerchief, he wiped clean everything in the small berth he thought he might have touched. He paid special attention to the knife, the watch, and the whiskey bottle, and closed Bates's fingers around each one. He restored the knife and the watch to their places in Bates's clothing and put the bottle on the table. He left the whiskey glass where it had fallen, next to the overturned chair.

This late, he hoped everyone else would be in bed, either their own or someone else's, anywhere, in fact, as long as they were not wandering the ship's halls. He put his ear to the door and listened for sounds of activity in the passageway.

His main concern was the roommate. Although he and his sweetheart spent most of their time humping in the darkness up on deck, Charles couldn't discount the possibility of a spat, or a crewmember interrupting their rut and sending them home. It would be hard going if he showed up now.

Charles flipped off the light and cracked the door, listening. The only sound was the boat's ceaseless hum. He pulled the door wider and poked his head out far enough to see both ways; the passageway was deserted. He flicked the lights back on and quickly stepped out of the room.

He took one last glance at the corpse swaying at the end of the rope—he hardly recognized the distorted and discolored face. He noticed a stream of piss running down under the trouser cuff, darkening the sock and dripping onto the carpet. He looked back up at the grotesque face. "Fuck you, Mr Steffens."

He closed the door and hurried away.

XXXIV

DAVID GOT TO THE LUGGAGE SHOP just as the proprietress was closing the door. He squeezed through and then apologized to excess for extending her workday. Unable to budge him, she backed away.

"What is it you want at this hour?" she asked, angrily, as she moved behind the counter.

"I need a satchel."

"A satchel," she repeated, dryly. "That's what cannot wait until tomorrow? A satchel?"

"I'm afraid it can't, uhhh... I didn't catch your name." Pouring on the charm, he smiled broadly. "I'm David."

"Miss Mitchell." She said it as a rebuke but, when she tried to hold his eyes, his smile caused her to redden and she had to look away. "Is there a particular satchel you had in mind?"

"Actually, yes, Miss Mitchell, there is. It's square-ish, like a doctor's bag. I'm hopeful you have one in black."

"I believe I know the bag. One moment."

She disappeared through a doorway into a storage area. David couldn't see the whole space but it was obviously very small. A moment later she returned, carrying a box and showing a slight, triumphant smile. "I think this might be what you're looking for."

She dug through the tissue paper and pulled out a perfect copy of the bag Charles had carried when he and David had their earlier encounter.

"It's become popular. I sold another just like it only a couple of days ago."

"Did you? Well, I'm not surprised. It's a handsome bag, and it'll suit me just fine. What do I owe you?"

XXXV

"SIT DOWN, LAD, and join us." Charles directed Billy Pruitt toward the settee next to him. "We're in a celebratory mood. Whiskey?" He lifted the bottle and found it nearly depleted. He emptied it into a glass and offered it, but Billy was distracted and didn't register the gesture. Nervously, Billy edged into the seat. He seemed unusually awkward and scanned the salon furtively. Sipping his own drink, Charles eyed him. "What's eating you, lad?" Billy avoided looking at Audrey and Charles wondered whether her presence was throwing him off.

"Uhhh, nothing. I just, uh... nothing at all." He sat back into the sofa, trying for nonchalance and failing.

"Waiter!" Charles caught the man's eye and waved him over. "Bring us another bottle of Glenfiddich, would you?"

The waiter scuttled away.

"You will join me, won't you, Master Pruitt?"

Billy nodded, then he blurted out, "I say, Pierce, would you... I mean, listen..." He lowered his voice almost to a whisper. "I want to invest more in your mine. I've got a lot of cash here; how much can I buy in for?" He dragged an envelope out of an inside pocket and cracked the top to show Charles.

Charles clucked. "Master Pruitt. Discretion, if you please." He waved a nervous hand at him. "Put it away."

"But I want in on the ground floor, Pierce. This could be big—anybody can see that. I want my father to... I want to be the first in. You know... grasp the... the brass ring, the..."

"Seize the day! Carpe diem! The main chance," Charles embellished. Pruitt didn't catch that he was being mocked.

"That's it. That's what I'm after, the main chance." His obvious discomfort made Audrey wince.

Charles understood the gut-level urge in Billy Pruitt, his desperate need to show his father that he could do a rich deal. His own father had been a tyrant who thought Charles had no skills, no future, and made no attempt to spare his feelings in telling him so. Long ago, he realized he was toiling to prove his father wrong. As soon as he could put that thought into words, to say it out loud, he found he no longer cared what his father thought.

Billy's father was going to be even more disappointed in the boy when this was all over. Charles tried to muster up a little pity for him but he couldn't manage it. Besides, nothing he could do or say would save Billy Pruitt from himself. He would have to take his lumps and learn from them.

Charles didn't appreciate the look of censure he found on Audrey's face. With a subtle frown, he cleared his throat softly and she averted her gaze.

"Audrey, let me have the ledger, please."

She didn't move right away, the hesitation intended to convey her disapproval of Charles accepting Billy's money. Charles sat with his legs crossed and his hand outstretched, waiting for her to comply. She pulled the cloth-bound book from her carryall and handed it to him, then she rose and moved to a table in a corner.

Charles took a pair of gold rimmed reading glasses from an inner pocket and ceremoniously wrapped the temple arms over his ears. Then he sat back and opened the ledger, as though it were St. Peter's Book of

Records. He leafed through the first few pages, drawing the moment out to keep Billy on the hook. One slow leaf at a time, he turned to the page of pledges and ran his finger down the columns. Billy craned his neck trying to see the figures but he couldn't make them out. Charles subtly tipped the book up so Pruitt couldn't read the entries.

"Well, let me see. I do have a few positions left. You're already in for a thousand. How much more are you thinking of investing?"

"Uhhh... three," said the boy, tentatively.

Charles eyed him. "Thousand?"

Billy nodded, tight lipped.

"Pounds? Or was that dollars?" He had a way of making dollars seem cheap and low class, and so very unwelcome. Charles looked at him over the top of his glasses.

"Uhh... p... pounds." The poor chump was stuttering now. Four thousand pounds was most of the money his father had given him to help him forget Sadie.

As Charles took his pen from his jacket pocket and unscrewed the top, the waiter appeared with the whiskey and set the service at his elbow. Charles signed for it and tipped the man. Then with a flourish, he made an entry in the ledger and turned to Billy. "Well, that almost closes the subscription. You're making a wise choice, Mr Pruitt." "Mister" was icing on the cake; only the servants at his father's mansion, the nameless people who kept his clothes clean and his dinner plate full, called Billy "Mister." Charles knew it would boost Billy's ego to have a man of business address him so.

"You're going to multiply your money many times." He made another notation in the ledger, then closed it dramatically.

Billy counted out the money, put it into an envelope, and took it to Audrey. He was too embarrassed to meet her eyes so he didn't catch the look of regret on her face as she took it. He went back to Charles, who stood and extended his hand, gripping Billy's in a firm grasp.

"Good show." Stepping in closer, he made a fist and tapped it twice into Billy's shoulder. In a low voice, as though welcoming Billy into a secret society, he said, "Let's mine some silver, Master Pruitt. Let's get very, very rich. Here, have a drink." He picked up the whiskey bottle and ostentatiously poured matching levels into two glasses. With a wink, he handed one to Billy. "This is the finest whiskey in the world, a suitable accompaniment to our partnership." He intended that this fine taste of aged, single malt whiskey would be Billy's only reward from this investment.

David was sitting at the bar. In the mirror, he watched the interaction between Charles and Billy, and marveled at Charles's smoothness. Sure, Pruitt was an easy mark but there was something special in Charles's style—he'd be hard to resist. And as if on cue, as Pruitt walked away, two other wealthy speculators sidled over to Charles and began negotiating with him about how much cash they could force on him. Charles almost succeeded in seeming put upon.

Just then, a commotion developed at the wide portside doors to the salon, leading onto the Promenade Deck. A man standing there was gesturing excitedly. A group formed around him at the doors; others rushed past and out onto the deck.

David walked over, wondering what could get this group of the self-involved into such a lather. When he got out to the deck and stepped to the rail, he saw what the object of interest was. About two hundred yards off the beam, and steaming almost directly at them at a good rate, was a submarine. It apparently had just surfaced and its black skin was glossy wet. Sailors clad in black poured out of a hatch and scuttered fore and aft on its deck, tending to various lines. Three of them rushed to the bow and began removing a cover from a cannon mounted there. Just as David started to wonder whether the boat would keep coming, it made a turn to run with the Queen, at a distance of less than 100 yards. The turn revealed the black and white Iron Cross insignia of the *Bundeswehr,* prominent on its tower.

Those crowded onto the deck buzzed about the sub's intentions, wondering if the gun crew was taking aim at them. David thought it was a training exercise, most likely; the sailors manipulated the gun, pointing it in various directions, and appeared to load it, but didn't fire.

Running on the surface, the U-Boat could not keep pace with the Queen. As she began to fall astern, David could see several men in the bridge, scanning the Queen through binoculars.

"What in blazes do they think they're doing!" Felix Hansen demanded. "This is an outrage; intimidation, pure and simple. They're not even supposed to have any submarines!"

"They're damned lucky there are no British frigates nearby," Worthington declared, in his highest dudgeon. "They'd be ducking out of sight, I'll wager, instead of waving that silly cannon around."

Apparently the U-Boat captain agreed. The gun crew re-wrapped the cannon, the sailors quit the small deck, and they all returned to the sub's interior. A light began blinking in the sub's bridge—a coded message to the Queen Mary. David craned to see if any answer was going out from the Queen's bridge but he couldn't tell from where he stood. The blinking from the sub stopped and the figures on its bridge disappeared. A moment later, the boat tilted forward, its bow planes bit into the sea, and it sank from view.

"I think a war is inevitable, don't you?" It was Sam Riverson. He had come up beside David at the rail and was offering him a cigarette from a gold case. David took one and smiled, then turned back to the sea, curious to see if the sub's periscope would pop up above the surface.

"I wish I didn't," he said. He took out his lighter and lit Riverson's cigarette, then his own. "It's going to be bloody; sure to chew up even more men than the last one."

"Worst is," said Riverson, "it's avoidable, I think. We have to stand up to this guy, Hitler."

David nodded. The two men stood at the rail, smoking their cigarettes, absorbed in their thoughts. David checked his watch. He was on the cusp of his own major challenge. He reminded Sam of the night's card game, then went to the washroom off the salon. In the glare of the light over the sink, he splashed cold water on his face and dried off with one of the thick terrycloth towels the ship provided in first class. He combed his hair, smoothed his jacket, and straightened his tie. It was time to open up play at the poker table for this, the last night of the voyage.

The stakes were high and involved more than money, now. Success tonight could help insure a future with Audrey. He felt like a soldier crouched in a foxhole, waiting for the whistle that would send him into the enemy guns. Would he make it? He had a plan for the battle—would it work? Would he carry the day? It worried him that he didn't have a solid feel for how this crucial night would go.

XXXVI

TRUE TO FORM, the first thing the players did on the final night was abandon the betting limits. Intent on getting their money back, they didn't want anything slowing them down. And even though he was back at the table after being absent the previous three nights, Michael Gallagher was particularly opposed.

They got off to a brisk start, suppressing small talk as each player focused on being strongest out of the gate. David had just dealt the last card in this early game. Looking at his hand, Gallagher champed at the stub of his cigar and let a faint smile show. The smile did not escape David's notice. Catching minutiae—small movements of a mouth, fingers picking lint from a sleeve—was the essence of his skills and they were fully engaged now.

David was not happy when Gallagher shouldered himself into this game, having opted out the previous three nights. Why would he sit in now, on the last night at sea, and test himself against David and the others? By reputation, Gallagher was a wily operator. His company, Bessemer Allegheny, was one of the most successful enterprises on the globe at the moment. Indeed, it was quite a bit more profitable than US Steel, much to their embarrassment. David felt no man capable of that trick, and so clearly not a novice at poker, would sit down at a hot table and expect much success.

He felt he knew the answer—Gallagher was spoiling for a fight. David's strategy had succeeded. After playing possum in those first sessions, he'd pocketed almost £3,000 over the previous two nights. That news traveled fast around first class and everyone knew that tonight's games would be something of a showdown. A working stiff taking on some of America's savviest businessmen...! Gallagher would feel it his duty to beat back such a challenge.

Music and voices filtered in from the ballroom and from the bars. Again, the players had tipped a waiter to spread one of the ship's blue banquet covers across two tables, to form the gaming arena.

"Your bet, Nelson," said Gallagher. He had an annoying way of taking charge, as though the game belonged to him in some way. His reading glasses again slid to the end of his nose and he repeated a gesture that David thought odd, pushing them back in place with his thumb. He'd just raised the stakes twenty pounds over David's open and was studying his hole cards. He was sitting forward, elbows plunked on the table and his head tilted back on his neck, as he scanned the cards through the steel-rimmed glasses. His small black eyes shot around the table periodically, taking the temperature of those still in the hand.

Although the other players still wore their dinner jackets, Gallagher was in shirt sleeves, his jacket draped over the back of his chair. He had also buttoned on a set of accountant's cuffs, proclaiming, "I'm just an ordinary Joe." Cute touch, David thought. Cuffs were the uniform of a working accountant, which Gallagher most decidedly was not. It made David all the more wary.

With Gallagher knocking around as though he owned the table, David tried to parse his mannerisms—what was real and what was part of a war dance intended to intimidate? He still didn't know what lay behind Gallagher's open display of personal animus on the first day out and he'd been too busy to think about it. David needed to take his time now, reading Gallagher, drawing him in, picking up on his tells. He had the advantage of having studied the other players for the past four days so tonight, he could focus on this surly opponent.

Riverson had folded early in this game, leaving Gallagher, Chandler, Brownlow, and David in the hand. Chandler was showing a pair of nines and he was betting as if his cards had a lot of strength. He met Gallagher's raise and tossed in another red chip—twenty pounds.

Brownlow was next. He paused, removed his glasses, and cleaned them with his handkerchief. David couldn't read much in his expression but that was a big clue in itself. When Brownlow had a good hand, he chattered away—Mr Jovial; less exuberance meant bad cards. He called Chandler's bet, but without enthusiasm.

David's turn again. He had a pair of tens, one of them in the hole along with an ace. With luck, it could turn into a hand he might stake some money on. But Gallagher had an ace showing and, watching him fidget, David suspected he had another one. If true, he'd be hard to beat.

"Fold," he announced, affecting disappointment. Now he could sit back and watch how Gallagher played the hand.

Gallagher's up-cards showed some strength. David was now sure he had the two aces but, having tracked the cards carefully, he was also sure that he didn't have more. Gallagher kept his eyes on his cards, rearranging them as though he couldn't decide which of a plethora of wonderful options he wanted to play. But he had failed to stifle a smile when David folded.

"My go?" asked Gallagher. He knew full well it was his play. This was another of his ploys; pretend you're a little green and having trouble following the status of play. David thought it unlikely that anyone at the table was taken in by it. Gallagher glanced at

Chandler and at Brownlow, the remaining players in the hand. Tossing two blue chips into the pot, he said, "I think I'm going to raise it another hundred?"

He put it as a question, as though he needed permission, another way to suggest inexperience. He was like a kid who'd eaten the whole pie—David was enjoying his performance.

Chandler, too, was feeling lucky, and trying to hide his enthusiasm for his cards. He pushed two blue chips into the pot, then added one more. "Call the hundred and raise fifty," he announced, a little too loudly.

"Crap!" said Brownlow, looking haggard. With a shrug, he threw his cards in and slumped back against the chair. "Damned cards! Don't know why I try."

"You're like me, Milton," said Chandler, smiling and smoothing his thinning hair with one hand. "Can't resist a wager, no matter how bad the odds."

David was pleased with tonight's pots—he had already pocketed one worth over £1,800. He was the only one at the table who really cared about this. For the others, these pots were loose change, of special interest only for what they would symbolize for the winner. For David, of course, they were crucial. The next pots would be higher still, maybe double, and he'd push it higher if he could, but even these guys began to get nervous when the raises bumped up towards £500.

A small gallery, mostly men but a few women as well, watched the play. Some sat at nearby tables but most stood, in the room's half light, in a rough semi-circle around the poker table, whispering to each other as the cards came out. Billy Pruitt was among them. He had lost a bundle when he sat in early in the voyage and, this time, he took the lesson to heart. He knew he was in over his head in this company. Plus, Charles Pierce and his sham mine had claimed a good chunk of Pruitt's spending money.

Only Gallagher and Chandler remained in this hand. "So, Mr Chandler, looks like all those corn flakes have made you a little reckless," Gallagher declared.

"No, Gallagher. Though I have many faults, recklessness is not among them." Chandler shifted in the chair. "And it's *wheat* flakes." Then he smiled coyly. "You know, all bluster and play acting aside, nothing succeeds in poker so well as a good hand."

"Well said, sir," he replied, his bluster undiminished. Again, he thumbed his reading glasses back into place. "Now with our nemesis, Mr. Bowen, out of the way for now, it's down to us, Nelson, and you're going to have to spend some more money to see these cards." He pushed in two more blue chips and turned a smug face toward Chandler.

"I thought you were more adventuresome than that, Mr Gallagher." The cereal purveyor took a moment to relight his pipe, producing a new cloud of blue smoke around his head. He pushed more chips in, matching Gallagher's bet and, pleased with himself, looked up at his adversary. "All done?" he asked, with an amused smile.

"Sure," Gallagher declared, laying his three hole cards next to the ones already showing on the table. "Flush," he announced. "Let's see what you have."

Chandler's face fell. He turned over his cards. A third nine in the hole gave him three of a kind, normally a pretty good hand. His face reddened; he'd been certain he would take this pot. "Damn!" He pushed his cards into the center of the table, as though they'd suddenly become contagious.

"Oh, don't take it too hard, Nelson," Gallagher laughed. "It's just money." He made a show of raking in the chips and stacking them. Again his face broke into a smile he couldn't suppress. He looked around quickly to see if anyone had noticed. The only eyes he did not find staring at him were David's.

"Did you hear?" Gallagher asked, trying to divert attention. "That mining engineer?"

Brownlow perked up. "That fellow who was so impressed with Charles Pierce's ore samples? Steffens, isn't it?"

"Yeah, that's him," said Gallagher. "Seems he killed himself." The table, as well as the gallery, erupted in shock. All except David, whose immediate reaction was suspicion.

"Suicide? You sure?" asked David. "Didn't he just put a chunk of money in that ore strike?"

"It's what the ship's officers say," answered Gallagher. "Hung himself. Drunk, apparently." He was putting the finishing touches on a stack of blue chips, making sure it was straight and tidy.

"What a shame," said Brownlow. "He seemed like a nice fellow."

David put two and two together and came up with Charles Pierce as the probable impetus for Steffens's "suicide." If he needed further grounds for his belief that Audrey was in danger, he now had them.

The players were settled in now and reduced to the core group. The pots had grown and, best of all for David, Gallagher was as lubricated as he was going to get, full of himself and certain he would be the night's big winner. All David needed were the cards to nail him with.

They came six games later. After several games in which he folded early to limit the damage, the cards in this new hand fell neatly into place. By the time the fifth card was out, David held a full house; three sixes and a pair of kings.

David, Chandler, and Gallagher were still in, and the pot stood at over £3,500. Riverson and Brownlow had bowed out early but Riverson, as dealer, was still running the deck. Sam Riverson had a high regard for good poker and good players, the way kids admired Mel Ott and Lou Gehrig. Unconcerned about his own wins and losses, he studied his tablemates and their styles of play as though they were the subjects of his dissertation.

Besides a pair of jacks, Gallagher had an ace showing, which gave him the lead bet. Riverson prompted him. "Your go, Mr. Gallagher.

David wasn't concerned much about Gallagher's ace—he knew the other three were in the dead pile. But he thought he might have a third jack, possibly a jacks-over-something full house, a hand that would win most poker games.

But David's hand was one of the best he'd seen in a while, the more so because its strength was hidden. His three up-cards, a king and two sixes, made it look unpromising but he had another king and another six in the hole. On 6th Street, the last up-card, he drew a three of hearts, perfect for the impression that he didn't have much. Still, what he did have wouldn't beat a full house with jacks on top, if that's what Gallagher was holding.

Characteristically, Gallagher bet as though the game was in the bag. He opened the round with another £40. Chandler matched him. David called, and raised 40. Eager to brandish the strength of his hand, Gallagher reached into his stack of chips. Without waiting for Riverson's prompt, he met the raise and threw in two blues. "Raise it another hundred. Any takers?"

Chandler hesitated, then matched Gallagher's raise.

Despite Gallagher's jacks, David wasn't ready to cede this game. He would not see a stronger hand tonight; he had to make these cards work. It wasn't certain that Gallagher had a winner. If he didn't have that third jack, David had him beaten. He matched the raise.

Then Riverson dealt the last cards, face down. When David lifted a corner of his, he found the King of Clubs winking up at him. He picked up the card, skewing down the corner of his mouth slightly as though he might have a toothache; the others would have been excused for thinking it was the last card he wanted to see. In fact, it made his full house in the other direction, kings over sixes, turning a strong hand into a powerhouse. Gallagher's jacks no longer concerned him.

They had pushed the pot to nearly £4,000. David stayed in by matching. As another betting round ended, Gallagher could hardly contain his excitement.

"More bets, gentlemen?" asked Riverson. He turned to Gallagher, still showing high. "Mr Gallagher?"

Again, Gallagher thumbed his glasses up the ridge of his nose. His cigar had gone out but he kept the stub clenched in the corner of his mouth. Then, as though they were nickels, he tossed in two more blue chips, accompanied by one of his smug faces, directed this time at Nelson Chandler.

"Your go, Mr Chandler. A hundred to stay," Riverson announced.

"Finally. Some real play," Gallagher spat, looking past his cigar stub at David. He was on his own little rampage, out for working-class blood.

David had seen similar dismissive behavior before, though it was a little odd for Gallagher, himself the product of the working class. His open disdain for David seemed to be a way of showing that his rough history was an anomaly, as if he'd been switched at birth. "What about it, Chandler? You staying in? Come on, help me run Bowen outta town."

Nelson Chandler cast a sidelong glance at Gallagher. He had no interest at all in such a proposition, and the steel monger was getting under his skin. He had one queen showing and one in the hole, and thought he had a fair chance this time. "Just for laughs, I'm gonna call the hundred..."

"Hot dog," Gallagher blurted. This *is* my lucky day. I..."

Chandler raised his voice to add, "...and I'm gonna push things up a notch." He pushed in another 400 pounds worth of chips.

Gallagher had been convinced that Chandler was finished. He jerked his gaze over to him, puzzled. David was surprised too. His reading of Chandler's cards didn't add up to such an aggressive bet. But he also knew Chandler was undisciplined and might just be going on crossed fingers.

"Whooop!" blurted Gallagher, "Now we're playing poker! What're you going to do, Bowen? You still in?"

David looked carefully again at Chandler's up-cards: a queen, a nine, and a pair of sevens. A possible high straight but the lack of any suit matches all but ruled out a straight flush. Only a straight flush or four-of-a-kind could beat David's cards and he doubted that Chandler had either one. Going over Chandler's betting in this round, it felt more mischievous than serious. He felt Chandler had stayed in to see how far he could go on the strength of two pair. He might even have a third queen but any way David analyzed it, nothing about Chandler's hand or his betting signaled a sure winner. He decided to keep to his strategy—he was certain he had the best hand there, by quite a bit.

Gallagher eyed David, unsmiling. A challenge, daring a working stiff to try staying in this game, and prepared to make it as expensive as possible. David was determined not to let his growing contempt for Gallagher show, or to rise to the tacit insult.

He looked back to the table and the cards he was holding. There was no question that he would call the bet. But could he get either man, particularly Gallagher, to come higher? More than £4,500 sat in the pot. Could he push it to £6,000?

"Yes, Mr. Gallagher, I'm still in." He met Chandler's raise and added 200, to set his hook more firmly in Gallagher's jaw.

"Good, good," said the steel baron. "I love it when the bushes rattle. Let me see..." He took another look at his hole cards and chewed on his cold cigar stub for a moment, then he brought out more blue chips. "How much is it, Bowen?" He knew how much the bet was but wanted David to restate it. David didn't respond. He let the silence underline the inanity of Gallagher's question.

Sam Riverson supplied the answer. "Two hundred to stay."

"Well that's just peachy," Gallagher declared. "Here's the two hundred, and two hundred more."

It was Chandler's turn to be stunned. He scanned Gallagher's up-cards again, recalculating the value of his own hand. Gallagher missed the cereal maker's hesitation; he had turned to David, with a smirk, prodding him to risk more.

Deflecting the challenge, David took the opportunity to take care of one of poker's courtesies. "You do remember that this has to be my last hand?" he said, glancing around the table. "I don't want to upset anyone when I have to leave without giving you more time to get even." He was not being coy. He was anxious about Audrey's safety. If she and Pierce were going to clash, he intended to be there.

Gallagher humphed, dismissing David's declaration, certain he was bluffing. He was irritated, exactly what David wanted.

Chandler's bet. He started to fidget. David's big raise made him realize he was probably in too deep. If he hadn't felt a need to stay the course to save some face, he would have folded. His tender was hesitant. "Uhh, I'll stay, uhh... plus fifty." His loss of confidence in his cards couldn't have been more palpable.

David smiled, pleased that Gallagher was going to be his main pigeon. He had worried whether the industrialist would be a challenge for him. Now he knew Gallagher was just another over-confident amateur, with bad behavior.

Time for the final push. Again, David studied the up-cards in front of his two opponents and, combined with his knowledge of the cards in the dead pile, he saw nothing to indicate a hand stronger than his own. The four-of-a-kind remained a possibility he couldn't rule out but, if probabilities, and his intuition, meant anything, neither of his opponents had it.

David leaned against the back of the chair and took a deep breath, letting the silence stretch out. He glanced from Gallagher to Chandler and back again, feigning uncertainty, careful not to let his optimism show. He examined his hand again, and checked Gallagher's and Chandler's up-cards—he was waiting for one of them to speak. The silence finally got to Gallagher. "Your bet, Bowen."

David looked up, reacting as though he'd been daydreaming. "Uhh... yes." He drew in a sharp breath and held it, then let it out in a long sigh and spoke haltingly. "I'm going to call your raise, Nelson, and I'll raise... five hundred."

As David pushed in the chips, his opponents stared at him, looking as though their faces had been slapped. David didn't look up for a long time. He kept his gaze on the tight little packet of cards in his hand, rearranging them as he dragged on his cigarette, and drained his glass of its rum-free rum and Coke.

The gallery had stilled. Only the strain of a saxophone solo, drifting in from the ballroom, pushed through the silence. Riverson looked at David with an appreciative smile. Milton Brownlow's mouth hung open, astonished at the sudden jump in the stakes. When the silence stretched to an unbearable length, David looked up and leveled his gaze at Gallagher. He spoke softly. "Is there a call?"

Gallagher let his eyes flicker up at David and then quickly and furtively away—his bravado had vanished. He glanced at Chandler, hoping to find help, and some way to make sense of David's wager. But Chandler was glum, vainly seeking salvation in his own cards.

Finally, clearing his throat, Gallagher had to call the bet. He might lose to David, this nobody he could buy wholesale, but he couldn't slink away with his tail between his legs. David read it all in Gallagher's expression, like a Pathé newsreel.

"Well..." Gallagher forced a smile and pushed in the chips—£550 worth. "I have to see what you have," he said flatly.

"Mr Chandler?" asked Riverson, after a beat.

Chandler examined his hand for another few seconds, then, irritated, he collected his up-cards and lobbed the hand into the dead pile. "I'm out."

David considered upping the wager again but it would have been an empty gesture. It was clear Gallagher was finished. He turned over his hole cards. "Full house, kings over sixes." A collective gasp came from the gallery; a man yelped, as though he'd been nipped by a dog. Someone began to clap but quickly caught himself.

David allowed himself a smile of satisfaction as he looked up squarely into Gallagher's face. Gallagher studied David's cards, no readable change in his expression. Then the merest flicker of a frown crossed his brow and he slumped back, letting out the long breath he'd been holding. Red faced, he turned his cards over. He did have a full house—three fives plus the two jacks—a costly and embarrassing bluff. David waited another beat before scooping in the chips. There were so many, he had trouble corralling them.

"Well, my friends," David said, standing. "Thank you very much for your company. It's been a pleasure playing with you these past few days and, I have to say..." smiling thinly, he looked directly at Gallagher, who's face was a mix of embarrassment and anger, "it's been an education."

That was all the consolation Gallagher would get. David did feel a little sorry for Chandler—he was an earnest guy just trying to improve his game. Like the others, he had ample wealth with which to fund those lessons.

As Brownlow converted chips into stacks of banknotes, David saw that he hadn't done too badly, considering the situation with Pierce. Still it annoyed him that Pierce's dubious bonanza had kept so many of the ship's moneyed men away from the poker table, particularly the profligate youngster, Billy Pruitt.

Then Chandler's voice intruded on his thinking. "I must say, David, you do seem to have a guardian angel sitting on your shoulder." David listened carefully for any hint of an accusation but he saw that Chandler was expressing genuine admiration. "You don't win every hand, not by any means, but damned if you don't win just about every time it really counts."

"Thank you, Nelson. I take that as a compliment. I do this for my living, as you know. When you do that..." he was careful to pitch this not as a lecture but as a simple statement of fact, "you acquire some level of skill..." He was arranging the bills Brownlow was stacking before him on the table. He paused and, with an edge to his voice, he spoke directly at Gallagher. "And you learn to be careful."

"Skill?" Gallagher blurted. "Skillful card playing, you mean...?" He took the cold stub of his cigar from his mouth and cleared his throat. "Is *that* what does it?" The gallery was thinning as people turned back to their drinking and seductions, nattering over the game's conclusion, but Gallagher's statement was loud and sharp enough to make them stop. They appeared to turn back on cue, alarmed, as if someone had suddenly brandished a pistol.

Gallagher fixed David with a look of open contempt, his mouth cocked into a sardonic smile. David returned his look, level, neutral, unblinking, as he quickly ran his alternatives through his mind. He would have enjoyed bloodying Gallagher's nose but a physical attack was out of the question. If he allowed himself that indulgence, he would be manacled and possibly prosecuted. If no one of Gallagher's social rank spoke up for David, he would be banished from the liners summarily—there was no court of justice he could appeal to. The decision would be made solely on Cunard's and White Star's concept of how best to protect their free spending first-class passengers, their exclusive catalogue of Michael Gallaghers. So whether Gallagher knew it or not, the accusation held a real threat for David. Although he intended to give up this way of life, David wasn't ready to burn those bridges yet.

Gallagher didn't feel confident enough to make a direct charge of cheating but doing it through innuendo, and publicly, did the same damage—David couldn't let the slur hang in the air unchallenged. His mind was racing. He had to force Gallagher either to make an open charge or back down, and he searched for the right words and tone. But as he took in a breath and started to speak, Chandler's voice cut through the pall.

"Aww, come off it, Gallagher. You should be ashamed. Don't you know when you've been beaten?"

Gallagher blanched. He snapped his head over and met Chandler's eyes, his mouth twisted in anger. "Shut up, Chandler!" he hissed. "I'm not talking to you!"

David couldn't have predicted what followed. In a quick move, Chandler bolted from his seat and bore in over Gallagher, who arched back in his chair, his eyes wide in surprise. Chandler now loomed over the man, one hand bearing on the table, the other on the back of Gallagher's chair. Although, by reputation, Gallagher would be picked as the scrapper in the group, it was clear that Chandler held no fear of him. And unlike Gallagher, Chandler was large and athletic, someone you wouldn't attack without thinking twice about it.

Gallagher tried to squirm out of his chair but Chandler was too close, Gallagher couldn't get his feet under him. Chandler bent closer; Gallagher slumped back into the seat. They were almost nose-to-nose—David braced for a punch that was sure to cause a major furor. There'd be hell to pay and he'd most likely end up doing the paying.

But instead, Chandler spoke, in a low, modulated tone that raised the hair on the back of David's neck. Both Riverson and Brownlow, who had risen to their feet, eased back into the gawking crowd of onlookers. "Mister Gallagher, I find your behavior unacceptable. When you sit down to a game of poker, you bring your honor as a gentleman with you, and if you know what the hell you're doing, you know within minutes whether your table mates have done the same." Gallagher was turned at an awkward angle in his chair, trying at the same time to meet Chandler's gaze and to edge away from his overbearing presence. He couldn't have been at a greater physical disadvantage. He tried to respond but could only manage an inarticulate splutter. Chandler cut him off.

"I've played poker with Mr. Bowen for several nights, now. One thing I know for sure, he's no cheater."

"No, I... I didn't mean..."

"Yes! Yes, you did."

"Well I...

"You've been beaten, Gallagher, by a better player. That's the long and short of it." Still hovering over the man, Chandler let the statement hang in the air for a few tense seconds. "Do you have anything else to say?"

Gallagher shook his head, and Chandler backed away a foot or so, enough to allow Gallagher to rise awkwardly. He struggled to his feet, grabbed his coat from the chair, and retreated a few steps in the direction of the salon. He cared nothing for David's feelings, of course, but having been taken down by the cereal mogul, he was eager to reclaim a semblance of lost dignity. "I'm sorry, Bowen. Really, I, uh... I didn't mean to..." He glanced at Chandler, whose expression made it clear he was not going to allow Gallagher to temporize. "I'm... look, I'm sorry, Bowen. Truly."

David straightened and nodded to him, "It's all right," he lied. "No offense taken."

Gallagher spun around and scurried toward the lounge, pulling his jacket on as he went. He still had his accountant's cuffs on his sleeves.

With the tension ramping down, the gallery dissipated. Brownlow eased back to the table. "Good show, Nelson," he said, admiringly. "I must say I find him difficult to like." Riverson grunted his agreement.

David turned to Chandler. "Thanks, Nelson. Thanks very much."

Chandler waved him off as he re-loaded his pipe. "I hate it when a fella can't lose like a gentleman." He packed the pipe's bowl with his silver tool. "I think it may be the best way to judge a man's character, how he handles himself at cards."

David nodded. He realized that he believed that too. He looked at Chandler, who had just lit his pipe, creating a bloom of smoke around his head. "You know, I believe you're right." He thrust his hand toward Chandler, who shook it with his firm, assured grip. The two smiled at each other before turning their eyes back to the battleground of the table, where Milton Brownlow had resumed the conversion of David's chips into cash.

David wanted to pause and savor his victory but his thoughts now turned to Audrey. He was certain Pierce was wrapping up his scheme around this time and if he planned to silence her, he'd soon be putting that plan into action. David would not let her face that alone.

XXXVII

CHARLES AND AUDREY STOOD arguing near the starboard rail, above the fantail at the aft end of the Promenade. The ship pushed forward through a faint pall of fog—the air was heavy and wet, and tasted faintly of salt. Audrey held a wrap around her shoulders; Charles was still in his tuxedo. A small lamp high on the superstructure lit the area dimly, mixing its light with a pale glow from a half moon that hung low in the sky.

Audrey paced. Every so often, her voice rose in anger and frustration. Charles chuckled derisively at her irritation. "Don't be ridiculous, my girl. Why would I even think of giving you that kind of money? Have you lost your senses?"

"Don't patronize me, you... thief. We'll see if you're ready to have your... your nasty scheme made public."

Charles eyed her at some length. The lamp overhead shadowed her face but there was light enough to read her expression—he did not like what he saw. Her jaw was set, her head cocked at a challenging angle as she stopped and placed a defiant fist on one hip.

He met her challenge with a disarming smile. "Forgive me, Audrey. You're right—we should treat each other as equals." He paused and lit a cigarette, using the interruption to rethink his plans for her. A long drag made the end of the cigarette glow bright red. "By the way, when I confronted your friend, Mr Bascomb, we had a fascinating little chat. He told me something quite surprising."

A twinge of fear clutched at her but she held on to her sense of indignation. "Friend?", she huffed. "He's certainly no friend of *mine*. What nonsense did he tell you?"

"He shared with me his suspicion that you are masquerading—that in fact, you're a Negro. Could that be true?"

She tried to see in his expression whether he believed it but as always, Charles's face revealed very little. "It's what he was saying—shouting—when he attacked me. Seemed to be his excuse."

"But is it true? Is that the secret behind your, uh... appeal?"

She hesitated. "Would it make a difference?"

Pulling on his cigarette, he thought for a moment. "I don't know—perhaps not, though I dislike being misled. Mostly, I'm curious."

"Misled?" she said. The implied accusation seemed to harbor several levels of irony. She looked past him into the black night, thinking, then drew her eyes back to his face, and raised the cant of her chin. "Martin Bascomb is wrong about many things but this time, he got it right. People like him like to make up funny names for people like me: quadroon, or octoroon, or something equally as stupid." He had glanced away—she waited until he was again focused on her. "Yes, there *is* Negro blood in my background—I'm not ashamed of it. And I don't accept that you've been misled."

She was surprised by her own boldness. Somehow, revealing the truth about her race strengthened her—it freed her and, though she felt some sense of fear, it was mixed with determination. Up till now, Charles had been her puppet master and she still found him intimidating. And she had never before dared to challenge a man in a position of power and authority over her. But she was determined to exert her will now, and was not going to let her black ancestry stop her. She had never let anyone call her tune, not even her mother, and she was not going to start with Charles Pierce.

Charles sensed the change in her—he flicked his cigarette into the sea. "I see you are resolved. Forgive me for underestimating you. Come, let's be friends." He took a step toward her, offering his hand. She hesitated. Despite her fears, she had convinced herself that making Charles back down would only require her to meet his force with force of her own. The strategy now seemed to be working; she was pleased with herself.

She extended her hand. He took it and she suddenly felt as if it were trapped in a vice. Charles yanked her in to him, spinning her so that he now embraced her tightly from behind. What's this?, she thought. Did *he* intend to rape her?!

Sputtering, she struggled to break away but Charles lifted her off her feet. Fear clutched at her when, in the next instant, he carried her toward the rail and the black water beyond. She grasped the rail with all her strength, screaming as loudly as she could. "What are you doing!? Let go of me!"

Now certain of his intent, she fought to free herself, struggling and kicking against his strength. Twisting around, she strained, in the faint light, to look into his face. His expression told her she would have to fight with everything she had. No emotion showed in his eyes, no sympathy she could appeal to. He didn't look at her, and didn't speak. He concentrated on her fingers, working to peel them off the rail with one hand while he maintained his hold around her waist. He hadn't expected such strength in her small body.

It was the strength of desperation. Audrey yelled for help but she knew how hopeless it was. Those who were still up at this late hour were either too far away, too involved in partying, or simply too smashed to hear her, no matter how loud her cries. And she had no chance against Charles's strength, regardless of how fiercely she resisted. She was utterly alone. Still she kicked and scratched at him, while cursing the biological whim that put her at so great a physical disadvantage against men.

She was tiring. One by one, Charles peeled her fingers off the rail while lifting her body higher, setting himself to loft her weight up and out over the water. As Charles pried one hand free, she gathered her strength for one last scream, certain she wouldn't have another chance. Then a voice cut through the darkness.

"Pierce! Pierce!!" Louder, then louder still. "Enough!!!" David came out of the shadows and stopped a dozen feet away.

Charles froze at the sound of David's voice. He was facing toward the sea, Audrey's body between him and the rail, and it took him an instant to identify the voice. Relaxing his grip on Audrey, he turned. David stood outlined in the weak light, his hands at his sides. Charles pushed Audrey away and bent to charge but, as he was about to spring, David brought his hand up and the silhouette of a long-barreled revolver pulled Charles up short. David leveled the gun at Charles's belly.

"Audrey," David called, holding out his hand. She took a step toward David but stopped and aimed a kick at Charles's shin. "Bastard!" She was on target.

"Aghhh!" Charles grabbed his leg and danced on one foot. "You ungrateful little..."

"Oh," she cried, mocking him. "I'm so-o-o-o grateful for your attempts to teach me how to cheat and lie—oh, yes, and how to swim. Yes, thank you!" She kicked at him again but he deflected this one. Barely able to contain her rage, Audrey moved next to David.

After a moment, Charles stopped attending to his leg and stood to full height. Putting his façade back in order, he straightened his jacket and patted at the wrinkles, and combed his fingers through his hair. "So, Bowen. More meddling. I'm getting rather fed up with it."

"Meddling? As you attempt to clear your slate—is that what you call it? I've tried to keep out of your way, Pierce, but when it comes to Audrey—as I told you earlier—I'm far from indifferent."

"So, what do you propose to do now?" Charles challenged, tilting his chin up and looking down his nose at them.

"I think we should go and have a talk with the captain. How's that sound?" David waved the gun barrel as an invitation for Charles to walk in the direction of the bridge.

Charles's laugh was forced. "And tell him what, old man? That you... stumbled upon us..." a wave of the hand paired him with Audrey, "in an argument over business, and that in your stupidity, you mistook it for an assault and began waving that silly weapon around?"

David couldn't resist a chuckle of admiration at Charles's chutzpah. "Argument. Do you always settle your arguments by flinging your opponents over the rail? Or perhaps the argument was over how fast the lady can swim—a bet on whether she could keep up with the ship?"

David had unconsciously allowed the gun barrel to droop, but when Charles reached toward his jacket pocket, he brought it back to bear. Charles hesitated, eyes fixed on David's; he sensed that David would welcome an excuse to put a hole in him. He continued, slowly, to reach into the pocket and withdrew his cigarette case. Methodically, he extracted one and lit up. He offered one to Audrey and to David; they both refused. Then he leaned back against the rail and, the soul of equanimity, exhaled a stream of smoke into the light breeze. "Again, what is our... or I should say, your, next step?"

"Look, Pierce, drop it. I'm on to your scheme, in all its particulars."

"You're not making a lot of sense here, Bowen, trying to play tough with that popgun." Taking another long drag, he cast a disdainful look at Audrey before turning his attention back to David. "You've seen too many American gangster films. Perhaps you'll skip the theatrics and tell me exactly what you mean."

"I hardly need to tell *you* all this, but I'll state it for Audrey's sake. She does have a right to know why you tried to kill her. So, here it is. There is no mine. You are no miner or mining engineer or any other such thing."

Audrey had turned to look at Charles as the tally of deception lengthened. Assured that she was all right, David took a couple of steps toward Charles and continued.

"And you murdered that poor fellow found hanging in his cabin the other night."

Audrey reacted in shock. "Murdered?! He was murdered?!"

"That's my thesis," answered David. "I haven't worked out how killing him fits into Pierce's scheme, although my guess is the man pushed too hard for a share of the take." He turned back to Charles. "And you intend to abscond with all that money—tonight."

Charles broke into a laugh. The very soul of self-assuredness, he took yet another unhurried pull on his cigarette. "You're imagination has got the better of you, old man. It's a fascinating story, though. Is that all?"

"Not quite. My guess is Audrey finally accepted the truth of what I've been telling her and confronted you with it. If you had not already planned to kill her, you decided it was too dangerous and inconvenient—not to mention, expensive—for her to remain alive."

Charles laughed again, the smile on his mouth clashing with the coldness in his eyes. "This is amusing. And I have to admit, it even sounds logical—I can see how you might have come to believe it. But don't you see, Bowen, even if the rest were true, the part about absconding—quite crucial to your theory—is totally fanciful." He swept an arm around the horizon, invisible in the dark. "We're in the middle of the Atlantic, old man." He affected a smile of triumph.

David crossed his arms, keeping the pistol visible. He glanced at Audrey, who had inched closer to him and was evaluating what Charles had said. "Pierce, you make the mistake of underestimating people—typical of men like you, and fatal in the con. As you know very well, the coast of France is only a few miles off the starboard rail." David gestured with the gun toward the unseen coastline over Charles's shoulder. "And unless I'm mistaken, that blinking red light, off to your right, is your contact, in a launch, here to pick you up."

Dropping his calm pose, Charles wheeled and looked out to sea. A dim red light, off the bow, blinked in short bursts, stopped, then repeated the pattern. David turned his attention to Audrey, looping his free arm across her shoulder and drawing her close. They smiled at each other for a long moment. Charles took advantage, bolting toward the dark side of the ship.

"Stop!" David yelled. He raised the gun and got off a shot.

Audrey grabbed at his arm. "David! Stop! You can't shoot at people like that! My God, did you hit him?!"

"Don't worry, darling. I'm a very good shot—it's the other thing I did at college. If I wanted to, I could easily have put a slug in his backside, even in this light."

He turned to face her. "Listen. I want you to go up forward and stash yourself in that little cocktail lounge. You know the one I mean?"

She nodded.

"I have to follow Charles and make sure he goes overboard."

"What?! I thought you wanted to take him to the captain!"

"Actually, no. No, that's the last thing I want. I'll explain it all when I get back. I won't be long." He started away, but stopped and turned back. "Stay away from your berth for a half hour or so—things could get a little dicey. And you may hear another shot or two. Don't worry, I won't hit him."

David took off running in the direction Charles had taken. The berth was about halfway between the bow and stern, a distance of about 150 yards. He wanted to drive Charles aft, so he ran to the forward end of the superstructure before entering the cabin section and took the stairs down to A Deck, two at a time.

He slowed as he approached the dim passageway leading to the rooms. Peering around the corner, he was in time to see Charles emerge from his berth, 100 feet away, dressed now in bulky, foul weather clothes and carrying a duffle. Charles's head was down as he walked briskly in David's direction, poking his hands into his pockets, arranging his clothing. David stepped into the passageway and stood so his pistol was silhouetted. "Pierce"!

Charles looked up. Without skipping a beat, he spun and sprinted away in the opposite direction.

"Hold it!" David tried to sound convincing as an enforcer. Charles stopped and looked back as he reached the cross passage at the far end but instead of running out, as David expected, he raised his free hand and David saw the gun. Before he could react, he saw the muzzle flash, an instant before the bullet cracked into the paneling above his head. He ducked, and Charles disappeared around the corner, toward the starboard stairwell.

David hadn't anticipated facing another gun. From its sound, he knew it was of a small caliber but that didn't mean it was harmless. He raced down the passageway and followed Charles's course up the stairwell and out to the starboard rail on the Promenade Deck. The weak moonlight, along with Charles's dark clothing, made him into an apparition, a dark figure against an inky blackness, running aft in the partially enclosed Promenade. As he followed, David glanced seaward and saw the red signal lights still flashing, but closer now.

He reached the end of the Promenade, exactly where Charles and Audrey had struggled moments before. The fantail was one level below, down a broad flight of stairs and Charles now stood at the rail there, thirty yards away, cinching the seal of his duffle bag. David brought his pistol up and laid the sights just off Charles's back.

"Pierce!" he shouted. Charles spun and fired wildly in David's direction. David wasn't even sure Charles could see him in the gloom; the bullet pinged off the ship's superstructure, well over his head.

David steadied his arm on the rail, held his breath, and squeezed the trigger, putting his shot close enough to Charles's ear that the snap of the bullet would make him doubt he would survive another one. Charles clambered over the rail, slung his duffle overboard, and followed it into the black water.

XXXVIII

LEANING ON THE RAIL where Audrey and Charles had struggled, David watched the motor launch dissolve into the darkness and the enveloping fog, and smiled, knowing that Charles Pierce, cold and soaking wet, was on it. But he didn't get much time to enjoy the moment. The sound of running feet and raised voices grabbed his attention. A ship's officer and a seaman emerged from a passageway. The officer carried a flashlight and splayed its beam around the deck. When the beam found David, the men hurried up to him. The sailor turned out to be Benny; David had seen the officer around the ship but didn't know his name.

"Oh. Bowen, it's you," said Benny.

"Hi, Benny," said David. He nodded a greeting at the officer. "I think I know why you're here."

"We got a report of shots fired," said the officer, a little out of breath. "Did you see anything?"

David had tucked his pistol inside his cummerbund at his hip but he was afraid it wouldn't stay put if he moved. He pressed against the rail to keep it in place and hoped his stance didn't seem too odd.

He drew out his cigarette case. "Yes. I was down the rail there, well forward, and thought I heard what might have been shots from around here. I came to look but I didn't find anyone. Are you sure it was gun shots?"

"Can't say we are," said the officer. "Seems unlikely, but..."

"Cigarette?" He took one and offered the open case to the two men. "Could it have been something else? Maybe something breaking on deck?"

"I suppose." The officer swung his torchlight around the area, searching aimlessly. "I don't see anything right off. It'll have to wait until morning. For now, I guess it's just a note in the log."

"Well, we're still afloat." David's lighter sparked and he lit the three cigarettes. "I suppose that's the important thing."

"Indeed," said the officer, sucking on the cigarette. "Thanks. Let me know if you see anything."

"G'night, Bowen," said Benny. Chattering, the men hurried toward the bow and turned into the passageway they'd appeared from.

David shifted his position and cinched the cummerbund tighter against the pistol. He pulled on his cigarette and took stock. His main opponent was over the side and motoring toward France. A few more things to go right and he could make a major change in his life. And with a little more luck, Audrey would be there to share it with him.

XXXIX

AUDREY DIDN'T KNOW whether she welcomed the knock on the door or not. It would be David, of course, and she wasn't sure if she wanted to see him right now. She was having difficulty sorting things out, especially the question of whether David was any different from the other hustlers on this floating pleasure palace. Was it possible that he was the worst of the lot?

The knock came again; she couldn't ignore it. She went to the door and opened it. David ducked through, smiling, eager.

In one motion, he shut the door and wrapped his arms her around her waist, and pulled her to him. "I was afraid you weren't here—I couldn't imagine..."

"What do you think you're doing?" she cried. "Let go!" She pushed hard against him and he understood she was serious. Dismayed, he released his grip and she slid away. He had looked forward to her embrace and all that it would mean. He felt he had earned this prize—a profound disappointment swept over him.

"Audrey, what's wrong? I thought, after..."

"After what? After you played your tricks on Charles and on me as well, you thought I'd let you do whatever you want with me. Is that what you think of me?"

"Audrey, why are you talking to me like this? Haven't I... My God, Audrey, I... I love you." He stepped closer and looked into her eyes—they were wide in surprise. Softly, he said, "Did you hear me? I love you. I want to care for you. I want us to be... together, for the rest of our lives. Don't you know that? I thought you wanted that, too—I *hoped* you did."

She hadn't expected such a straightforward statement. And he didn't stumble and stutter, as he so often did. His earnestness touched her. She looked at him, searching for the essence of this David Bowen. She stepped away, not speaking, her emotions in turmoil.

"Audrey, listen. Don't you know what happened out there just now?"

She spun and turned her frustration on him. "You chased Charles away—with a gun! Did you shoot him? You don't expect me to make my life with someone like that, do you? A gunman!?" She turned again and moved further away. "What's happened to Charles? Did you kill him?"

"What?! No. Of course not!" He threw up his hands, completely perplexed. "You really can be pigheaded!"

"Thank you, David Bowen. Do all your women appreciate your calling them by such affectionate names?"

This made him angrier. He faced her squarely, hands on hips. "Let me see where I've gone wrong. From the very beginning, I've been telling you I distrusted Pierce. You resisted the notion because of the 'good' treatment you had at his hands. Little by little, you came to understand that his work here on this ship is as close to mining as... as ballet dancing.

"What happened then? I couldn't hear everything out on deck but it sounded like you were trying to bargain with him—threatening to expose him?" He cocked his head and examined her face. She gave a telling motion of her head.

"Yeah. I was afraid of that. That's why I kept an eye on you tonight, and why I brought my pistol along. As I told you before, using you in his scheme without letting you in on it meant he was likely to want to... silence you. Charles Pierce doesn't like partners, as that man Steffens discovered.

"Oh, he..."

"So when you tried to extort some of the take from him, to all intents, you put a gun to your own head."

She was flustered. Seeing this side of David— worldly, cynical—blurred the sweet memory of how he had saved her earlier.

Still miffed, he went on. "So I follow you two out on deck and, sure enough, Pierce tries to toss you into the drink. I stop him and chase him off. Then I come here, hoping for a little, uhh, recognition, expecting a certain level of... of gratitude, I admit, and what happens? You treat me as if I'm a criminal, as if... goddammit, as if *I* were Charles Pierce!"

"Oh, David!" She collapsed onto the bed, crying, and buried her face in the coverlet. David let her cry for a few moments, then he went and sat next to her. He was still peeved but, at the same time, all he wanted was to hold her, and for her to seek the comfort of his arms.

"Dry your eyes," he said softly. "I've something to tell you."

She pulled herself together and sat up. "I'm sorry, David, I..."

"No. Not another word. Ready to listen?"

She nodded.

"OK. Best of all, for now at least, we're rid of Charles Pierce."

"'Rid' of him?" She stiffened. "You *did* kill him!?"

"No!" he retorted, exasperated.

"What then?! Tell me!" She was angry again, feeling duped.

"Stop it!" he demanded. "I chased him off the ship!"

"You mean... you purposely...?"

"Of course, purposely. What was I going to do, let him stay onboard and have another go at you?"

"But you've *killed* him!"

"No! Look, don't you remember those flashing lights?"

She thought for a moment. "I know you said they were there. I never really saw them. What lights. What about them?"

"A reddish light—off the beam. Flashing a signal. That was Pierce's accomplice. He intended all along to go over the rail after he collected all his money from the scam. Remember? I told you that had to be his plan, after feeding you to the sharks first. His partner picked him up within minutes of him hitting the water; they're chugging toward the French coast right now. I don't suppose they've realized it yet but they're missing what they came for."

Audrey sprang to her feet, agitated. "You are maddening! Stop talking in riddles and tell me what's happened! What are they missing?"

"The loot. The bonanza. The satchel with all the money in it."

"Charles wouldn't leave his money behind."

"Not knowingly—that's true." He smiled, coyly.

She studied him. "I suppose you have it."

"You suppose correctly, my love. Pierce was in too much of a hurry dodging bullets to check his bag before making his exit. That's exactly what I wanted, and that and only that is why I sent a few rounds in his direction. I had already swapped the bag for one just like it."

"You're so smug. You're like the little boy who's stolen the pie off the window sill." She bit her lip and turned away from him, upset by this man who had just pledged his love to her. "What *does* he have?"

"I gave him a couple of pairs of shoes—nice shoes, though. Plus a pound or so of salt from the galley—you know, to make the weight right." An impish smile animated his face.

Audrey plunked down on the bench at the foot of the bed. "So now you've stolen from Charles and taken all that other money..."

David scooted forward. "Now here's what I'm thinking. You and I get off this ship and go get ourselves married, and then we go down to Cornwall and put a healthy down payment on a wonderful piece of land I have on hold there. And then we..."

"Wait!" She held up her hand; David's patter lurched to a halt. "Did I hear you say something about getting married?"

"Well... yes. Yes, of course. That's what people do, you know, when they love each other. You've heard of it, haven't you?" Grinning slyly, he edged closer to her, but she slid back, restoring the distance between them.

"I must have been sleepwalking... because I don't remember agreeing to marry you."

"Well, no, you haven't agreed. Not exactly. Not yet. Maybe I..." He slid off the bench onto one knee. "Audrey, look. I've been head over heels for you since the moment I first saw you, when you came up the gangway last Tuesday.

He softened his voice and leaned closer. "You know, since I've been working these ships, I've seen a thousand girls; some of them beautiful, stunning. Then later, I talk with them, and I find they're either vapid or cruel, or so self-centered there's no room at all for anyone else. Before I know it, I'm looking for an excuse to get away before I collapse from boredom.

"That didn't happen with you. And somehow I knew it wouldn't. Something about you, when you first came on the ship, sashaying arm-in-arm with Mr Charles, 16-to-the-ton Pierce, something told me you were pure gold—the real McCoy. Now that I know you, I know that first impression was right. You *are* the real thing, and I want to have you in my life, for the rest of my life."

His intensity was more than she could bear. "David, I..."

"Audrey, I'm being as honest with you as I know how. I love you. I want you to be my wife. I'm here on my knees so you'll know I mean it, and... and I feel my heart's about to split wide open." He moved closer. His eyes moistened and his voice went hoarse. He stopped to get a lung full of air. "Audrey. Will you marry me?"

His plea was earnest and open, utterly sincere, completely vulnerable. She dropped her gaze to the handkerchief she was unconsciously wringing in her hands. She didn't know what to say. She wanted to put her arms around him; she wanted him to hold her. But she felt it would be unfair to him. She thought she loved David, but David was a gambler. A part of her equated that with cheat, with ne'er-do-well, possibly with violator. None of that applied to him as far as she could tell but she'd been taught to think that way. And now, after all this nasty business with Charles, and gunshots, and phony mines, her feelings were muddled.

And something important remained, something David didn't know about her. She thought of her mother, standing in the family kitchen back home, rolling out the dough for one of her delicious pies. Her hard-working, sainted mother, who could quote chapter and verse from the King James. And there she is, Audrey, introducing David as her new husband. David, gambler and... what was the term...? Hustler! The disappointment she imagined on her mother's face crushed her soul.

Two wealthy men on this ship had essentially proposed marriage to her. Most likely neither of them had been serious but even if they were, she didn't want them. They were weak, protected, arrogant. One, a tall man, actually went around with his chin held strangely high so he literally did look down his nose at others. David was real and fresh and... exciting. And a gambler. And white.

"Please, David. Give me time. I don't know what I want right now. I had no thought of marriage when I started this trip. I accepted Charles's offer because it was a way to get to London and Paris and the fashion world. You *have to* let me think about it."

He sat back, trying not to show his disappointment. "Of course, darling. I won't rush you. But will you come off with me and let me show you the farm? It's unbelievably beautiful—plenty of room for sewing machines." He smiled puckishly at his joke.

"I don't know. I..."

"Audrey! Everything has changed! Your deal with Pierce is out the window—he tried to kill you. He's gone now but he's still out there somewhere. And you're alone."

She looked down at her hands as she rolled this uncomfortable thought around in her head. Alone. It made her shiver. Her mind rushed back to her struggle with Charles at the ship's rail, to the terror she felt when she realized he intended to drop her into the water and how desperately alone she felt as she fought him. She never wanted to feel that way, ever again. She looked into David's eager face. "Yes. I'll go with you. Just to look."

A wide smile swept over his face he took her hands in his. "Wonderful. Just wonderful!" Still on his knees, he leaned forward and embraced her. They indulged in a series of lingering, delicious kisses and all the good feelings she had toward David coursed through her. She returned his embraces and surrendered to his. Her arms circled him inside his coat and she could feel his muscled back through the fabric of his shirt—she wanted to wish the shirt away and touch his bare skin. She felt completely open to him. If he began to undress her now, she would put up no resistance, she would help him. And part of her very much wanted him to undress her. But she couldn't maintain her hold on these sweet feelings; harsher feelings disturbed them, feelings she could not keep at bay. With David's proposal, her secret had forced its way to the front of her mind and she had to deal with it.

Was she demented? She couldn't let David take her to his farm, to his dream home, expecting she would become his wife. Not as things stood now. Did she love him? She wasn't sure. She thought probably she did; she wished she didn't have to ask that question. Her dreams of a life in fashion in London or Paris never included marriage, being tied to a man, to children. For heaven's sake—why had this happened?! Why had David come along now, when her life was finally moving along just the right route?

Oh, she *did* love him—of course she did. But she couldn't say she would marry him, not now; that wasn't on her horizon. Most important, she needed to know whether his love was strong enough to overcome the problems her heritage would surely create for him.

She realized he was chattering at her.

"...so I think we're ready for the final move. Getting off the ship without Pierce seeing us is going to be difficult but I think we can manage it. I..."

She stopped him, putting her fingers to his lips. "David, there's something we have to talk about... something you need to know about me."

Audrey, darling, we're really pressed for time. Can it wait 'til..."

"No! No, it cannot wait."

With a sigh, he rose from his knees and sat on a chair next to her bureau. He focused his attention on her and tried not to look anxious.

"You asked me to marry you," she said, as though he needed reminding.

"Yes, I did. Is that what this is about? Are you saying you'll..."

"No. I'm not saying that. I'm not saying no, either. I told you I want time to think and I still do."

She needed to put some physical distance between them; she paced to the opposite wall. "I think I may love you, David, but I'm not sure. Even if I did, I'm not sure I could marry you, since all you want to do is raise sheep. But there's something important we have to sort out first. You're doing all this planning and plotting and it's all based on the assumption that we'll be together."

"It sure is. I'd do anything to make that happen."

His earnestness was beguiling. She was profoundly sad to crush it with something that might ruin their chances for a future together. But she had no choice.

"Well, that's the problem. I don't know if you'll still want to when you hear what I have tell you."

He sat forward. "Well, tell me then. I can't imagine it'll make any difference but let's see. What is it? Babies? How many have you murdered?" Putting on a comic face, he mimed the action of strangling a small neck.

She liked that he always looked for the humor in things. She wanted to laugh but this was too serious. He was seated next to the bureau—she went to it and opened a drawer, and took out a package. She unwrapped it and withdrew a cluster of black-and-white photos, portraits and small groups, some framed, others not, and arranged them on the bureau's top.

David watched as she lined them up. Their subjects all seemed dark-skinned and foreign. "Who are these funny people?" he asked.

He picked up one picture in a thin, hammered silver frame, and turned it in the light. The photo, in black & white, showed a tall, brown-skinned man dressed in a morning coat and bowler, carrying a medical bag and standing next to a horse and buggy. He was slender, with wooly white hair, closely cropped.

"Who's this?" David asked. The man in the photo was looking directly into the lens and his expression, shaded from the sun under the bowler's brim, was direct, serious, a man whose dignity was a chip on his shoulder.

"That's Emanuel Simmons. Dr Simmons. He was my father."

David's face showed no reaction—Audrey wasn't sure he had heard her. She picked up another photo and pushed it toward him. It was of a tan-skinned woman with strong Indian features, her gray-flecked hair in two thick braids wrapped around her head. Her round, chubby face could not hide her prominent cheekbones. "This is Sarah Waltrice, my grandmother."

A look of disbelief spread across David's face. He blinked several times, as if to clear his vision, and his mouth hung open. Still seated, he looked up at Audrey, then back at the pictures, then back again at her, struggling to find her likeness in them.

"Audrey, is this a joke? If it is, it's not a very good one. This can't be..."

"It's not a joke, David!" she said, with a tinge of irritation. "These are pictures of my family. I know I *look* white but I'm not. I'm a Negro, and part white and

Indian, too." She thrust another picture at him. "This is my mother and my two brothers." The stiff-backed, unframed picture showed a handsome, elegant woman in a long gown, seated in a photographer's studio tableau, complete with brocaded drapery and a stuffed peacock. Her complexion was light but other features, her frizzy hair, full lips, her cheekbones, marked her as Negro. Behind her stood three young people; two bright-eyed, swarthy, teenaged lads, and between them, Audrey, fair-skinned, a little older than the boys, a little more mature, with a faint, knowing smile on her lips. The facial structure of the boys made them easily recognizable as Audrey's kin, despite their darker skins.

One picture was of a Caucasian man, gaunt, bearded, pale, with long gray hair, in a suit coat and vest and a western hat. He stared into the lens with apprehension, as though the camera might bite him. He looked ghost-like next to the others, with their richly toned skins. "This is my grandfather on my mother's side. He was Scotch-Irish."

She looked into David's face, not knowing what she expected to find there. Horror? Disgust? All she could identify was confusion. She laid a hand on his shoulder. "If we were to marry, David, these would be your in-laws. You'd be sitting down to eat with them at Thanksgiving and Christmas. Our children could look like any one of them."

David slumped forward, dropping his elbows on his knees, and buried his face in his hands. He sat like that for a long time, breathing deeply, saying nothing. Finally he looked up at her. "I don't... you're living a lie. Everybody believes you're white. It's... it's so..."

"It's what, David?" Her tone was sharp. "What name do you want to put on it? Do I deserve to be beaten... or lynched, maybe? Is that what you would like to do to me now?"

He recoiled. "No, Audrey. No, I don't, but... why did you... how can you live like this? I don't understand..."

"I had no choice. Not if I wanted a career in fashion in the U.S. I assume you're aware that Negroes in America don't have full rights. We're not allowed an equal chance at jobs... or an education. We're expected to clean, labor, and serve, but never to advance, never to excel. Did you know that?" He looked away, embarrassed by the implication in her question. He never thought about the discrimination colored people automatically dealt with every day.

Audrey went on. "Ads for jobs as clerks or secretaries, accountants, lawyers, black people aren't expected to apply for them. It's assumed we're not qualified. And the education system tends to ensure that we won't be. Offers for an apartment... they come right out and say 'White Only,' or 'No Colored,' or if they don't want to be too crass, 'Restricted.' Whites only want to see us when there's some mess to clean up.

"Well I want to work in fashion, to design clothes—I'm good at it." She picked up the photo of Emmanuel Simmons and held it up to him. "How far do you think I would get in the States if I let on that this was my father?"

David couldn't take it all in. "We're not given an equal chance..." she had said! "We"! She meant the people everyone looked down on! Everyone bad-mouthed them, everyone called them vile names! How could his beautiful, perfect Audrey define herself as one of them? It was impossible, profoundly confusing—he could hardly stand to hold the notion in his head. He took the photo of Emmanuel Simmons from her and looked at it closely.

"Your father. He's a doctor?!" The idea that a Negro might be a doctor—or would ever see a doctor—had never entered his head.

"Yes, David, he was. A family doctor in Baltimore, where I grew up. Ironically, if you manage to overcome all the restrictions, all the obstacles, you can be a professional, a doctor or a dentist. Then you have a monopoly on all the black patients. So a black doctor in Baltimore is automatically a successful, fairly well-to-do man. Yes, he was a doctor. Still, every week or so, some raggedy white man, usually drunk, would call him a... well, you know the word."

David looked away. Yes, he knew the word. He knew guys who used it a lot. He didn't like it but he never really objected when they started in. Now Audrey was saying that she felt scarred by that word and the mindless hate behind it, that it was personal.

He tried to recall his own encounters with blacks. Had he treated them well? With respect? Had he seen them as human beings? Had he seen them at all? Or had he treated them the way most people he knew did, the way Audrey had described? He thought his own record was not very commendable.

His thoughts shifted to their current situation. "What about Pierce? Does he know?"

"He didn't. But that... cretin, Martin Bascomb, somehow figured it out and told him. Bascomb's rare. Most white people never cotton on."

She moved to the bed and sat. "But that's not the issue, is it? The important question now, David, is about you. A few minutes ago, you said you wanted to marry me."

He was dazed, as though she had punched him. Looking at her now, he saw a stranger—someone he was seeing for the first time. He didn't really know what to feel. He didn't know who she was or what her presence in his life might mean now.

He rose and looked around the room, avoiding Audrey's eyes, uncertain what to do next. He walked to the door. As he reached for the handle, he turned to her. "It's my turn to think. This is all very new to me." He looked at his wristwatch. "We're so short of time. I wish you'd told me sooner."

"David, I never thought it would come to this. A relationship? Marriage? They were the furthest things from my mind when I boarded this ship."

David nodded distractedly, gnawing at his lip. "I'll be back," he said flatly. He pulled the door open and shut it behind him.

Audrey slumped against the bedhead, drained. A deep sadness enveloped her. She thought of her mother and of her family, Jessie and Daniel, her brothers, and what all this might mean to them. She wished she could talk to them now, especially to her mother. It was agony to be separated from them, unable to share her fears and hopes about David.

She felt completely vulnerable, completely alone. Would he come back? She couldn't guess. She buried her face in the pillow and sobbed.

XL

WITH A CLEAR DAWN spreading over the southern English Channel, tugboats nudged the Queen against the pier at Cherbourg; the pier's stubborn joints creaked and cracked as the ship's mass leaned into the fenders. A team of men, co-ordinating with the boats, shouted instructions, protests, and insults at each other in French, as they secured the Queen's thick lines around steel cleats at bow and stern.

At the end of a troubled, sleepless night, David now stood on the Promenade deck and studied the dock through a pair of borrowed binoculars. Sheltering behind a post, he scanned the dock's full length. A growing crowd of people, bundled against the chill and toting luggage, shuffled toward the ship in the half light, waiting for the gangways to be deployed so they could board for the trip across the Channel. David saw no one he recognized.

He had planned to leave the Queen here at Cherbourg and disappear—along with Audrey—before Charles Pierce and his friends got themselves organized. But this time, his luck failed him. In the night, as the ship neared France, she'd been ordered to lie off while a dredge completed work at the mouth of the inner harbor. They sat dead in the water for almost three hours, the landfall just out of reach. David went over the timing again and again, aided by maps borrowed from the bridge, and he couldn't see any way that Pierce and company could have failed to get here before them. They were down there somewhere, he was sure, waiting for him and bent on revenge.

And as if David's thoughts had conjured him into form, the figure of Charles Pierce filled his view in the glasses. He had stepped from a café onto the dock, along with another, taller man. The two talked for a moment, then Charles went to stand near the bottom of the forward gangway while the other man took a position near the one aft.

So there it was, a watch on the ship's exits. What were the odds that he and Audrey could slip through? David thought he stood a good chance of getting past the accomplice but disguising Audrey would be difficult. With a general description, plus the fact that she and David would find it hard to dress down to the level of the third class passengers, an alert sentry would have a good shot at making them.

No. They'd have to take their chances in Southampton. With luck, Charles wouldn't get there ahead of them—he'd have to hire a fast boat. And David was familiar with Southampton, which would up their chances.

He backed away from the rail and left the deck, heading toward Audrey's cabin. In a couple of hours, they'd be steaming North across the Channel toward the Queen's home berth; by noon, British longshoremen would be securing the ship. By then, David knew, everything had to be ready. And he had to know where things stood with Audrey.

Making his way toward her berth, his thoughts slipped back to all that had happened in the past few days and hours. His plans to win big at poker had gone well, thanks largely to Michael Gallagher's arrogance. And though Charles Pierce's con had cut into the take, he'd won more than £7,000 in all—about $35,000. He also had Pierce's satchel. He hadn't had time to count it but was sure it was stuffed with two or three times as much. So he had more than enough to secure the farm he had his eye on, near Truro in England's southwest corner.

Best of all, he had saved Audrey and driven Pierce off the ship. He felt a special satisfaction at the memory of the unflappable con man's panicked leap into the sea, after his last shot zipped past Pierce's head.

Then something shocking—completely unexpected—occurred, and it threatened to throw all his dreams into a cocked hat. He told Audrey of his feelings for her and asked her to share his life. And instead of the joyful acceptance he hoped for and thought he might get, she told him something he could hardly believe, something that knocked all the wind out of him.

He couldn't help feeling sucker punched. He had worked and planned and taken risks to win her, this golden prize, and it dissolved into sand in front of him. She knew that everyone thought she was white—it was a wicked deception.

But after going off to calm down and think, he found he couldn't name her crime. All she had done was let people make their own assumptions about her. When she explained why she had to do it, he readily understood—if she were forthcoming about her race, she wouldn't get anywhere in fashion in the U.S. People did make assumptions about blacks—negative ones; they were untrustworthy, unclean, less capable, a range of things that were a poor fit to the world of high fashion, or much of anything else.

When he realized *he* had made those same assumptions, a wave of shame struck him like a fist. How could he have treated other people that way, people he knew nothing about? He had just gone along with others, of course—the neighborhood kids, his high school and college buddies. Was that any kind of excuse?

David had never thought much about race before—hardly at all. It was a thorny topic and he didn't *want* to think about it. He just operated on the common assumption: There were white people and black people and a lot of shades in between, and the white people were best—the good ones and the smart ones and the ones with all the power, because they were better. Black people came in last—that was the way the world worked. He almost didn't think of them as being people, whole human beings, with all the needs and desires and rights that "real" people had.

He had almost no experience of coloreds and that was the main issue; they were foreigners to him. Oh, he was aware of them, growing up as he did in New York. Their music was the rage but that happened mainly up in Harlem, where neither he nor any of his friends ever dared go. There didn't seem to be very many of them, and except for the music, they had all the crap jobs. He'd never actually known one to say hello to and discuss things with. They were an afterthought in his world, a parallel population, there mostly to do the hard labor and keep things clean.

When he was in college, there was a black guy from Jamaica who shined shoes in front of the barbershop David used. And he *was* black—along with the whitest teeth and the whitest eyes, he had the darkest skin David had ever seen, like coal.

Every once in a while, David had his shoes done and he would talk with this guy because that's what you did, you shot the shit with him about whatever was going on in the news, while he laid on the polish and snapped his shine rags and all that. And the guy—his name was Jonah and he liked to joke that he went for a swim one day and a whale swallowed him and spat him up on Coney Island—he would laugh and joke because he got the best tips that way, sending you off with your shoes shined and a smile on your face.

And David remembered that once, when he was playing cards and guzzling beer with his pals one night in the dorm, something came up about blacks. It was in the papers. There'd been an incident down in the South—in Georgia, he thought. A woman had accused a couple of Negroes of raping her and a crowd of men stormed the jail and dragged them out, and lynched them in a particularly savage way.

The guys talked about how awful it was and about blacks in general, how odd they seemed and somehow less than whites, and somebody mentioned the Jamaican shoeshine guy. They started laughing at him and imitating his accent and strange speech patterns.

Then David's friend, Jake—he was a linguistics major, which none of them even knew what that meant—he startled them all. He said, "But have you ever listened to him, really *listened?*" They all said of course they had, what the hell did he mean? And he said, "If you really listen to him—past all that slang and the Jamaican accent and everything—he speaks the most correct English of just about anybody. He's got a huge vocabulary. And he makes more sense than most people, too."

And Jake was right, Jonah was no fool, and his English was really almost perfect, better than most of the guys sitting around that table. It kind of shut them all up for a minute.

Shame again swept over him as he remembered this. Why had he been so ready to make Jonah the butt of stupid, college boy jokes? Why had he dismissed him, withheld the presumption of common needs, of common experience, of membership in the human club, that every white man automatically gets? And now it turned out that Audrey was Jonah's kin in a way and in dismissing him, he was dismissing her, too—insulting her. The ugly truth of it tore at his conscience.

And now he had an uncomfortable new reality to deal with. This beautiful woman, whom he had shaped his future around in his imagination, whom he had dreamed of settling down with and having a family with, was a Negro. The picture she showed him of her father was of a man unmistakably African. What the hell should he do? Just walk away from her, as if they'd never met, never talked, as if they'd never held each other, never kissed? Before this, holding and kissing her was all he wanted to do, and those urges hadn't ebbed.

She said that any child of theirs might look like the people in those family photographs. He thought about those faces, in various shades of brown, their hair mostly tight curls, some kinky. Could he bear to have a child that looked like them? What if his son looked like the Jamaican bootblack? Or Audrey's grandmother—would he be ashamed if their daughter reflected the Cherokee ancestry so apparent in *her* features? Would he reject her?

She said she was a Negro; it was a label she had hung on herself. He was white. What did that mean, except to give him license to disparage her people—people who were different from him—for the sin of being different?

Different. That was the problem, wasn't it? Negroes were so obviously different, and that automatically meant not as good, so you could dump on them as much as you wanted. That's what he and his buddies had done, without a thought for what it meant to those on the receiving end, because he'd never allowed himself to know them as people. He feared them. His head was full of negative thoughts and feelings about them, thoughts that mostly came from other people, who didn't really know blacks any better than he did, but thought they did.

His friends—Benny and all his shipmates? Kelly and the other guys from college? What would he say to them? "Oh, and by the way, she's a Negro" ...and dare them to laugh or jeer? How many noses would he have to break, how often have his own nose busted, over this incendiary fact?

He knew what he would hear, or overhear: "Did you know, that wife of his is a..." The word stuck now. He'd never used it all that much. It hardly meant anything to him—just a casual, dismissive way to describe someone different, someone dark-skinned, someone who wasn't part of your clique, your clan. Now he was ashamed to say it, ashamed he had ever thought it, that it came so readily to his mind and to his tongue.

He'd never been so conflicted, never imagined an ambivalence so deep, so gnawing. He had wanted Audrey so much—almost desperately. There were so many things about her that he cherished—he'd been willing to do anything to win her. How could this one new thing suddenly turn his feelings upside down?

And what about his mother? And his two sisters? They were sure to be shocked, just as he had been. But would they object to Audrey? Try to talk him out of marrying her? He didn't see them much these days but he knew they all worried about him—they worried most that he was alone; they wanted to see him married and happy. His older sister, Sharon, was married and had one child—his mother wanted more grandkids. He'd never heard his mother utter a word against blacks but what would she do if she thought her grandchildren might look black?

He imagined introducing Audrey to his family. If that introduction had taken place yesterday, if yesterday, they had all bumped into each other on the street in New

York, nothing out of the ordinary would have occurred. He could see his mom's and sisters' approving smiles and knowing glances as they gushed over Audrey.

Today, that meeting would feel entirely different. What had changed? Today, he knew something new about Audrey that somehow made a monstrous difference, though outwardly, it made no difference at all.

As far as he could tell, as he tried to look into himself, his feelings toward Audrey hadn't changed. She was still this amazingly beautiful person that he ached to embrace, if only he could ignore her race. What should he do? What was the right thing to do? He couldn't find the answer and it was driving him crazy.

And all mixed up in it was everything he had done—and still needed to do—to protect her. Charles Pierce was still out there somewhere and they both had cause to fear another encounter with him. Would she let him help her deal with Pierce? He hoped at least that wouldn't be too much of a hard sell. But then what? He had no answer.

He reached her cabin and tapped softly on the door. It took several tries before her sleepy voice came through from inside.

"Who is it?" She knew who it was. "Don't you know what time it is?"

"It's me. Let me in."

There was a long silence. Finally, he heard the latch thrown and the door cracked open.

"David," she protested, sleepily, "you can't burst into my room at your whim."

"Audrey, please. We need to talk." He smiled, "Don't worry, I won't attack you."

She turned away to hide her own smile. She hadn't slept much either. She'd been thinking about David constantly since she told him about her heritage. If it worked out the way she hoped, if David could somehow not care about her race, she thought she might get used to the idea of being "attacked" by him, and had been thinking of the ways she would assist him if he did. She pulled the door open and switched on the overhead light as he ducked in.

She turned back to her bed. She was wearing creamy silk pajamas that fell seductively across her figure as she yawned and stretched, putting a lump in David's throat. She fell onto the bed and burrowed into a wad of blankets there but her mind was alert—this was a crucial moment for them. She closed her eyes and waited to see what her future would be.

David sat on the edge of the bed and laid a hand on her shoulder. Through the silk, he felt the elemental warmth of her body. Tousled and disheveled as she was, without lipstick or makeup, he still thought her the most beautiful creature he had ever seen. She opened an eye and bristled at him.

"What are you staring at?"

He laid on the bed beside her, fitting his knees and hips in behind hers, and draped his free arm over her. His nose was buried in her thick hair—it smelled of soap and perfume.

Tangled in his embrace, she could move only one arm. She folded it in and draped her hand along his neck. She closed her eyes and focused on the sensations in her fingertips as she stroked lightly along his throat, exploring. She felt the warmth of his skin and the taut cord of muscle in his neck, and next to it, the faint pulse of his heart. His mouth had settled near her ear.

"I'm so confused," he whispered. "I don't know what to feel or what to do. I love you, Audrey. I love you, but..."

Her heart sank. Her hopes for an unclouded future with David were evaporating, like a dream she'd been awakened from and couldn't hold on to.

A deep sadness swept through her. She wanted him so much. She had wished fervently for a wholehearted declaration of his love, but it hadn't come.

"We still have important things to take care of," he whispered.

"What things?" she asked, heavily, her spirits at the lowest ebb of her entire life. This whole episode, leaving her job, her family, her mother, skulking away to England with Charles Pierce, no longer seemed to make any sense. For a fleeting few seconds, she wondered whether she could possibly go back to New York and beg Chez Moreau to take her back?

David sat up and held her at arm's length. "We still have Charles Pierce to deal with."

He got up and pulled a chair next to the bed and sat. She sat up and they talked in low voices, their heads close together. "We're going to be disembarking at Southampton in a few hours," he began. "It's likely that Charles and his partner will be waiting there for us. They'll be in a foul mood."

"It's all about that money, isn't it? I've been thinking... it's almost like you robbed a bank. Shouldn't you just give it back?"

Shocked, he sat back and looked at her, searching for the sensible, pragmatic person he was sure was behind those intense green eyes. He admired her, respected her. She was like his sister, Marian. Marian was younger. She'd always had a steely sense of right and wrong but she was also capable of sudden detours into fantasy.

He had to overcome that now; Audrey had to see the situation as he did. "Y'know, you're right about Charles's money. And if it had come out of the pockets of people who have to scratch for a living, like the poor schlubs down in the lower decks, who these guys don't even know exist, if it came from them, I wouldn't hesitate to return it. But the men who gave Charles that money are unimaginably rich, every one of them. They don't scratch. They hardly do anything at all for their caviar and pheasant. Felix Hansen, for one. While he's been lounging around upstairs, making merry with Chris and Sarah every day, his tenants have poured a fortune into his accounts."

"But you told me you don't cheat."

"I don't. This isn't cheating—most of that money would have been mine anyway. If Charles hadn't been here with his mining scam, I'd have won much more of their excess cash. Charles got to them with his seductive scam."

Her brow wrinkled. "What about Billy Pruitt?"

"What about him?"

"He's an innocent. And the money he gave Charles was not idle change for him. He has no money of his own."

David rose and walked across the room. "I can't be responsible for every snot-nosed kid who thinks papa's money makes him special." He was pacing now, angry, his hands thrust into his pockets. "I told you about Billy. He's been the center of every society scandal in New York for the past five years, most of them involved getting into gambling trouble with his father's dough."

She watched him move back and forth across the cramped space. As he went on, her feelings for him cooled.

"So what does he do? He gets on this ship and throws every extra dollar in his pocket into a transparent con game!"

She didn't like this side of David. Her own recent education, through him and through Charles, had put a new patina on life, one that didn't shine quite so brightly as before. In response, she held more tightly to her own sense of right and wrong. It distressed her to hear David trying to turn black and white into shades of gray.

"I understand your feelings about people like Hansen and the rest", she said. "And it's true, they won't miss the money they lost. But I think you should return Billy's money."

"Why him?! He's possibly the richest of the lot!"

She rose and went to him. She held his arms and looked into his eyes, so he couldn't mistake her seriousness.

"No, David. It's his father who's rich. The money Billy invested with Charles was the bulk of his travel funds. He's desperate to make a good impression on his father. If he has to wire and tell him he's lost all his money in some scheme, he'll lose any chance to get his father's respect."

David understood that Pruitt had touched her, that she had developed a maternal interest in him. Still, he resented Pruitt's ability to be so careless about money, and to have someone like Audrey at hand to bail him out. He knew Billy had lost thousands of Pruitt Mercantile's cash, had gambled it away, at about the same time his own father was struggling to make any kind of living, after his talents for caring for horses became obsolete almost overnight.

And now, another war was brewing, one that would consume the lives of tens of thousands... *hundreds* of thousands of young men of Billy's age. Their blood and bowels would be dumped onto the battlefields like so much fertilizer. But William Pruitt III would not be among them. If he participated at all, his father would see to it that he remained far from the assault of bombs and bullets, artillery shells and poison gas even now being assembled to flay and corrupt their flesh.

So David had trouble being sympathetic. People like Billy Pruitt needed to know what it meant to be poor and he was more than willing to provide that lesson.

He stared at the carpet while his thoughts calmed. He was framing them into a speech so Audrey would understand why Billy shouldn't be let off the hook. When he glanced up at her, watching him as he paced, he saw something in her face—a look of resignation—that he hadn't seen before. He saw that she understood his feelings about the Billy Pruitts of the world—and probably agreed with them. But that wasn't the issue. The question was: What would he do now? How would he deal with the power he held over Billy?

After a long moment, he sighed. "OK. We'll give Pruitt back his money."

He had said, "We." It carried the assumption that they were together, working as one, and the conflict in this assumption sat heavily on his brow. He felt he had to act for them both, although it meant acting on behalf of a couple whose existence he'd been set to celebrate just a few hours before, but which now he wasn't sure of. It was disconcerting, but watching the furrows disappear from Audrey's brow and a smile sparkle in her eyes was like watching clouds give way to a bright, summer sun.

Too soon, the smile faded and a look of anxiety clouded her face again. "So what are we going to do about Charles?"

David held her by the shoulders. "I do have an idea about that. It involves cutting your hair."

XLI

THE THIN, PALE YOUTH with close-cropped red hair, dressed in plus fours and a matching jacket, argyle knee socks, solid oxfords, and slumped on the stateroom bed, was Audrey. No lipstick or powder, no earrings, her unpainted nails trimmed short, she came close to looking like a schoolboy, as she and David intended. But a platoon of ship's officers, uniformed police constables, and plain-clothes detectives surrounded her, standing almost shoulder-to-shoulder in the small room. So she was uneasy, her face clouded with concern.

Leading them was a solid, stocky Irishman, Inspector Sheridan, in a brown twill suit and sturdy shoes. A full, reddish brown beard, edging toward gray, covered much of his face. It was neatly trimmed and he stroked it when deep in thought.

He and his officers were there because, on the last leg of the Queen's journey, steaming between Cherbourg and Southampton just after sunrise, Charles Pierce's absence began to be noticed. By the time breakfast was cleared, the men who had favored Charles with their trust and money knew they had been duped. Telegrams were sent, ship-to-shore calls made, the Captain consulted, and Charles—and Audrey, too—thoroughly vilified. Trying to deflect suspicion from Audrey, David went to the Captain and laid out everything he knew or suspected about Charles's mining dodge, including his doubts about the mining engineer's suicide. The Captain radioed ashore and when the ship docked, squads of British policemen swarmed aboard.

Now Inspector Sheridan paced Audrey's stateroom, stroking his beard. He stopped and bent toward her. "I'm sorry, Miss Simmons," he said, with a sigh. "You seem to be an earnest young woman but I find your story difficult to accept."

Audrey pleaded. "I know it sounds awful, but... well, I've been trying to get the details from him ever since I first met him. He was always vague... I suppose I should have pressed him, but..." She stopped, fearing that finishing the thought would make her seem either an idiot or a liar.

The Inspector thought Audrey hardly fit the profile of a confidence hustler but, on the other hand, despite her current attempt to look like an adolescent boy, he had little trouble imagining that men would make fools of themselves over her. "I'm afraid, Miss, I'm going to have to detain you. Now, can you tell me where...?"

David, out of breath, burst into the room, surprising the constable standing at the door. He rushed to the bed. "Audrey! I heard that they were questioning you. Are you all right?"

"David! They think I took all that money!" She dissolved into tears. "They want to arrest me!"

David spotted Sheridan and sprang to him. "Look, sir, I can vouch for her. She had nothing to do with Charles Pierce's phony mine. I spent most of the voyage trying to convince her it was bogus. She didn't want to believe me."

"And who are you, sir?" asked the inspector.

"My name is Bowen. David Bowen."

The Inspector's eyes widened, in obvious delight. "Ah, yes. Bowen."

"I'm a gambler..." He looked over at Audrey. "Right now, my main concern is this young woman and..."

"Now that's very sweet, Mr Bowen. My heart is fairly thumping in my breast. But you see, I'm here investigating a crime, two crimes, perhaps, and your intentions toward the young lady are of little interest to me. What I would like to hear is what you know about this Charles Pierce, and the sale of shares in his alleged mine."

David hesitated. "Well, there's a difference between what I know and what I suspect..." He stopped and thought for a moment, then lowered his voice and leaned toward the policeman. "Is there a chance we could speak in private?"

"That's most irregular sir. What would your motive be?"

"Well, I have some rather 'irregular' things to say and I believe they're critical to your investigation."

The Inspector scratched at his beard for a moment, glancing at David, then away, then back again. He turned to a younger man in plain clothes, standing nearby. "Detective Deason, would you please take over for a moment while I go for a private interview with this young man?"

"Aye, guv'nor," said Deason.

"Constable," he spoke to the man guarding the entrance to the room. "Just step out into the passageway and keep a sharp eye on us if you don't mind. Blow your whistle if you see Mr Bowen here on the point of koshing me."

The constable broke a smile and nodded, and stationed himself at the junction of the main passageway and its off-shoot into Audrey's cabin. David and the Inspector walked down the passageway.

"So what was it you wanted to say?" asked Sheridan. The question was soaked in skepticism.

"Well, from the first, I knew Pierce was a flim-flam artist, dangling his vials of silver ore in front of his pigeons. I don't know—there was something... wrong about it. Oh, believe me, he's very convincing. And he had all the bases covered—a telegram at just the right time, plus a masterstroke of a shill, a man named Steffens, who came forward at the right moment and endorsed the ore samples. As soon as he'd played his part, they found him with a noose around his neck."

"Yes, we're aware of Mr Steffens."

"I strongly suspect Pierce engineered that 'suicide'. I told the Captain so last night."

"So you are the source of that particular bit of conjecture."

"Most important, uhh... Detective?"

"Inspector, if you please."

"Well, most important for me, Inspector—not only is Audrey innocent of any knowledge of Pierce's scam, the opposite is true—he scammed her, too. And last night he tried to kill her, to throw her over the side. I intervened—and I chased him. The ship's officers will confirm that they had reports of shots fired last night—I fired them. I missed him—on purpose—and I saw Pierce jump over the rail and get picked up in a motor launch." He stopped and made sure he had eye contact with the policeman. "Now that's the main thing, Inspector. That boat could only have been there by pre-arrangement."

Inspector Sheridan gave David a sidelong look, smoothing his beard with one hand. "Now why would he do a thing like that do you suppose—jumping off the ship?"

"He thought he was escaping with his money."

"*Thought* he was escaping with it?"

"Yes, in a satchel he bought for the purpose. It was close to £20,000."

"Are you suggesting that he didn't have the money?"

"Yes, that's right. I had it."

The Inspector's brows arched. "*You* had it?!"

"Yes, I swapped the satchel for an identical one. You see, Pierce and I had clashed and he was keeping players away from my table with his bogus mine. I didn't trust him *and* I didn't like him. Plus he threatened me when I asked him about his intentions toward Audrey. I felt he owed me and..."

"Well, sir, it's to your credit that you're owning up to all this but I'm not certain a magistrate would share your opinions. Where is this satchel?"

"I asked a friend of mine, Benny, one of the crewmen, to take it off the ship with him. He's putting it in freight storage at the rail station here. He's to keep the tag until I contact him and tell him where to send it." David dug a small key out of his pocket and dangled it in front the policeman. "The bag is locked; he doesn't know what's in it."

"I see," said Sheridan, "leaving only the question of how to slip away." He scratched at his beard again and cast a look at David that contained a hint of a smile. With a nod, he turned their stroll back toward the berth. "I suppose that has something to do with why Miss Simmons is done up like a school lad?"

"Yes. I hoped to get us free without a run-in with Pierce."

"The pair of you, plus Pierce's loot."

"Uhh... our money, too." He hoped this small lie would help get the policeman on their side. "All my winnings were in with the other cash."

"Well, I have to tell you, sir, you've been quite reckless. You say you want to vouch for Miss Simmons but you've just admitted to a handful of serious crimes, and implicated her, and other friends of yours, in them as well. I'm not sure they'll thank you for that. I should add that I have only your word for the notion that Pierce, who *is* missing, went over the side of his own volition, or that there was any boat there to pick him up. You admit shooting at him. How do I know you didn't kill him? You certainly appear to have motive enough."

David bit his lip in frustration, realizing he'd made things worse.

The Inspector took in a deep breath. "Mr Bowen, I'm afraid I'm going to have to place you..."

David broke in. "Listen, Inspector. Please, I see, now that you put it in words, that I have been... reckless, but... well, your primary interest is in Charles Pierce, right?"

"Yes, that's a fair statement. If he's still alive, we certainly want him to answer for the swindling of your fellow passengers. And of course, there's the death of Mr Steffens."

"Inspector, Charles Pierce is going to turn up here this morning. He's probably already here, down on the dock someplace. If we're sharp, we can grab him."

Sheridan's eyebrows arched again. "Can we now?"

"I'm certain of it. He's not the kind to be conned out of a big score like this and just walk away. He'll be looking for his money *and* for me, and he'll have blood in his eyes."

The Inspector scratched at his beard and pondered. "And what is it exactly that you're proposing, Mr Bowen?"

XLII

STILL DRESSED AS AN ADOLESCENT BOY, Audrey pushed through the turnstile into the public pavilion of the Southampton docks, carrying her portfolio and a valise. She, David, and Inspector Sheridan had agreed that her schoolboy costume, topped with a tweedy cheese-cutter cap, was convincing enough if viewed from a little distance. Plus, the goal was that it only look like an *attempt* to disguise her, one that didn't quite succeed.

David, in a corduroy coat and a wide-brimmed hat pulled down to mask his face, trailed a few dozen steps behind, along with a porter, trundling their baggage on a noisy carrier. The porter was one of Sheridan's men.

They had all agreed that if Pierce was there, he'd be sure to keep back, too easily recognized by the people he'd scammed. So they were looking not for Pierce but for an accomplice. They assumed there would be just one—presumably the man who piloted the boat that plucked Pierce out of the water. His actions, as he tried to spot David and Audrey, should be distinctive enough to betray him.

Audrey had instructions to act as much as possible as if she hadn't a care in the world. And until she engaged a cab and got her luggage into it, she and David would pretend to be strangers.

Sheridan had scattered his men around the pavilion; besides the porter, she thought she'd spotted one or two of them—the man in the phone booth near the entry, and probably the newsagent, in the stall outside the wall of windows enclosing the area.

She pushed through the exit door while David and the policeman/porter stopped just inside, and David pretended to examine the timetables posted there. She walked to the curb and scanned the street for a cab. Without any imminent boardings or dockings, the traffic was light and there were no taxis, either waiting for fares or delivering passengers. She looked along the road. She was confused at first, with the few cars that did pass driving on the wrong side of the road.

Finally a boxy, shiny black taxicab, fronted by an angular, brightly polished bronze radiator, drove into the forecourt and stopped next to Audrey at the curb, its engine idling noisily. The driver got out and came to her. Reacting to her unusual costume, he gave her an inquisitive look.

"'Morning, Miss. Let me help you with that case." He smiled at her as he picked up her suitcase and set it in the luggage bay next to his seat. She held on to her portfolio and smiled shyly at the driver, embarrassed by his attentions. With a gesture, he invited her to take a seat in the cab's passenger compartment, which seemed nearly as big as the parlor in her home in Baltimore. But she remained standing at the curb, trying to keep David in sight and searching for anyone who might stick out amid the crowd as Charles Pierce's partner.

Looking toward the pavilion through the big window, she could see David inside—he seemed to be unaware of her. Then, to her relief, he and the porter pushed through the door, apparently on a signal, moving in her direction at a brisk pace.

When their luggage was all lashed down and Audrey and David had settled themselves in the cab, they scanned the forecourt, exchanging puzzled glances after failing to catch any sign of Pierce or a likely accomplice.

Then, just as the driver got in and started the meter, the door jerked open and a man in a raincoat and a hat leaned in. The hat brim hid his features as he stooped to fit through the door. He pressed the jump seat down and dropped onto it, bringing his face into view—it was Charles Pierce.

He directed a cold stare at Audrey, holding it for a long beat, then shifted his look to David. His expression was contemptuous. He drew his right hand from the pocket of his coat and kept it low, out of the driver's view; it held a snub-nosed revolver, pointed more or less at David's midriff.

"Thank you for holding the cab for me," he said, his voice raised for the driver's benefit. Then speaking through the window separating the driver from the passenger's space, he added, "We can go now, my good man."

The cabby edged the car out onto the main road and Charles turned and faced his captives with an arch grin. "Well, isn't this cozy? Unexpected, I'll warrant." He looked disdainfully at Audrey. "You do look ridiculous in that costume."

David's mind raced. "Look, Pierce, you're off base again. We don't have your money..."

The cabbie interrupted, calling back through the window. "Still going to the rail station, Guv'nor?"

Charles glanced at Audrey and David, then turned to the driver. "Uhh, yes. The railway station." Then, reaching for the knob on the sliding window, he added, "Don't take this personally, will you? We have some business to discuss." As he slid the window closed, David spoke up again, more emphatically.

"Pierce, listen. The money isn't..."

Charles lashed out, backhanded, driving the butt of his pistol into David's stomach. With a loud grunt, David doubled over.

"Charles!" Audrey shouted. "You beast! What are you...?!"

He glanced at her, sidelong, his eyes full of rage. The look stopped her, rekindling the fear she'd felt just hours before, struggling to keep him from throwing her into the sea. She drew back into the corner. Charles leaned close to David, who was still doubled over and straining to catch his breath. With a sneer, he spoke into David's ear.

"You interfering, obnoxious little man. I warned you about meddling in my affairs." He moved back slightly, as though David might contaminate him. "And that you would actually steal from me?" His derisive laugh made it clear that the notion of such a thing succeeding was unthinkable.

His face contorted, David glanced up, unable to draw a full breath, the pain still sharp in his belly. Charles continued, hissing in anger.

"When we get to the train station, Mr Bowen, we will find a corner where we won't be disturbed and you will open these cases, and produce the money you took from me." He sat back and drew a deep breath, letting it out slowly through his nostrils. And as suddenly as his rage had emerged, it seemed to vanish.

He addressed them as if speaking to a class of unruly children. "Once I'm satisfied that it is intact, I probably will release you." He grimaced, as though he had just bitten into spoiled food. "It goes against the grain, I have to say. You can count yourselves lucky that I haven't time to waste on you. Normally, anyone who dared cross me as you have..." He let the thought trail off with a dismissive wave of one hand. He glanced up just then, through the rear window, and his eyes widened in alarm.

"Ohh! What's this? The police?"

David and Audrey turned and looked—a black police cruiser kept pace behind them, three cars back. They glanced at each other, smiling faintly. But the mood did not last.

"Good," said Charles. "They're turning off."

Looking back quickly, David and Audrey saw the police car turn down a side road. They looked at each other with failing spirits; David bit his lip as Charles spoke.

"You should be pleased. I don't know what precisely would have happened had they been on our track; I can assure you that neither of you would have survived it."

David's breathing had settled enough to allow him to talk. "Your money's not here, Pierce..."

Charles lashed out again, a slap across the face that spun David's head. Audrey yelped and pulled David to her, vainly trying to shield him. Charles ignored her. "Damn it, Bowen, don't trifle with me! And don't make the stupid mistake of thinking that I'm as naïve as the lambs you fleece."

David's cheek stung—a tooth had cut into the flesh and the metallic taste of blood was in his mouth. His reflex was to strike back but he had already discarded the idea of a fight in the car. Pierce would not be a pushover—too much chance of the gun going off.

Still looking for a strategy, David weighed his words carefully. "Believe me, Pierce, nothing would please me more than to hand you your money and get you the hell out of our hair, but it isn't that easy. Once again: It isn't here." Warily, he repeated what he'd told Inspector Sheridan.

"The bag is probably at the station already but I couldn't tell you exactly where."

Charles sat back against the seat and gazed through the window, weighing his options. When he looked back, his demeanor had shifted again and he was in character as the suave, unruffled man-about-town. "Well, we're approaching the station now. We'll have a look, shall we?" He indicated the cases stacked in the luggage bay, next to the driver. "And if what you say is true, it appears that we'll have to endure each other's company for a while longer, while we sort out this problem."

Minutes later, the cab pulled into the broad forecourt of the Southampton Central railway station. The three stepped out onto the platform amid a bustle of people laden with trunks and cases, scrambling to make trains, or scurrying to catch cabs, buses and private cars. Sounds of the steam engines, huffing and hissing on the tracks and exercising their whistles, filtered out of the concourse. A porter appeared and Charles instructed him to load their luggage on his cart. The group set off with Charles at the rear, the pistol concealed in the pocket of his raincoat.

Just inside the concourse entrance, they stopped at a rank of dark, leather-covered booths that formed the seating area of a cafe. The porter quickly stacked the cases and Charles dismissed him with a few shillings.

"Now, Bowen. Let's have a look." He pointed to the largest trunk, a leather-bound case cinched by two broad straps, threaded through sturdy brass buckles. "Sit down, Audrey," he ordered.

Audrey had no courage to challenge him. Glowering, she eased into the nearest booth and slid back until the wall stopped her retreat.

David wanted to protest rooting through their luggage but he knew it was fruitless. Even if Pierce believed the story, he would still have to see for himself that his money wasn't there. That left a bigger problem. He had told Inspector Sheridan that he'd mixed his money in with Pierce's. In fact, his winnings were in an envelope tucked into a corner of the small case Audrey was tending and he couldn't think of any way to conceal it.

With a shrug, and still hurting from the ache in his mid-section and the wound in his mouth, he bent to the case and began unbuckling the straps. He moved as deliberately as he could, trying to buy time to think. As he worked at the buckle, he happened to glance up and he hesitated—he thought he recognized a man approaching from the cafe, carrying a mug of tea, as one of Inspector Sheridan's men. He quickly returned his attention to the case, releasing the latches, but his mind was racing. If he was right, it was an astounding stroke of luck. But how could he signal to the policeman without Charles noticing?

Almost as he framed the question, the answer came in a loud crash that echoed in the space. The man had stumbled into a trashcan, knocking it over and dropping his tea; the mug shattered on the cement floor. As everyone's attention went to this ruckus, two burly men rushed up behind Charles, one at each arm—in an instant, they had him face down on the floor, with the knee of one of them pressed firmly into his back, and his arms twisted painfully behind. Charles writhed and bellowed in protest as they fixed a set of manacles around his wrists. As they trussed him, and passers-by gawked, his pistol slipped from his pocket and clattered to the floor. One of the men picked it up.

Audrey left the booth and rushed to David. "What's going on?!"

"Well, believe it or not," he said, with a broad smile, "I think we're saved. It looks like the police were not so easily thrown off. Look!"

He nodded in the direction of the cafe door— Inspector Sheridan walked through and came toward them, with several uniformed constables trailing behind.

He put two fingers to the brim of his hat in a salute as he walked up, stopping just in front of Charles, who was still prostrate, and whose only view of Sheridan was of the scuffs and stitching on the policeman's sturdy brown shoes.

"Get him up on his feet, please, gentlemen," he said to the two men.

David thought that the mixture of anger and dismay on Charles Pierce's face, as the men lifted him to a standing position, might have been worth all that they had suffered at his hands.

Inspector Sheridan turned to them. "Do you recognize this man?" he asked, gesturing toward Charles.

"That's Charles Pierce," Audrey blurted. "He tried to murder me."

"Yes. That's him," said David.

Charles turned his most threatening face on David. "Damn it, Bowen. You're...?"

"What, Pierce?" David challenged, stepping forward. "Look, you needn't worry, 'old man'," he said, injecting all the sarcasm he could into Pierce's favorite phrase. "Cash in some of that 16-to-the-ton ore of yours, 'old man', and you can hire a pretty good lawyer."

Charles's eyes bulged with anger and he began to utter another threat but, realizing that almost everyone within hearing was a policeman, he decided not to say more.

"Take him away," Sheridan said to the officers. They marched Pierce out through the cafe; Sheridan, Deason and the others looked on with satisfaction.

The Inspector turned to his detective. "Good job with that waste bin, Deason," he said. "You'll be playing the West End any day now."

Deason smiled self-consciously. "If you don't mind, sir, I'll stick to the Christmas pageant."

David and Audrey joined the Inspector. "I thought we were done for," Audrey gushed, "when your patrol car turned off the road. How'd you ever find us?"

"Oh, Miss Simmons, please give us a little credit," said Sheridan—David thought "avuncular" might serve as his middle name. "We never lost you. Besides the patrol car, we had two other cars on your tail." David and Audrey broke into surprised laughter and hugged each other.

Their euphoria lasted only a few moments before David found himself working hard to remain free, as Inspector Sheridan settled down to a talk with them, over mugs of hot tea from the cafe.

"I'll turn that tag over to you the minute I get it in my hands," David pleaded. "You wouldn't have caught Pierce if it weren't for us. Certainly you can trust me that far."

Sheridan was studying the graffiti carved in the tabletop and scratching at his whiskers, but he looked up sharply in response to David's plea and shook his head. "I'm not paid to trust suspects, Mr Bowen. You probably don't appreciate being spoken of in such terms but you're an intelligent man—once you think for a moment, I'm sure you'll understand. Thanks to you, we do have Mr Pierce now—I'll grant you that. But tens of thousands of pounds are missing and you, and your fiancée here, are my only link to it."

Audrey perked up at Sheridan's reference to their relationship. Fiancée—a woman who has been asked by a man to marry him and has accepted. She wondered whether David had described her as his fiancée to the Inspector, or had Sheridan's orderly mind provided him with a label that seemed to fit their intimacy. The word didn't fit her situation precisely—not yet, anyway—and she wondered if it ever would. She liked Sheridan, despite the wringer he was putting them through; he was more like a benevolent uncle than a policeman. If only she could unravel the knot of barriers that were keeping his description from being true.

"If I let you go, simply on your word," Sheridan explained, "I'd be looking for a new job by the end of the week."

Audrey was wondering what she might do to help when she glanced toward the platforms. She saw a familiar figure in line at the entrance, about to pass through the gate and head for the trains.

"Excuse me for a moment?" she asked Sheridan.

The Inspector hesitated. His reflex was to keep her corralled but she wasn't a prime suspect any longer. And intuition told him that, if he had David, he essentially had her too; he decided to trust it. He nodded and she left at a run toward the platforms.

As she hurried to the gate, she was certain now that the man just going through, wearing a seaman's blue shirt and a pea coat, was Benny.

"Benny!" she called, as she jogged up to him. He looked up, puzzled, wondering who this redheaded lad, with a high voice and an awkward gait, might be.

"Benny, I'm so glad to see you."

"Audrey?! Is that you?! What in...? What happened to you? I mean, your... your hair, and...?" He was making his way back toward her, against the flow of train-bound travelers.

"Oh, it's a long story." As he broke from the crowd, she grabbed his arm and pointed him toward the tables, where David and the others stood. "We'll tell you the whole thing sometime, over a pint." Showing him a conspiratorial smile, she added, "We need your help."

* * * * * *

"You present me with a problem, Mr Bowen," Inspector Sheridan declared. A twinge of embarrassment caused him to revert to official jargon. "I'm afraid I have to ask you to accompany us to the police precinct, where you will be arraigned before a magistrate."

David's heart sank. He had been high on success since winning so decisively at the poker table, just hours earlier. Now his fortunes had reversed completely.

"I expect you won't be detained for long," Sheridan stood and beckoned David to his feet. "Once the luggage ticket you've alleged is in the court's hands and we can retrieve the satchel, you'll probably be released." He gestured to a constable, standing nearby. "I regret this, Bowen, but I have no choice." He nodded to the constable, who stepped behind David and asked him to put his hands behind his back.

With a heavy sigh, David complied. The clench of the manacles on his wrists sent a wave of sadness and defeat through his frame. All his planning, his careful play at the poker table, his efforts to gain Audrey's respect and start to build a life with her, had come down to this disgrace. He shook his head—how could things have gone so far off track?

Audrey's voice cut through the gloom. "David! Look! Here he is!"

He looked up—she strode toward them, Benny in tow. He couldn't have been more surprised. "Benny! I thought you'd left!"

"I did. Came up here and checked the bag, like we said, and got a bus. But I had to come back..." David's eyes widened. "That old uncle of mine—the one who moved?" David nodded. "I was all the way past Winchester before I realized I'd left the letter behind with his address. 'Bloomin' nuisance." He looked around at the police activity. "What's all this?"

"It's all about Charles Pierce," said Audrey. "He's been arrested."

"I'm so glad you forgot that letter," David said.

Benny was bewildered. Sheridan broke in. "You'll excuse me, but perhaps you'll tell me who this gentleman is?"

David was quick to answer. "This is Benny, Inspector. He's the one I told you about, the one I gave the satchel to."

The Inspector's eyes shifted to Benny like a cat on the hunt. He held up his ID wallet. "I'm Inspector Sheridan, Mister uhhh..."

Benny's eyes widened. "Uhhh... Hogarth. Benny Hogarth... Benjamin. What...?!"

"Mr Hogarth. May I have a quick word with you?" He took Benny by the arm and walked with him, back toward the platforms and the hissing trains, and out of David and Audrey's hearing.

Watching them, Audrey slipped her arm through David's and she sensed something wrong with the way he was holding his body. She looked behind and saw the manacles. "Oh, David! You're handcuffed!"

"I'm so sorry, Audrey. I..."

"No! Stop!" She placed two fingers against his lips and shook her head, forbidding his apology. Then she went up on her toes and put her lips in place of her fingers, pressing her mouth against his. Backing away slowly, she held his gaze, then she wrapped her arms around his waist and laid her head on his chest, watching as Sheridan questioned Benny.

David bent to her. He could only lay his cheek on her head, with his nose pushed into the fabric of her cap. Breathing in, the faint perfume of her hair mixed with the musk of the warm wool. He savored her scent and the gift of her embrace, and tears welled in his eyes.

After many minutes, Sheridan returned, with Benny following. "Well, you two, this may yet be your luckiest day." He held up a green cardboard tag. "Mr Hogarth confirms your story, Mr Bowen, and tells me that this is the magic ticket. We'll soon know." He found Deason.

"Have one of your men go over to Left Luggage and bring us back what they give him in exchange for this tag." He turned back to David. "This should clear you. Of course, it's possible that I'll be over-ruled but I see no benefit in pressing charges. I wouldn't get your hopes up, though, about separating your winnings from the other cash. Mixing them might not have been quite the smartest thing you've ever done."

Audrey cast a quizzical glance up at David, whose face held a look of disappointment.

"In the meantime," Sheridan turned to the constable, "please remove the shackles from Mr Bowen and let him have a seat."

XLIII

THE CROWD OF POLICE OFFICERS had scattered. Inspector Sheridan stayed behind long enough to admonish Audrey and David not to disappear, as they were sure to be wanted during the investigation. Finally, they found themselves alone amongst the ceaseless flow of travelers in the Southampton railway station.

Audrey's suitcase lay open on the floor of the cafe. Still dressed in her schoolboy costume, she was on one knee, rifling through her clothing as if she were taking inventory. A look of sadness tinged her face.

David sat nearby, at the end of a booth bench, watching her. He was hunched over, his elbows on his knees, and his face reflected the deep sense of uncertainty that overshadowed him. Moments before, with his wrists manacled and his spirits at their lowest ebb, Audrey had kissed him, had wrapped her arms around him and held him tight, an embrace he ached to return. He felt then that they were together again, they were one, and the cloud of doom hanging over him began to disperse. But with Charles Pierce and the police gone, Audrey had separated from him, and now busied herself making preparations to leave.

He watched as she drew a parti-colored silk scarf from the suitcase and draped it around her neck. Before closing the case, she dug out the small envelope containing the money she'd brought with her from New York. She counted it carefully.

"I don't know that I have enough here," she said, looking up at him. "Will you lend me some so I can get established in London? I'll pay you back as soon as I can."

"What are you talking about, Audrey? You're going off to London, just like that?"

"Don't sound surprised, David." She tugged the case closer to the booth. "You knew that was my plan from the start. Yes. I'm going to London."

Ever since their talk, when she knocked the wind out of him with the story of her background, much of Audrey's behavior had confused him. Now, once again, he couldn't make sense of her actions. Was she really going to walk out of his life, as though they meant nothing to each other? Did she think she could just drop down in London without knowing a soul?

He had tried to envision what would happen to them in the coming days and weeks. He wanted time to think things over, time to decide if he could see a future with her, time to design that future. He hadn't had much success forming a picture of it. His dreams of the two of them, happily tending sheep or cows, all too readily became jumbled with premonitions of unpleasant, even violent encounters with boorish, racist men and scandal-mongering women. Still, each time he tried to imagine his future; at the farm, in the town, at the stock auctions, it automatically included the two of them, together.

"You can't do this, Audrey. You can't just go off to London on your own like this."

Her brow knitted in a frown. "How dare you tell me what I can and cannot do? When did you earn that right?"

Embarrassed, his mouth scrunched into a thin line. "I'm sorry. I..." He stood. Nervously, he combed one hand through his hair. "It's just that... well, you have no contacts or anything. London's like New York,

Audrey. With no support, you'll become a victim there, fast. There are lots of unscrupulous people—Charles Pierce types, just without the fancy veneer."

Audrey thought for a moment, looking along the line of puffing steam engines being oiled and watered and coaled. They were being readied to carry people to the various corners of the country. One of them, she thought, would soon bear her away to London, and away from David. "I'll have to take my chances. London is why I came here. Nothing else makes any sense for me."

He stepped closer. "Please, Audrey. Come with me down to Truro. I have to go and sign some papers, and put some money on the farm so they don't sell it out from under me. Come with me and see it, at least."

She looked at him without speaking, listening for words that would make her change her mind. Unnerved, he began pacing as he continued. "Then I'll go with you up to London. I have friends there. They'll help you get settled, so you won't have to sleep on a park bench. Maybe one of them knows somebody in the fashion business."

"I can't do that, David."

"Why not?!" he snapped. "It's the only sensible thing! Do you hate me so much?"

Anger flashed briefly in her eyes—she bit her lip to avoid lashing back at him. She knew he didn't mean it but still, his question was an affront. She loved David and he knew it. She desperately wanted to express her love to him, to hold him, to be held by him.

He knew why she was determined to leave, that the obstacle to their togetherness lay in him, his fear of a black stain that just might be hidden within her, in her womb, ready to infect their children and expose him to the world, to make him uneasy and ashamed. Dredging all this up made her want to cry but she was determined not to show him any weakness. "Where would we stay, there?" she demanded.

"Oh, there are plenty of inns and bed-and-breakfast places. We'll be snug as bugs."

"Sleeping in the same room, like married people? What will your friends there think of me?"

He winced at the size of the hole in his thinking. He pondered for a moment.

"OK. We'll get separate rooms—whatever it takes. I can't let you go to London alone—it's impossible. Dangerous. I'm serious."

She looked at him intently, gauging his sincerity, and trying to see her own intentions through his eyes. She hadn't given any thought to the possibility of danger in London. Such dangers existed in New York and she always took them into account as she moved around there. But she had created a London and a Paris in her mind that were without blemish—shining cities that welcomed visitors with a warm smile and a protective embrace. It was to that fairy tale London that she was headed—she now had to discard that fantasy.

"OK. We'll go to Truro. Separate rooms." She let a thin smile soften her expression. "And thank you for your concern for me, David. I appreciate it."

"Of course, Audrey. I feel responsible for you. I..."

"What, David?"

"Nothing." He turned abruptly and beckoned to a passing porter. "Come on, let's get out of this station." He began gathering their cases. "I think we should start out on the bus—we'll get a better look at the scenery. We'll go to Lymington first. Then we can decide if we want to stay on the bus, or catch a train at Bournemouth."

She didn't care how they got to Truro. It was all new to her and she was ready to take whatever route

David suggested. But she could hardly bear the change she now saw in him. His discomfort was painful to watch. The confident, surefooted man she'd fallen in love with had disappeared and a hapless, hesitant stranger had taken his place. It broke her heart.

XLIV

WITH THEIR LARGE BAGS CHECKED at Left Luggage, Audrey and David carried only the valise, plus Audrey's portfolio, as they boarded a red, double-decker bus at the side of the Southampton rail station. Exhausted, they dropped onto the rear seat. It was a storybook summer day in southern England, bright sun in the bluest of skies, dotted here and there with cotton-ball clouds.

As the bus chugged out of the city and steered toward the Southwest, they sat for a long moment in silence. Then Audrey leaned against David, laid her head against his shoulder and closed her eyes. The small gesture surprised him; he was getting used to coolness coming from her.

Despite her bright scarf, Audrey still looked like an Eton sixth-former, including her dark red hair trimmed as short as a corporal's, and they drew stares from new riders walking by them as they boarded at the rear of the bus. It wasn't long before all the passengers were craning, with varying degrees of subtlety, to get a glimpse. When finally she noticed them gawking and realized why, she sat up and fished in her pocket for her makeup bag. With a few strokes of lipstick, a daub of powder and a pair of small, pearl earrings, she had her femininity back on parade, her boyish costume now just a fashion statement. In a final flourish, she gave her scarf another turn round her neck, sending most of the staring eyes back to their magazines and knitting.

David's heart lightened as she transformed herself. Her physical appeal hadn't vanished but as she made herself up, the familiar feminine accents re-emerged—the icing on this beautiful cake. He studied the details in her face for a long moment. She looked up.

"You're staring at me."

"It's fascinating," he said, a bemused smile on his lips. "Every time I look at you, I see something new. I remembered the pictures you showed me of your father and, just now, I thought I could see him in your face—in your nose and around your eyes. But it's fleeting—maybe a change in the light. I can't see it now, separately like that."

Audrey wondered if it's really possible to pick apart a person's ancestry in the details of her appearance. She toyed with the catch on her earring as she mulled this over, then she turned and looked into David's face, gazing intently at each feature.

"What?" he said, uncomfortable in her scrutiny.

"Nothing," she said. "I was just wondering if I could see *your* ancestry in the features of your face." She turned away and settled back into the seat. "I suppose I could if I knew what your mother and father looked like. Without that..." she let the thought trail off.

"I know you're mocking me, Audrey. I wish I could find the humor in it."

She looked up at him again. His expression was pained, his lips drawn into a tight line. He couldn't look at her. She opened her mouth to speak—she was going to apologize and tell him it was all right, that she understood—but she caught herself.

It wasn't all right. And she couldn't really say that she understood why, if David loved her, he couldn't simply act on that feeling. Mixed couples were rare but they existed, even in the US. She knew of some who appeared to live happily together. True, they lived in black neighborhoods and they were careful about being seen together outside those borders. But the situation in Britain and in Europe was different—that's what people said.

It frustrated her that their feelings for each other carried so many complications—it made her angry. Not with David, but with all the things she felt constantly pulling her back, forcing her down, preventing her from reaching her goals; being a Negro, being "small town", being female—it seemed that so much about her was not the best thing to be.

She had made another, very personal decision recently and that, too, was showing signs of being wrong. She didn't really know if she had been saving her virginity for her life's partner, as her mother always said she must. But if she had, she thought she had found him. If David could commit to her, she wanted to be a woman for him, to put girlhood behind her.

Within the space of a few hours, her life had taken a new path, as she gave in to the fact that she loved David. It was the path of womanhood, of full participation in life. She wanted to embrace it fully, in partnership with him, and she needed first to take him inside her and bind with him in a way that could not be taken back, to demonstrate that she was now his partner, in love and in life.

She smiled to herself, thinking back a couple of days, on the ship, when the notion of becoming David's lover was taking shape in her mind. She knew little about the gritty details of sexual intimacy, and even less about contraception. So she did something she could not have brought herself to do just days earlier—she asked Molly and Chris for help. Diaphragms had been available for a few years and Chris's friend, Sarah, who was about the same size through her hips as Audrey, had an extra one she was willing to part with.

Audrey told them she was only *thinking* about sleeping with him but the women refused to accept it as anything but a certainty. By the time they had spent part of an afternoon celebrating, aided by some fine scotch, and teaching her, very much hands-on, how to put the latex barrier in place, they had become fast friends.

Now, it all looked like a futile exercise. As David hesitated, her hopes for a sweet, intimate coupling with him were crumbling to dust.

They rode on in silence. Audrey began taking notice of the landscape, which had been field and forest for some time, but was dotted now by clusters of cozy-looking red brick and timber-framed homes as they approached Lymington, a small town sheltered from the English Channel by the Isle of Wight. Once again, cars driving on the wrong side of the road confused her and it took her a moment to remember why.

"Where are we going?"

David smiled at her. "Lymington first, then Bournemouth—we'll probably hop a train there for Truro."

She took in the passing row houses and semi-detached cottages as the bus climbed the shallow grade at the outskirts of the town. The houses huddled closer together and more and more people walked or cycled by.

All the roads were narrow, only two lanes wide. Lots of people rode bicycles and Audrey was amused that so many of them appeared to be housewives, in skirted woolen suits and blocky shoes. They sat upright, on practical bikes with fenders on the wheels, and wide handlebars supporting oversized baskets filled with groceries.

The pub signs beckoned from another time; The Hart and Ferret, The King's Head, The Crown and Scepter. Audrey felt a sudden urge to see what life was like behind those ancient walls and beneath those old slate roofs, capped with potted chimneys. She wanted to compare them with Barney's, wondering whether she would like them better.

"I'm hungry, aren't you? Let's stop and eat in one of these pubs... like that one, the... what's that word? P-l-o-u-g-h." She pointed to a yellow, brick and flint building passing by on the left. "Pluff? The Pluff and Hearth!? What's a pluff?"

David laughed. "It's plow. That's how they spell it here."

The Plough and Hearth was set back from the road. Bicycles and motorcycles, plus a handful of cars, edged its forecourt. Audrey turned to the rear window to get another glimpse as it receded. "It looks so... real."

He chuckled. "What do you mean, real?"

"Real. Not made up, like in a story. The only pubs I've ever known about have been in stories. Can't we stop?"

Someone had pulled the cord and the bus was slowing. "Sure," David shrugged. "Let's get off."

He rose and pulled Audrey to her feet. Again her looks drew stares—a mix of amazement and disapproval—from the mostly middle-age women passengers. Audrey refused to be intimidated. As they moved toward the door, a woman in a heavy, check-patterned coat and black pillbox hat couldn't take her reproachful gaze off her. Audrey cocked her cap at an angle. Smiling as they passed, she addressed the frump.

"Isn't it a beautiful day?"

The woman recoiled. "Cheek!" She turned away sharply, snugging her bag closer to her bosom. Audrey laughed as the bus jerked to a stop at the curb. David grabbed the valise, she picked up her portfolio case and they tumbled off.

Still laughing, they turned toward the Plough and Hearth, three short blocks back. The sidewalk took them past a row of small shops: a bakery, still busy with the morning's customers; a cheese shop; a florist and at the corner, a news agent, the small shop bursting with newspapers, magazines, tobacco and cigarettes, and an astonishing variety of hard candies and chocolates.

They crossed the side road, bringing them along the front of a garage and petrol station. A small black coupe sat at the station's two pumps and the car's owner was leaning over the fender, under the open, bi-fold hood of the engine compartment, checking his oil. At the nearby pump, an attendant, working a long handle back and forth, forced gasoline up into the large glass bottle on top, which was marked on its side in half-gallon increments. When the bottle was full, he drained the contents into the car's tank.

A vicar, wearing a black cassock trimmed in red, approached on the sidewalk. Audrey smiled at him as he passed and he was taken aback by this amiable, spirited boy who turned out to be a captivating young woman. He turned and gazed, open-mouthed as they strode by, one hand frozen in the act of tipping his biretta. Audrey smiled and waved a salute.

David looked at Audrey as if examining a new bicycle. Her mood had lightened—almost too much, he thought, considering what they'd just been through. She caught his gaze.

"What's the matter?" she asked.

"I don't know. Suddenly you seem... happy."

"Oh, well, Mr Grim," she mocked, refusing to allow the question hanging over them to spoil her introduction to England. "I shouldn't be too happy, should I? Here, how about Mrs Fishface on the bus—I'll be like her." She worked her face into a grimace.

David laughed. "Stop. You win," he declared. "Happy is much better." He draped his arm around her and they continued walking.

David didn't speak for a long time and she sensed that something was working at him. "What?" she demanded, turning to him as they walked. He glanced at her, then looked away. She could see him preparing his speech.

"So look, I don't understand," he said, soberly. "You don't seem the least concerned about the future. What about money?"

She glanced at him, sidelong. "Oh, no, I'm not concerned," she said, jauntily. "Not about me. Why should I be? I believe in myself."

She had a knack for statements like that and they charmed him to his core. He knew that they differed in many ways and, if there were any future for them together, it would have many ups and downs. He, too, believed in her, though he had doubts about her hopes in the fashion industry—his belief contained a certain dread of the traps and obstacles the world would put in her path. *She* believed the way one believes the sun will rise. He couldn't resist trying to pull her closer to Earth, if only a little. "Yes, but you haven't any prospects for a job."

"Oh, I don't know about that," she answered coyly, subtly swinging her portfolio in his direction. "I imagine that, the minute these fashion people in London see what I can do, I won't want for much." She adopted a sauntering gait and her mouth curved into a self-satisfied smile that puzzled him. He couldn't decide whether she was unbelievably green, or good at fashion and style in a way he couldn't appreciate. Most likely, he thought, she overestimated her skills in the marketplace and was setting herself up for a major disappointment.

"By the way," she said, "you told Inspector Sheridan you mixed your winnings in with Charles's money. Unless I'm mistaken, they're in that case you're carrying."

His eyes widened in surprise. "My God, you knew! How...?"

"Well of course I knew. What do you take me for? I never thought you'd be silly enough to put the money you won in with Pierce's. If you had," she teased, "I'd have to change my thinking about you."

David looked at her, his mouth half open in astonishment.

"Why'd you tell him that fib, anyway?" she asked.

"I was trying to get him on our side. Didn't work all that well."

"That's an understatement," she said, arching her eyebrows at him.

They approached the entrance to the pub, a wide, solid, dark wooden door with a window of cut glass panes in the upper half and set in a sturdy, yellow stucco wall. The large sign, in a wrought iron frame hanging over the door, displayed a crude painting of logs burning in a stone hearth. An incongruous, single-bladed plow stood in front of the fire, its long curved handle propped against the mantle. The name, The Plough & Hearth, occupied the space above, scrawled in white script against the black background of the painting. The sign jutted from its footings in a roof of ancient black slate, splotched with algae growths in a variety of pastel colors.

As he opened the door and let Audrey pass, David chuckled. "What is it?" she asked.

He shook his head. "Your whole approach to life is so... fresh, as though evil didn't exist, as though Charles Pierce was just a bad dream." He smiled at her in admiration. "I don't know... probably I should try to stop underestimating you."

She knuckled him playfully in the ribs. "Yes," she said. "Perhaps you should."

XLV

THEIR FIRST DAYS IN TRURO were a delight. The charm of the town; the warmth of its people; visits to farms, where sheep and cows cropped the grasses relentlessly; the manicured look of the fields; the homey, smoky atmosphere of British pubs; it was all a fascinating revelation to Audrey.

David was greeted as the Prodigal Son. Some of the elders remembered his father and treated David as though his arrival was in some way the natural completion of the elder's journey. And they automatically took Audrey to be his wife. Even when she explained their relationship, they found it hard to grasp and quickly substituted their own versions. And even though, as Audrey insisted, they slept in separate inns each night, tongues began to wag.

By the end of a fortnight, it was clear to her that things weren't working out. David's business, securing the farm, was stalled, and she was tagging along behind him, sitting in on conversations, in banks and in farmhouse kitchens, where her opinions weren't sought and her presence made everyone uncomfortable. Even her hair was a problem. Still short from their adventure, she didn't have enough colorful scarves and berets to deflect the gossip, and the questions about why she was shorn. She and David thought the real story could only make matters worse.

David did everything he could think of to make her feel included but he couldn't find the will to do the one thing that might have made a difference. Audrey watched—and grew anxious—as he inched closer to his goal of becoming a farmer. Finally, she couldn't wait any longer.

One afternoon, as they walked from the bank to the pub they favored for lunch, and David was explaining why the real estate sale was stalled, she broke in.

"David, I'm leaving for London. I can't stay here any longer."

"What?! Audrey, no! Don't you...?!" He waved a hand in the general direction of the town center. "I mean, I thought you were starting to get used to this... to this place and the whole idea and..."

"It's charming, David. I have nothing against anyone here, or any thing, though I can't say I'm too comfortable with the way the cows stare at me. But it's not what I came here for."

"Audrey, please don't go." He clutched at her arm and they stopped, facing each other in the middle of the narrow street. "I... I don't know what I would do without you."

His statement carried a special depth of feeling, like a confession, and she looked at him intently. "What are you saying, David?"

"I'm saying..." He gazed around nervously while he searched for the words. "I'm saying I love you, Audrey. I love you and I think you love me. Stay here. We'll get married—whatever you want."

"Oh David! No!" she cried, burying her face in her hands. She turned and hurried away, blinded by tears, her goal only to put distance between them.

Perplexed, David followed. He caught up with her on the sidewalk, pacing in front of a shop window full of bridles and boots, and holding a handkerchief to her face.

"No, no, no!" she cried, as he approached. "It's too late." She pounded her small fist into his chest. "Too late! And you're too steeped in this town and your new life. I don't have a place here." Before he could answer, she turned and hurried away, heading for the inn.

When she reached her room, she flung her cases on the bed and jerked them open. She was frustrated, and angry with him, but she also felt an unexpected sense of relief. David's indecision had saved her from facing a choice she dreaded, between life with him, on his farm, in a place almost no one had ever heard of, versus London, and an earnest attempt at a career in fashion.

She gave rein to the fury, and began stuffing her clothing into the cases, hampered by a stream of tears she was unable to stanch.

XLVI

THE CONDUCTOR'S WHISTLE cut through the soft gray haze shrouding the Truro station and Audrey's train began to move. David watched, pleadingly, from the platform, his eyes full of anguished tears.

He felt as though he was being stood up against a wall to be shot, that he'd been shown up as a coward. He'd failed to muster the courage to claim Audrey, his great prize, afraid of what others would say and do. Now, she was leaving, to pursue her private dream. He didn't know if he would ever see her again.

The train gathered speed and he ran to keep up, calling out an apology that she couldn't hear. Forced to stop at the end of the platform, he covered his face with his hands to hide his tears.

Audrey's heart ached as she watched from her compartment window. She waved at him as the train gathered speed but she forced her own tears back until he was too far away to see them. Then, devastated, heartsick, she sank into the seat and wept. She tried to muffle her sobs. The other passengers in the car, two men traveling on business and an older couple, sitting across from her, did their best to ignore her, to spare her embarrassment.

Tears flooded from her eyes. She couldn't help feeling that David's change of heart was a betrayal. She hadn't any thoughts of meeting a man or falling in love when she decided to take her voyage. David wooed her and she responded to him, she returned his attentions

364 ❖   *Robert L. Grant*

and he stitched himself into her heart. And now he had retreated, unable to freely declare his love for her, and had left her to deal with the wreckage of her emotions, forced to squelch her yearnings for a life with him.

When she was cried out, she looked up from behind her sodden handkerchief to find the woman opposite smiling warmly at her. Drying her eyes, she smiled back. They lapsed into conversation. The woman, Clara, quickly pegged Audrey's accent as American and it piqued her curiosity. Audrey was grateful that Clara didn't ask her why she'd been crying. Instead, she asked what had brought Audrey to England—what was awaiting her in London? Audrey told her of her plans to work in fashion—Clara was immediately interested. "Oh, how delightful," she said. "I'd love to see your work."

Over the next half hour, Clara studied Audrey's portfolio, ooh-ing and ahh-ing over each new rendering. They were a spectrum of beautiful gowns, sports clothes, dresses and suits, each displaying Audrey's artistic flare. She believed in colors and textures, and used them liberally and artfully as accents to set off the basic material of an outfit. Most of the drawings were accompanied by samples of the materials, pinned along the edges.

"I must say, Audrey," said Clara, as she closed the portfolio, "you are immensely talented. I'm envious."

"Thank you," said Audrey, embarrassed. "With a little luck..."

Clara grasped Audrey's hands in both of hers, and waited until she looked up. "I'm sure that luck will come, dear," she said, "because you will make it come." She leaned in closer and whispered. "Forget the problems you left back in Truro, whatever they were," she said. "Go after your dream."

Hours later, in a heavy rain, the landscape began a subtle change. With the train slowing on its approach to

London, farms and fields gave way to scattered clusters of homes and businesses. Soon the view through the window was a tableau of wet slate roofs and rain-streaked brick walls, dark and dreary under leaden skies, as the train picked its way toward Paddington Station. Audrey followed the lead of the other passengers and rose to assemble her luggage. She retrieved her portfolio from the overhead rack—Clara nudged her husband to pull Audrey's cases down.

When she looked again through the window, a new image greeted her—the station platforms at Paddington, passing slowly as the train crept in. Men and women, bundled in their traveling clothes, stood in clumps along the platforms, or strode past, leading porters who were pushing cartloads of luggage. There were nearly as many dripping umbrellas as people, though they were all folded now, unneeded beneath the station's roof.

The train's halting set loose a flood of activity—the passengers rushed to reach the platform, as though the train might suddenly start backing out before they could get themselves and all their luggage onto firm ground. On the platform, Clara helped Audrey find a porter. Then she wished her good luck and she and her husband hurried away.

While the porter arranged her cases on his cart, Audrey looked around the huge train shed. Along the platforms, long lines of cast iron stanchions projected high into the air, expanding at their tops into a tracery of mullions in the shed's arched glass roof—a loud tattoo rattled down from the roof as the rain intensified. Just beyond the shed roof, trains chugged in and out, shifting from track to track across a web of rain slick switches, their steam exhausts and whistles competing for intensity with the noise of the downpour. Audrey wondered what genius coordinated their movements and prevented them from crashing into each other as they came and went.

London.

Finally, she was standing in the place she had set her heart on. She walked toward the platform exits and into the pavilion, a sense of exhilaration building inside her, an exhilaration tempered with sadness. She had hoped she would share this moment with David, that they would walk together into this new world as a couple, as lovers, hand in hand. But all she had of him was a hastily scribbled note in her bag, which he'd given her at the station in Truro.

Walking through the high-ceilinged pavilion, she was struck by the crush of people scuttering to and fro, catching other trains, heading into the Underground, making for the various exits, all in a great hurry. It was exciting, even more, she thought, than the helter-skelter of Grand Central Station. She was amazed by the variety of people and costumes, the kaleidoscope of skin tones and hairstyles and materials, dyes, and patterns.

"Do you have an umbrella, Miss?" asked the porter, stopping near the entrance to a small shop at one end of the pavilion. He was a tall, sturdy man, middle aged. A thick, grey-flecked mustache covered his upper lip and curved down around the corners of his mouth. His black slicker and broad hat were still shedding water from previous forays into the weather.

"No, I haven't," she said, feeling a little foolish.

"There's a shop just here. Theirs ain't posh but they'll do a fair job of keeping the rain off."

He reached to take her portfolio. With a shy smile, she surrendered it and stepped into the crowded store. It displayed an astonishing array of goods that filled every imaginable square inch of space; cheap luggage; coats and hats; plates and tins of cookies and biscuits, decorated with images of the royal family; other souvenirs. There were shelves of hard candies and chocolates, plus magazines of many kinds, and newspapers from places around the world she had never heard of and in languages she'd never seen before in print.

In a dark corner, their handles hooked over a thick pipe near the ceiling, hung a dozen or so umbrellas, identically black. Even on tiptoe, they were too high for her to reach. She worked her way to the register and enlisted the shop assistant to pull one down for her.

The porter nodded approvingly as she rejoined him, brandishing the umbrella. He handed back her portfolio and got the cart moving, toward the main doors. "May I ask you, Miss—what's in there?"

"They're my drawings," she said, with a smile. "Clothing designs—dresses and things."

"Hmm. I can't say that's something I think about very much. I suppose someone does draw up all those crazy things women wear these days. You don't make that kind, do you, Miss?"

"No, no," she said, laughing. "Well, I have to find a job first, of course, but I promise not to draw up anything crazy."

"You're American, are you?"

"Yes," she replied, miffed that it was so easy for people to peg her as an outsider. "Is it tattooed on my forehead?"

"It's the accent, Miss. No offense—it's charming." She was grateful for his broad, friendly smile.

They reached the large doors that opened onto the station's expansive front. Audrey wasted no time getting the umbrella open as they pushed through to the outside, into a driving rain.

"Welcome to England, Miss," the porter said. With raindrops battering every exposed surface, he had to raise his voice to be heard. "Good country for ducks."

"Thank you, sir," said Audrey, with a faux curtsey. "Do you think we'll be able to get a cab in all this rain?"

"Oh, I dare say there'll be one available soon. We'll just splash down to curbside and make our presence known."

He turned to take the cart down a ramp to street level. Audrey followed, gazing from beneath the umbrella at the traffic surging through the broad plaza in front of the station. Horns blared; cars, trucks, taxis, and buses jockeyed for position, along with an occasional horse-drawn rig; pedestrians, clad in a variety of waterproof coats and shoes and galoshes, under a solid layer of black umbrellas, did their best to dodge both the vehicles and the surging run-off, as they coursed back and forth. Audrey was mesmerized. She thought, if the activity here was any clue, London might have its dangers but it was never going to be dull.

The porter brought the cart to a stop at the curb. "Do you know where you're going, Miss?"

Juggling the umbrella, Audrey dug in her coat pocket for the folded square of paper David had pressed on her, before she stepped into the carriage at Truro. He had hurriedly written the address of some friends with a flat in Putney, and the name of an hotel, which he promised would be cheap but well-run. Her breath caught now, as she unfolded it and saw his handwriting. She stood frozen for a moment, gazing at this scrap of paper, the only remaining connection she had to David.

"Yes. Here." She thrust it in the porter's direction, hoping he would attribute the dampness on her cheeks to the weather.

A taxi pulled up and the porter grabbed the door, claiming it while its passengers settled with the driver. He didn't take the paper from Audrey but busied himself getting her cases into the cab. "Just tell the driver where you need to go. These cab men know the city like the backs of their hands."

She handed him two schillings from her coin purse, which produced a broad smile on his face. "Thank you, Miss." He leaned in toward the driver, a youngish man with a dark mustache.

"Make sure she's well settled, won't you?" he said with a nod. "There's a good lad."

Audrey sat back in the seat with her portfolio on her lap. "Good luck, Miss," he said, smiling as he closed the door.

As the cab edged out into the traffic, she held the porter's gaze. Something about his parting wish struck her as more than polite chat. As he and Paddington Station receded into the background of the crowded plaza, she wondered just how much luck she would need, and whether it would show up at the right time. Then the driver's voice cut into her thoughts.

"Where to, Miss?"

ACKNOWLEDGEMENTS

There are many whom I must thank for their help in bringing this book into existence. First, Arlene Richman, who lavished so much of her time and intellect on editing the book that it would be impossible for me ever to repay her. Arlene was creative and tough, and kept me well grounded—I am in awe of her skills.

Next, Jim Krusoe, author/teacher/guru. He teaches creative writing at Santa Monica City College. Without Jim's key insights, the book would never have achieved whatever level of significance and relevance it can now be said to have. Also, my friend, Dan Saucedo, deserves a nod. A marvelous writer in his own right, Dan gets credit both for encouraging me, and for introducing me to Jim.

Special mention goes to fellow writers who gave of their precious time to read the book and to offer me their insights and advice: Norma Dawson, Attila Domokos, Elizabeth Graham, Susan Marangell, Pamela Jaye Smith, and Tamala Whittley. In addition, my colleagues from Jim's classes have provided me with key suggestions and much encouragement. I thank them all.

Others who took a deep interest in the book and offered advice, material aid, and/or moral support, include: Kathy Babcock, Ken and Sherry Grant, Piper Grant, Sharon Hoppas, Barbara King, Sergio Saucedo, Kristin Shannon, Tom and Patty West

By no means least, my incomparable spouse and life partner, Julia Pennbridge. She has endured and aided the gestation of this book with a patience and a serenity that are truly marvelous. Julia has read the manuscript more times than could possibly have held her interest. She has suffered my absences—both mental and physical—and produced numerous cups of delicious tea, all to help me push through to the end.

My eternal gratitude to you all.